AN EQUAL MUSIC

Vikram Seth

CHIVERS PRESS
BATH

First published 1999
by
Phoenix House
This Large Print edition published by
Chivers Press
by arrangement with
Orion Publishing Group Limited
2000

ISBN 0 7540 1435 5

British Library Cataloguing in Publication Data available

Printed and bound in Great Britain by
REDWOOD BOOKS, Trowbridge, Wiltshire

FOR PHILIPPE HONORÉ

Perhaps this could have stayed unstated.
Had our words turned to other things
In the grey park, the rain abated,
Life would have quickened other strings.
I list your gifts in this creation:
Pen, paper, ink and inspiration,
Peace to the heart with touch or word,
Ease to the soul with note and chord.

How did that walk, those winter hours,
Occasion this? No lightning came;
Nor did I sense, when touched by flame,
Our story lit with borrowed powers
Rather, by what our spirits burned,
Embered in words, to us returned.

And into that gate they shall enter, and in that house they shall dwell, where there shall be no cloud nor sun, no darkness nor dazzling, but one equal light, no noise nor silence, but one equal music, no fears nor hopes, but one equal possession, no foes nor friends, but one equal communion and identity, no ends nor beginnings, but one equal eternity.

JOHN DONNE

AN EQUAL MUSIC

PART ONE

1.1

The branches are bare, the sky tonight a milky violet. It is not quiet here, but it is peaceful. The wind ruffles the black water towards me.

There is no one about. The birds are still. The traffic slashes through Hyde Park. It comes to my ears as white noise.

I test the bench but do not sit down. As yesterday, as the day before, I stand until I have lost my thoughts. I look at the water of the Serpentine.

*　　　*　　　*

Yesterday as I walked back across the park I paused at a fork in the footpath. I had the sense that someone had paused behind me. I walked on. The sound of footsteps followed along the gravel. They were unhurried; they appeared to keep pace with me. Then they suddenly made up their mind, speeded up, and overtook me. They belonged to a man in a thick black overcoat, quite tall—about my height—a young man from his gait and attitude, though I did not see his face. His sense of hurry was now evident. After a while, unwilling so soon to cross the blinding Bayswater Road, I paused again, this time by the bridle path.

Now I heard the faint sound of hooves. This time, however, they were not embodied. I looked to left, to right. There was nothing.

*　　　*　　　*

As I approach Archangel Court I am conscious of being watched. I enter the hallway. There are flowers here, a concoction of gerberas and general foliage. A camera surveys the hall. A watched building is a secure building, a secure building a happy one.

A few days ago I was told I was happy by the young woman behind the counter at Etienne's. I ordered seven croissants. As she gave me my change she said: 'You are a happy man.'

I stared at her with such incredulity that she looked down.

'You're always humming,' she said in a much quieter voice, feeling perhaps that she had to explain.

'It's my work,' I said, ashamed of my bitterness. Another customer entered the shop, and I left.

As I put my week's croissants—all except one—in the freezer, I noticed I was humming the same half-tuneless tune of one of Schubert's last songs:

I see a man who stares upwards
And wrings his hands from the force of his pain.
I shudder when I see his face.
The moon reveals myself to me.

I put the water on for coffee, and look out of the window. From the eighth floor I can see as far as St Paul's, Croydon, Highgate. I can look across the brown-branched park to spires and towers and chimneys beyond. London unsettles me—even from such a height there is no clear countryside to view.

But it is not Vienna. It is not Venice. It is not, for

4

that matter, my hometown in the North, in clear reach of the moors.

*　　　*　　　*

It wasn't my work, though, that made me hum that song. I have not played Schubert for more than a month. My violin misses him more than I do. I tune it, and we enter my soundproof cell. No light, no sound comes in from the world. Electrons along copper, horsehair across acrylic create my impressions of sense.

I will play nothing of what we have played in our quartet, nothing that reminds me of my recent music-making with any human being. I will play his songs.

The Tononi seems to purr at the suggestion. Something happy, something happy, surely:

> *In a clear brook*
> *With joyful haste*
> *The whimsical trout*
> *Shot past me like an arrow.*

I play the line of the song, I play the leaps and plunges of the right hand of the piano, I am the trout, the angler, the brook, the observer. I sing the words, bobbing my constricted chin. The Tononi does not object; it resounds. I play it in B, in A, in E flat. Schubert does not object. I am not transposing his string quartets.

Where a piano note is too low for the violin, it leaps into a higher octave. As it is, it is playing the songline an octave above its script. Now, if it were a viola . . . but it has been years since I played the

5

viola.

The last time was when I was a student in Vienna ten years ago. I return there again and again and think: was I in error? Was I unseeing? Where was the balance of pain between the two of us? What I lost there I have never come near to retrieving.

What happened to me so many years ago? Love or no love, I could not continue in that city. I stumbled, my mind jammed, I felt the pressure of every breath. I told her I was going, and went. For two months I could do nothing, not even write to her. I came to London. The smog dispersed but too late. Where are you now, Julia, and am I not forgiven?

1.2

Virginie will not practise, yet demands these lessons. I have worse students—more cavalier, that is—but none so frustrating.

I walk across the park to her flat. It is over-heated and there is a great deal of pink. This used not to unnerve me. Now when I step into the bathroom I recoil.

Pink bath, pink basin, pink toilet, pink bidet, pink tiles, pink wallpaper, pink rug. Brushes, soap, toothbrush, silk flowers, toilet paper: all pink. Even the little foot-operated waste-bin is pale pink. I know this little waste-bin well. Every time I sleep here I wonder what I am doing with my time and hers. She is sixteen years younger than I am. She is not the woman with whom I want to share my life. But, having begun, what we have continues. She wants it to, and I go along with it, through lust and loneliness, I suppose; and laziness, and lack of focus.

Our lessons are a clear space. Today it is a partita by Bach: the E major. I ask her to play it all the way through, but after the Gavotte I tell her to stop.

'Don't you want to know how it ends?' she asks cheerfully.

'You haven't practised much.'

She achieves an expression of guilt.

'Go back to the beginning,' I suggest.

'Of the Gavotte?'

'Of the Prelude.'

'You mean bar seventeen? I know, I know, I should use always my wrist for the E string.'

'I mean bar one.'

Virginie looks sulky. She sets her bow down on a pale pink silk cushion.

'Virginie, it's not that you can't do it, it's just that you aren't doing it.'

'Doing what?'

'Thinking about the music. Sing the first phrase, just sing it.'

She picks up the bow.

'I meant, with your voice.'

Virginie sighs. In tune, and with exactitude, she goes: 'Mi-re-mi si sol si mi-fa-mi-re-mi . . .'

'Can't you ever sing without those nonsense syllables?'

'That's how I was taught.' Her eyes flash.

Virginie comes from Nyons, about which I know nothing other than that it is somewhere near Avignon. She asked me twice to go there with her, then stopped asking.

'Virginie, it's not just one damn note after

another. That second mi-re-mi should carry some memory of the first. Like this.' I pick up my fiddle and demonstrate. 'Or like this. Or in some way of your own.'

She plays it again, and plays it well, and goes on. I close my eyes. A huge bowl of pot-pourri assails my senses. It is getting dark. Winter is upon us. How young she is, how little she works. She is only twenty-one. My mind wanders to another city, to the memory of another woman, who was as young then.

'Should I go on?'

'Yes.'

I tell Virginie to keep her wrist free, to watch her intonation here, to mind her dynamics there, to keep her détaché even—but she knows all this. Next week there will be some progress, very little. She is talented, yet she will not apply herself. Though she is supposedly a full-time student, music for her is only one of many things. She is anxious about the college competition for which she will perform this partita. She is thinking of selling her Miremont, and getting her father—who supports her unstudentlike standard of living—to buy her something early and Italian. She has a grand circle of acquaintance here, scores of friends from all over France who descend on her in every season, vast linked clans of relatives, and three ex-boyfriends with whom she is on good terms. She and I have been together for more than a year now.

As for the one I remember, I see her with her eyes closed, playing Bach to herself: an English suite. Gently her fingers travel among the keys. Perhaps I move too suddenly. The beloved eyes turn towards me. There are so many beings here,

8

occupied, pre-occupied. Let me believe that she breathes, that she still exists, somewhere on this chance sphere.

1.3

The Maggiore Quartet is gathering for a rehearsal at our standard venue, Helen's little two-storey mews house.

Helen is preparing coffee. Only she and I are here. The afternoon sunlight slants in. A woman's velvety voice sings Cole Porter. Four dark blue armless chairs are arranged in an arc beneath a minimalist pine bookshelf. A viola case and a couple of music stands rest in the corner of the open-plan kitchen-living-dining room.

'One? Two?' asks Helen. 'I keep forgetting. I wonder why. It's not the sort of thing one forgets when one is, well, used to someone's coffee habits. But you don't have a habit with sugar, do you? Sometimes you don't have any at all. Oh, I met someone yesterday who was asking after you. Nicholas Spare. Such an awful man, but the more waspish he gets the more they read him. Get him to review us, Michael. He has a crush on you, I'm sure he does. He frowns whenever I mention you.'

'Thanks, Helen. That's all I need.'

'So do I, of course.'

'No crushes on colleagues.'

'You're not all that gorgeous.'

'What's new on the gardening front?'

'It's November, Michael,' says Helen. 'Besides, I'm off gardening. Here's your coffee. What do you think of my hair?'

Helen has red hair, and her hairstyle changes annually. This year it is ringleted with careless care. I nod approval and concentrate on my coffee.

The doorbell rings. It is Piers, her elder brother, our first violinist.

He enters, ducking his head slightly. He kisses his sister—who is only a couple of inches shorter—says hello to me, takes off his elegant-shabby greatcoat, gets out his violin and mutters, 'Could you turn that off? I'm trying to tune up.'

'Oh, just till the end of this track,' says Helen.

Piers turns the player off himself. Helen says nothing. Piers is used to getting his way.

'Where the fuck is Billy?' he asks. 'He's always late for rehearsal. Has he called?'

Helen shakes her head. 'That's what happens, I suppose, if you live in Loughton or Leyton or wherever.'

'Leytonstone,' I say.

'Of course,' says Helen, feigning enlightenment. London for her means Zone 1. All of us except Billy live quite centrally, in or near Bayswater, within walking distance of Hyde Park and Kensington Gardens, though in very different conditions. Piers is quite often irritable, even resentful, for a few minutes after arriving at Helen's. He lives in a basement studio.

After a while Helen quietly asks him how he enjoyed last night. Piers went to listen to the Steif Quartet, whom he has admired for many years, play an all-Beethoven concert.

'Oh, OK,' grumbles Piers. 'But you can never tell with the Steif. Last night they were going in heavily for beauty of tone—pretty narcissistic. And I'm beginning to dislike the first violinist's face: it looks

10

more and more pinched every year. And after they finished playing the *Grosse Fuge*, they leapt up as if they had just killed a lion. Of course the audience went mad . . . Has Erica called?'

'No . . . So you didn't like the concert.'

'I didn't say that,' says Piers. 'Where is bloody Billy? We should fine him a chocolate biscuit for every minute he's late.' Having tuned up, he plays a rapid figure in pizzicato quartertones.

'What was that?' asks Helen, almost spilling her coffee. 'No, no, no, don't play it again.'

'An attempt at composition à la Billy.'

'That's not fair,' says Helen.

Piers smiles a sort of left-handed smile. 'Billy's only a fledgling. One day twenty years from now, he'll grow into the full monster, write something gratingly awful for Covent Garden—if it's still there—and wake up as Sir William Cutler.'

Helen laughs, then pulls herself up. 'Now, now, no talking behind each other's backs,' she says.

'I'm a bit worried,' continues Piers. 'Billy's been talking far too much about what he's working on.' He turns to me for a reaction.

'Has he actually suggested we play something he's written?' I ask.

'No. Not actually. Not yet. It's just a pricking of my thumbs.'

'Why don't we wait and see if he does?' I suggest.

'I'm not for it,' says Helen slowly. 'It would be dreadful if we didn't like it—I mean if it really sounded like your effusion.'

Piers smiles again, not very pleasantly.

'Well, I don't see the harm in reading it through once,' I say.

11

'What if some of us like it and some don't?' asks Helen. 'A quartet is a quartet. This could lead to all sorts of tensions. But surely it would be worse if Billy's grumpy the whole time. So there it is.'

'Helenic logic,' says Piers.

'But I like Billy—' begins Helen.

'So do we all,' Piers interrupts. 'We all love each other, that goes without saying. But in this matter, the three of us should think out our position—our joint position—clearly, before Billy presents us with a fourth Razumovsky.'

Before we can speak further, Billy arrives. He lugs his cello in exhaustedly, apologises, looks cheerful when he sees the chocolate biscuits that Helen knows are his favourites, gobbles down a few, receives his coffee gratefully, apologises again, and begins tuning.

'Lydia took the car—dentist. Mad rush—almost forgot the music for the Brahms. Central Line— terrible.' Sweat shines on his forehead and he is breathing heavily. 'I'm sorry. I'm sorry. I'm sorry. I'll never be late again. Never ever.'

'Have another biscuit, Billy,' says Helen affectionately.

'Get a mobile phone, Billy,' says Piers in a lazy-peremptory prefect-like tone.

'Why?' asks Billy. 'Why should I? Why should I get a mobile phone? I'm not a pimp or a plumber.'

Piers shakes his head and lets it go. Billy is far too fat, and always will be. He will always be distracted by family and money worries, car insurance and composition. For all our frustration and rebuke, he will never be on time. But the moment his bow comes down on the strings he is transfigured. He is a wonderful cellist, light and profound: the base of our harmony, the rock on which we rest.

1.4

Every rehearsal of the Maggiore Quartet begins with a very plain, very slow three-octave scale on all four instruments in unison: sometimes major, as in our name, sometimes minor, depending on the key of the first piece we are to play. No matter how fraught our lives have been over the last couple of days, no matter how abrasive our disputes about people or politics, or how visceral our differences about what we are to play and how we are to play it, it reminds us that we are, when it comes to it, one. We try not to look at each other when we play this scale; no one appears to lead. Even the first upbeat is merely breathed by Piers, not indicated by any movement of his head. When I play this I release myself into the spirit of the quartet. I become the music of the scale. I mute my will, I free my self.

After Alex Foley left five years ago and I was being considered as a possible second violinist by Piers, Helen and Billy, we tried out various bits of music together, rehearsed together, in fact played several concerts together, but never played the scale. I did not even know that for them it existed. Our last concert was in Sheffield. At midnight, two hours after it was over, Piers phoned me in my hotel room to say that they all wanted me to join.

'It was good, Michael,' he said. 'Helen insists you *belong* to us.' Despite this little barb, aimed at his sister, doubtless present at the other end, he

13

sounded almost elated—quite something for Piers. Two days later, back in London, we met for a rehearsal and began, this time, with the scale. As it rose, calm and almost without vibrato, I felt my happiness build. When it paused at the top before descending, I glanced at my new colleagues, to left and to right. Piers had slightly averted his face. It astonished me. Piers is hardly the sort of musician who weeps soundlessly at the beauty of scales. I had no idea at the time what was going through his mind. Perhaps, in playing the scale again, he was in some sense letting Alex go.

Today we are running through a couple of Haydn quartets and a Brahms. The Haydns are glorious; they give us joy. Where there are difficulties, we can understand them—and therefore come to an understanding among ourselves. We love Haydn, and he makes us love each other. Not so Brahms. He has always been a cross for our quartet.

I feel no affinity for Brahms, Piers can't stand him, Helen adores him, Billy finds him 'deeply interesting', whatever that means. We were asked to include some Brahms in a programme we are due to perform in Edinburgh, and Piers, as our programmer, accepted the inevitable and chose the first string quartet, the C minor.

We saw valiantly away through the first movement without stopping.

'Good tempo,' says Helen tentatively, looking at the music rather than at any of us.

'A bit turgid, I thought. We aren't the Busch Quartet,' I say.

'You'd better not say anything against the Busch,' says Helen.

'I'm not. But they were them and we are us.'

'Talk of arrogance,' says Helen.

'Well, should we go on? Or clean up?' I ask.

'Clean up,' snaps Piers. 'It's a total mess.'

'Precision's the key,' says Billy, half to himself. 'Like with the Schoenberg.'

Helen sighs. We begin playing again. Piers stops us. He looks directly at me.

'It's you, Michael. You're sort of suddenly intense without any reason. You're not supposed to be saying anything special.'

'Well, he tells me to express.'

'Where?' asks Piers, as if to an idiot-child. 'Just precisely where?'

'Bar fifteen.'

'I don't have anything there.'

'Bad luck,' I say shortly. Piers looks over at my part in disbelief.

'Rebecca's getting married to Stuart,' says Helen.

'What?' says Piers, jogged out of his concentration. 'You're kidding.'

'No, I'm not. I heard it from Sally. And Sally heard it directly from Rebecca's mother.'

'Stuart!' says Piers. 'Oh God. All her babies will be born brain-dead.' Billy and I exchange glances. There is something jerky, abrasive, irrelevant about many of our conversations during rehearsals which sits oddly with the exactitude and expressivity we are seeking to create. Helen, for instance, usually says the first thing that comes into her head. Sometimes her thoughts run ahead of her words; sometimes it's the other way around.

'Let's go on,' suggests Billy.

We play for a few minutes. There is a series of

15

false starts, no sense of flow.

'I'm just not coming out,' says Billy. 'I feel like such a wimp four bars before B.'

'And Piers comes in like a gobbling turkey at forty-one,' says Helen.

'Don't be nasty, Helen,' says her brother.

Finally we come to Piers's high crescendo.

'Oh no, oh no, oh no,' cries Billy, taking his hand off the strings and gesticulating.

'We're all a bit loud here,' says Helen, aiming for tact.

'It's too hysterical,' I say.

'Who's too hysterical?' asks Piers.

'You.' The others nod.

Piers's rather large ears go red.

'You've got to cool that vibrato,' says Billy. 'It's like heavy breathing on the phone.'

'OK,' says Piers grimly. 'And can you be a bit darker at one-oh-eight, Billy?'

It isn't usually like this. Most of our rehearsals are much more convivial. I blame it on what we're playing.

'We're not getting anywhere as a whole,' says Billy with a kind of innocent agitation in his eyes. 'That was terribly organised.'

'As in organised terribly?' I ask.

'Yes. We've got to get it together somehow. It's just a sort of noise.'

'It's called Brahms, Billy,' says Piers.

'You're just prejudiced,' says Helen. 'You'll come around to him.'

'In my dotage.'

'Why don't we plan a structure around the tunes?' Billy suggests.

'Well, it sort of lacks tunes,' I say. 'Not melody

16

exactly, but melodicity. Do I mean that? What's the right word?'

'Melodiousness,' says Helen. 'And, incidentally, it doesn't lack tunes.'

'But what do you mean by that?' says Piers to me. 'It's all tune. I mean, I'm not saying I like it, but . . .'

I point my bow at Piers's music. 'Is that tune? I doubt even Brahms would claim that was tune.'

'Well, it's not arpeggio, it's not scale, it's not ornament, so . . . oh, I don't know. It's all mad and clogged up. Bloody Edinburgh . . .'

'Stop ranting, Piers,' says Helen. 'You played that last bit really well. I loved that slide. It was quite a shock, but it's great. You've got to keep it.'

Piers is startled by the praise, but soon recovers. 'But Billy now sounds completely unvibrato'd,' he says.

'That was me trying to get a darker colour,' counters Billy.

'Well, it sounds gravelly.'

'Shall I get a new cello?' asks Billy. 'After I've bought my mobile phone?'

Piers grunts. 'Why don't you just go up the C-string?'

'It's too woofy.'

'Once more, then? From ninety-two?' I suggest.

'No, from the double-bar,' says Helen.

'No, from seventy-five,' says Billy.

'OK,' says Piers.

After a few more minutes we pause again.

'This is just so exhausting to play,' says Helen. 'To get these notes to work you have to dig each one out. It's not like the violin . . .'

'Poor Helen,' I say, smiling at her. 'Why don't

17

you swap instruments with me?'

'Cope, Helen,' says Piers. 'Brahms is your baby.'

Helen sighs. 'Say something nice, Billy.'

But Billy is now concentrating on a little yellow score that he has brought along.

'My deodorant experiment isn't a success,' says Helen suddenly, raising one creamy arm.

'We'd better get on with it or we'll never get through it,' says Billy.

Finally, after an hour and a half we arrive at the second movement. It is dark outside, and we are exhausted, as much with one another's temperaments as with the music. But ours is an odd quadripartite marriage with six relationships, any of which, at any given time, could be cordial or neutral or strained. The audiences who listen to us cannot imagine how earnest, how petulant, how accommodating, how wilful is our quest for something beyond ourselves that we imagine with our separate spirits but are compelled to embody together. Where is the harmony of spirit in all this, let alone sublimity? How are such mechanics, such stops and starts, such facile irreverence transmuted, in spite of our bickering selves, into musical gold? And yet often enough it is from such trivial beginnings that we arrive at an understanding of a work that seems to us both true and original, and an expression of it which displaces from our minds—and perhaps, at least for a while, from the minds of those who hear us— any versions, however true, however original, played by other hands.

1.5

My flat is cold, owing to the perennial heating problems here on the top floor. The ancient radiators of Archangel Court, tepid now, will scald me in the spring. Each winter I promise myself double glazing, and each spring, when prices are discounted, decide against it. Last year the money I'd set aside was soaked up by some primordial pipework that had rusted, almost rotted, into the concrete, and was dripping onto my seventh-floor neighbour's head. But this year I must do my bedroom at least.

I lie in bed, I muse, I doze. The brass flap is lifted; letters shuffle onto the wooden floor. The lift door slams. I get up, put on my dressing gown, and walk to the front door: a phone bill, a postcard from one of the students I give lessons to, a travel brochure, a letter.

I open my post with the silver letter-opener that Julia gave me a year to the day that we first met. The bill goes into the guilt-pile, where it will sit for a week or two. The brochure goes into the waste-paper basket. I enter the kitchen, shivering a bit, fill the kettle, switch it on and take the letter back to bed.

It is from my old teacher, Carl Käll—pronounced, with typical contrariness, 'Shell'. We haven't been in touch for years. The stamp is Swedish. Professor Käll's handwriting on the envelope looks cramped. It is a short note, astonishingly unabrasive.

He is no longer teaching in Vienna. He retired last year, and returned to his small hometown in Sweden. He says that he happened to be in

Stockholm when we played there. He was in the audience, but chose not to come backstage after the concert. We played well. In particular, he has this to say: he had always told me to 'sustain', and sustain I did. He has not been in the best of health lately, and has been thinking of some of his old students. Perhaps he was a bit rough on some of them, but the past is the past, and he can't make amends, only hope that the gain will outlast the damage. (In Professor Käll's German this last sentence sounds odd, as if he were translating from Martian.) Anyway, he wishes me well, and hopes that if I ever teach, I will have learned something from him of how not to. He has no plans to visit England.

The kettle clicked itself off a few minutes ago. I go to the kitchen and find myself unable to remember where the teabags are. There is something troubling in the letter. Carl Käll is dying; I feel sure of it.

*   *   *

Someone is hammering slates onto a roof. A few sharp taps, a pause, a few sharp taps. I roll up my blinds and the light floats in. It is a clear, cold, blue-skied day.

I can smell the professor on a day like this. He is standing in a grey classroom and staring at five edgy students. He has come back from lunch at Mnozil's and his charcoal overcoat exudes an aura of garlic and tobacco. *'Und jetzt, meine Herren . . .'* he says, ignoring Yuko, 'our colleague from the morning-land', as he sometimes calls her. He taps his bow on the piano.

20

I stay behind after the class for my own session with him. As soon as they have left, he rounds on me.

'If I have you here as a *Gasthörer* it is because certain things are understood.'

'I understand, Professor Käll.'

'I wanted the Kreutzer Sonata, and you prepare this instead!'

'I happened to get hold of a facsimile of this manuscript, and Beethoven's handwriting for once was so clear, I was amazed. I thought you wouldn't mind—'

'Amazed. Excited, also, no doubt.'

'Yes.'

'Amazed and excited.' The great Carl Käll savours the words, rich alien growths on the corpus of music. Yet it was not his fame but the excitement in his playing that first drew me to him, and it is this excitement that his playing retains—and transmits to those happy enough to hear him. But how many concerts does he choose to give these days? Five a year? Six?

'I thought that another sonata . . . the one just before the Kreutzer . . .'

Carl Käll shakes his head. 'Don't think, I do not recommend it.'

'Julia McNicholl and I have spent two weeks practising it. I've asked her to join us in half an hour.'

'What is today?'

'Friday.'

Professor Käll appears to be pondering something.

'That silly Yuko goes to the *Zentralfriedhof* to lay flowers on Beethoven's grave on Fridays,' he says.

21

Despite myself, I smile. I am not surprised. Yuko does all the things that young Japanese women students are expected to do: practise obediently, suffer terribly, and visit all the Beethoven and Schubert houses they can locate. But Yuko also does what I know I should do—would, indeed, if I knew how to. She ignores the fact that Carl ignores her, annuls his insults by not rising to them, and sifts out a musician's message from his playing, not his speech.

'I want the Kreutzer by Monday,' continues Carl Käll.

'But, Professor—' I protest.

'By Monday.'

'Professor, there is no way I can—or even if I could, that a pianist could—'

'I am sure Fraulein McNicholl will assist you.'

'Our trio had set aside this weekend for rehearsing. We have a concert coming up.'

'Your trio manages with not much apparent practice.'

I say nothing for a few seconds. Carl Käll coughs.

'When are you playing next?'

'In a couple of weeks—at the *Bösendorfer Saal.*'

'And what?'

'We're beginning with an early Beethoven—'

'Are you being deliberately unspecific?'

'No, Professor.'

'Which?'

'Opus 1 number 3. In C minor.'

'Yes, yes, yes, yes,' says Carl Käll, provoked by my mentioning the key.

'Why?'

'Why?'

'Yes, why?'

'Because our cellist loves it.'

'Why? Why?' Carl looks almost demented.

'Because she finds it amazing and exciting.'

Carl Käll looks carefully at me, as if wondering which of my cervical vertebrae it will cause him least trouble to snap. He turns away. I used to be one of his favourite students. It was at a masterclass in my last year at the Royal Northern College of Music in Manchester that we briefly met, and it was he who suggested, to my disbelieving joy, that I should come to study with him in Vienna as an older student outside the regular curriculum. He thought that I was capable of—and that I would want—a solo career. Now he is perhaps as disillusioned with me as I with him.

'You spend too much of your time on chamber music,' he says. 'You could have a better career.'

'I suppose so,' I say, bothered by his assumption of what 'better' is, but not disputing it.

'You should be guided by me. That is why you are here, is it not? You are very self-willed. Too much so.'

Carl's voice is temporarily gentle. I say nothing. He hums a phrase from the Kreutzer, reaches his hand out for the facsimile manuscript, looks at it with fascination for a few minutes, but won't relent.

'Till Monday, then.'

*   *   *

My tea has overbrewed: it is bitter, but still drinkable. I turn on the television—and return to the present. Four plump humanoid creatures, red, yellow, green and purple, are frolicking on a grassy hill. Rabbits nibble the grass. The creatures hug each other. A periscope emerges from a knoll and tells them they must say goodbye. After a little protest, they do, jumping one by one into a hole in the ground.

Carl Käll, that old man, that stubborn magician, brutal and full of suffocating energy, did not, unaided, drive me from Vienna. It was as much my younger self, unyielding, unwilling to exchange a mentor for a dictator, or to sidle past a collision.

If I had not met him I would not have brought to life the voice in my hands. I would not have gone to the *Musikhochschule* to study. I would not have met Julia. I would not have lost Julia. I would not be adrift. How can I hate Carl any more? After so many years, surely everything is subject to the agents of change: rain, spores, webs, darkness. Maybe I could have learned more from him if I had swallowed my sense of self. Julia must have been right, she must have been right. But now I think: let him die, his time has come, I cannot reply. Why should he foist on me this responsibility for absolution?

I could not have learned more from him. She thought I could, or hoped I could, or hoped at least that for her sake I would remain for a while in Vienna. But I was not learning, I was unlearning, I was unravelling. When I came apart at the concert, it was not because I had been ill, or because I had not prepared what I was playing. It was because he had said I would fail, and I could see him in the audience and knew he willed me to.

24

1.6

'We seem to irritate so much each other tonight,' says Virginie. She turns towards me without raising herself from the pillow.

I shake my head. I was looking up at the ceiling, but now I close my eyes.

'I will bite your shoulder.'

'Don't,' I say. 'I'll bite you harder, and it'll end very badly.'

Virginie bites my shoulder.

'Stop it, Virginie,' I say. 'Just stop it, OK? It hurts, I'm not into it. No, don't pinch me either. And I'm not irritated, just tired. Your bedroom's too hot. We had a really long rehearsal today, and I just don't feel like seeing some late-night French movie on TV. Why don't you tape it?'

Virginie sighs. 'You're so boring. If you're so boring on Friday night, I can't imagine what you'll be like on Monday night.'

'Well, you won't need to know. We're going to Lewes on Monday and then to Brighton.'

'Quartet. Quartet. Phuh.' Virginie kicks me.

After a while, she says, rather reflectively: 'I've never met your father. And you never want to meet mine, even when he's in London.'

'Oh, Virginie, please, I'm sleepy.'

'Doesn't your father ever come to London?'

'No.'

'Then I will go with you to Rochdale. We'll go in my car to the English North.'

Virginie has a little Ford Ka in what she calls 'panther-black' metallic paint. We have made short forays with it to Oxford and Aldeburgh. When I'm driving, she insists on saying, 'Take that turn,' when

25

she means 'this'. This has led to many detours and altercations.

Virginie is immensely proud of her car ('nippy, zippy, natty,' is how she describes it). She hates all four-wheel drives with a passion, especially since the suspended spare tyre of one of them produced a little indentation on the bonnet of her parked Ka. She drives with the flair and imagination she usually withholds from her playing.

'Somehow, I can't see you in Rochdale,' I say a bit sadly, probably because I can hardly see myself there any more.

'Oh, why?' she demands.

'The shops are not elegant, Virginie. No nice scarves. You would be a gazelle in a cement factory.'

Virginie half-rises from her pillow. Her panther-black eyes are smouldering and, with her black hair falling over her shoulders and down to her breasts, she looks delicious. I take her in my arms.

'No,' she says, resisting. 'Don't be so condescendant. Do you think that I am interested only in shopping?'

'No, not only in shopping,' I say.

'I thought you were sleepy,' she says.

'I am, but this is not. Anyway, what's ten minutes here or there?' I open the bedside drawer.

'So practical you are, Michael.'

'Mm, yes . . . no, no, Virginie, don't. Don't. Stop it. Just stop it.'

'Relax, relax,' she says, laughing; 'it only tickles if you're tense.'

'Tickles? Tickles? You're biting me and you think it tickles me?'

Virginie is overcome with laughter. Instead of

26

this distracting me, I get completely carried away.

After a hot shower in the pink bathroom, I set the alarm clock.

'Why?' asks Virginie, sleepily. 'It's Saturday tomorrow. We can wake up at noon. Or are you going to practise, to set for me a good example?'

'Water Serpents.'

'Oh no,' says Virginie in disgust. 'In that filthy freezing water. You English are mad.'

1.7

I dress in the dark without waking Virginie, and let myself out. She lives on the south side of Hyde Park, I on the north. It was while walking from her house one freezing Friday morning that I noticed a couple of heads bobbing in the Serpentine. I asked the closer of the two heads what he thought he was up to.

'What does it look like I'm up to?'

'Swimming. But why?'

'Why not? Join us. We've been swimming here since 1860.'

'In that case you look young for your age.'

The swimmer laughed, emerged from the water and stood shivering on the bank: twentyish, about my height, but a bit more muscular. He was wearing a black Speedo swimsuit and a yellow cap.

'Don't let me stop you,' I said.

'No, no, I was getting out anyway. Three or four minutes at this temperature is enough.'

He was hugging his body, which was completely red from the cold—lobster-red, as Virginie might have said. As he dried himself off, I looked at the murky shallows of the Serpentine.

'I suppose it's treated?' I asked.

'Oh, no,' said the cheerful young man. 'They chlorinate it in the summer, but in winter there's nobody but us Water Serpents, and we had to fight the park authorities and the Department of Health and the council and God knows who else to retain our right to swim here. You have to be a member of the club and sign away your health rights, because of all the rat-piss and goose-turds, and then you can swim between six and nine in the morning any day of the year.'

'Sounds complicated. And unpleasant. All that in a stagnant pond.'

'Oh, no, no, no—it's not stagnant—it flows underground into the Thames. I wouldn't worry. We've all swallowed the occasional mouthful and no one's died yet. Just turn up tomorrow morning at eight. The whole gang will be here. On Saturdays we swim races. I swim on Fridays and Sundays too, but then I'm a bit weird. Oh, I'm Andy, by the way.'

'Michael.' We shook hands.

A couple of joggers stared at Andy incredulously and continued on their way.

'Are you a professional swimmer?' I asked. 'I mean, what's the general standard in the club?'

'Oh, don't worry about that. A few of us have swum the Channel, but others can barely swim up to that yellow buoy there. I'm just a student. I'm studying law at University College. What do you do?'

'I'm a musician.'

'Really? What do you play?'

'The violin.'

'Excellent. Well, swimming's the best exercise for the arms. See you tomorrow then.'

'I'm not sure you'll see me tomorrow,' I said.

'Give it a try,' said Andy. 'Don't be scared. It's a great feeling.'

I did turn up the next day. Though I'm not particularly athletic, I was tempted by the quirky luxury of swimming in the open air in the heart of London. It was a masochistic luxury for winter, but after a couple of weeks I actually began to enjoy it. The water jolted me more than fully awake and braced me for the day. The coffee and biscuits in the clubhouse afterwards, the mainly male comradeship, the discussion of Giles's whimsical handicapping of us in the race, the reminiscences of the old-timers, the exchange of small talk in an amazingly wide variety of accents, all admitted me to a world outside Archangel Court and the Maggiore Quartet and Virginie's flat and the past and future and the ungiving pressure of my thoughts.

1.8

As for my own accent: what has become of it? When I return to Rochdale I find myself donning, sometimes even affecting what I once hid. From the start it was drummed into me by my mother that I should 'talk proper'. She felt there was nothing for me in the distressed and constrained town in which we lived. The way for her only child to escape was via a decent school—my comprehensive had been the old grammar school—and later, if possible, a university and the professions. My insistence on my vocation was met by both my parents with incomprehension, the withdrawal of support, and the repeatedly voiced sense that I had betrayed what had been for them real sacrifices. My father had a butcher's shop in a small street. No one in the family had ever dreamed of going to university. Now here was someone who had a chance of getting in, and who was refusing even to try.

'But, Dad, what's the point of filling out the forms? I don't want to go. What I want to do is to play music. There's a music college in Manchester —'

'You want to be a violin player?' asked Dad slowly.

'A violinist, Stanley,' interposed my mother.

He hit the roof. 'It's the bloody fiddle, that's what it is, the bloody fiddle.' He turned back to me. 'How will you support your Mum with the bloody fiddle after I've gone?'

'What about doing Music at university?' suggested my mother.

'I can't do that, Mum. I'm not doing A levels in Music. Anyway, I just want to play.'

'Where's playing going to get you?' demanded Dad. 'It won't get you a blooming pension.' He tried to speak more calmly. 'You've got to think ahead. Will you get a grant at this music college?'

'Well, it's discretionary.'

'Discretionary!' he shouted. 'Discretionary! And if you go to university, you get a mandatory grant. Don't think I don't know all that. Your head needs looking at. Look at what's happened to us and the shop this last year. Do you think we can support you when you're fiddling away?'

'I'll get a job. I'll pay my own way,' I said, not

looking at either of them.

'You'll have to return your violin to the school,' said Dad. 'Don't count on us to get you another.'

'Mrs Formby knows someone who can lend me one—for a few months, at least.'

My father's eyes flashed fire and he went stomping off. When he returned a couple of hours later, he was less furious but even more bewildered and aggrieved.

'I've been up to the school,' he said slowly, looking back and forth from Mum's face to mine, 'and that Mr Cobb he told me, "Your Michael's a very bright boy, very clever, he could try for languages or law or history. He'd get in and he could do it if he wanted." So what is it? Why don't you want to do it? That's what I want to know. Your mother and me, we've worked and worked so that you could have a better future—and you'll end up playing in some pub or nightclub. What sort of future is that?'

It took years and the intercession of others for us to be reconciled. One of them was his sister, Auntie Joan, a sort of irritant peacemaker, who ticked off both of us till we could hardly stand it any more.

We came together for a while after Mum's death, but it was clear that Dad thought I had, by turning my back on her dreams, deprived her of a happiness she was due.

Later, he attended my first recital in Manchester, but grudgingly and suspiciously. At the last moment he tried to rebel, and an elderly neighbour, Mrs Formby, had to virtually bundle him into her car. That evening he heard me receive the applause of an urbane world far outside his ken

31

and, after a fashion, conceded that there might be something to my chosen line of work after all. He is proud of me now, and curiously uncritical.

When I left for Vienna, Dad did not object. Auntie Joan too salved my conscience by insisting that one person was more than enough to look after him. Perhaps the shocks of life have, by breaking his spirit, made him milder. If there is something a bit unsettling about the way he concentrates his attentions on our cat Zsa-Zsa, at least there is little left in him of the old anger that once used to terrify me—and occasionally drew forth from me something similar, slow to enkindle and slow to disappear.

1.9

Returning from my weekly swim, I'm humming something from Schubert as I enter Archangel Court. I have my little black electronic tab-key out, but I hear the click of the unlocking glass door even before I pass it over the sensor.

'Thank you, Rob.'

'Not at all, Mr Holme.'

Rob, our so-called head porter, but really our only one, sometimes calls me by my first name, and sometimes by my last name, and there is no apparent logic to this.

'Miserable day,' he says with some enthusiasm.

'Yes.' I press the lift button.

'You haven't been swimming again, have you?' he asks, noting my bedraggled hair and rolled-up towel.

'Afraid so. It's an addiction. Talking of which,

have you got your lottery ticket for today?'

'No, no, we always get ours in the afternoon. Mrs Owen and I discuss the numbers over lunch.'

'Any input from the kids?'

'Oh, yes. By the way, Mr Holme, about the lift—it's due for servicing on Tuesday morning, so you might want to make a note of that.'

I nod. The lift growls down and stops. I take it up to my flat.

I often think how lucky I am to have what many musicians do not—a roof above my head that I can call my own. Even if the mortgage weighs on me, it is better than paying rent. I was fortunate to find my flat when I did—and in the dreadful condition that I did. Its three small, ceiling-sloped rooms, for all their quirks of water and heat, are a refuge of light that I could never afford to buy in today's market. I love the view. There is no one above me, so I hear no stomping overhead, and at this height even the sound of traffic is muted.

The building, despite its staid exterior of red brick, is various, even in some ways strange: custom-built, I think, in the thirties, it contains flats of very different sizes, from one bedroom to four, and, as a result, a diversity of residents: young professionals, single mothers, retired people, local shopkeepers, a couple of doctors, tourists who are sub-leasing, people who work in the City, which is an easy commute via the Central Line. Sometimes sounds penetrate my walls—a baby cries, a saxophone warps itself around 'Strangers in the Night', a drill judders through; but for the most part, even outside my soundproof cell, it is quiet.

A man who came to look at my TV told me that some of the residents have their sets connected to

33

the security system so as to observe the goings-on of their neighbours as they enter and leave the building or stand in the lobby waiting for the lift. For the most part, if we meet at all, it is in the lift or the lobby. We smile, hold the door open for each other, and wish each other good day. Over us presides the benevolent Rob, skilfully balancing his multiple roles of terminus manager, weather discussant, handyman and psychiatric counsellor.

Back in my flat, I turn to the newspaper I bought on the way back, but cannot concentrate on the news. I have an odd sense of compulsion. There is something I must do, but I am not quite sure what it is. I try to think it through. Yes, I must call Dad. I haven't spoken to him for almost a month.

The phone rings more than a dozen times before he answers. 'Hello? Hello? Is that Joan?' He sounds cross.

'Dad, it's Michael.'

'Who? Michael? Oh, hello, hello, how are you, Michael? Is anything the matter? Are you all right? Is everything going well?'

'Yes, Dad. I called to ask how you were.'

'Fine, fine, never been better. Thank you for calling. It's good to hear your voice.'

'I should call more often, but you know how it is, Dad. Suddenly I realise it's been a month. How's Auntie Joan?'

'Not very well, you know, not very well at all. Between you and me, she's getting a bit soft in the head. Yesterday, she got a parking ticket because she couldn't remember where she'd left the car. To tell you the truth, with her arthritis she shouldn't be driving at all. She'll be sorry to have missed you. She's just gone down to the shops. I'll tell her you

34

asked about her.'

'And Zsa-Zsa?'

'Zsa-Zsa's in the dog-house.' He chuckles.

'Oh. Why?'

'She scratched me two weeks ago. My hands. It took a good long time to clear up.'

'Did you bother her in some way?'

'No. Joan had gone out. I was watching Inspector Morse with Zsa-Zsa on my lap, and the phone rang. I thought it was part of the programme, and then I realised it wasn't. So I jumped up to answer it, and she scratched me. But I got to the phone in time.'

'Oh?'

'Oh, yes. I got there in time. Bloodstains on the receiver. The Inspector would have made something of it. When Joan got back she called the doctor. He bandaged me up. It could have got septic, you know. Joan took Zsa-Zsa's side, of course. Said I must have been mithering her in some way.'

My father sounds frail.

'Dad, I'll try to make it up north in a fortnight or so. And if I can't, I'll definitely be there for Christmas. We aren't going on a tour or anything.'

'Oh? Oh, yes, good, it'll be very good to see you, Michael. Very good indeed.'

'We'll go to Owd Betts for lunch.'

'Yes, that'll be good.' He sighs. 'I dreamed of the carpark last night.'

'It's just a parking ticket, Dad.'

'No, the other carpark. Where the shop was.'

'Oh.'

'They ruined our life. They killed your mother.'

'Dad. Dad.'

35

'It's the truth.'

'I know, Dad, but it's, well, it's the past.'

'Yes. You're right.' He pauses a second, then says, 'You should settle down, son.'

'I am settled.'

'Well, there's settled and there's settled. Are you seeing any pretty girls these days or is it just your violin?'

'I am seeing someone, Dad, but . . .' I trail off. 'I'd better go, we've got a rehearsal this afternoon, and I haven't looked at the music properly. I'll call you soon. Don't let Zsa-Zsa and Auntie Joan gang up against you.'

My father chuckles again. 'Last week, she delivered some fish to the door.'

'Who did?'

'Neighbours were thawing it on the window ledge. Zsa-Zsa smelt it and brought it over, plastic package and all.'

I laugh. 'How old is Zsa-Zsa now?'

'Sixteen last August.'

'Getting on.'

'Yes.'

'Well, bye, Dad.'

'Bye, son.'

For a few minutes after the call I sit still, thinking of my father. When he came to London three years ago the lift went out of order for a couple of days. He insisted on climbing, in slow stages, to my eighth-floor flat. The next day I booked him into a small hotel nearby. But since his only reason for coming to London was to visit me, this somewhat defeated the purpose. He rarely leaves Rochdale now. Very occasionally he goes to Manchester. London makes him jittery. One of the many things he dislikes about it is that the water doesn't lather properly.

After my mother died, he was adrift. His widowed sister believed he would not survive the loneliness, so she moved in with him and rented out her home. Zsa-Zsa, my parents' notoriously unsociable cat, then very young, took immediately to Auntie Joan. My father has coped. But he has never got over my mother's death.

As for the shop and the carpark, that was a bitter business. The council, planning to expand a main road, placed a compulsory purchase order on our butcher's shop, which was just off it, on a small side street. It was more than our shop; it was our home. A number of our neighbours' houses were taken over too. The compensation was derisory. My parents tried to fight it for years but got nowhere.

During this period I myself was in Manchester, trying through a series of odd jobs both to earn a living and to save in order, later, to go to college. I could not help at all at first, and very little later on. Besides, relations were still strained between us. After two or three years, about the time I got into the Royal Northern College of Music, my father, his work and purpose gone, fell ill with a series of bronchial ailments. My mother exhausted herself trying to nurse him, to earn a living working as a dinner lady in a school, and to fight the case. Though it was he who was ill, it was she who died— quite suddenly, of a stroke.

After a few further years of dithering, the council decided not to expand the road after all. The acquired land was sold to developers. The small shops and houses, now mainly derelict, were smashed. Where Stanley Holme, butcher, once practised his trade there is now only asphalt. It is a carpark.

1.10

When I say I come from Rochdale, people in London smile, as if the name itself were amusing. I no longer feel resentful, let alone puzzled, by this. Indeed, if there is any object of resentment here, perhaps it should be the town itself. But what happened to us could have happened anywhere, I suppose.

Besides, as a boy, I was quite happy in Rochdale. Our house was not too far from the edge of town, and once I got a bike I could cycle out towards the moors, sometimes with a schoolfriend, more often by myself. Within minutes I would be in the open countryside. Sometimes I would walk on the tops, sometimes just lie in the grassy hollows where I could no longer hear the sound of the wind. The first time I did this, I was held by surprise: I had never heard such silence before. And into that silence after a minute or two fell the rising song of a lark.

I would lie there for hours sometimes, my bike parked quite safely at the isolated inn of Owd Betts below. Sometimes a single lark would sing; sometimes as the voice of one thinned higher and higher into the sky, another's would begin to rise. Sometimes, when the sun came out after a drizzle, there would be a whole scrum of skylarks.

In London, high up though I am, there is no natural silence. Even in the middle of the 600 acres of the park, I can hear the traffic all around, and often above. But some mornings I take a camp stool and walk over to the sunken garden near the Orangery. I sit down in one of the gaps in the tall lime hedge and look out across the sinking ledges of colour to the calm oblong pool. Among the water-lilies the fountains play, obscuring any noise that the hedges have not dampened. Squirrels run boldly about, small mice timidly. A pigeon coos fatly at my feet. And—in the right season, at the opposite month of the year to this—the blackbirds sing.

Today, as I walk around the sunken garden, a conversation with Julia comes back to me. Our piano trio was playing in a concert somewhere near Linz, and afterwards the two of us went for a walk in the woods behind our host's house. It was a full moon night and a nightingale was singing frantically.

'Very flash,' I said. 'The Donizetti of the bird world.'

'Shh, Michael,' said Julia, leaning against me.

The nightingale paused and Julia said: 'Don't you like it?'

'It's not my favourite bird. Is it yours?'

'Yes.'

'That must be your Austrian blood.'

'Oh, don't be silly. How about a kiss?'

We kissed, and walked on.

'If it really is your favourite bird, Julia, I take back what I said.'

'Thank you. And what's yours?'

'The lark, of course.'

'Oh, I see. "The Lark Ascending"?'

'Oh, no—it's nothing to do with that.'

'It's a drab-looking sort of bird, isn't it?'

39

'Well, your nightingale's no bird-of-paradise either.'

'I suppose there aren't that many good-looking composers,' said Julia after a while. 'Schubert was a bit of a frog.'

'But a frog you would have kissed?'

'Yes,' said Julia without hesitation.

'Even if it distracted him from his composing?'

'No,' said Julia. 'Not then. But I don't believe it would have. It would have inspired him, and he would have finished his Unfinished.'

'I believe he would have, my darling. So it's a good thing you never kissed him.'

It began to drizzle slightly, and we turned back towards the house.

1.11

When I was being considered for the Maggiore Quartet, Helen asked me how Julia was. They knew each other because our trio and their quartet—both recently formed—had met at the summer programme in Banff in the Canadian Rockies.

I said that we'd lost touch.

'Oh, what a pity,' said Helen. 'And how's Maria? Marvellous cellist! I thought the three of you played awfully well together. You belonged together.'

'Maria's fine, I think. She's still in Vienna.'

'I do feel it's a pity when one loses touch with friends,' babbled Helen sympathetically. 'I had a schoolfriend once. He was in the class above me. I adored him. He wanted to be, of all things, a dentist . . . Oh, it's not a sensitive subject, is it?'

'No, not at all. But perhaps we should get on with the rehearsal. I've got to be somewhere at five-thirty.'

'Of course. You told me that you were in a hurry, and here I am, nattering on. Silly me.'

To lose touch—and hearing and smell and taste and sight. Not a week passes when I don't think of her. This after ten years: too persistent a trace in the memory.

After I left Vienna, I wrote to her, perhaps too late. She did not write back. I wrote again and again into a void.

I wrote to Maria Novotny, who replied, saying that Julia was still very upset and that I should give her time. My letters were disturbing her studies in her final year. Perhaps I should ease off. Maria, though, was always Julia's friend more than mine. They knew each other before I came on the scene and after I so suddenly exited it. She told me no secrets and gave me no hope.

When Julia's course was over, she disappeared off the face of the earth.

I wrote to the *Musikhochschule*, asking them to redirect my letter. I never heard from her. I wrote to her at her parents' home near Oxford, to no effect. I wrote to her aunt in Klosterneuburg, and got no reply. I wrote to Maria again. Maria wrote back to say that she hadn't heard from Julia either. She was sure she wasn't in Vienna, though.

Finally, more than a year after we parted, and overcome with loss, I phoned her parents. Her father had spent a day with us when he visited Vienna for a historical conference. He was an Auden fan, and had taken us on a little pilgrimage

41

to Kirchstetten, the small village where Auden spent his last years. In the evening, back in Vienna, we'd gone for a meal and a concert. We had taken to each other immediately.

A woman picked up the phone. 'Hello,' I said. 'Is that Mrs McNicholl?'

'Yes, it is. May I know who is speaking?' I could detect an Austrian accent buried there somewhere.

'This is Michael Holme.'

'Oh, yes, yes, I see. Please hold on. I will call my husband.' Something like panic had replaced self-assurance.

In a few seconds Dr McNicholl came on the line. He was not unfriendly in tone, but gave the impression of someone who wanted very quickly to get out of a jammed lift.

'Hello, Michael. I suppose it's about Julia. I have been sending your letters on, but, well, it's really up to her to reply.'

'How did she do in her exams?' Maria had already told me she had done quite well, but I was now flailing around to keep the conversation going.

'She passed.'

'She is all right, isn't she?'

'Yes, she is,' he replied firmly.

'Would you tell her I called? Please.'

A pause, and then, with reluctant mendacity: 'Yes.'

'Where is she now? Is she there—I mean—is she with you in Oxford?'

'For God's sake, Michael, haven't you hurt her enough?' Dr McNicholl's courtesy gave out, and he put down the receiver.

I too put it down, trembling with sadness, knowing it was no use.

1.12

My first task today is a lesson of mutual drudgery with a twelve-year-old boy who would much rather be playing the guitar. When he leaves, I try to turn to quartet work. I look over the music for our next rehearsal, but cannot concentrate on it. Instead I put on a CD of Beethoven's piano trio in C minor, the one that Carl Käll questioned me about so many years ago.

What wonderful things are his first self-numbered works, a trio of trios that say to the world, yes, these I could bear to be known by. Of them, this is the gem: the opus 1 number 3. Carl, of course, disagreed with me; he thought it the weakest of the three.

It was Julia's favourite among all Beethoven's trios. She particularly loved the minor variation in the second movement, though it was almost as if the cello and violin were, in that calm melancholy, robbing her of her own prominence. Whenever she would hear it or play it or even read it in the score, she would move her head slowly from side to side. And she loved the unflamboyant close of the entire work.

Though I have often listened to it, I haven't once played it these last ten years. In the occasional ad hoc trios I participate in, whenever it is suggested as a possibility, I persuade the others out of it, sometimes by telling them I do not care for it. As for the recordings: none of them remind me of how she played it, though some of them do ease my heart.

But what has ever reminded me of the way she played? Sometimes a phrase or two at a concert,

43

sometimes a bit more, but never anything that lasts very long. To say that there was a naturalness to her playing does not say very much: after all, everyone plays according to their nature. Rightful surprise, intensity, inwardness—it is pointless to try to convey what she conveyed. I could as little describe the beauty of her playing as explain what I felt when I first met her. Sometimes in the last few years when I have turned on the radio I have heard someone playing who I have felt convinced must be Julia. But some turn of phrase unconvinces me; and if I still have a hope or a doubt, the announcement at the end puts me right.

Last year I heard a snatch of Bach, in a taxi of all places. I rarely take cabs, cabs rarely play music, any music they do play is rarely classical. I had almost arrived at the studio when the cab-driver suddenly decided to tune in to Radio 3. It was the end of a prelude and the start of a fugue: strangely enough, in C minor. This is Julia, I said to myself. This is Julia. Everything spoke of her. We arrived; he turned off the radio; I paid him and ran. I was late for a session, and anyway I knew that I must be wrong.

1.13

Virginie calls me to cancel a lesson. When she fixed the date she hadn't looked at her diary. Now she realises that she is double-booked. A friend has just arrived from Paris. The friend will not understand, but I will, and anyway she made the other booking first, so would I mind very much?

'Who is this friend?' I ask.

'Chantal. I've told you about her, haven't I? She's Jean-Marie's sister.' Jean-Marie is Virginie's last boyfriend but one.

'OK, Virginie.'

'So what date should we make it?'

'I can't discuss that now.'

'Why not?'

'I'm busy.' The fact is, I'm quite put out by Virginie's approach to things.

'Eh-oh!' says Virginie reproachfully.

'Eh-oh yourself.'

'You sound so grumpy, Michael. Have you opened at all your windows today?'

'It's a cold day. I don't always want fresh air.'

'Oh, yes, the great Arctic swimmer is afraid of the cold.'

'Virginie, stop being tedious.'

'Why are you in a bad mood with me? Are you in the middle of something?'

'No.'

'Have you just finished something?'

'Yes.'

'What?'

'I've been listening to some music.'

'What music?'

'Virginie!'

'Well, I'm interested.'

'What you mean is that you're curious—which is entirely different.'

'No, it's just a little different. So?'

'So, what?'

'So, what is this mysterious music?'

'Beethoven's trio in C minor, sorry, in *ut mineur*, for pianoforte, violin and violoncello, opus 1 number 3.'

45

'Be just nice, Michael.'

'I'm trying.'

'Why did that music annoy you with me?'

'It did not annoy me with you, as you put it. I'm not annoyed with you. If I'm annoyed at anyone, it's myself.'

'I like that trio very much,' says Virginie. 'Did you know he arranged it himself into a string quintet?'

'What nonsense, Virginie. Oh, all right, let's fix a date for the lesson and get it over with.'

'But he did, Michael. He did not transpose it or anything.'

'Virginie, believe me, if there had been a string quintet in C minor by Beethoven, I would definitely have heard of it, I would almost certainly have listened to it, and I would very probably have played in it.'

'I read it in my *Guide de la Musique de Chambre*.'

'You couldn't have!'

'Wait. Wait. Just wait.' She is back at the phone in a few seconds. I can hear her turning the pages. 'Here it is. Opus 104.'

'What did you say?'

'Opus 104.'

'But that's crazy. That's at the wrong end of his life. Are you sure?'

'You're not too busy? You want to talk to me now?' asks Virginie, raised eyebrows audible in her voice.

'Oh, yes. Yes. What does it say?'

'Let's see,' says Virginie, translating quite fluently from her book. 'It says that in 1817 he re-arranged the third piano trio in opus 1 as a string quintet . . . Some amateur did it first, and

46

Beethoven writes down a, how do you say, a humoristical appreciation that the amateur's horrible arrangement was a quintet in three voices, and Beethoven has made it properly into five voices, and converted it from a big miserability to a presentable aspect. And the original three-voice arrangement by the amateur is now offered in a solemn holocaust to the infernal gods. Am I clear?'

'Yes, yes. But how incredible! Anything else?'

'No. For a commentary it refers you to the trio.'

'Do you always read your way through reference books, Virginie?'

'No, I was just bruising through, as you English say.'

I laugh. 'This Englishman doesn't.'

'Are you happy now?' asks Virginie.

'I think so. Yes. Yes, I am happy. Thank you, Virginie. Thank you. I'm sorry I wasn't very nice earlier on. When do you want to have your lesson?'

'Thursday next week at three o'clock.'

'Isn't that rather a long time from now?'

'Oh, no. Not very long.'

'Well, keep practising.'

'Oh, yes, of course,' says Virginie brightly.

'You're not inventing all this?' I ask. 'It just seems so unbelievable.' But she couldn't possibly have invented so many plausible details on the spot.

'Don't be silly, Michael.'

'And it's two violins, two violas and a cello—no strange combinations, right?'

'No. That's what it says.'

'Opus 104?'

'Opus 104.'

47

'Opus 104?'

'Opus 104.'

'That's very strange, sir. In C minor? Well, it's not in the CD catalogue. I can't see it under Beethoven's string quintets.'

'Perhaps it's listed under the piano trio for some reason.'

'I'll check . . . no, I'm sorry, it's not there either. Let me try the computer. I'll key in 'String quintet in C minor' and see what it spits out. No, it's not being very helpful. It says, 'No records satisfy your enquiries' . . . Let's see what happens if I try opus 104 . . . Sorry, I'm afraid all I'm coming up with is Dvorák . . . you don't mean Dvorák?'

'No. I don't mean Dvorák.'

'Well, would you like me to order the trio instead, sir?'

'No, thank you.'

*   *   *

The voice of the girl at Chimes is somewhat incredulous. 'A string quintet in C minor by Beethoven. Have you heard this piece yourself, sir?'

'No, but a friend has told me about it. It's well-documented.'

'Well, sir, I'm afraid we don't have any score of that description. Perhaps if you left us your phone number . . .'

'Look, you must have a list of Beethoven's opus numbers somewhere. Could you please look up one-oh-four?'

48

A half-sigh, half-snort. 'I suppose so.'

When she returns, her tone is puzzled, apologetic. 'Well, sir, you appear to be right.'

'I *appear* to be right?'

'I mean, you are right. Well, I don't know what to say. I'm sorry. We don't have it, and it's not in print.'

'But this is Beethoven, not Engelbert Humperdinck. Are you absolutely sure you can't order it from somewhere?'

There is a second of silence. Then she says: 'I've just thought of something. Would you hold on a minute?'

'For a week if necessary.'

When she returns, she says, 'I've been looking at the microfiche. I don't know what you're going to think of this. Emerson Editions does it in an arrangement for clarinet quintet. Score and parts. We could order that for you. It's thirty-two pounds altogether. It would only take a couple of weeks if they have it in stock. But that's all that exists.'

'Clarinet quintet? This is absolutely crazy. Well, order it, I suppose. No, no, don't order it. I'll get back to you.'

*   *   *

The main public music library in London opens, astonishingly enough, at one in the afternoon, so I decide to try the one in Manchester instead.

I phone the Henry Watson Music Library, my second home when I was a student in Manchester—and, even more crucially, for three years between school and college when I had to earn a fitful living there. I could not afford scores

49

and music in those days. If this library had not existed, I don't know how I could have held onto my dream of becoming a musician. I owe it so much; surely it will allow me to owe it a little more.

A deep male voice comes onto the line. I explain what I want.

There's a tone of slight surprise in his response. 'This arrangement, it's by him, you mean? Yes, of course, of course, if there's an opus number it would be, wouldn't it? . . . Just a moment.'

A long wait. Two, three minutes. Finally:

'Yes, we do have a set of parts for a number of quintets by Beethoven: your one's among them. Let's see now: there's 4, 29, 104, and 137. This edition is published by Peters, but I don't know if it's still in print. We've had it for yonks. Since the twenties, if not earlier. And you'll be pleased to hear that we also have a miniature score—one of the Eulenburgs. Pretty ancient too. This one has "10th August, 1916" on it. Well, one learns something every day. I must admit I'd never heard of opus 104.'

'I can't thank you enough. Now the only problem is, I'm in London.'

'That shouldn't be difficult. We do interlibrary loans, so any reputable library could ask us for it.'

'The Westminster Music Library for example?'

'Yes, I suppose so. They've had their, well, tribulations, but they should still, I suppose, be able to tell a trio from a quintet.'

I smile. 'You're right, it's not in the best of shape,' I say. 'But I hear you've had a few problems of your own these last few years. Council growlings and so on.'

'Well, there's been a lot of turmoil ever since

1979. We haven't fared too badly compared to some. The thing is to keep going.'

'I have a lot to thank your library for,' I say. 'I was in Manchester myself for seven years.'

'Ah.'

As we speak, the curve of the walls comes to my mind, the light through the windows, the heavy mahogany shelving. And the books, the wonderful scores, which I could borrow even before I joined the RNCM—when I was scrabbling about to survive and save, unsupported by any academic or musical institution at all.

'By the way,' I continue, 'the last time I was in Manchester I noticed you had equipped yourselves with modern shelving and got rid of the lovely old mahogany stuff.'

'Yes.' He sounds a bit defensive. 'It's good solid shelving, but, well, a bit slippery. Once we've overcome the slipperiness it'll suit our needs very well.'

'How do you plan to do that?'

'Tape. Or sandpaper.'

'Sandpaper?'

'Yes, sandpaper—it works very well. Yes, I'm in favour of sandpaper myself. Odd thing about sandpaper: it seems to know how to make smooth things rough and rough things smooth . . . Well, I won't reshelve these. I'll keep them aside, shall I, with a note saying we're expecting a loan request from London?'

'If you would. Thank you. Thank you very much indeed.'

*   *   *

51

I can hardly believe it. I will play this quintet as soon as I get the music. The Maggiore can borrow a second viola player. I know that, unlike with the trio, nothing will seize me up or paralyse my heart and arm. But now I am hungry to hear it. Somewhere in London there must surely be a recording of it.

I get the bus and sit upstairs at the very front. It is a freezing, clear day. The wind pries through the edges of the pane in front of me. The dried plane leaves have been blown onto the road. I can see through the bare trees to the Serpentine.

Soon, though, I am on Oxford Street, the antithesis of greenery and water. Red buses and black cabs, like two hostile species of giant ants, take over the traffic lanes. On the packed pavements, pre-Christmas shoppers scurry about like demented aphids.

I go to every store I can find—Tower, HMV, Virgin, Music Discount Centre, the works—and talk to innumerable sales clerks and strain through reams of fine print in the CD bible before it really comes home to me that there is no CD of this work and that there has almost certainly never been one.

Frustrated, I phone Piers and ask him for advice. He tells me he thinks he's heard of the piece, but can't advise me on how to get hold of a recording. I then phone Billy, who, oddly enough for a thoroughly modern composer, is a great believer in the virtues of vinyl.

'Mm,' says Billy, 'it's a long shot, but you could try Harold Moore's. They have a whole lot of old records: there might be something there. You're in the area anyway. No harm in giving it a shot.'

He gives me directions and adds: 'It would be

52

wonderful to play if there is such a thing.'

'There's no 'if' about it, Billy. I've managed to locate parts and a score.'

'Oh, I'd love to examine the score,' says Billy with fervour, his compositional persona coming to the fore. 'I'd love to. I mean, it's recycling, isn't it, but it's not just recycling. He would have had to make a lot of changes—I mean real changes. How can a single cello do double duty? And what about the broken chord passages on the piano? That wouldn't suit strings at all, would it? And . . .'

'Billy, I'm really sorry, I've got to go. But thanks a lot. Really. See you this evening.'

I rush off on my quest, revitalised, and locate the shop. After the glass-and-chrome titans of Oxford Street, frenetic with escalators and decibels and security guards, Harold Moore's is a Dickensian haven, with a few dubious-looking people flicking their way sleepily through cardboard boxes. I am directed to the basement, and look through whatever's on offer. I talk to an old man, who is quite helpful but, in the event, unable to help.

'You're sure you don't mean opus 29?'

'No.'

'Well, write down your name and address on this card, and if anything comes in we'll contact you.'

Upstairs, I notice a preoccupied-looking man standing behind a counter at the back of the shop. I am on my way out, and I know it is hopeless, but I try him on the off-chance.

He closes his eyes and taps his lips with his index finger. 'You know, this rings a bell. I don't want to be too optimistic, but would you mind going downstairs again? There's a pile of Eastern European recordings that have been lying around

53

for a while. I haven't yet classified them under composers, but I have a faint inkling . . . Of course, I may be wrong—or even if I'm right, it could have been sold already.'

In five minutes he pulls a record out, examines both sides of the sleeve, and hands it to me.

1.15

On Regent Street I catch the bus home. The front seat is taken, so I sit by a window halfway along. Behind me half a dozen French schoolgirls are giggling and chattering and arguing.

I savour the precious record. The photograph on the sleeve portrays a large room, stately in brown and dull gold, the floor gleaming with elaborate parquetry, an uncluttered assortment of vases and paintings arranged here and there, a chandelier, a Persian rug, a valanced door opening out to a further room, and that to a room beyond, the whole suite full of light: a pleasing prelude to the vinyl delights within. The one slight oddness is a wooden stand in the middle of the floor, of the kind that I imagine is usually attached to plush red ropes that keep back the public. Could it not have been moved? Is it stuck to the floor? Is it in fact an article of furniture: a hat-stand for a single hat?

As the bus turns into Oxford Street, the French schoolgirls start to applaud.

There are two Beethoven string quintets on the LP: my C minor, so desperately sought, so astonishingly found; and one in E flat major, another complete surprise, though I recall the librarian mentioning in passing its opus number, 4.

54

They were recorded (with an extra viola player) by the Suk Quartet and issued in 1977 under the Czech label Supraphon. According to the sleeve note, the members of the quartet, being attached to orchestras, 'enjoy only limited opportunities for concert appearances, but they have made the most of them. They make a systematic effort to present some less popular works which they feel are being unfairly neglected, and invite outside instrumentalists for joint performances of works for unusual combinations, which the public otherwise hears only rarely.'

Bravo. Bravo Suk. Bravo Supraphon. What would I have done if it had not been for you? In twenty minutes I will be back in my flat, but I won't listen to it immediately. Late tonight, after the rehearsal, I'll come home, light a candle, lie down on my duvet, and sink into the quintet.

As the bus trundles fitfully along Oxford Street, held up by bus-stops, traffic lights, congestion and the odd crazy pedestrian weaving his way across, the French schoolgirls turn animatedly to what I think is a discussion of the merits of rival cosmetics. I turn back to the sleeve.

The Suk Quartet, founded in '68, was originially called Quartet '69, a name quite clearly not thought through. One year later, however, 'it adopted, with the agreement of the executors of the estate of the composer Josef Suk, its present name.'

So my first impression that its name must have had something to do with the violinist Josef Suk was entirely wrong. Or maybe it wasn't, because I notice that the German text doesn't mention the word 'composer', and nor does the French. But the violinist was, after all, the great-grandson of the composer . . . who, if I recall, was himself the son-in-law of Dvorák, who, like me, was a butcher's son. My thoughts are rambling furiously now, and I look up from my record to see why we aren't moving.

We are stuck behind a line of buses just after the traffic light at the midpoint of Selfridges. I turn my head back slightly to see one of my favourite landmarks, the grandiose lapis-robed statue of the Angel of Selfridges, with her attendant mermen kneeling in homage. She and her eccentric building are the only things on Oxford Street that make me smile.

My eyes do not reach the Angel of Selfridges.

Julia is sitting five feet away from me, reading a book.

1.16

In the bus directly opposite, at the window directly opposite, is Julia. Her bus has stopped at the traffic light.

I begin to pound the window and shout, 'Julia! Julia! Julia! Julia! Julia!'

She cannot hear me. We are in separate worlds.

Stop reading, Julia. Look. Look out of the window. Look at me. Oh God.

Around me the passengers stop talking. The schoolgirls gasp. In the bus opposite no one seems to notice.

I keep pounding the window. At any moment her bus or mine could move off.

She smiles at something in the book, and my heart sinks.

A man sitting behind her notices me and the commotion that has resulted. He looks mystified but not alarmed. I gesticulate and point desperately—and, with great hesitation, he taps Julia on the shoulder and points at me.

Julia looks at me, her eyes opening wide in what? astonishment? dismay? recognition? I must look wild—my face red—my eyes filled with tears—my fists still clenched—I am a decade older—the lights will change any second.

I rummage around in my satchel for a pen and a piece of paper, write down my telephone number in large digits, and hold it against the glass.

She looks at it, then back at me, her eyes full of perplexity.

Simultaneously, both buses begin to move.

My eyes follow her. Her eyes follow me.

I look for the number at the back of the bus. It is 94.

I grab my record and get to the stairs. I am given a wide berth. The schoolgirls are whispering in tones of wonderment: *'Fou.' 'Soûl.' 'Non. Fou.' 'Non. Soûl.'*

The conductor is coming up the stairs. I can't get past him. I have to stand aside. I am losing time, I am losing it.

Finally I get down, push my way past a couple of people, and jump off the moving bus.

Weaving across the traffic, I get to the other side. I have lost too much time. Her bus has moved away. It is far ahead, with a number of buses and taxis in between. I try to push through the crowd, but it is too thick. I will never catch up.

A taxi lets out a passenger. A young woman, her hands full of shopping, is about to grab it when I interpose myself. 'Please,' I say. 'Please.'

She takes a step back and stares at me.

I get into the cab. To the taxi-driver I say: 'I want to catch up with the Number Ninety-four in front.'

He half turns around, then nods. We move forward. The lights turn yellow against us. He stops.

'Couldn't you go through?' I plead. 'It's not red yet.'

'I'll get my licence took away,' he says, annoyed. 'What's the hurry anyway? You won't save much time.'

'It's not that,' I blurt out. 'There's someone on that bus I haven't seen for years. I've got to catch it. She might get off it.'

'Take it easy, mate,' says the driver. But he tries his best. Where our single lane broadens out for a bus bay, he overtakes a bus or two. Then the street narrows and we can do nothing. Suddenly everything slows down again. Only couriers on bicycles squeeze swiftly through between the lanes of traffic.

'Can't you try to get off Oxford Street and join it further along?'

He shakes his head. 'Not here you can't.'

After one more tricky feat of overtaking the driver says: 'Look, mate, I'm nearer but, to be quite honest, I won't make it, not on Oxford Street. It's usually slow but not as slow as this. Your best bet now is to get out and run for it.'

'You're right. Thanks.'

'That's two pounds sixty.'

I only have a five-pound note in my wallet and I can't wait to be given the change. I tell him to keep it and grab my satchel.

'Hey! Not that door,' he shouts as I open the one on the right. But I know I have no chance against the crowds on the pavement. My one hope is to run between the opposing streams of traffic.

Sweating, diesel-gassed, unable to see clearly through my most inconvenient tears, I run and gasp and run. On the other side the traffic speeds up, but ours remains blessedly still.

I catch up with the bus a little before Oxford Circus. I cut across and get on. I try to run up the stairs but can't. I walk up slowly, in hope and in dread.

Julia is not there. Where she was sitting are a small boy and his father. I go to the very front and look back at every face. I go downstairs, I look at every face. She is not there.

I keep standing. People glance at me and turn away. The conductor, a black man with grey hair, seems to want to speak, but doesn't. I am not asked for my fare. The bus turns onto Regent Street. At Piccadilly Circus, I get off with all the others. I cross streets, moving where those around me move. The wind blows about small pieces of debris. I see the sign of Tower Records in front of me.

I close my eyes in shock. My satchel is on my shoulders but my hands are empty. I have left my record in the taxi.

Under the arrow of Eros I sit down and weep.

1.17

Under the statue of Eros, among the tourists, drug-pushers and rent boys, I sit. Someone speaks to me but what he says I cannot fathom.

I get up. I begin walking down the length of Piccadilly, through an underpass peopled by the cold and wretched, across Hyde Park, till I get to the Serpentine. I have disburdened myself of what coins I had. A white sun slants low. Geese honk. I sit on a bench and put my head in my hands. After a while I walk on. Eventually I get home.

The light on my answering machine is flashing and I press the button quickly. But there is nothing: a message from Billy; a message from the double-glazing people; a message from someone who thinks I am the London Bait Company.

How could it have been? How could anyone in a few seconds memorise seven random illegibly scrawled digits? But I am in the phone book. Surely, having seen me, she will know how I am to be traced.

It was her. I know it was her. And yet could I have been as mistaken with my eyes as with my ears: when someone else was playing on the radio and everything said to me that it was her? Her gold-brown hair, worn longer now, her grey-blue eyes, her eyebrows, her lips, her whole well-loved face, there could not be two such faces in the world. She was no further from me than the seats on the other side of the aisle, but she could have been in Vienna. Her expression—it was Julia's expression—even the tilt of her head when she read, the way she smiled, the absorption.

A black coat against a day such as this, a peacock-blue scarf at her neck. What is she doing in London? Where was she going? Where did she go? Did she get off to look for me? Did we cross each other? Was she standing on the pavement somewhere, scanning the multitude and crying?

The two layers of glass between us, like a prison visit by a loved one after many years.

Buses are infamous for travelling in convoys. Could there have been another Number 94 just in front in which she was still sitting when I had given up hope? Why think of this now, what use in thinking of it?

Has she been in London these last ten years? No, I would surely have got to know of it. In England then? What is she doing here now? Where is she?

My stomach heaves. I feel sick. What is it? My cold walk after sweating? I have eaten almost nothing all day.

What could I read in her eyes? Puzzlement—alarm—pity? Could I read love? In that woman's eyes could I read love?

PART TWO

PART TWO

2.1

I get through the rehearsal. A day passes, then another. I buy bread and milk. I eat, I drink, I bathe, I shave. Exhausted by wakefulness, I sleep. I teach. I attend rehearsals. I turn on the news and absorb words. I exchange greetings with our porter and the other denizens of our building. As once before, after I fled Vienna, my brain and body direct themselves.

Julia, if she lives in London, does not have a listed number. If she does not live in London, she could be anywhere.

Nor can I trace the lost LP. The taxi-driver, I learn, should have taken it to a police station, and they would have sent it on to the London Carriage Office. I phone them. Do I remember the number of the cab? No. I should call again in a couple of days. I do, to no avail. Two days later I call once more. They are not hopeful. Maybe the next passenger in the taxi picked it up. That sort of thing happens all the time with umbrellas. If they hear anything, they'll get in touch. But I can tell that I will not see that record again. I will not now hear what I came so close to hearing.

I talk to Erica Cowan, our agent. She is surprised to hear my voice. Piers usually deals with her. I ask for her advice in tracing Julia McNicholl.

She asks a few questions, takes down a few details, then says: 'But why so suddenly, Michael, after so many years?'

'Because I saw her the other day in London, on a bus, and I have to find her. I have to.'

Erica pauses, then says, seriously and hesitantly: 'Michael, could you have been mistaken?'

'No.'

'And you're sure you want to revive your acquaintance after this, well, hiatus?'

'Yes. And, Erica—please keep this under your hat. I mean, I don't want Piers, Helen and Billy to go on about this.'

'Well,' says Erica, with evident pleasure at our complicity, 'I'll ask around in this country and I'll ask Lothar in Salzburg if he can help.'

'Would you, Erica, would you really? Thank you very much. I know how busy you are. But—talking of Austria—there's a cellist, Maria Novotny, who's quite active in the musical world in Vienna, and who was—is, I should think—a friend of Julia's. The three of us were students at the *Musikhochschule* and played in a trio together. That may be—I don't know, but that may be a lead.'

'It may,' says Erica. 'But wouldn't you rather follow that one up yourself?'

'I'm not sure,' I say. 'I just feel that an enquiry from an agent—a local agent like Lothar probably—would work better.' At the back of my mind there is a sense of unease: that Maria might know where Julia is, but not want to tell me.

'And you think your friend Julia McNicholl still performs?' asks Erica. 'She couldn't have given up music?'

'It's unimaginable.'

'How old would she be—approximately?'

'Thirty. No, she'd be thirty-one, I suppose. No, thirty-two.'

'When did you last see her? Before London, I

mean.'

'Ten years ago.'

'Michael, you're sure you want to meet her again?'

'Yes.'

'But ten years—isn't that a bit excessive?'

'No.'

There is a pause, and Erica becomes pragmatic. 'Any A in the Mac? One L or two?'

'No A, two Ls. Oh, and an H after the C.'

'Is she Scots? Or Irish?'

'Well, I think her father's one quarter Scots, but for all practical purposes she's English. Well, English and Austrian, I suppose.'

'I'll give it a try, Michael. This may be the start of a whole new career for me.' Erica, as almost always, sounds hugely upbeat.

If Erica, our Big White Chief, with her mixture of matronly and shark-like qualities can't find her, I don't know who can. But again the days pass and, with each of Erica's bulletins of unsuccess, my reserves of hope drain away.

Finally I tell her that Julia's parents live in Oxford.

'Why on earth didn't you tell me before?' asks Erica, taking down the particulars, unable to keep some annoyance out of her voice. 'It would have saved time.'

'Well, Erica, you're right, but I thought it would be best to try the professional route first. I didn't want to waste your time, but I couldn't bear to hassle her parents.'

'Michael, I'm going to have to leave this bit of it to you.'

'I can't. I really can't. I tried once, years ago, and

was frozen in my tracks. You've been so kind, I hate to ask you to consider this. It's just that I can't do it myself.'

Erica sighs. 'I'm not sure how to put this. I don't feel completely comfortable about this, well, project. But I like you, Michael, and I'll give it one last try. If I do find her, all I can really do is to make sure that she knows how to get in touch with you.'

'Yes. That's fair enough. I accept that.'

Erica phones me the next weekend. 'Guess where I'm calling from.'

'I've no idea—no, I can guess. Erica, you needn't have gone to so much trouble.'

'Well,' says Erica, 'Oxford's not much further away than parts of London. A true sleuth goes to the source. Besides, I had to meet someone here anyway,' she quickly adds.

And?'

'Michael, the news isn't good,' says Erica in a rush. 'The college lodge told me that Dr McNicholl died five or six years ago. They think Mrs McNicholl went back to Austria, but they don't have an address for her any longer. As for Julia, they don't know anything about her at all. The telephone number you gave me still works—you've got to add a 'five' in front, by the way—but it's someone completely different. And I visited their house on the Banbury Road. The present owners bought it from someone else, so it's changed hands at least twice.'

I can't think of anything to say. Erica continues:

'The trail's run cold. I'm so sorry. I was beginning to enjoy it, and for some reason this morning I was certain I'd succeed. Well, there it is.

But I thought I'd call you from Oxford to tell you—and to ask you if you can think of anywhere else in this city that I might try.'

'You've tried everything,' I say, hoping to disguise my disappointment. 'You've been wonderful.'

'You know, Michael,' says Erica, suddenly confidential, 'someone once disappeared completely out of my life. Just walked out. It took me years to—not to understand, I never did that—I suppose I still can't understand why it happened with so little warning—but to reconcile myself to it. But now, when I look at my husband and my children, I think, thank God.'

'Well—'

'We must have you over for supper sometime soon,' says Erica. 'By yourself. No, with the others. No, by yourself. How about next Thursday?'

'Erica . . . I'd rather just lie low for a bit.'

'Of course.'

'It's really very good of you.'

'Not at all. Pure self-interest. Feeding my flock. Grooming my stable. And, as I said, I had an appointment here. It's lovely in Oxford this afternoon, everything's just *glistening* after the rain. But parking's hell. Always is. Ba-yee.'

This is followed by two audible kisses, and Erica rings off.

2.2

Days pass. I cannot bear to be in the company of others, but when I am alone, I am sick with memory.

69

I cling to routine in a life that, by its nature, consists—apart from the lessons, whose times I arrange myself—of arbitrary dates: for performances with the quartet, for rehearsals, for session work, for playing as an extra with the Camerata Anglica.

I teach Virginie, but find some reason not to stay over. She senses a problem. How could she not? At times she looks at me with an expression of pain mixed with angry puzzlement.

The one fixed point in my week is my Saturday morning swim. If I lapse here, I will lose all pattern to my days.

Today, however, there is a difference. The Water Serpents are being filmed for TV. All of us are doing our best to appear phlegmatic.

It's not too cold as November mornings go, though since the programme is going to be aired sometime around Christmas it'll appear colder. The three pretty girls hired by the studio introduce the action. They stand on the long diving platform, shivering in their swimsuits, squealing exaggeratedly. Phil and Dave let out strident wolf-whistles, and are shushed by the camera crew. 'Oooooh,' says one girl, 'we'll be back after the break, we're absolutely mad to be doing this, but . . .' The camera pans to the swans and geese floating on the lake and wandering around the shore. The little Lido looks remarkably tidy. It appears that Phil has swept their filthy droppings, mounds of them, into the water. 'Where else?' he says, and shrugs.

A golden retriever appears and swims with his master. The shot is unsatisfactory. Soggy dog and frozen master are directed into the water again.

Then our race begins. Giles assigns us handicaps based on our previous results. We get onto the board, and dive off, the slowest first, then the rest of us one by one as the passing seconds are shouted out on shore. Andy, the young law student, dives off last of all. His handicap is usually so heavy that he doesn't have a chance.

Everyone emerges shivering and virtuous. Back in the clubhouse, the cameras are ejected.

'You can't come in 'ere, it's private.'

'What, Phil, you got something you're ashamed of?' asks Dave. 'Let the totties come in. And their crew.'

Andy, suddenly worried, puts his shirt on and pulls his shirt-tails down before taking off his swimsuit.

'Nun joke! Nun joke!' shouts Gordon. 'Silence for the nun joke. There were these four nuns and they got to the pearly gates . . .'

'Shut up, Gordon. This used to be a nice club,' laughs someone.

'Before my time,' says Gordon proudly.

The kettle whistles. While Phil makes tea, the lugubrious Ben locks me into conversation. Ben, before he retired, was a meat inspector.

'I'm on a diet. I've been eating pears,' he says with gravity. 'Pears and water.'

'Sounds rather faddish,' I say.

'Six pounds of pears.'

'Why?' I ask, wondering—but not enquiring—whether this is his daily or weekly quota, and whether this is all he is allowed to eat.

'Prostate.'

'Oh,' I murmur sympathetically, unenlightened yet not thirsting for light. 'Ah, tea. Let me get you a mug.'

The golden retriever is barking and begging. Phil dips his oatmeal biscuit in his tea, and gives the dog half.

Dressed again, I wish everyone goodbye.

'So long, Mike.'

'See you next week.'

'Don't get into mischief, mate.'

Three swans fly low over the water and land. On the far bank, a troop of cavalry clip-clop along, helmets and breastplates flashing in the sun. On the triple-arched bridge to my left the traffic stops and starts. The TV crew is standing on the diving platform, but there is no sign of the three glamorous girls.

I walk back under the bridge, along the lake. By the Bayswater Road I stop to have a drink. The water-fountain is topped by a little bronze statue of two bears, hugging each other in affectionate play. I find myself smiling. Having drunk, I pat their heads in thanks, and make my way back home.

2.3

In front of Archangel Court there is an area of lawn enclosed by a low box hedge. Some flower-beds, a small goldfish pond, a tallish holly tree covered with a cyclamen creeper: our part-time gardener, a cousin of Rob's, takes care of this zone. He is usually as taciturn as Rob is chatty.

I am walking across this little field of green when I notice a blazered, trousered woman—gaunt, heavily made-up, I'd guess in her late fifties—walking briskly along the path. I glance at her and she at me, presumably wondering whether, as strangers heading for the same building, we should exchange a friendly greeting.

As I join the path, she looks at me very directly. 'I don't think you should be walking across the grass,' she says in the kind of disdainfully diphthonged accent, thick with horse-dung, that sets my teeth on edge.

I take a second or two to recover. 'Well, I don't usually,' I say, 'but occasionally I think it's very pleasant to. Thank you for your views on the matter.'

There is a pause, and we walk on side by side. I open the outer glass door for her, but—since I've never seen her before and, anyway, am not feeling excessively gallant—not the inner one. I have my black tab in my hand, but wait for her to fumble around in her bag. She looks rather flustered by our proximity, sandwiched as we are between two slices of glass.

'By the way,' I say, 'why on earth did you feel it necessary to talk to me if that was all you wished to say?'

Rather mutedly but still firmly she says: 'I was just thinking of the grass.

Rob, from his desk in the lobby, raises his head from the *Daily Mail*, notices us and clicks open the door. The woman walks down the corridor to the far lift. I wait by my own lift, the near one.

'Making friends with Bee?' Rob asks me.

I tell him about our strange exchange, and he laughs.

'Oh, yes, well, Bee, she can be a little sharp . . . They're new here—come up once a week from Sussex. Her husband can't stand it when people walk across the grass. A few days ago he said to me, 'Rob, there are children playing on the grass.'

'How wonderful,' I said. 'After all, what is grass for?'

A courier in black leather gear buzzes, and is let in.

'Package for number twenty-six. Will you sign for it?' he asks Rob, evidently in a rush to continue his round.

'Number twenty-six—that's Mrs Goetz. She's still in—you'd better give it to her yourself. Far lift ... Oh, that reminds me, Michael. A taxi-driver left this for you. You were out, so he left it here.'

He reaches down to the shelf below his desk, and hands me a white plastic bag. I stare at it.

'Are you all right?' Rob asks.

'Yes—yes,' I say, sitting down on the sofa.

'Nothing wrong, I hope, Michael,' says Rob. His phone rings. He ignores it.

'Nothing wrong at all,' I say. 'I'm sorry ... I just can't believe that anyone would ... Did he leave a note or anything? Did he say anything?'

'No, just that you'd left it in his taxi, and that he was glad he'd tracked you down.'

'What did he look like?'

'I didn't pay much attention, you know. White. Spectacles. Fortyish. Short. Clean-shaven. He'll be on the security videotape if you want to check up on him. It was just twenty minutes ago.'

'No, no—I think I'll go up now.'

'Yes, yes, you do that. Means a lot to you, that record?' says Rob, a little bemused.

I nod, and press the button for the lift.

2.4

Without washing the Serpentine off myself, I put the string quintet on. The sound fills the room: so familiar, so well-loved, so disturbingly and enchantingly different. From the moment, a mere ten bars from the beginning, where it is not the piano that answers the violin but the violin itself that provides his own answer, to the last note of the last movement where the cello, instead of playing the third, supports with its lowest, most resonant, most open note the beautifully spare C major chord, I am in a world where I seem to know everything and nothing.

My hands travel the strings of the C minor trio while my ears sing to the quintet. Here Beethoven robs me of what is mine, giving it to the other violin; there he bequeaths me the upper reaches of what Julia used to play. It is a magical translation. I listen to it again from beginning to end. In the second movement it is the first violin—who else?—who sings what was the piano's theme, and the variations take on a strange, mysterious distance, as being, in a sense, variations one degree removed, orchestral variants of variations, but with changes too that go beyond what could be explained by orchestration alone. I must play this with the Maggiore, I must. If we're simply playing it through with a friendly viola, Piers will surely not mind my being first fiddle for once.

I still don't know how the cabbie found me. The only possibility I can think of is that he examined the bag or the receipt—that he went to Harold Moore's the very day I left it behind—that someone there recognised the record—that the old man downstairs remembered I'd just filled out an address card. But was Bayswater out of his way for so many days on end? Was he perhaps on holiday? And what moved him to such effort, to such kindness? I do not know his name or the number of his taxi. I cannot trace him or thank him. But somewhere in this music, interfused in my mind with so many extra-musical memories, this strange action too has found a sort of home.

2.5

I write to Carl Käll: an awkward letter, wishing him well in his retirement and saying little of myself. I do say that I am happy he heard us in Stockholm, and that he was not ashamed of his student. I know I have not built the kind of career he envisaged for me, but I am making music I love. If I think of Vienna at all, it is of the early days. This is hardly true, but why widen a rift between strangers— between those estranged? I add that if I am exacting with myself, I owe it to him, and to my admiration of him. In large part this is true.

He was a mocker: 'Oh, you English! Finzi! Delius! It would be better to remain in a land without music than to have music like that.' And a charmer: when Julia and I played for him once, he took pains to praise her, casually, intelligently, extravagantly. She couldn't understand what fault I found in him, either then or later. She loved me, yes, but saw this as a mote in my own eye. Yet when I met him in Manchester, had he not equally charmed me?

Why did we call him Carl among ourselves?

Because that is what he would most have hated. 'Herr Professor. Herr Professor.' What did the noble sound he created have to do with such bowing and scraping, such subservience of soul? But why fret about all that when I have the present to address? December deepens. One morning, early, I am walking along the path just outside Archangel Court when I stop suddenly. Ten yards ahead of me is a fox. He is staring intently at a laurel bush. The light is grey, and a street-lamp makes sharp shadows. I thought it must be a cat at first, but only for a moment. I hold my breath. For a good half minute neither he moves nor I. Then, for some reason—an inadvertent sound, a change of breeze, intuitive caution—the fox turns his head and looks at me. He holds my eyes for several seconds. Then he pads calmly across the road towards the park and is lost in the mist.

Virginie is going to Nyons for a few weeks to spend Christmas with her family, then on a little round of old schoolfriends: Montpellier, Paris, St-Malo. I realise that it is a relief.

I imagine her zipping along the autoroutes in her little black Ka. I don't own a car myself. Piers or Helen or Billy—my sympathetic strings—usually give me a lift when we play out of town. I like driving; perhaps I should buy something second-hand. But I don't have a great deal by way of savings, and I have too many expenses to think about: actual, like my mortgage; potential, like a good violin of my own. My Tononi is borrowed—it has been generously lent, and has been in my hands for years, but there is no piece of paper to back my right to this piece of wood. I love it, and it responds to me, but it belongs to Mrs Formby, and at her wish, it could be taken from me and lie unplayed, unloved, unspeaking in a cupboard for years. Or she could die soon, and the violin be swallowed up into her estate. What has happened to it in the last two hundred and seventy years? Whose hands will follow mine?

The church bell rings out eight o'clock. I lie in bed. My bedroom walls are blank: no painting, no hanging, no pattern in wallpaper: just paint, white and magnolia, and a small window from which, lying thus, I can see only the sky.

2.6

Life settles into a bearable aloneness. The return of that record has changed things. I listen to sonatas and trios that I have not heard since Vienna. I listen to Bach's English suites. I sleep better.

Ice begins to form on the Serpentine, but the Water Serpents swim on. The real problem is not the cold, which can't fall below zero anyway, but the sharp little slivers and needles of floating ice.

Nicholas Spare, the music critic, invites me and Piers (but not Helen or Billy) to his pre-Christmas party: mince-pies, strong punch and virulent gossip interspersed with carols thumped out by Nicholas himself on an untuned grand piano.

Nicholas irritates me; why, then, do I go to his annual party? Why, for that matter, does he invite me?

'My dear boy, I'm absolutely besotted with you,' he tells me, although, being just a couple of years younger, I can't very well be Nicholas's dear boy.

Also, Nicholas is besotted with everyone. He looks at Piers with unfeigned (but slightly exaggerated) lust.

'I met Erica Cowan at the Barbican last night,' says Nicholas. 'She told me your quartet is soaring, that you are playing all over the place—Leipzig, Vienna, Chicago, she rattled off the names like a travel agent. "How terrifying," I said. "And how do you manage to get them such wonderful venues?"'

'"Oh," she said, "there are two mafias in music, the Jewish mafia and the gay mafia, and Piers and I between us have both bases covered."'

Nicholas emits a sort of snorting laugh, then, noticing that Piers is smouldering with unamusement, bites into a mince-pie.

'Erica's exaggerating,' I say. 'Things are pretty uncertain for us—as for most quartets, I suppose.'

'Yes, yes, I know,' says Nicholas. 'Everything's awful except for the Three Tenors and Nigel Kennedy. Don't tell me. If I hear that once again, I'll scream.' His eyes stray across the room. 'I've got to listen to you again sometime, I really must. Such a pity you don't have any recordings. Aren't you playing at the Wigmore next month?'

'Why don't you write something about us?' I say. 'I'm sure Erica must have suggested it. I don't know how it is we're getting better known. No one ever reviews us.'

'It's these editors,' says Nicholas shiftily. 'All they want us to cover is opera and modern music. They think that chamber music is a sort of backwater—the standard repertoire, I mean. You should commission something from a really good composer. That's the way to get reviews. Let me introduce you to Zensyne Church. That's him over there. He's just written a marvellous piece for baritone and vacuum cleaner.'

'Editors?' says Piers with contempt. 'It's not the editors. It's people like you, who're only interested in what's glamorous or trendy. You'd rather go to the world premiere of some trash than a great performance of something that you'd find boring because it's good.'

Nicholas Spare basks in the attack. 'I do so love it when you get passionate, Piers,' he says provocatively. 'What would you say if I came to the Wig and reviewed you? And put it in my weekly highlights of future concerts?'

'I'd be speechless,' says Piers.

'Well, I promise to. That's my word of honour. What are you playing?'

'Mozart, Haydn, Beethoven,' says Piers. 'And there's a thematic connection between them that you might find interesting. Each quartet has a fugal movement.'

'Fugal? Marvellous,' says Nicholas, his attention wandering. 'And in Vienna?'

'All Schubert: *Quartettsatz,* Trout Quintet, string quintet.'

'Oh, the Trout,' says Nicholas, sighing. 'How sweet. All that tedious charm. I hate the Trout. It's so county.'

'Fuck you, Nicholas,' says Piers.

'Yes!' says Nicholas, brightening up. 'I hate it. I loathe it. It makes me ill. It's so kitsch. It knows exactly what the right moves are, and it makes them all. It's light and it's trite. I'm astonished that anyone still plays it. No, on second thoughts, I'm not astonished. Some people should have their ears tested. Actually, Piers, do you know, your ears are far too big. Well, as I was saying, I'm not a snob—I like a lot of light music—but . . .'

Piers, livid, pours a glass of warm punch on his host's head.

2.7

We have a rehearsal the next day at Helen's house. Brother and sister are both looking subdued. Piers's behaviour has made the rounds. Helen has been ticking him off for antagonising Nicholas Spare, especially after he had promised to review us. But, as Piers says, Nicholas has made the same promises several times in the past, always backed up by his sacred honour, has avoided Piers for a month or two after the unreviewed concert, and then dear-boyed him as if nothing had happened.

'I didn't know you liked the Trout so much,' I say to him.

'Well, I do,' says Piers. 'Everyone treats it as if it's a sort of divertimento—or worse.'

'I do feel it's one movement too long,' I say.

'Helen, could I have a cup of tea, please,' mutters Piers. 'The hotter the better.'

'I take it back,' I say quickly. 'Looks like Billy's late as usual. What is it this time? The wife, the kids or the Central Line?'

'He did call,' says Helen. 'He couldn't get his cello into its case. The spike was stuck. But he's on his way now. Should be here any minute.'

'That's an original one,' says Piers.

When Billy arrives, he apologises profusely, then announces that he has something very important to discuss. It's something structural to do with our

Wigmore Hall programme. He's been thinking about it all day. He looks very troubled.

'Tell us, Billy,' says Piers in a patient tone. 'There's nothing I enjoy more than a good structural discussion.'

'Well, that's it, you see, Piers, you're determined to be sceptical.'

'Come on, Billy, don't let Piers put you off,' I say.

'Well, you know,' says Billy, 'that by doing the Haydn, the Mozart and the Beethoven, in that order, we're getting the key relations all mixed up. It's total confusion. First three sharps, then one sharp, then four. There's no sense of progression, no sense of progression at all, and the audience is bound to feel structural stress.'

'Oh, no!' says Piers. 'How terrible. Now if we could get Mozart to write a piece in three-and-a-half sharps . . .'

Helen and I laugh, and Billy joins in weakly.

'Well?' says Piers.

'Just change the order of the Mozart and the Haydn,' says Billy. 'That solves the problem. Ascending order of sharps, sense of perceived structure, no problem.'

'But, Billy, the Mozart was written after the Haydn,' says Helen.

'Yes,' says Piers. 'What about the audience's chronological stress?'

'I thought you'd say that,' says Billy with a guileful look—as guileful as Billy is ever capable of. 'So I have a solution. Change the Haydn A major. Do a later Haydn, one that was written after the Mozart.'

'No,' I say.

'Which one?' asks Helen. 'Just out of curiosity.'

'The one in opus 50 that's in F sharp minor,' says Billy. 'It's also got three sharps, so nothing else changes. It's terribly interesting. It's got all sorts of—oh, yes, and it too has a fugal last movement, so that doesn't disturb the overall theme of the concert.'

'No, no, no!' I say. 'Really, Billy, audiences don't give a damn about the order of sharps.'

'But I do,' says Billy. 'We all should.'

'Doesn't it have a movement which goes into six sharps?' asks Piers a little dubiously. 'I remember playing it through once as a student. It was a nightmare.'

'And in any case I'm sure it's too late to get the Wigmore to change the programme,' I say quickly. 'It's probably all printed up.'

'Well, let's call them and find out,' says Billy.

'No, no!' I say. 'No. Let's get on with the rehearsal. All this is a complete waste of time.'

The other three look at me, surprised.

'I love the A major,' I say. 'I won't give it up.'

'Uh,' says Billy.

'Oh,' says Piers.

'Ah,' says Helen.

'No, I won't. As far as I'm concerned, that Haydn's the highlight of the concert. In fact, it's my favourite string quartet of all time.'

'Oh, OK, it was just an idea,' says Billy, gently backing off, as one would from a lunatic.

'Really, Michael?' says Helen. 'Really?'

'Of all time?' asks Piers. 'The greatest string quartet of all time?'

'I didn't claim it was the greatest,' I say. 'I know it's not the greatest—whatever the greatest means, and I don't really care what it means. It's my favourite, and that's all that matters to me. So let's get rid of the Mozart and the Beethoven if you like, and let's play the Haydn three times over. Then there won't be any structural or chronological stress at all—and no need for an encore either.'

There is silence for a few seconds.

'Oh,' says Billy again.

'Well,' says Piers. 'There we have it. No change in the programme—Michael's vetoed it. Sorry, Billy. Well, actually, I'm not all that sorry.'

'Talking of the encore,' says Helen, 'do we stick to our mystery plan? It'll be a bit of a shocker for the audience, but, Billy, that's one of your ideas that really is brilliant.'

'Yes, brilliant, Billy,' I say. 'After a concert like that, what else would be right?'

Billy is mollified.

'Well,' says Piers, 'Michael's the one who's got the toughest job in that encore, and if he likes the idea, let's go ahead. But I don't know if we really can bring it off. Assuming the audience likes us enough to want an encore.' He pauses for a few seconds. 'Let's start by working on that today. All except that one problem note that Michael has. That way we'll get a sense of what we're aiming for before we weigh him down.'

Billy looks as if he's about to say something, but thinks better of it and nods.

And so, having tuned up and played our ritual scale, we practise the four-minute encore for more than an hour. We sink into its strange, tangled, unearthly beauty. At times I cease to breathe. It is unlike anything we as a quartet have ever played before.

2.8

It is three days before Christmas. I am going north.

The train is packed. Faulty points outside Euston station have caused half an hour's delay. People sit patiently, reading, talking, or looking out of the window at the wall opposite.

The train moves. Crossword squares fill up. Plastic stirrers agitate cups of tea. A child starts crying loudly and purposefully. Mobile phones beep. Paper napkins crumple. Outside the window the grey day darkens.

Stoke-on-Trent, Macclesfield, Stockport; and, at last, Manchester. It is a windless but freezing day. I am not going to linger here. I pick up the car I have booked to drive out towards Rochdale. It is a bit of an extravagance, but gives me the chance to wander off around the moors whenever I want and to take Mrs Formby for a ride.

'All our cars are alarmed,' the girl says in broad Mancunian. She glances down at my address as she hands me my keys. Already I can feel a bit of my own accent returning.

Past the civic-heroic statuary in Piccadilly Square I drive, past the glass-and-black building that once housed the *Daily Express*, past the Habib Bank and the Allied Bank of Pakistan, the clothing warehouses, a Jewish museum, a mosque, a church, a McDonalds, sauna, solicitors, pub, video shop, Boots, bakers, sandwich bar, kebab house . . . past a grey telecom tower with its pustules of transmitters and receivers, a devil's delphinium. I drive until the fringes of Manchester give way to daubs of green and against the darkening day I can see a horse in a field, a farmhouse or two, leafless chestnut and plane trees and, soon, the dark Pennine spur that shelters my birthtown.

All my schoolfriends from Rochdale have moved away. Apart from my father and Auntie Joan and Mrs Formby and one old German teacher, Dr Spars, I have no living ties with this town. Yet what has happened to it, its slow evisceration and death, fills me with a cold sadness.

The sky should be swept by a sleety wind. It is too calm a day. But snow is forecast. Tomorrow the three of us will go to Owd Betts for lunch. On Christmas Eve we will go to church. On Boxing Day, as usual, I will drive Mrs Formby out to Blackstone Edge. I do not wish to visit the cemetery. I will sit for a while in this alarmed and centrally-locked white Toyota in the carpark where we once lived and lay a white rose—her favourite flower—on the flat and, I hope, snow-covered site of my mother's life.

2.9

My father sits with Zsa-Zsa on his lap and dozes off. He has been feeling a bit under the weather the last couple of days. Our plan to go to Owd Betts has been shelved till after Christmas. He doesn't feel up to going to church this evening either. Auntie Joan believes he is slacking.

Holly and mistletoe decorate the small front room, but there has been no Christmas tree since Mum died. The house is full of cards: no longer strung up as they used to be, but distributed over all the flat surfaces of the house. It is difficult to put down one's glass.

A few people drop by: some old friends of my parents or of Auntie Joan, folk who used to know us from the time we had the shop, neighbours. My mind wanders. Our next-door neighbour but one has died of liver cancer. Irene Jackson has got married to a Canadian but it won't last. Mrs Vaizey's niece had a miscarriage in her fourth month. As if it weren't enough that an articulated lorry had crashed through the front of her shop the previous month, Susie Prentice's husband ran off with her best friend, an exceptionally plain woman, and they were tracked down to a hotel in Scunthorpe.

'Scunthorpe!' exclaims Auntie Joan, delighted and appalled.

For better for worse, unto us a child, ashes to ashes.

Zsa-Zsa and I get restless and walk outside. A robin is hopping about on a patch of gravel below the pebble-dash wall. The sharp air clears my head. Zsa-Zsa eyes the robin attentively.

When I was in junior school, I went through a phase where I had to have white mice. I managed to buy two. My mother was terrified of them and wouldn't allow them in the house, so their home was an old outdoor toilet near the dustbins. One morning I came across a scene of horror. One mouse had died. The other had then eaten its head.

Zsa-Zsa lowers her shoulders and creeps forward. The neighbour's gnome smiles impassively on.

2.10

When we had the shop, Christmas was a complicated and busy time. Almost everyone wanted to collect their turkeys at the last minute— or have them delivered. As a teenager, I would help with the deliveries. I could manage a couple on my bike at a time (two were always easier to balance than one) but though Dad suggested it often, I refused to fix a wire basket in front. As long as I got the job done somehow, why should I ruin the appearance of my bike, which, next only to my radio, was my most valued possession?

The huge wooden refrigerator—more a wardrobe than a fridge, covering an entire wall of the cellar—was packed full of pink carcasses in December. It clicked shut with a grand mechanical cadence. And when the fierce motor down on the left-hand side, complete with fly-wheel and metal guard, kicked on, a huge chugging noise juddered into the living room above.

On my sixth birthday, while I was playing a game of hide-and-seek with friends, I decided that the fridge would make a brilliant hiding place. I put on a couple of sweaters, crawled in and, with a bit of effort, managed to pull the door shut. Just a few seconds in that cramped, dark, freezing place, however, and I was ready to quit. What I had not realised was that once the door had clicked, I wouldn't be able to open it from the inside.

My thumping and yelling were almost drowned out by the growl of the motor and the shouts of the game. Still, it could not have been more than a couple of minutes before someone in the rooms above heard me and came to my rescue. When I was brought out I was in a state of suffocated terror, screaming still but almost incapable of speech. For months afterwards I had nightmares about the incident and would wake up in a sweat, inarticulate with claustrophobia and panic.

The fridge also figured in my first major rebellion over food. When I was ten or thereabouts, Dad and I drove down in a van to collect a number of birds from a turkey farm. Some turkeys were having their heads chopped off, some their feathers plucked, some were still running around gobbling. I was so unhappy at the thought of the very birds I was looking at turning into the lifeless mounds that stocked our fridge that I promised I wouldn't eat my Christmas turkey, then or ever. Despite the aroma of the stuffing to tempt me and my father's scoffing to goad me, I kept my resolve for one Christmas.

My mother's apple sauce has given way, under Auntie Joan's regime, to cranberry sauce, and Dad invariably complains about this. It's not really Christmas without apple sauce, cranberry sauce is an American import, it is too tart and gives him indigestion.

It is not going to be a white Christmas this year after all, but the usual drizzly nondescript one. But I am in good spirits after a huge meal culminating in Christmas pudding with a white rum sauce. Auntie Joan's attempt to replace this a few years ago with brandy butter was successfully repelled. I have bought a bottle of champagne, and my father has had several glasses.

'A little of what you fancy does you good,' he says.

'Yes,' says Auntie Joan, 'and I suppose that a lot

of what you fancy does you better.'

'It's good for my heart,' says my father. 'Isn't that your Serpents?' he asks, pointing at the TV.

Indeed, the Water Serpents are on the news, doing their annual hundred-yard Christmas Day swim. About half the old gang are there, horsing around, but there's a whole host of one-timers on the divingboard. A crowd has gathered and is cheering them on. I am very happy to be where I am, snugly stroking Zsa-Zsa behind the ears. I wonder idly when the programme they shot of us will be shown. Perhaps it's been on the air already.

'I never forgave Maggie Rice,' says Auntie Joan, her eyes on the TV.

'What was that, Auntie Joan?'

'Maggie Rice. I never forgave her.'

'What didn't you forgive her?'

'She tripped me up at the Whit Friday races.'

'No.'

'Her excuse was that I had won twice before. I never spoke to her again.'

'How old were you?' I ask.

'I was seven.'

'Oh.'

'Never forgot, never forgave,' says Auntie Joan with satisfaction.

'What's happened to her since?' I ask.

'I don't know. I don't know. She might be dead for all I know. Quite a nice girl, really.'

'Was she?' I ask. I am feeling very drowsy.

Auntie Joan looks across at Dad, who has nodded off with a pleased expression on his face.

'Her father had a shop on Drake Street,' continues Auntie Joan. 'But Drake Street's dead— killed off by the shopping precinct. And they've

90

even sold Champness Hall.'

'I'm going for a walk,' I say. 'I might give the Queen's speech a miss this year.'

'Oh, all right,' says Auntie Joan to my surprise.

'I might walk over to Mrs Formby's with some of your Christmas pudding.'

'Her husband was with the council,' says my father, his eyes still closed.

'I'll be back in an hour or two,' I say.

2.11

Mrs Formby laughs with pleasure to see me at the door. She is a fairly rich, very ugly woman, with pebble glasses and buck teeth. Her husband, who died some years ago, was also quite ugly, though I saw less of him when I was a child. They were, for me, an excitingly exotic couple. He had been—of all things—a roller-skating champion in his youth, and she had been a violinist in an orchestra, though it was difficult to imagine them ever having been young, so old did they appear to me even then. They lived in a large stone house with a big garden full of brilliant flowers, quite close to our humdrum cobble-streeted neighbourhood of small terraced houses and shops. How they met, where their wealth came from, or how her husband was associated with the council, I still have no idea.

'Hello, Michael, how nice to see you today. I thought it was tomorrow you were going to come over to give me my run.'

'I'm on foot today. Just walking off my lunch.'

'What's that? Is it for me?'

'Some of my aunt's Christmas pudding. Weeks in

91

preparation, seconds in consumption. Rather like music.'

The Formbys had no children of their own. I, being an only child, had no natural companionship at home. Mrs Formby in particular took to me, and insisted I go with her to all sorts of things that were, and would have remained, outside my ken. It was she—not he—who taught me to roller-skate, and who took me, when I was only nine, to hear the great 'Messiah' at Belle Vue.

'Have you met my nephew and his family? We've just had dinner. But our pudding's only from M&S. Why don't you join us in a glass of something?'

'I think I'll just continue on my way, Mrs Formby.'

'Oh, no, no, no, Michael, none of that, you just go through now.'

The nephew, a bald, florid man of about fifty, a chartered surveyor from Cheshire, acknowledges me with, 'Oh, yes, the violinist.' He looks appraisingly and somewhat disapprovingly at me. His wife, much younger, has her hands full with the three girls who are pulling each other's hair between whining recriminations, and quarrelling about which channel to watch.

Once I have a glass of wine in my hands, Mrs Formby settles herself down in a comfortable armchair and sits calmly through the noise. I drink my wine as quickly as I politely can, and take my leave.

I am now close to my old neighbourhood. There is very little traffic about. My feet turn towards the carpark where our shop stood. It is bound to be empty today. But at the last moment something stops me, and I stand still, uncertain of purpose, afraid of the descent of unpeaceful thoughts.

Into my mind comes an extraordinarily beautiful sound. I am nine years old. I am sitting between Mr and Mrs Formby in a state of anticipation. On the seats all around us are people chattering and rustling programmes. Into the circus ring enter not elephants and lions but a group of men and women, many of them bearing amazing instruments, gleaming and glowing. A small, frail man enters to applause such as I have never heard before, followed by the strange, absolute silence of a multitude.

He brings down a stick and a huge and lovely noise fills the world. More than anything else I want to be part of such a noise.

2.12

On Boxing Day I drive Mrs Formby along the road past Blackstone Edge. When I left home to go and live in Manchester, it was an old friend of hers who lent me a spare violin. But when she heard that I was going to Vienna to study under Carl Käll himself, she insisted I take her own Tononi with me. It has been with me ever since. She is happy that it's being played, and that it's I who am playing it. Whenever I come to Rochdale I bring it with me. She calls this annual drive the rent for her violin.

The sky is clear with only a few clouds. I love the light near Blackstone Edge. We should be able to see far into the distance, across the whole of the plain, past Rochdale and Middleton to Manchester, even into Cheshire.

'Everything all right at home?' she asks. Mrs Formby's relations with our family have had their peaks and troughs. She was always one of the best customers at the shop, but for a while she was mainly viewed as the one who had beguiled me away from university.

'Yes,' I say. 'Everything's fine. Dad's been a bit out of sorts, but, well, he's getting on—'

'And in London?'

'Everything's going fine there too.'

'Have you got a window box yet?' Mrs Formby often chides me about my flower-less existence. Having the run of her garden as a child I learned a certain amount about plants from her. But I'm too lazy, I travel too much to take care of them, the park is so close to me anyway, and the constitution of Archangel Court frowns on window boxes. I tell her so, as I already have once or twice before.

'Are you travelling a lot?'

'About the usual amount. We've got a concert in Vienna next May. It's the sort of thing you'd enjoy. Nothing but Schubert.'

'Yes,' says Mrs Formby, her face lighting up. 'Schubert! When I was young we used to have Schubert evenings. A friend of mine tried to infiltrate some Schumann. I didn't allow it. I called him the wrong Schu! . . . That reminds me, Michael. Our local music society was wondering whether your quartet might want to perform here in Rochdale at the Gracie Fields Theatre. I said I thought not, but I promised I'd ask you. Believe me, I'm simply relaying a request, so I don't want you to feel any pressure one way or the other.'

'Why did you think I might not want to, Mrs Formby?'

94

'Just a sixth sense. Well, the music society is still quite active. It's our one bright spot, culturally speaking, in my opinion. Of course it is silly that the only decent auditorium in town is inaccessible by public transport . . . But what do you think?'

'I just don't know, Mrs Formby,' I say at last. 'I would like to do it—I mean, I would like us to do it. But I just don't feel I'll do justice to what I play here. I don't think I can even explain it. It sounds stupid, I know, and somehow, well, even a bit small-minded.'

'It sounds neither, Michael,' says Mrs Formby. 'You'll play here when you're ready. And, quite frankly, if it isn't in my lifetime, I won't mind. Some things can't be forced. Or at any rate, if they are, no good comes of them . . . By the way, you must thank your aunt. That Christmas pudding was quite delicious.'

'Did you eat any of it, or did you feed it all to your grand-nieces?'

'Well,' says Mrs Formby, laughing, 'I did eat a little. How is our violin?'

'It's doing wonderfully well. I took it for a few adjustments earlier this year. It was buzzing a bit, but it's singing like a lark now.'

I have stopped the car by the side of the road and am looking out over the sharp green slope. I used to cycle down this road full tilt, with the wind raking through my hair. Where do larks go in winter?

'You know I want you to play it, Michael,' says Mrs Formby in a troubled voice.

'I know. And I love it, Mrs Formby,' I say with sudden anxiety. 'I didn't tell you, did I, that we're going to Venice after Vienna? So I'll be taking it

95

back to its birthplace for a visit. That should make it happy. You aren't thinking of taking it back, are you?'

'No, no, not really,' says Mrs Formby. 'But my nephew's been pestering me about setting up a fund for my grand-nieces' education and making a will and so on. I don't know what to do. And he's been making enquiries and he tells me that it's very valuable now—the violin.'

'Well, yes, it is, I suppose,' I say sadly.

'It didn't cost me very much so many years ago,' she continues. 'It actually bothers me that it's gained so much in value. I don't like my nephew but I'm fond of my grand-nieces.'

'If you hadn't lent it to me, I could never have afforded to buy it,' I say. 'You've been very generous.'

As both of us know, if it hadn't been for her, I would very likely not have become a musician at all.

'I don't think I could bear it to be played by a stranger,' says Mrs Formby.

Then give it to me, Mrs Formby, I want to say. I love it and it loves me. We have grown to know each other. How can a stranger hold and sound what has been in my hands so long? We have been together for twelve years. Its sound is my sound. I can't bear to part with it.

But I cannot say it. I say nothing at all. I help her out of the car, and we stand for a few minutes by the side of the road looking past the tower blocks that landmark Rochdale to the vaguer plains beyond.

2.13

When I was just nine years old, our rowdy, chattering, sweet-paper-crinkling, paper-aeroplane-throwing class was taken to a Schools' Concert. It was my first experience of live music. When I visited Mrs Formby the next day I told her all about it. What I particularly remembered was a piece about a lark—'The Lark in the Clear Air' I think it was called.

Mrs Formby smiled, went to the gramophone and put on what she told me was another piece inspired by the same bird. From the first note of 'The Lark Ascending' I was enchanted. I had noticed a couple of violins lying around among the many marvels of the house and I knew Mrs Formby used to play the violin, but I could hardly believe it when she told me she used to play that piece herself. 'I don't often pick up the violin now,' she said, 'but I'd like to read you the poem that led to that piece.' And she read me the lines by George Meredith that had inspired Vaughan Williams. It was strange fare for a nine-year-old, still stranger as I watched Mrs Formby's face, the ecstatic expression in her eyes magnified by her thick glasses.

He rises and begins to round,
He drops the silver chain of sound,
Of many links without a break,
In chirrup, whistle, slur and shake . . .

For singing till his heaven fills,
Tis love of earth that he instils,
And ever winging up and up,

Our valley is his golden cup
And he the wine which overflows
To lift us with him as he goes . . .

Till lost on his aerial wings
In light, and then the fancy sings.

Mrs Formby did not bother to explain the poem to me. Instead she told me that they wanted to go to hear Handel's 'Messiah' in a few weeks—a niece of theirs from Sheffield was singing in it—and that, if my parents agreed, they would take me along. It was thus that I heard and saw the small and ailing Barbirolli re-create in the King's Hall at Belle Vue the soaring sound that rocked my head for days, and that, together with 'The Lark Ascending', made me beg Mrs Formby to teach me to play the violin.

For a while she taught me on the small violin she had used as a child. It supplanted roller-skating as my prime obsession. While I was still at junior school, she managed to get me a good teacher. My parents were nonplussed, but felt that it was a sort of social grace and at any rate would keep me out of mischief for a few hours a week. They paid for it, as they did for my school trips, my extra tuition, books that I felt I had to have, all the things that would, as they saw it, broaden my mind and help me on my way to university. They had no particular fondness for music. There had been a piano in my grandparents' parlour, and the furniture was arranged around it, as it would be around a TV today, but it was never played except by an occasional visitor.

Because the comprehensive I went to had been

98

the old grammar school, it had a fine tradition of music. And the services of what were known as peripatetic music teachers were provided by the local education authorities. But all this has been cut back now, if it has not completely disappeared. There was a system for loaning instruments free or almost free of charge to those who could not afford them—all scrapped with the educational cuts as the budgetary hatchet struck again and again. The music centre where the young musicians of the area would gather to play in an orchestra on Saturdays is now derelict. Yesterday I drove past it: the windows were smashed; it has been dead for years. If I had been born in Rochdale five years later, I don't see how I—coming from the background I did, and there were so many who were much poorer—could have kept my love of the violin alive.

The handsome town hall presides over a waste— it is a town with its heart torn out. Everything speaks of its decline. Over the course of a century, as its industries decayed, it lost its work and its wealth. Then came the planning blight: the replacement of human slums by inhuman ones, the marooning of churches in traffic islands, the building of precincts where once there were shops. Finally two decades of garrotting from the government in London, and everything civic or social was choked of funds: schools, libraries, hospitals, transport. The town which had been the home of the co-operative movement lost its sense of community.

The theatres closed. Every one of the five cinemas closed. The literary and scientific societies shrank or disappeared. I remember my despair when I heard our bookshop was going to close. We now have a few shelves at the back of W.H. Smith's.

In the next few years my father will die, Auntie Joan will die, Mrs Formby will die. I doubt I will visit Rochdale after that. If I myself am then determined to cut my ties with my town, by what right do I mourn for it so angrily now?

2.14

On the way back to London, I spend a few hours wandering around in Manchester.

About noon I find myself at the Bridgewater Hall. I have come to consult the huge, smooth-curved touchstone outside. Today, when I pass my hands over it, it gives me an initial sense of peace; but from somewhere in its cold heart emanates a delayed impulse of danger.

At the Henry Watson Music Library I browse around. I have not yet ordered the score and parts of the Beethoven string quintet from London. I am eager to play it, yet filled with uncertainty. Here I am, however, in the very place where the music is housed. The librarian, after checking my credentials, permits me to use my old card.

On the train down to London I look at the score. When, after early nightfall, I get to London, I phone Piers.

'Well,' says Piers, 'how was Christmas?'

'Fine. And yours?'

'Awful in the usual way. Charades. Endless fucking jollity. I quite enjoyed it, except that Mother's become a complete alcoholic. The parents have finally given up on me. Helen's getting the marriage-and-babies flak now. Did you get any of that?'

'No, my father didn't talk much about my settling down this time. He usually does.'

'Well, what's up?' asks Piers.

'You remember that Beethoven quintet we talked about once?'

'Yes, C minor, wasn't it, based on the trio? You said you'd tracked down the music. Did you manage to get hold of a recording?'

'Yes. And I've just borrowed the parts from the music library in Manchester.'

'Excellent! Well, let's get hold of a viola player and run through it. Who should we get? Emma?'

'Sure—why not? You know her better than I do. Will you give her a call?'

'Righty-ho.'

'There's one other thing, Piers. Would you mind terribly if I played first violin just this once?'

There is a second's silence. 'It's not just a question of *my* minding,' says Piers.

'Well, should we ask the others?'

'No, Michael,' says Piers with a touch of annoyance. 'Whatever they may say, I don't think it's a good idea. When Alex and I kept alternating between first and second violin, it not only drove us mad but Helen as well. She kept saying she couldn't adjust to the other parts, particularly to the second violin. And Billy too said it was like playing with a different quartet each time.'

'But this is just a one-off thing. We're not playing it professionally.'

'What if we like our playing of it? What if we do want to play it professionally? Then we'll be stuck with that configuration.'

'Piers, it's just that the piece means a lot to me.'

'Well, then, why not get a few colleagues from the Camerata Anglica together on an ad hoc basis and play it through?'

'It wouldn't work for me without our quartet.'

'Well, it won't work for me with our quartet.'

'Just think it over, Piers.'

'Michael, I'm sorry, I have thought it over.'

'Of course you haven't,' I exclaim, angry at what seems closer to selfishness than neutral rigidity.

'I have. I've thought it over in advance. I've gone over it hundreds of times in my head. When Alex left,' says Piers a bit shakily, 'I asked myself endlessly where we had gone wrong. There were other things too, but I'm sure that this was at the heart of it.'

'Well, you know best,' I say, too upset to be sympathetic. And indeed, I'm not delighted by the regretful mention of Alex: after all, if he and Piers hadn't broken up, I wouldn't have been in the quartet at all.

'Michael,' says Piers, 'I went through hell when he left. I know I'm no good as a second violinist now, if I ever was.' He pauses, then continues: 'If I were ever to take that part with our quartet, it would remind me of those times, and affect my playing. It would be no good for any of us.'

I remain silent.

'Well,' he says, 'we've got a rehearsal the day after tomorrow at five at Helen's. That's still OK with you?' Piers has raised his visor again.

'Yes. Why shouldn't it be?'

'Well, see you then.'

'Yes. See you.'

2.15

I never knew Alex well, though we met off and on during those weeks we spent in Banff. Even Helen, who loves gossip, does not talk of him and of his effect on all of them; and I have always felt that it isn't for me to ask about what exactly happened before my time. At first it seemed to me that the other three deliberately avoided talking about their former partner, and later, when I felt at ease with them and they with me, it seemed beside the point.

His name rarely came up. When it did, Piers would quite often simply disappear into thoughts of his own. Sometimes, if it was Helen who mentioned him, he would snap like a wounded lynx.

If I had known that six years later I would fill the place he left, I would have been more curious about Alex when we first met. On the surface, he was a cheerful man, full of energy, easy-going, fond of attention, quick to make jokes or recite humorous verse, very gallant towards women, and quite possibly attracted to them too. Julia liked him a lot. From hearing him play sometimes first, sometimes second violin when they performed (both then in Canada and later at the odd concert in London that I went to), it was obvious to me not only what an excellent player he was but also what a flexible one—more flexible than Piers, who stuck out a bit when he played second violin. Perhaps, as Piers intimated, if Alex had been content to play only second violin they might have stayed together, and I would never have joined the Maggiore. But perhaps, being both lovers and fellow violinists, what they had was fated to fray. When tension entered either relationship, it must have stressed and twisted the other. And Piers, at the best of times, is never an easy person to be with.

Alex left Piers, the quartet and, indeed, London, and took up a position with the Scottish Chamber Orchestra. Piers was bereft. He was without a partner for more than a year after I joined the quartet. And then Tobias entered the picture—or, more exactly, crashed through the frame.

Tobias Kahn was a very powerful, concentrated, serious violinist. Music was his life—he had no other interests—and he believed with complete conviction that there was a correct way to make music and a wrong way. He was a member of another string quartet. Piers came under his sway.

Piers and Alex had been equals. But with Tobias it was almost as if Piers was taking orders from a superior, an invisible fifth person who was perpetually present among us. It was a strange and unsettling episode, and one of the things that brought home to me how precarious, for all their strength, the ties between us are.

Piers is, was, has always been a natural musician: he is very focused, very disciplined, but not rigid in his musicianship. When he plays something, he lets the moment as well as the structure guide him. Under the influence of Tobias, he became obsessed with the holy writ of theory: what a piece is, what it should be, what it must be, what it couldn't not be. A bar or a phrase or a passage had a certain tempo; one had to stick to it, come what may. Our job was to realise a reproduction of the score. Anything else—an imaginative idea, a fluctuation in pace, a whim, anything that smudged the template—was an abomination. There was no sense of 'ah!' to our music at all. We attained a lifeless lucidity.

104

Piers was playing entirely against his grain, and it was hell for the rest of us. The unconstrained things, the things that make a movement work from minute to minute, disappeared—at first they were excised, then not even attempted. At times it was almost Tobias and not Piers who was playing and arguing. It is difficult to explain this fairly, even with the passage of time. It was a bit like *The Invasion of the Body Snatchers*.

Helen couldn't fathom what had got into her brother. Tobias was an odd fellow—he almost didn't have a personality, just a mind in the grip of powerful and serious ideas—and she couldn't see what Piers saw in him. He was, after all, almost the antithesis of Alex. Even Billy, who is interested enough in matters of theory, was deeply unhappy. He saw the Tobias line as a self-indulgent pandering to the will. Rehearsals were a torment. Sometimes we talked around things for three hours and didn't play a note. It ate into our lives. It nearly split us, and would have if it had gone on a little longer. Helen wanted to leave before she in effect lost a brother. Once, when we were in Japan, she said she was going to quit as soon as the tour was over. But, after more than a year, the fever abated. Piers somehow exorcised Tobias, and not just he but all of us gradually became ourselves again.

We never mention Tobias if we can avoid it. We skirt around the subject but do not touch it. The experience of that year, the unprepared-for pain of it, is something none of us are likely to forget.

Many musicians—whether players in orchestras or freelancers—consider quartet players to be an odd, obsessed, introspective, separatist breed, perpetually travelling to exotic destinations and

105

garnering adulation as if by right. If they knew the costs of that too-uncertain adulation, they would not resent us quite so much. Quite apart from our shaky finances and our continual anxiety about getting bookings, it is our proximity to each other and only to each other which, more often than we recognise, constricts our spirits and makes us stranger than we are. Perhaps even our states of exaltation are akin to the dizziness that comes from lacking air.

2.16

On my answering machine are a number of messages from Virginie. I call her and get her answering machine. Late at night, when I have almost drifted off to sleep, the phone rings.

'Why didn't you call me at Christmas?' demands Virginie.

'Virginie, I told you I wouldn't. I was up north.'

'And I was down south. That's what phones are for.'

'I told you I wouldn't call you—that I wanted to be on my own.'

'But how could I believe you would be so horrible?'

'Did you have a good time in—where exactly were you at Christmas? Montpellier? Saint-Malo?'

'Nyons, of course, with my family, as you perfectly well know, Michael. Yes, I had a good time. A very good time. I don't need you to have a good time.'

'Yes, I know, Virginie.'

'The more it goes, the less I understand you.'

'Virginie, I was half asleep.'

'Oh, Michael, you're such a bore,' says Virginie. 'You're always half asleep. Such a boring old git,' she adds proudly.

'Virginie, you're ODing on your English idioms. Yes, well, I've been thinking about that. I'm sixteen years older than you.'

'So what? So what? Why do you always tell me you aren't in love with me?'

'I didn't say that.'

'No, but that's what you meant. Do you like to teach me?'

'Well, when you respond.'

'And do you like to talk to me?'

'Well, yes, when it's not too late.'

'And do you like to make love to me?'

'What? . . . Yes.'

'I am content with that. I practised two hours every day when I was in France.'

'Making love?'

Virginie starts to giggle. 'No, silly Michael, violin.'

'Good girl.'

'We have a lesson tomorrow, and you will see the progress I've made.'

'Tomorrow? Look, Virginie, about tomorrow—I wonder if we could postpone it by a couple of days.'

'Why?' An audible pout.

'You know that Beethoven string quintet you told me about? I've got hold of the music, and we'll be playing it through the day after tomorrow. I want to have a good look at it first.'

'Oh, but that's wonderful, Michael. Why don't I join you to play it?'

'Now, Virginie, wait a second—'

107

'No, listen. You play the second viola since you always say you miss the chance to play the viola, and I will play the second violin.'

'No, no, no, no—' I cry, warding off the thought like a swarm of bees.

'Why are you so violent, Michael?'

'It's just that . . . Piers has already asked someone else.'

'But I only suggested it.' Virginie sounds bewildered.

What a cruel fool I am. But I won't make it worse by elaborating.

'Michael,' says Virginie. 'I love you. You don't deserve it, but I do. And I don't want to see you tomorrow. I don't want to see you or talk to you until after you have played that stupid music. I told you about it. You didn't even believe it existed.'

'I know. I know.'

Virginie puts down the phone without a goodnight or goodbye.

2.17

We meet at Helen's to play the Beethoven quintet. I have spent the previous day studying my part and the score.

Neither Piers nor I refer to our conversation. I have accepted the status quo as second violin, even for this. The parts of the quintet have been distributed to the other players and we have tuned up. Emma Marsh, whom Piers knows from his student days at the Royal College of Music, has joined us as second viola. She is a short, plump, pretty young woman who plays the viola in a quartet of her own, so she should blend in well with us. Billy and Helen look at each other and make operatic gestures of separation.

'All repeats?' asks Helen.

'Yes,' I reply.

Billy examines his part with intense interest, and asks to see the score. He will be playing almost without pause in the quintet, unlike in the trio that was its original avatar, but some of his higher lyrical lines have gone to Helen.

Piers looks uncomfortable. Good.

I have never before now felt unhappy with my position as second violinist, though I agree with whoever said it should more properly be called 'the other violinist'. Its role is different, not lesser: more interesting, because more versatile. Sometimes, like the viola, it is at the textural heart of the quartet; at others it sings with a lyricism equal to that of the first violin, but in a darker and more difficult register.

Today, though, I am unhappy and aggrieved. I have had to wean myself from the expectation of playing the part that I had come to see and hear as mine. Piers cannot imagine how qualmlessly I would stab him with the poisoned tip of my bow. I never expected him to be so ungiving.

But now he breathes in a swift little crotchet-sniff of a cue, and we are off, allegro con a lot of brio.

Within a minute I have forgotten all resentment, all rights and pleasures due to me. They are irrelevant within this lovely, vigorous music. We play the first movement without stopping, and do not get entangled once. It ends with Piers playing a tremendously zippy set of ascending and descending scales, followed by a huge resonant chord from all five of us, ebbing swiftly away in three softer chords.

We look at each other, beaming.

Helen shakes her head. 'How come I've never heard this? How come no one knows about this?'

'It's delicious,' is all Emma can say.

'Thank you, Michael,' says Piers, his face radiant. 'It's a real discovery. But it makes you sweat.'

'You'll thank me even more after the second movement,' I say. 'It's a beauty.'

'But it must have been written a good twenty years after the trio,' says Billy. 'What else was he composing at the time?'

'Not much,' I say, having researched it. 'Well, what do you think? *Avanti*?'

'Avanti,' cries everyone, and, after a few quick re-tunings of our instruments and re-initialisings of our hearts, we enter the slow theme-and-variations movement.

How good it is to play this quintet, to play it, not to work at it—to play for our own joy, with no need to convey anything to anyone outside our ring of re-creation, with no expectation of a future stage, of the too-immediate sop of applause. The quintet exists without us yet cannot exist without us. It sings to us, we sing into it, and somehow, through these little black and white insects clustering along five thin lines, the man who deafly transfigured what he so many years earlier had hearingly composed speaks into us across land and water and ten generations, and fills us here with sadness, here with amazed delight.

For me there is another presence in this music.

110

As the sense of her might fall on my retina through two sheets of moving glass, so too through this maze of motes converted by our arms into vibration—sensory, sensuous—do I sense her being again. The labyrinth of my ear shocks the coils of my memory. Here is her force in my arm, here is her spirit in my pulse. But where she is I do not know, nor is there hope I will.

2.18

I met Julia two months after I arrived in Vienna, in early winter. It was at a student concert. She played a Mozart sonata. I told her afterwards how entranced I had been by her playing. We got talking about ourselves, and discovered we both came from England—different Englands, though, since her father taught history at Oxford. Her parents had met after the war: like us, in Vienna. After weeks of struggling in German, it was such a pleasure, such a relief to speak English again that I babbled on much more than usual. She smiled when I said I came from Rochdale—but then somehow drew me into talking about my town in a way that I never had before. I asked her out to dinner. It was a cold night, with bits of snow and slush on the ground, and Vienna was at its greyest and grimmest. We walked to the restaurant. I slipped, and she stopped me from falling. I kissed her instinctively—amazed at myself even as I did it—and she was too surprised to object. She wore a grey silk scarf around her hair—she was always fond of scarves. I looked into, and away from, her eyes, and realised, as she must have, that I was far gone.

From the moment of our first meeting I could think of nothing but her. I don't know what she saw in me other than my almost desperate longing for her, but within a week of our meeting we were lovers. One morning, after a night of making love, we tried making music together. It did not go well; we were both too nervous. Later in the week we gave it another try, and were taken aback by how naturally, how responsively—to each other, to the music—we were playing. Together with a cellist— Julia's friend and classmate Maria—we set up a trio, and started performing wherever we could, in and out of Vienna. At a friend's suggestion we sent off a tape and an application, and were accepted for the summer school in Banff. That winter, that spring, that summer, I lived in a waking dream.

She was five years younger than I was—a regular student, not someone there as a sort of graduate appendage attached to a particular teacher. In many ways, though, she seemed older. She was at ease in our shared city, where she had already lived for three years. Though she had spent all her life in England before coming to Vienna to study, she had grown up speaking both German and English. She had been brought up in a world unreachably different from mine, where art and literature and music are absorbed without effort or explanation— from speech and travel, from books and records, from the very walls and shelves. For all my studies at school and all my autodidact's reading, sometimes random, sometimes obsessive, during those years in Manchester, it was she who became my best teacher, and for this as for everything else I gave my heart into her hand.

112

She taught me to enjoy art, she improved my German enormously, she even taught me bridge. She showed me things about music simply through her playing; the joy I got from making music with her, alone or in our trio, was as great as the joy which the quartet has given me. I later realised that even about music I had learned more from her than from anyone else, for what I learned from her I was not taught.

She sometimes went to church, not every Sunday but from time to time, usually when thankful or when troubled. That was a world opaque to me, who had not prayed even ritually since my schooldays. No doubt it was one of the bases of her confidence, but I felt awkward about it and it was clear that she too did not want to talk about it, though she never said so outright. She had an acuity, a gentleness unlike anything I was used to. Perhaps what she saw in me was a corresponding strangeness—a volatility, a sense of resistance, of scepticism, roughness, impulsiveness, even, at times, of dark panic, almost brainsickness. But how could any of this have been attractive? She said that because I had had to work to earn my living for years, I was different from the other students she knew. She said she loved my company although she never knew what to expect of my moods. She must have felt how much I needed her when I sank increasingly into depression. Most of all she must have known how much I loved her.

A second winter came. Early in the year, my third finger began giving me difficulty. It responded slowly, and was only effective after a long warm-up. Carl reacted with fury and impatience: my slack trills were yet another insult to him, and my anxieties reflected my fecklessness. It was as if one of the potential diamonds on his crown was proving itself to be merely carbon, convertible to its ideal form only under intense and continuous pressure. He applied it, and I crumbled.

Through winter into spring she tried to talk to me, to coax me into courage, to stay where I had planned to stay for the rest of the year, if for nothing else, then for the sake of love. But I could not speak to her of the bleakness in my mind. She told me not to leave on bad terms with my teacher, and again and again reminded me of what I had first seen in Carl, what I could see she still saw in him: someone whose playing went deeper and farther than his virtuosity, whose music conveyed nobility of spirit in every phrase. But my conflict with him had pressed itself so deeply into my skull that her defence of him appeared to me an unbearable betrayal on her part: worse in a sense than his, for from him I no longer expected understanding.

I left. I became, in effect, a fugitive in London, for I could not bear to return home either. I did not write or call her on the phone. It was only gradually that I was able to see things through eyes less injured and less blind, to understand how honestly she had acted, and with what love, and to realise that I might well have lost her through my sudden departure and silence. I had. Two months had gone by. When I at last wrote, she must have been past caring.

I tried to phone, but whoever picked up the common telephone in the students' hostel always returned, after a minute or two, to tell me she wasn't in. My letters went unanswered. Once or twice I thought of going to Vienna, but I had very little money, and I was still afraid of the memories of my collapse, and of the presence of Carl Käll, and of how Julia might greet any explanation from me. Besides, by now it was the summer holidays, and she could be anywhere. Months passed. In October the next term began, and still I heard nothing from her.

The sharp consciousness of losing her gave way in London to a numbed state of self-preservation. After a while I lost hope, and with it the edge of that anguish. I still had two-thirds of my life to live. I subscribed to a diary service that arranged work for me. After a year or so I auditioned for the Camerata Anglica, and was taken on. I played; I survived; in time, I even saved a bit, since I had no one I wanted to spend it on. I visited museums, galleries, libraries. I walked everywhere. I acquainted myself with London and the facilities of London, but could not have felt less a Londoner. My mind was elsewhere, north and south. In the paintings I saw, in the books I read, I recalled her, for she had in many ways been the making of me.

When I listened to music, it was often to Bach. It was after all in her company, through her playing, that my feeling for his music had grown from admiration to love. Sometimes she and Maria had played the gamba sonatas, sometimes she and I had played his violin and keyboard music, a few times she had even made me thump out the pedal part of an organ work at the far left of the piano. There was one choral prelude, 'An Wasserflüssen Babylon', which had overcome me even as we played it. But it was when she had played by herself, to herself—a suite, say, or an invention, or a fugue—that I had

115

most completely yielded my being to Bach, and to her.

I had slept with other women before, and she had had a boyfriend once, but I was her first love, as she was mine. Nor have I ever been in love since. But then I have never fallen out of love with her—with her, I suppose, as she then was, or as I grew afterwards to realise or imagine she had been. What is she now, who is she now? Am I with such inane fidelity fixated on someone who could have utterly changed (but could she have? could she really have changed so much?), who could have grown to hate me for leaving her, who could have forgotten me or learned deliberately to expunge me from her mind. How many seconds or weeks after seeing me on that bus did I survive in her thoughts?

How could she forgive me when I cannot forgive myself? When I hear Bach, I think of her. When I play Haydn or Mozart or Beethoven or Schubert I think of their city. She showed me that city, every step and stone of which brings her back to me. I have not returned there for ten years. But that is where we are due to go next spring, and nothing, I know, can anneal me against it.

2.19

For the last three months or so, a strange fellow has been following us around: a sticky fan. At first we took him to be a harmless sort of enthusiast: tie, spectacles on a string, the sort of jacket worn by an academic. He followed us here and there, greeted us in green rooms, hosted rounds of drinks, latched

116

onto us with monopolistic mania, talked knowledgeably about what we had played, insisted we let him take us out. We slithered out of most of this. Helen was the most wary among us, and—unlike her usual self—quite sharp with him a couple of times. Sometimes he seemed almost wild with excitement, but what he said was such an odd compound of irrelevance and sense that it was not easy to dismiss him completely. When he said he knew how we had got our name, Piers looked upset and angry: it is supposed to be something of a quartet secret.

Last month in York the sticky fan hijacked a party. The host, who had something to do with the local music society, had invited a number of people to his house for dinner after the concert. The sticky fan, having followed us so far north, was somehow taken to be a friend of ours. He tagged along and took over. To our host and hostess's amazement, caterers appeared from nowhere, providing food and drink to supplement needlessly what was already provided. By now it had become clear that this man was not someone the quartet had voluntarily brought along, but it was too late: he was entrenched. He became a sort of master of ceremonies, moving people here and there, summoning waiters, asking that lights be dimmed. He talked, he sang to illustrate his points, he danced. He rose to compose a paean to art and to our artistry. He fell on his knees. At this point our host discovered that he had a flight to catch very early the next morning and, with many apologies for his own inhospitality, pushed everyone out of the house. The fan danced in the street for a while, then sat in the caterers' van and sang. Every so often he coughed violently.

This was the most extreme behaviour he had ever displayed, and we didn't know what to do.

'Shouldn't we make sure he's all right?' asked Billy, starting the car.

'No,' said Piers. 'He's none of our responsibility. He can take care of himself. I hope to God we never see the bastard again.'

'Oh, come on, Piers, he's harmless,' said Billy. 'But, well, I feel bad for our hosts.'

'Save some sympathy for yourself. I doubt we'll be invited here again.

'Oh, Piers,' said Helen.

'What on earth do you know about all this?' demanded Piers, turning around from the front seat to glare at her. 'I'm the one who'll have to tell Erica about what happened and get her to repair the damage. Not that she's so brilliant at damage control. And what if he turns up at our next concert?'

Helen seemed shaken by the thought of this. I put a reassuring arm around her. Strangely enough, I think Piers's anger may have been heightened by his sense of how upset Helen was.

'If he's in the audience in Leeds,' she said, 'I'll just stop playing. No, keep your arm there, Michael.' She sighed. 'I'm so tired tonight. Here's a question: how can you end up with a million pounds as a string quartet player?'

'Start out with ten million,' said Billy.

'Billy, you cheat, you've heard that one before,' said Helen.

'Inherit it from your aunt,' muttered Piers, not looking back this time. Helen said nothing, but I felt her shoulders tense.

118

'Piers,' I said. 'Enough's enough.'

'Shall I give you some advice, Michael?' said Piers. 'Just keep out of family matters.'

'Oh, Piers,' said Helen.

'Oh Piers, oh Piers, oh Piers!' said Piers. 'I've had enough. Let me out. I'll walk to the hotel.'

'But we're already there,' said Billy. 'Look—there it is.'

Piers growled and let it go at that.

2.20

It is 7:30 on a February evening. The skylight above the audience is dark. As we walk to our chairs, my eyes go to where Virginie is sitting. Behind us is a creamy gold curved wall and above us a semi-cupola adorned with a bizarre and beautiful relief. We sit down. The applause dies. We do a bit of fine tuning, and are ready to begin. Piers raises his bow to play the first note. Then Billy sneezes, very loudly. He quite often sneezes before a concert, never—thank God—during one. There is a swift ripple of amusement, quite sympathetic, through the audience. We look at Billy, who has flushed red, and is fumbling in his pocket for his handkerchief. Piers waits a few seconds, assures himself that we are all ready, smiles at Billy, brings his bow down, and we are off.

A winter evening in the Wigmore Hall, the sacred shoe-box of chamber music. We have spent the last month practising intensively for this night. The fare is simple—three classical quartets: Haydn's opus 20 no. 6 in A major, my most beloved quartet; then the first of the six quartets that

Mozart himself dedicated to Haydn, in C major; and finally, after the interval, Beethoven's steeplechase-cum-marathon, the ethereal, joky, unpausing, miraculous, exhausting quartet in C sharp minor, which he composed a year before his death, and which, just as the score of the 'Messiah' had consoled and delighted him on his deathbed, was to delight and console Schubert as he lay dying in the same city a year later.

Dying, undying, a dying fall, a rise: the waves of sound well around us even as we generate them: Helen and I at the heart and, to either side, Piers and Billy. Our eyes are on our music; we hardly glance at each other, but we cue and are cued as if Haydn himself were our conductor. A strange composite being we are, not ourselves any more but the Maggiore, composed of so many disjunct parts: chairs, stands, music, bows, instruments, musicians—sitting, standing, shifting, sounding— all to produce these complex vibrations that jog the inner ear, and through them the grey mass that says: joy; love; sorrow; beauty. And above us here in the apse the strange figure of a naked man surrounded by thorns and aspiring towards a grail of light, in front of us 540 half-seen beings intent on 540 different webs of sensation and cerebration and emotion, and through us the spirit of someone scribbling away in 1772 with the sharpened feather of a bird.

I love every part of the Haydn. It is a quartet that I can hear in any mood and can play in any mood. The headlong happiness of the allegro; the lovely adagio where my small figures are like a counter-lyric to Piers's song; the contrasting minuet and trio, each a mini-cosmos, yet each contriving to sound unfinished; and the melodious, ungrandiose, various fugue—everything delights me. But the part I like best is where I do not play at all. The trio really is a trio. Piers, Helen and Billy slide and stop away on their lowest strings, while I rest— intensely, intently. My Tononi is stilled. My bow lies across my lap. My eyes close. I am here and not here. A waking nap? A flight to the end of the galaxy and perhaps a couple of billion light-years beyond? A vacation, however short, from the presence of my too-present colleagues? Soberly, deeply, the melody grinds away, and now the minuet begins again. But I should be playing this, I think anxiously. It is the minuet. I should have rejoined the others, I should be playing again. And, oddly enough, I can hear myself playing. And yes, the fiddle is under my chin, and the bow is in my hand, and I am.

2.21

We get the last two chords of Haydn's fugue perfectly: no massive *Dämmerung* of some daemonic wrestling-match—we'll keep that for the three enormous twelve-note chords at the end of the Beethoven—but a jovial *au revoir*, light but not slight.

We are applauded off and back onto the stage several times. Helen and I are grinning from ear to ear, Piers is trying to look statesmanlike, and Billy gets in a couple of sneezes.

Next comes the Mozart. We sweated far more rehearsing this than the Haydn, although it's in a more natural key for our instruments. The others like it, though Helen has one or two reservations. Billy finds it fascinating; but then, I have rarely found a piece that Billy did not, from a compositional point of view, find fascinating.

I'm not mad about it. Piers, the most opinionated being I know, claimed that I was being opinionated when this emerged in rehearsal. I tried to explain myself. I said that I didn't like the epidemic of dynamic contrasts: they seemed fussy. Why couldn't he let us shape even the opening bars ourselves? Nor did I like the excessive chromaticism. It seemed strangely laboured, un-Mozartean even. Piers thought I was mad. Anyway, here we are, playing it well enough. Luckily, what I think about this piece hasn't conveyed itself to the others. Indeed, if anything, their enthusiasm has brought my own playing to life. As with the Haydn, the trio is my favourite bit, though this time I too have to play for my pleasure. In the fugal—or, rather, fugue-ish—last movement, it's the non-fugal bits that really come alive, and do what a fugue—especially a quick one—should do: take flight. Oh well. Inspired or not, we accept our applause happily enough.

We sit in the green room in the interval, relieved and tense. I pat my violin nervously. It is sometimes a temperamental beast, and I won't be able to retune it for forty minutes: there is no gap between the seven movements of the Beethoven.

Billy is tinkling away at the upright piano, and this makes me still more tense. He is playing a few bars of the curious encore we have so carefully prepared, and humming various parts to himself, and as a result I am suffering all kinds of advance agonies. At the best of times I hate intervals.

122

'Please, Billy!' I say.

'What? Oh—oh, I see,' says Billy, and stops. He frowns. 'Tell me,' he says, 'why do people have to cough immediately after a movement ends? If they've held back for ten minutes, can't they hold back for two seconds more?'

'Audiences!' says Piers, as if that explained it all.

Helen offers me a sip of whisky from a little silver flask she keeps in her bag.

'Don't get him drunk,' growls Piers.

'Just medicinal,' says Helen. 'Nerves. Look, poor Michael, he's trembling.'

'I'm not. Not more than usual, anyway.'

'It's going very well,' says Helen soothingly. 'Very well indeed. They all seem to like it.'

'What they really like, Helen,' says Piers, 'is your red dress and bare shoulders.'

Helen yawns ostentatiously. 'Billy, play us a bit of Brahms,' she says.

'No, no—' cries Piers.

'Well, then how about silence?' asks Helen. 'No unpleasant remarks, no bickering, lots of collegiate love and sympathy.'

'Very well,' says Piers in a conciliatory tone, coming over and stroking his sister's shoulders.

'I'm looking forward to it really,' I say.

'That's the spirit,' says Piers.

'That slow opening fugue, it makes me shiver,' says Billy to himself.

'You boys are so *wet*,' says Helen. 'Can't you be a bit less *dewy* about music? Then you'd be less nervous.'

We are quiet for a while. I stand up and look out of the window, resting my hands against the radiator.

'I'm worried about my fiddle staying in tune,' I say almost under my breath.

'It'll be fine,' murmurs Helen. 'It'll be fine.'

2.22

Forty minutes later we are taking our applause. Billy's shirt is drenched with sweat. He once said about the C sharp minor quartet: 'You give everything of yourself in your first four bars, and where do you go from there?' but he, and we, have answered that in our own way.

It is a piece after which there can be no encore, and should be none. The fourth time we are called back on stage, we could have left our instruments behind to indicate as much, but we have brought them with us, as before, and this time we sit down. The applause dies instantly, as if at the downbeat of a baton. There is a murmur of expectancy, then silence. We look at each other now, concentrate entirely on each other. For what we are to play we need no music. It is in our cells.

I have made a small adjustment to the Tononi backstage. I now check it almost silently, and tell it not to let me down.

Normally Piers would announce the encore. Instead, he and the others look at me and nod almost imperceptibly. I begin to play. I take my first two notes on open strings, almost as if they were a transition from tuning into music.

As I play the first few slow notes I hear from different points of the dark hall the indrawn breath of startled recognition. After my four lonely bars, Piers joins me, then Billy and then Helen.

We are playing the first contrapunctus of Bach's 'Art of Fugue'.

We play almost without vibrato, keeping the bow on the string, taking open strings wherever they fall naturally, even if it means that our phrases do not exactly replicate one another's. We play with such intensity, such calm, as I never imagined we could either feel or create. The fugue flows on, and our travelling bows follow its course, guided and guiding.

As I move to the tiny quaver, the minuscule quibble of a note that was the source of all my anxiety, Helen, who has a rest here, turns her head slightly and looks at me. I can tell that she is smiling. It is the F below middle C. I have had to tune my lowest string down a tone in order to be able to play it.

We play in an energised trance. These four-and-a-half minutes could be as many hours or seconds. In my mind's eye I see the little-used clefs of the original score, and the sinking and rising, swift and slow, parallel and contrary, of all our several voices—and in my mind's ear I hear what has sounded and is sounding and is yet to sound. I only have to realise on the strings what is already real to me; and so have Billy, and Helen, and Piers. Our synchronous visions merge, and we are one: with each other, with the world, and with that long-dispersed being whose force we receive through the shape of his annotated vision and the single swift-flowing syllable of his name.

2.23

Piers and I have changed out of our dinner jackets into easier clothes. This is an operation that we have got down to ninety seconds flat. People are standing outside the green room and along the stairs.

We open the door and Erica Cowan marches in with her arms spread in welcoming rapture. She is followed by twenty or thirty people.

'Marvellous, marvellous, marvellous, mwah, mwah, mwah!' goes Erica, dispensing lateral kisses. 'Where's Billy?'

'In the shower,' says Piers.

Billy rushed off down the corridor before the arrival of the public. He will be back with us in a few minutes, unsweaty and presentable. Lydia, his wife, is talking to Virginie. Piers, his eyes half-closed, is leaning against the coat-stand. Appreciative members of the audience are milling around. 'Thank you, yes, thank you, delighted, delighted you enjoyed it . . . Hey, Luis!' he says with sudden enthusiasm, seeing someone he recognises.

All of us would rather be by ourselves but the Maggiore must smile to live.

Piers, unable to disentangle himself, is being asked his least-favourite question—the reason for our name—by an earnest young woman. He sees his parents across the room, waves them over, and engages them immediately in domestic conversation.

The sticky fan is here, adhering to Helen, resplendent in red. Luckily, however, he is soon diluted by a couple of students of hers from the

Guildhall.

Needless to say, Nicholas Spare is nowhere in sight, though after what Piers did, it would have taken improbable nobility of spirit for him to turn up. Nor has he honoured his promise to include us in his musical highlights of the week. In fact, according to a source we have in the management of the hall, there are no critics here at all. It is immensely frustrating—a wonderful performance, and not a scrap of newsprint to tell the world it happened. Not, I suppose, that the world would get many column-inches in the newsprint of the universe.

'Oh, *c'est la guerre,*' says Erica to Piers when he complains. 'Critics don't matter, really.'

'That's nonsense, Erica, and you know it,' says Piers shortly.

'It's too wonderful an evening for fretting,' says Erica. 'Ah, that's Ysobel Shingle there. Ysobel with a Y, would you believe it! She's from Stratus Records . . . Ysobel, Ysobel,' shouts Erica, waving wildly.

A tall young woman, who looks as grey as if she'd never seen the sun and with a forehead fraught with worry approaches and, with tremulous eagerness, tells Erica and Piers how much she enjoyed the concert.

'Offer us a contract,' says Erica with abandon.

Ysobel Shingle smiles in a hunted way. 'Well, I have a sort of idea,' she says. 'But I don't, you know, think that this is quite the place to . . .' She trails off.

'Ten thirty tomorrow morning, I'll be in your office,' says Erica.

'Well, you know, Erica, I, er, let me call you to . . .

Let me think things through. I just wanted to tell all of you how very much I . . .' She twists her palms outwards in a tortured gesture, then, almost in a panic, turns to leave.

'What a very odd woman,' says Mrs Tavistock, who, judging from Piers and Helen's unfilial accounts, is quite an odd woman herself.

'She's the power behind the success of Stratus,' says Erica.

'Really?' says Piers, unwillingly impressed.

'It's fantastic that she was in the audience tonight,' says Erica. 'I'll follow this up like a bloodhound.'

Ten minutes later Helen and I are chatting with a young woman from the hall management when we overhear the tail-end of one of Piers's conversations. 'I'm so sorry,' Piers is saying. 'It's a problem I've had since I was a child . . . I've never been able to deal with stupid questions.'

'I'd better go and gag him,' says Helen.

The initial hubbub has died down; the crowd has thinned a bit. Billy and Lydia have gone home to relieve Billy's parents, who are baby-sitting Jango, their three-year-old son. The sticky fan has somehow dematerialised. But there are still quite a few people around.

Virginie too has gone. She offered me a lift, but I decided I'd go with Helen instead. I want to have a quick post-mortem with her and Piers in the car.

I look around the room, tired but in a way content, the Bach still sounding in my head.

'Michael,' says Julia as my eyes fall on her.

'Julia.' The name forms on my lips, but I speak no sound, no whisper.

She looks at me, I at her. Some sort of dark-leafed lily is on her right, and she is wearing green. It was her; it is her.

'Hello,' she says.

'Hello.'

There is an intentness to her gaze. The green silk swims into the deep green leaves, the shot green of the tablecloth, the olive green of the chairs, the thick velvety green of the curtains, the grass-green of an inchoate painting. I look down. The carpet, a rich veridian, is patterned with little red measles.

'Have you been here long?' I ask.

'I was waiting outside. I couldn't decide what to do.'

I examine the measles. They are irregular in shape, arranged in regular rows. 'And so, you're here,' I say.

'I didn't know you were in the Maggiore,' says Julia. 'I simply saw the monthly programme, and thought of Banff, and how we met them there.'

'I joined some years ago.' Is this what we are to talk about after all? I look at her. 'You came to the concert not knowing that I was playing?'

'It was a wonderful concert,' she says. Her eyes are moist.

My eyes move towards the window. Outside, in the back street, it is raining. A mound of black plastic rubbish bags stands at the entrance of a cul-de-sac. The street-lamp plays on their slick skins.

'It was you on the bus. I knew I couldn't be

129

wrong.'

'Yes.'

'Why did you wait so long to get in touch with me? Why didn't you look for me in the phone book?'

There is a pause. People are speaking all around us. I can hear Piers lay down the law on some point of theory. Julia takes a step towards me.

'I couldn't face seeing you again.'

'Then why are you here?'

'After the Bach I knew I would come backstage. I can't explain why. It probably wasn't a good idea. I've been standing in the corridor all this time. But it is good to see you again, not just to hear you play.'

There is no ring on her hand, but on her wrist is a small gold watch with a braided golden strap. Around her neck hangs a small diamond pendant. Her eyes seem more green than blue. From her voice, from the way she clutches her handbag, I know she is about to go.

'Please don't go,' I say, grasping her hand. 'I have to see you again. Do you live in London now? Will you call me? I'm doing nothing much tomorrow.' She looks at me, bewildered. 'What are you doing just now, Julia? Have you eaten? Do you have a car? You can't go out in this rain. You really can't.'

Julia begins to smile. 'No, I won't call you. I've never been very good on the phone. But we'll meet somewhere.'

'Where? And when?'

'Michael, let go of my hand,' she whispers.

'Where?'

'Oh, anywhere,' says Julia, looking around. 'How

130

about the Wallace Collection? At one?'

'Yes.'

'I'll see you at the entrance.'

'Julia, give me your phone number.'

She shakes her head.

'What if you aren't there? What if you change your mind?'

But before she can reply, Helen has come up to us. 'Julia!' says Helen. 'Julia! It's been ages! Ages! Canada, wasn't it? Banff. What a marvellous time. How have you been? Are you just visiting from Vienna? Michael said you'd lost touch, but here you are!'

'Yes,' says Julia, with her acute, gentle smile. 'Here I am.'

'Piers!' says Helen. 'Look who's here. Julia.'

Piers, deep in conversation with a young man, shakes his head a bit distractedly. Julia makes for the door.

'Let me walk you to your car,' I say.

She puts on her coat and opens the door to the corridor. 'I'm fine, Michael. You should stay behind for your post-mortem. A concert without a post-mortem . . .'

' . . . is like bridge without the mayhem. Yes.'

'But where's Billy?' asks Julia.

'He's gone home. Baby-sitter.'

'Billy has children?' Julia says, almost in wonderment.

'A child. A son.'

'When I saw the four of you take your bow, I thought of the first phrase of Beethoven's fifth,' she says. She matches her gesture to the notes: three tall thin players, and one short robust one.

I can't help laughing at the image. How has she

131

changed? Her hair is much longer, her face a bit more drawn—but this seems the work not of ten years, but of two.

'Do you have anything else to say about our performance?' I ask, trying to keep her talking.

'Well . . . I wish I couldn't see the name 'Haydn' through your music rack when you were playing the Mozart.'

'And?'

'And—nothing. It was lovely. But I must go. I really must . . . How is your finger?'

'Well, it hasn't troubled me much lately. In fact, hardly at all these last five years—ever since I joined the quartet, actually . . . Strange, isn't it, when your own body rebels against you, and then suddenly decides it doesn't want to any more.'

I get a felt pen out of my pocket and take her hand. I write my phone number on the edge of her palm. She looks at me, astonished, but doesn't object.

'That's a phone and answering machine and fax. Transcribe it before you go to bed,' I say. I lean down to kiss her palm, its life-line, its loveline. My lips move to her fingers.

'Michael, no, no, please.' There is a desperation in her words that stops me. 'Let me be. Please let me be. I'll see you tomorrow.'

'Goodnight, then, Julia, goodnight.' I let go her hand.

'Goodnight,' she says quietly, turning away.

I go to the window. In a few moments she emerges from the back door. She opens her umbrella, then appears for a second or two to be uncertain which direction to take. The rain falls on the back street, on the black rubbish bags. Why the

Wallace Collection of all places, I wonder—not that it matters much. How will I sleep tonight, or even believe all this when I am alone? For a few moments her face is lit, too dimly for me to read much on it. She may be older, but she is as beautiful as she was. How much have I changed? She turns to the right, and I watch her till she moves round the corner onto the main street, out of the reach of my eyes.

PART THREE

PART THREE

3.1

She is there a little before one. A nervous glance at me, a quick, tentative smile. I don't take her hand nor she mine.

'I've never been here before,' I tell her.

'Never?'

'No. Though I've often meant to.'

'Well, should we wander around?' she asks.

'Yes. Or we could go somewhere else for a coffee instead, if you'd like. Or a bite.'

'I've had lunch,' she says. 'But if you haven't—'

'I'm not hungry,' I say.

'The first time you went to an art gallery in Vienna it was with me, wasn't it?'

'Yes,' I reply.

'So it's only appropriate that I should be your guide here as well.'

'Except that Vienna is your city, and London is mine.'

'Since when has London been your city?' Julia smiles.

'No, it's not really,' I say, then smile back at her. 'But I'm getting naturalised.'

'Against your will?'

'Not entirely.'

'The others are Londoners, aren't they? In the Maggiore, I mean.'

'Sort of. Billy's London born and bred, Piers and Helen are from the West Country originally, but they're basically Londoners now.'

'I remember Alec most of all.'

'Alex,' I say.

Julia looks a bit puzzled, then nods. 'It was a shock to see you there instead of him.'

'Naturally.'

'I remember him reciting some Canadian poet, to the astonishment of our hosts. Service?'

'Yes. Rollicking stuff.'

'And I remember lying awake in Banff listening to the trains,' says Julia.

'So do I.'

'Why did he leave? Weren't Piers and he lovers?' Julia is looking at me with a very direct gaze, tender and attentive.

'I suppose so,' I say. 'But after a few years—well, anyway, Piers doesn't like to talk about it. Things just fell apart, I think, as they sometimes do. Musically as much as anything else. You remember, they used to alternate first and second violin.'

'Recipe for disaster.'

'Yes. We don't do that since I joined five years ago . . . And you—are you naturalised in London? Oh, by the way, I'm so sorry about your father.'

Julia looks startled.

'Julia, I'm sorry that sounded so casual,' I say, suddenly feeling guilty and dismayed. 'I didn't mean it in that sense. After I saw you that day, I tried to track you down again. But the trail petered out in Oxford. I am so sorry. I liked him. And I know you adored him.'

Julia looks down at her gentle, tapering fingers, which she crosses, and then slowly disengages, as if to let her thoughts run through them.

'Should we look around?' I ask.

She doesn't answer for a while, then looks up and says: 'Well, should we go in?'

I nod.

When she met me first, my mother was dead, and now her father is. Though he shut me off from knowledge of her when I most needed it, he was at heart a kind man. Pacific by nature, he wrote with objective clarity about the history of warfare. Julia takes after him, I think, in cast of mind. But how can I draw such conclusions, who met him only once and that just for a day?

3.2

We wander around for two hours, walking from room to room, hardly talking at all. This is not a neutral environment but a competing one. She is preoccupied—sometimes with a painting, sometimes with nothing explicable. She seems to attend to the expression on the faces of those portrayed, to sink into them, to be unaware of my presence, unresponsive to my comments. She stands for a while before Velazquez's 'The Lady with a Fan'.

'I'm sorry, Michael—I was far away.'

'No, no, that's fine.' She looks at the lady, I at her. But why be frustrated? She was always a bit like this when in a gallery. There was a painting in Vienna—a Vermeer—that she stood in front of for half an hour before I tapped her shoulder and broke her trance.

I follow her steps and her gaze. A young, unreadably inward-looking black archer; a naughty, fluffy young woman on a swing kicking off her pink slipper to her lover; Rembrandt's son Titus. Who are these people, and what chain of chance has brought them to the common shelter of this building? How many scores of faces have each of us added to our lives these last ten years?

We find ourselves in a room in which an attendant is performing discreet callisthenics. The walls are covered with paintings of Venice. Surely this can't be why she has brought me here.

She turns her gaze from the paintings to the attendant, then to me: 'Well, have you been there after all?' she asks.

'No, not yet.'

'I have,' she says quietly.

'Well, you wanted to so much.'

'I?' she asks with a trace of tension.

'We.'

She stands before a painting of a domed church with a tower, far out across the water. Though I have never been there it looks familiar.

'Maria and I went a few months after my final exams,' she says. 'There was a thunderstorm the first night we were there, with lightning flashing out over the whole lagoon. I kept crying, which was stupid because, after all, it was beautiful.'

'Not so stupid.' I want to touch her shoulder, but don't. I feel this whole scene is being acted out between strangers.

'You should go,' she says.

'I am going,' I reply. 'In fact, we're going there this spring.'

'Who is we?'

'The quartet.'

'What's taking you there?'

'A couple of concerts—and, well, Venice itself. We're flying there from Vienna.'

'Vienna?' says Julia. 'Vienna?'

'Yes,' I say. Since she remains silent, I add,

'We're playing an all-Schubert concert at the *Musikverein*.'

After a second she says in an even voice: 'I'll tell my mother to watch out for it. She lives there now. And my aunt.'

'And you? Won't you come?'

'I live in London now.'

My face lights up. 'You *do* live in London. I knew it.'

Suddenly something occurs to her and she becomes white with anxiety. 'Michael, I must go. It's after three. I had lost track of the time. I've got to . . . to pick someone up.'

'But—'

'I can't explain now. I must go, I really must. I shall be late. I'll see you tomorrow.'

'But when? Where?'

'At one?'

'Yes, but where? Here again?'

'No—I'll leave a message on your machine.'

'Why not phone me later on?'

'I can't. I'll be busy. I'll leave you a message by the time you get back.' She turns to leave. She seems close to panic.

'Why don't you phone them to say you'll be a bit late?'

But she does not turn back or pause to reply.

3.3

That was the sum of our meeting. Nor did we touch in parting. We spoke for not even five minutes— and what we said was stilted, bitty. I know nothing of what she now thinks or now is. I find myself

141

empty. A bit of her perfume remains on the air, light with lemon. I wander around the rooms, staring at weaponry: swords, scimitars, daggers, cuirasses, helmets. A horse armoured in black steel bears down on me like a tank. A roomful of children painted by Greuze, fat with false innocence, smile through me or gaze tremulously heavenwards. A black-orbed clock shows two golden figures, a goddess and a young man: a king or prince. She towers over him in size, but her tiny fingers rest incongruously on his huge hand. Upstairs and downstairs I drift along, uneasy, entranced, seeing, unseeing: allegory, myth, landscape, royalty, lapdogs, dead game. The attendant has his hands crossed behind his head, which he is moving to left and right. He flexes his fingers. In this room I hear the voice of my violin. Venice surrounds us—the serene Canaletto of turquoise water, the grubby, visionary mergings of Guardi.

We did not share these hours. We were sealed in separate absorptions. This is the only room where we talked at all. Yet how can one urge on a reacquaintance such as this? She didn't seem bitter; she even said she wanted to see me again.

All the portraits where she paused, I now pause at. I see and hear her: her tense shoulders as she stood before the lady with a fan, her laughter as she looked at Fragonard's pink-frilled coquette on the swing.

I stand in front of the painting and remember her laugh. Is she happy? Why does she want to see me again? Why, of all places, did she ask me here? Was it simply what first came to mind after the concert? Surely it could not have been because of

Venice.

Her laughter held delight. Yet she was suddenly anxious and sad.

The flushed face looks mischievously at the slipper flying through the air over a froth of leaves. The ropes disappear into a misty tumult of darkness above. The picture has charm. It held her here for a moment. Why look for another reason?

3.4

The world enters my head through my answering machine. There are seven messages: a bumper crop. The first is from Julia. She suggests we meet at one tomorrow in the Orangery in Kensington Gardens. This is just a few minutes' walk from where I live, but she couldn't possibly know that.

There are a couple of calls relating to the Camerata Anglica and various rehearsals that I am, according to their office, to 'pencil in' or 'pencil out'.

Erica Cowan calls to rave about our concert last night, and to say that Helen has told her that Julia came backstage afterwards. How marvellous. She is so happy for me; everything comes to those who wait. And she has some interesting news to impart to the quartet, but it will have to keep till tomorrow.

A message from Piers. He feels I was a bit distracted when we discussed the concert on the way home. He'd like us to have a quick review. And Erica has something she wants to share with us. Could we meet at Helen's at two tomorrow afternoon?

I call Piers. How about five instead of two? Fine with him, he says; he'll check with the others. What is this interesting news of Erica's, I ask him. Piers is cagey. Erica thinks we should all be together to consider it.

The next message is in a female voice, somewhat irate, wondering why the London Bait Company is not answering her calls in the middle of a working day.

A message from Virginie, sounding very cheerful. She loved the concert and is interrupting her practice—yes, she promises she is practising— to tell me how inspiringly we played.

The phone rings, and my heart leaps up. But it is Erica again. She sounds as if she's had much too good a lunch.

'Michael, darling, it's Erica, I felt I had to call you, I had to, the concert last night was absolutely brilliant.'

'Thanks, Erica. I've just been listening to your message.'

'But that's not why I'm calling. It's just this, Michael, dear, you must be very very careful. Life is never simple. I've just had lunch with an old old friend of mine, and I can't help feeling that things are meant to happen when they happen. You do understand what I mean?'

'I don't really—'

'Of course it could be physical or spiritual or, well, anything. Helen told me, of course.'

'But Erica—'

'Do you know, when you get to forty, you become intensely physical. I'm not interested at all in any men my age, I'm only interested in younger men, who by and large are absolutely gorgeous, but

144

entirely unavailable. Earlier I used to be terribly picky, and all these people were wafting around with endless desire, and you were saying oh no, no, and now it's all changed. But the trouble is that even if you want to be naughty, all these young men want to do is to ask you to introduce them to people to help them get jobs.'

'Well—'

'So you've got all this desire, but you're an old bag. Sometimes I look in the mirror and I don't recognise myself. Who is she? Where did these wrinkles come from? I used to have a round face, rather moonlike, and I longed to be gaunt, but now of course I'm gaunt, terribly gaunt, and I'm not terribly keen to be an old bag. I could do with that moonface again.'

'You're not gaunt, Erica, you're attractive and drunk.'

'You're not forty yet, you don't know,' says Erica resentfully. 'And you're a man.

'Where did you go for lunch?' I ask.

'Oh, the Sugar Club, they have all these unpronounceable ingredients in their food like jicama and metaxa—do I mean metaxa?'

'I'm not sure.'

'But they have a brilliant wine list.'

'Apparently.'

'Naughty boy! My husband took me there for our anniversary last year and it was a real discovery. Now I take all my friends there. Try the kangaroo.'

'I will. Erica, what's this interesting news you have for the quartet?'

'Oh, that? I think that Stratus are going to offer us a recording.'

I can hardly believe my ears. Stratus! 'You're joking, Erica,' I say. 'You can't be serious.'

'There's gratitude for you.'

'But that's amazing! How did you swing it?'

'I had a lovely long chat with Ysobel this morning—but let's talk about all this tomorrow at two.'

'Not two. Five.'

'Five?'

'Five. Write it down.'

'Oh, I'll remember.'

'Erica, you won't remember a thing. Not after your liquid lunch.'

'All right. But don't tell the others what I've told you. I want it to be a surprise. Remember, mum's the word.'

But I have no doubt that Erica has phoned each of us to swear us to secrecy.

Before I get off the phone I tell her to drink lots of water, take a Nurofen, and attempt to pronounce 'Ysobel Shingle' ten times in rapid succession.

3.5

Thinking of Julia and unable to sleep, I watch a desultory thriller late at night, and drift off at three in the morning.

At eleven it is fresh and clear, but it darkens, and around noon there is a heavy and continuous downpour. But Julia does not phone to change our place or time of meeting.

At a quarter to one, umbrella'd, capped, and padded against the weather, I step out into the dark day. The old leaves, long since fallen, are whirled up and around. The rain cuts across and soaks my trousers below the knee. The umbrella with its weak spokes becomes a crazy black sail. The park is almost completely empty, for who would take a stroll in this weather?

On each of the larger boughs of a plane tree sit about a dozen pigeons, including a few brown ones, facing the wind, ruffled and uncooing, like fat fruit. A crow struts around beneath, calm, cawing, proprietorial. A couple of miserable joggers pass by.

I get to the Orangery. A few people, presumably trapped by the storm, are sipping cups of tea or reading newspapers. It is a beautiful building from the inside: a very high white rectangle with alcoves, its southern wall made up of tall pillars alternating with huge windows to let in the sunlight—or whatever scene the weather holds. There is no sign of Julia.

The place echoes at the best of times, but today the howling wind, the rain striking the tall windows at a shallow diagonal, the wail of an unhappy baby and the random clangs from the kitchen create the sort of effect that would doubtless delight Billy.

Julia comes in a few minutes later. She is utterly bedraggled. Her blonde hair is matted and almost brown, her dress soaked. There is an anxious look in her eyes as she glances quickly around the Orangery.

I am by the door in a second.

'This umbrella,' she says, struggling.

I laugh and embrace her, and kiss her on the mouth without thinking, like that first time so many years ago.

She half responds, then draws quickly away. For a few seconds she looks away from me, as if trying to collect herself.

'What a storm,' she says, passing a hand through her hair.

'Why didn't you phone me to change the place?' I ask. 'You're soaked through.'

'Oh—it would have been too confusing.'

'Stand by the radiator.'

She stands by the radiator, shivering, and looks out at the rain. I stand behind her, my hands on her shoulders. She does not shake them off.

'Julia, I still love you.'

She says nothing. Is it my imagination, or do I feel her shoulders stiffen?

When she turns around it is to murmur: 'Let's have some coffee. Have you been waiting long?'

'Julia!' I say. It's one thing to ignore my words, but why this deliberate banality?

She reads the hurt in my eyes. Still she says nothing. We sit down. A waitress comes and we order something: coffee and ginger cake.

For a minute or so we do not speak, then Julia asks hesitantly: 'Do you have any news of Carl Käll?'

'I had a letter from him a few months ago.'

'He wrote to you?'

'Yes. You probably know that he's in Sweden now.'

The waitress brings our order. Julia looks at her plate. 'The rumour is that he's very ill,' she says.

'Something in his letter made me think so.'

She senses I don't want to talk about him, and moves to other matters. We touch on subjects carefully, one by one, as if they might suddenly rear up and strike: casual acquaintances, the likelihood of the storm letting up soon, the décor. I learn that Maria, after her string of artsy boyfriends, is now married to a good solid burgher.

I touch the red mark on the left side of my chin—the violinist's callus. In all this openness and space, something seems to close in on me. Again I think of Carl. His bow went up and down like a little switch while he told me what to do. For him an orchestra was what a pub or a nightclub was to my father. Even chamber music was not what he expected of me. When he played I heard a sound so noble—round, warm, unaffected—that I wanted to emulate it, but when I tried his techniques they did violence to my own style. Why could he not permit me to form myself—with guidance, not constraint?

Her eyes are on my face—almost warily. Then she says something which I lose in the noise around me. There is a loud clanging somewhere, and the baby three tables down is yowling lungfully.

'I'm sorry, Julia—this place is impossible. I didn't hear that.'

'For once—' she says, and I can read both tension and a touch of amusement in her expression.

'For once what?'

'Nothing.'

'But what was it you said?'

'I'll have to tell you, Michael, sooner or later. It's better sooner.'

'Yes?'

'I'm married.' Softly she repeats it, almost to herself. 'I'm married.'

'But you can't be.'

'I am.'

149

'Are you happy?' I strive to keep the misery out of my voice.

'I think so. Yes.' Her finger is moving in a small quadrant round the edge of her blue-and-white plate. 'And you?' she asks.

'No. No. No. I mean, I'm not married.'

'So you're alone?'

I sigh and shrug. 'No.'

'Is she nice?'

'She's not you.'

'Oh, Michael—' Julia's finger stops its movement around the edge. 'Don't do this.'

'Children?' I ask, my eyes holding hers.

'One. A boy. Luke.'

'And you all live happily together in London.'

'Michael!'

'And you still play music, of course.'

'Yes.'

'So that's all I need to know. Except—why don't you wear a ring?'

'I don't know. It distracts me. It distracts me when I play the piano. I look at it and I can't concentrate on the music. Michael, it was you who left Vienna.'

It's true. What can I then say? Only my own unblunted truth will do.

'I couldn't breathe with Carl around. I didn't know I couldn't do without you. I never thought that I'd lost you—that I'd lose you.'

'You could have written after you left, explaining things.'

'I did write—'

'Months later. After I'd slowly gone to pieces.' She is quiet for a moment, then continues: 'I didn't trust myself to open your letters when they finally

150

started coming. I had thought of nothing but you—every hour, every day, when I slept, when I woke. No.' She speaks from a surveying distance, almost beyond the memory of hurt or anger.

'I'm so sorry, my darling.'

'Michael, don't call me that,' she says sadly.

We don't speak for a while, then Julia says, 'Well, that was then.'

The rain has stopped. The garden outside is in clear view, with its huge green sand-turrets of topiary. The sky is clear.

'Listen,' I say. 'A robin.'

Julia looks at me and nods.

'You know,' I continue, 'I often come here—not to the Orangery so much as the sunken garden there. Sometimes in the spring I just come and listen to the blackbirds. And you—are you still in love with your nightingales?'

There are tears in Julia's eyes.

After a while I say: 'Look, let's get out of here and take a walk. I live close by.'

She shakes her head, almost as if she was denying what I've just told her.

'You need to get dried off properly,' I say.

She nods. 'I don't live far away either. My car's parked nearby. I'd better go.'

'You don't want me to have your phone number?' I ask.

'No,' she says, dabbing at her eyes.

'Well, here's my address,' I say, taking a yellow sticker out of my wallet and scribbling it down. 'Now write down yours. I'm not going to lose you again.'

'Michael, I'm not here to be gained.'

'You know that's not what I meant. I'm not such

a fool.'

'I don't know what you meant,' she says. 'And I don't know what I'm doing here.'

'Well, give me your address,' I say.

She hesitates.

'In case I want to send you a Christmas card. Or, who knows, even another letter.'

She shakes her head and writes down her address. It's in Elgin Crescent, in Notting Hill, only a mile or so from where I live.

'And are you still McNicholl? For professional purposes?'

'No. I took my husband's surname.'

'Which is?'

'Hansen.'

'Oh, so *you're* Julia Hansen. I've heard of you.'

Julia smiles despite herself. But, presumably seeing the wretchedness in my eyes, she stops.

We walk across the park, not saying much, I towards my flat, she to her car.

3.6

'No, she's not, Piers darling,' says Erica, setting down her Scotch on one of Helen's square table-cum-stools. 'Eccentric, yes, neurotic, yes, but not mad.'

'But, Erica,' says Billy, 'couldn't you dissuade her? Couldn't you? I mean, couldn't you tell her that we can't do it, and that there are dozens of things in our repertoire that we'd love to do? Dozens.'

Erica shakes her head vigorously. 'I sat in her office for two hours going round and round the subject, but it was either this or nothing. She's not interested in anything else we can offer. She says the quartet repertoire is over-recorded, and she won't contribute to it.'

'I don't understand it,' says Helen. 'She listens to the whole concert and then battens onto the encore.'

Erica smiles maternally. 'I told her it isn't the sort of thing you usually play. She said, "More's the pity: if I offer them this recording they'll have to." Really, Helen, I have very very rarely seen Ysobel Shingle as enthusiastic about anything as she was about the way you played the Bach. To get an offer from Stratus is a big deal. I don't mean money,' adds Erica quickly. 'You won't get much. But it'll definitely be noticed.'

'It could go badly wrong,' says Billy. 'A recording of the "Art of Fugue" on the Stratus label will be widely reviewed—and if people don't like it, we could be orbiting in outer darkness.'

'Yes,' says Erica. 'And if they do like it, you could be dazzled by the limelight. Well, there it is. It's for you to decide. But I'm willing to spend two hours trying to persuade you, since I couldn't dissuade her. Or deflect her, rather.'

'It's crazy,' says Piers. 'It'll distract us from our regular repertoire.'

'It's a challenge,' says Erica.

'That's a glib response,' says Piers shortly.

Erica turns to me, unfazed. 'You haven't said much, Michael.'

'He hasn't said anything,' says Helen. 'What on earth's the matter with you, Michael? You look completely out of it. Are you all right?'

Billy glances at me. 'What do you think?' he

153

asks.

'I don't know,' I say. 'I'm still quite stunned.' I turn to Erica, trying to concentrate. 'Is this why you didn't tell us over the phone what she was offering?'

'Perhaps,' says Erica. 'Yes. I wanted to enjoy your reactions. And I didn't want anyone to pre-empt everyone else's opinions.'

Piers grunts.

'How long is the "Art of Fugue", Billy?' I ask.

'An hour and a half—two CDs.'

'And all we've ever played of it is four and a half minutes,' says Piers.

'But we enjoyed it,' I say.

'Yes,' says Helen, 'more than almost anything I've ever played.'

'You played it superbly, superbly!' cries Erica, lathering on the enthusiasm. 'And the audience was silent for five whole seconds before clapping. One, two, three, four, five! I've never seen anything like it.'

'It's a seriously bad idea,' says Piers, unimpressed. 'It'll deflect us from what we want to do. It'll compete with our performances, not complement them. We can't *perform* the whole damned thing, only record it. Quartets don't do that sort of thing on stage. Besides, Bach didn't write it for string quartet.'

Billy gives a little pre-disquisitional cough. 'Um, you know, I'm sure if the string quartet existed in his time he'd have written for it.'

'Oh, yes, Billy, your hotline to Bach again?' says Piers.

'In fact, it's not really clear what he wrote it for,' continues Billy calmly. 'I'm pretty sure he wrote it

154

for the keyboard, since it falls under the hands, but some people think it wasn't written for any particular instrument. Others think it wasn't even written to be played, just as a sort of offering to God or the spirit of music or something—but I think that's silly, and so does Jango. No, there's no harm in us performing it.'

'And the viola does as much as everyone else, for a change,' says Helen meditatively.

Piers looks upwards at the ceiling.

'Both violas, actually,' says Billy to Helen.

'What do you mean?' she asks.

'Well,' says Billy with a Buddha-like air, 'you remember that Michael had to tune his lowest string down a bit at the Wigmore? If we had been recording it as opposed to performing it, he could just as well have played the whole of that fugue on the viola instead of the violin, and avoided the problem. And there are several other fugues where his part goes so low that he would really *have* to play on the viola.'

My face lights up at the thought of getting the chance to play the viola again.

'So?' says Erica, having poured herself a full and rather undiluted glass of whisky. 'What's the sense of the meeting? What shall I tell Ysobel?'

'Yes!' says Helen before anyone else can say anything. 'Yes! Yes! Yes!'

Billy gives a funny shrug with shoulder, head and right hand which says, in effect: well it's a risk, but on the other hand, what's life for, and Bach is so fantastic and Helen is so eager, so, well, yes, fine.

'I wonder whose viola I could borrow,' I say.

Piers is normally our programmer, but if he tries to lay down the law now, he will be faced with

155

rebellion.

'Let's suggest a different programme and call her bluff,' he says.

Erica shakes her head. 'I know Ysobel,' she says.

'Well, when would we be expected to record?' asks Piers irritably. 'If we were to agree, that is.'

Erica smiles a small smile of anticipated triumph. 'Ysobel's surprisingly flexible on that, though she does want an answer from us very soon about whether we'll do it at all. It could become a hole-in-the-catalogue issue for her, and if we delay or refuse she might start looking for someone else to fill it. She suddenly started talking—or whispering, in that way of hers—à propos of nothing in particular, or maybe I just missed the connection, which would be typical of me, of course, about how very much she liked the sound of the Vellinger Quartet . . .'

'We shouldn't rush into things,' says Piers, struggling in the face of Erica's tactics.

'No, but we shouldn't dawdle out of things, either,' says Helen. 'We aren't the only decent quartet around. You remember when we delayed getting back to the Ridgebrook Festival and they got the Skampa instead?'

'You know, Helen,' says Piers, rounding on her, 'you're a great enthusiast about everything at the beginning, but—do you remember the potter's wheel? You made everyone's life hell until Father got you one, and then you threw one pot on it—not a particularly attractive one, either, if I recall—and gave it up. It's still sitting in the garage.'

'I was sixteen,' says Helen, stung. 'And what does that have to do with this? If the Vellinger steal a march on us, we'll only have you to blame.'

156

'Oh, all right,' says Piers. 'All right, all right, let's tell the crazy Shingle that we're dumb enough to consider her idea. But we need time to think it through. We can't decide immediately. I refuse to. Let's go home and think about it. For a week. For at least a week.'

'Calmly,' suggests Helen.

'Yes, calmly, of course,' says Piers, smouldering.

3.7

Night comes down on a strange day, so full of change. I need to take a walk around my neighbourhood. Just as I am about to step outside Archangel Court, the silver-haired, immaculate and rather mysterious Mr Lawrence—Mr S.Q. Lawrence—accosts me.

'Um, Mr Holme, could I perhaps have a word with you? About the lift—we've been talking to the management agency, and . . . a word with Rob . . . some inconvenience . . . but rather a happy outcome, wouldn't you agree?'

I hear little of what he is saying. Stray phrases like shooting stars on a horizon enter my mind. But I wonder what the Q in his name stands for.

'Yes, yes, I agree completely.'

'Well, I must say,' says Mr Lawrence, looking surprised and relieved, 'I was rather hoping you'd say that. And of course we have the other long leaseholders to take into consideration . . . unsatisfactory performance . . . especially inconvenient for you . . . of course one could change to Otis . . . service agreement . . . swings and roundabouts . . . well, there it is.'

157

'I'm so sorry, Mr Lawrence, I must rush. Etienne's will be closing soon. Croissants, you know.' I open the door and step out into the moist night.

Why did I need to explain that I was going to buy croissants? I ask myself.

When will I see Julia again?

The girl at Etienne's has changed; she is fresh-faced, even so late in the day, and looks and sounds Polish. I walk past Greek restaurants, an Australian pub, ranks of telephones with the cards of call-girls attached to the inside with Blu-tack. I need emptier streets. I turn to the white squares to the west.

Their hearts are full of inaccessible trees. Their pavements are almost unpeopled. I walk for an hour here and there. The sky is clouded, the air mild for winter. Somewhere, far away, a car alarm starts up, sounds for half a minute, then stops.

I said I loved her and she did not respond. My hands rested on her shoulders, and I felt them tense. She looked in front of her through the huge windows at the bare, wind-battered branches of the horse chestnuts.

When we walked back across the park, she said hardly a word. Twigs lay scattered about the Broad Walk, gulls cried above the Round Pond. A disjointed conversation was what we had, as if she did not want to address what I had to say.

The dull silver domes of the Stakis Hotel; we parted there.

Mr and Mrs Hansen and their son Luke. A cat? A dog? Goldfish? The telephone must not ring in their home, their haven.

If I could talk to her tonight it would ease my heart. If I could hold her again I would be at peace.

3.8

I drop off to sleep about midnight, imagining I am
with her. I sleep dreamlessly, perhaps because I am
so tired.

At ten in the morning, someone rings from
below on the intercom. I look at the miniature blue
screen and see her face, a bit distorted. A scarf
covers her hair.

It's astonishing: as if the thought of her had
conjured her up.

'Michael, it's Julia.'

'Hello! Come on up. I'm just shaving. First lift,
eighth floor,' I say, and press the buzzer.

She looks a bit nonplussed by the entrance
procedure. She pulls open the inner glass door and
smiles. After what seems ages I hear the sound of
the lift, then the bell to the front door. I open it.

'Oh, I'm sorry—you're in the middle of things,'
she says, looking at me. There is a towel around my
shoulders, foam on my chin and neck, and an
idiotically broad grin on my face. 'I didn't realise
you were shaving,' she continues.

'I'm amazed I haven't cut myself,' I say. 'What
brings you here?'

'I don't know. I happened to be in the area.' She
pauses. 'What a view! It's wonderful. And there's
so much light.'

I step towards her, but she quickly says, 'Please,
Michael.'

'OK, OK, it's fine—foam on my face—I
understand. Would you like some music? I'll be out
in no time.'

She shakes her head.

'Don't disappear,' I say. 'You're not just a
159

shaving reverie?'

'No.'

In a few minutes I'm out of the bathroom. I follow the smell of coffee to the little leg of my sitting room that acts as my kitchen. Julia is looking out of the window. When I'm just behind her, she turns around, startled.

'I hope you don't mind,' she says. 'I've made some coffee.'

'Thank you,' I say. 'It's been some time since anyone's done that for me here.'

'Oh? But I thought—'

'Well, yes—but she never stays here.'

'Why?'

'We don't live together. I visit her sometimes.'

'Tell me about her.'

'She's a violin student. French: from Nyons. Her name's Virginie.'

'Would I like her?'

'I don't know. Possibly not. No, I don't mean that—you wouldn't dislike her, you just wouldn't have much in common. I like her, though,' I add quickly, feeling disloyal.

'I didn't see any photographs in the living room—except of your family,' says Julia.

'Actually I don't have any photographs of her,' I say quickly. 'Not accessible, anyway. I suppose I could describe her: black hair, black eyes . . . no, I can't. I'm no good at describing people's faces.'

'Well, I like the aftershave she's given you.'

'Hmm.'

'What's it called?'

'Havana.'

'Like the capital of Cuba?'

'What other Havana is there?'

160

'Well, none, I suppose.'

'And I like this lemony thing you've got on. What is it?'

'Michael, don't pretend you're interested in the name of my perfume.'

'A present from your husband?'

'No. I bought it myself. Just a month ago. You'd like James,' says Julia.

'Of course,' I say meaninglessly.

'I don't know why I've come. It's stupid of me. I was curious about where you lived,' she continues. 'Even that day I saw you on Oxford Street I knew you lived near me.'

'How could you have known that?' I ask.

'The first three digits.'

'I see.'

'I looked up your name in the phone book, in fact. I couldn't remember the number fully.'

'So you did look it up after all.'

'Yes.'

'And you didn't call me?'

'I remember thinking, as I was looking at those names—Holland, Holliday, Hollis, Holt, and so on—"These are just names. Just ordinary names." And of course, in the Vienna phone book, I read Kind, Klimt, Ohlmer, Peters—nothing happens in my head, nothing stirs in me.'

'What are you saying, Julia?'

'Beethoven, Haydn, Mozart, Schubert—don't you see what I mean? They're just names—names out of a phone book, I sometimes think. No, you don't see, I can tell. But it's so high up here—so high above everything.'

'Yes. Well,' I say, grabbing onto something that I can at last grasp. 'There's lots of light, as you said.

161

And a distant view of St Paul's to compensate for low water pressure.' I turn to point out a socket. 'If you plug the Hoover in there, you can vacuum the whole flat. Three small rooms—it's no palace, but it's bigger than in Vienna. Do you like it?'

'Milk but no sugar, I suppose?' asks Julia, countering the question.

'Neither, nowadays.'

'I'm sorry?' She sounds flustered, as if this change in my habits signified more than it does.

I smile at her confusion. 'I've gone off milk.'

'Oh? Why?'

'I keep forgetting to buy it. What's in the fridge is usually past its date. So rather than ruin my coffee, I've just got used to having it black.'

We take our mugs to the other end of the room and sit down. I look at her, she at me. What is all this chatter and all this silence?

'Are you glad I've come?' she asks.

'Yes, but I can't believe it,' I say. 'It is incredible.'

'I'm not disturbing you?'

'No. And so what even if you were? But I don't have any lessons this morning. We've got a rehearsal in an hour, though. The strangest thing happened yesterday. Well, the second-strangest.'

'What was that?'

'We were asked to record the "Art of Fugue".'

'The "Art of Fugue"? All of it?'

'Yes. By Stratus.'

'Michael, that's absolutely amazing.' Julia's face lights up with pleasure, with happiness at the thought—and surely for me.

'Yes, isn't it?' I say. 'You used to play bits of it. Do you still?'

'Sometimes. Not often.'

162

'I've got the music. And there's an upright in the next room.'

'Oh, no, no—I can't, I can't.' She protests almost violently, as if warding off some terror.

'Are you all right?' I touch her shoulder, then cup it with my palm.

'Yes. Yes,' she says. My hand moves to the side of her neck. She gently moves it away.

'I'm sorry if I upset you. It's just that I'd love to hear you play again. I'd love to play something with you.'

'Oh no!' she says sadly. 'I knew you'd want us to play together. I shouldn't have come. I knew I shouldn't. And I've disappointed you.'

'Julia—what are you saying? I'm not disappointed that you're here. How could I be?'

'Luke's school is just around the corner. I dropped him off, then sat in the car wondering what to do.' She looks stricken. 'Even after I decided to call you I couldn't, because I thought it would be too early. So I sat in a café for an hour and changed my mind every ten minutes.'

'Why didn't you phone me? I've been awake since nine.'

'I had to think things out myself. It wasn't simply that I was in the area. I wanted to see you. I want to see you. You were such a huge part of my life. You are. But I don't want anything from you—anything complicated. Anything at all. Not that it was simple then.'

I feel as if the brunt of the conversation has been forced onto me.

'What does James do?' I ask. I force the name out as casually as I can, but everything in me rebels against it. I'd rather call him 'your husband'.

'He's a banker. He's American. From Boston. That's where we've lived since we've been married. Until we came to London.'

'When was that?'

'More than a year ago . . . Luke misses Boston. He often asks when we're going back. Not that he's unhappy here. He's a bit of a leader in his group.'

'And how old is he?'

'Almost seven. Six and ten twelfths, according to him. He's into fractions—but he's not a little nerd, he's a darling.'

I feel a physical agitation in my heart. 'Julia, when did you get married? How soon after I came back to England?'

'About a year.'

'No. No. I can't believe that. I can't. That's not possible. I spoke to your father around that time. He didn't tell me anything.'

Julia says nothing.

'Was James around when I was there?'

'Of course not.' There is a trace almost of disdain in her voice.

'I can't bear it.'

'Michael, I'd better go.'

'No, don't.'

'Your rehearsal.'

'Yes. I'd forgotten . . . Yes, I suppose you'd better . . . But can't you come tomorrow? Please. I'll be up and about by nine. Earlier, in fact. When does school begin?'

'Eight thirty. Michael, I can't just drop Luke at school and then come and see you. I can't. It would be too—I don't know—too dismal.'

'Why not? What have we done?'

Julia shakes her head. 'Nothing. Nothing. And I

164

don't want anything. And nor do you. Fax me in a day or two. This is my number.'

'*Fax* you?'

'Yes. And—Michael, I know this sounds stupid—fax me in German . . . It's a machine we both use, and I don't want James to worry—'

'No. Incidentally, your eyes are extremely blue this morning.'

'What?' She looks dismayed. 'I don't understand—'

'Your eyes. Sometimes they're blue-grey, sometimes blue-green, but this morning they are simply blue.'

Julia blushes. 'Please stop it, Michael. Don't talk that way. It upsets me. I really don't like it. I'm not twenty-one any more.'

I stand with her outside my door. The lift comes. She enters. Her face is framed by the little noughts-and-crosses grid of glass in the outer door. There is a click, and the inner door, smooth steel, slides swiftly across her troubled smile.

3.9

We have gathered for a rehearsal of a programme of twentieth-century quartets—Bartók, Shostakovich, Britten—but all that has gone by the board. For the last half hour we have been discussing among ourselves the question of whether to take up the Stratus offer.

Helen is glaring at Billy. Billy is looking uncomfortable.

The problem that Billy has just pointed out is easy to state and hard to solve. If the 'Art of Fugue' is to be performed by a string quartet in its designated key of D minor—and Billy will hear of nothing else—some of the passages for the second-highest voice (played by me) fall below the compass of the violin. I can play them on a regular viola, and this presents no real difficulty. But in addition, a number of passages for the third-highest voice (played by Helen) fall as much as a fourth below the compass of the viola. And here's the rub.

'I can't tune it down a fourth, Billy. Don't be idiotic. If you insist on the same key, we'll simply have to transpose those bits up an octave,' says Helen.

'No,' says the adamantine Billy. 'We've been through all this before. That's just not an option. We've got to do it right.'

'Well, what can we do?' asks Helen, desperate.

'Well,' says Billy, not looking at anyone in particular, 'we could get a cellist to do those particular contrapuncti, and you could do the rest.'

All three of us turn on Billy.

'No way,' say I.

'Ridiculous!' says Piers.

'What?' says Helen.

Billy's little son, Jango, has been playing by himself in the far corner of Helen's living room. He senses his father is under attack and comes over. Occasionally Billy's wife, Lydia, who is a freelance photographer, leaves Jango with him, and if it's a rehearsal day Billy—and the rest of us—have to manage as best we can. Jango is a nice kid, and very musical. Billy says that when he's practising, Jango listens to him for hours, and sometimes dances along. But he isn't likely to disturb us when

166

we're playing, despite the dissonances of our century.

Now Jango looks at all of us, worried.

'Upsadaisy,' says Billy, and hoists him onto his knee.

Helen is still shaking her red-ringleted head at Billy in a Medusa-like manner. 'I wish Erica had never mentioned this wretched idea. I was getting so psyched up,' she says.

'*Can't* you tune the viola down a fourth—at least the lowest string? Or would it become impossibly slack?' says Billy.

His artless suggestion meets with a look of disgust.

'Sometimes, Billy,' says Helen, 'I think you are the most idiotic of us all. I've just told you I can't.'

'Oh!' is all Billy can say by way of response.

'So—do we say no to Erica?' asks Piers calmly. 'It was never such a brilliant idea in the first place.'

'No, we don't, Piers, we do nothing for another week. I need time to think,' says Helen.

'Think about what?'

'Just to think,' says Helen sharply. 'This is the one absolutely amazing thing I get to do, and you're taking it away from me. I won't let you. It's just like you, Piers. You're obviously delighted by all this.'

'Come on, come on,' says Piers. 'Shall we get on with the rehearsal? We've got a lot to get through.'

'Can we, I wonder—' says Billy tentatively. 'Just before the rehearsal, I mean—'

'Can we what?' asks Piers, exasperated.

'I promised Jango a bit of Bach if he promised to be good.'

'For heaven's sake,' says Piers. Even I am a bit

taken aback by Billy's insensitivity.

'Oh, why the heck not?' says Helen to our surprise. 'Let's do it.'

So I tune down quickly, and we play through the first contrapunctus of the 'Art of Fugue'. Poor Helen. I glance to my left, but now she is showing no obvious distress. I notice that Piers is looking at her as well, with a certain brotherly awareness. Billy is gazing at his son, who is sitting in front of him with his head at an angle. How much he is getting out of all this at his age is unclear, but from the expression on his face he is clearly enjoying it.

It is too quickly over.

'That was not a farewell,' says Helen with decision. 'That was an *au revoir*. We are *not* going to let it go.'

3.10

The phone rings early the next morning. I am lying in bed thinking of Julia, but don't succeed in conjuring her up on the line.

'Michael?'

'Yes. Yes. Helen—?'

'It's a good thing it is. Remember, if you hear a woman's voice, never volunteer a name. If you're wrong, she'll be upset.'

'Helen, do you know what time it is?'

'All too well. I haven't slept a wink. I look frightful.'

'What's all this'—I yawn—'about?'

'Why is Billy like that?'

'Like what?'

'Unchocolatey. Soft with a hard centre.'

168

'Billy's just Billy.'

'Talk to him. Please.'

'On something like this it'll do no good at all.'

'You think it'll harden his position?'

'No, Helen, you know as well as I do, it won't harden his position, it simply won't change it.'

'Yes, I suppose I do. Which is why you're to help me.'

'Helen, I love Bach, and I would love to take up the viola again, and for once the two of us would have really fantastic parts, but there it is. What can I do? Piers has probably told Erica by now, and she's told La Shingle.'

'No, he hasn't. I made bloody Piers promise not to say anything to bloody Erica for a week.'

'Well, where do I come into it?'

'You're going to help me find a viola that I can tune down a fourth.'

I take a couple of breaths. 'Helen, you know and I know that the viola—any viola—is way too small even for the sound it makes. You can't tune it down further. You certainly can't tune it down a fourth.'

'I will. I have to. I'll get a socking great seventeen-inch Gasparo da Salo, and enormous fat strings and . . .'

' . . . and an osteopath, and a physiotherapist and a neurologist, and even then it wouldn't work. Helen, even I find anything above sixteen inches uncomfortable. I'm telling you, as someone who's had problems with his fingers—'

'Well, I'm as tall as you,' says Helen, obsession obliterating vanity. 'And you are used to the violin, so of course you'd find a big viola difficult. And I've spoken to Eric Sanderson. And he thought it was possible.'

169

'Did he really?'

'Well, he . . . he said it was an interesting proposition. We're going round to see him at three. I assume you're not doing anything this afternoon? I'll take out a loan if I have to, and get him to make me an instrument.'

'When did you speak to Eric Sanderson?'

'Just before I called you.'

'Helen! You're a public menace.'

'Well, he has a couple of young kids, so I expect the family wakes up at seven.'

'And he sounded bright-eyed and bushy-tailed did he, our master luthier?'

'No, he sounded a bit sleepy and surprised, rather like you, but perfectly capable of conversation.'

'And why am I to accompany you?'

'For moral support. I need it. We middle voices must stick together. And because you'll learn a lot. And because he's the best instrument repairer in the business as well as the best instrument maker, and you need to work out why your violin sometimes buzzes. And because I'll let you borrow my lovely lovely viola for those places in the "Art of Fugue" where you need it and where I'm using the deeper one.'

'You are more cunning than I thought possible, Helen.'

'I am, as Ricki Lake puts it, *all that.*'

'I am afraid I don't watch Ricki.'

'Then you're missing out on the best life has to offer. If only I took her advice, I'd have a man in my life and a song in my heart and—oh, yes, high self-esteem. And so would you.'

'I don't want a man in my life.'

170

'I'll pick you up at two fifteen. His workshop's in Kingston.'

'Oh, British Rail land. I'm amazed you're venturing so far into the jungle.'

'Desperate diseases,' says Helen. 'See you just after two.'

3.11

I put down the phone and lie in bed with my hands behind my head. I have not heard from Julia for three days. I get up and pad around the flat, putting up the blinds.

I turn on Radio 3. For me, even with a rackful of CDs to choose from and in a city as rich in concerts as London, this is, morning or evening, an almost instinctive reaction. Now it often brings me pleasure and surprise; but when I lived in Rochdale it was my lifeline, virtually my only source of classical music. Once a year the Halle Orchestra performed in Champness Hall, three or four times a year Mrs Formby would take me to a recital organised by the local music society or something special in Manchester, but that was the sum of my contact with professionally performed live music. My small radio, which plucked music from the public air, was everything to me; I would listen to it for hours in my room. As with the public library in Manchester, I don't see how I could have become a musician without it.

In the lessening darkness I look for Venus. Dawn is breaking—a horizontal upwelling of pink, with one almost vertical gash of a contrail, like Lucifer hurtling down the sky. I turn the kettle on and

171

empty a vase full of thick twigs of holly, the berries by now almost black, into the rubbish.

A Bach cantata is being performed: *'Wie schön leuchtet der Morgenstern . . .'* The word puts me in mind of one of Julia's favourite comic poets. I compose a note in German, attempting the style he liked to deflate, and print it out:

The non-undersigned begs to submit evidence of his continued existence, and requests the presence (not in triplicate) of the recipient in his humble albeit elevated quarters between nine and ten tomorrow morning, failing which, the day after. Should she be accompanied by the spirit of Johann Sebastian of blessed memory, he will manifest joy and gratitude in equal and exorbitant measure.

Tendering assurances of the highest consideration, he remains steadfastly, indeed, irremediably, her obedient servant.

Over the name Otto Schnörkel I sign with a grand, self-important squiggle. This was the sort of stuff that used to amuse her, but, as she says, she is no longer one-and-twenty.

Consulting the manual of my fax machine, I remove my name and phone number from the information that would ordinarily be printed at the top of the message upon transmission, and send it to her.

It is a tangled web that I am weaving. If I have survived ten years of absence and vacant regret, why are three days so unbearable?

3.12

Virginie calls me around noon.

'Why haven't you phoned me, Michael?'

'I've been really busy.'

'You played so well, and I left you at least three messages.'

'You didn't ask me to ring back.'

'You don't appreciate my appreciation.'

'I do, but I really didn't realise there was something urgent to discuss.'

'Well there is not anything urgent,' says Virginie, annoyed.

'I'm sorry, Virginie, you're right, I should have called you back, but there's been a lot on my mind.'

'What?'

'Oh, this and that.'

'And the other?'

'The other?'

'Yes, Michael, you always say 'this, that and the other' when you are being evasive.'

'I'm not being evasive,' I say, irked.

'Who is she?'

'Who is who?'

'Are you seeing someone new?'

'No! No, I am not seeing anyone new,' I say with a force that surprises me as much as Virginie.

'Oh,' she murmurs with a touch of contrition which makes me feel guilty.

'Why did you say that?' I ask.

'Oh, I just felt—but—you're not—you're really not—sleeping with someone else, Michael?'

'No. I'm not. I'm not.'

'Then why aren't you sleeping with me?'

'I don't know. I just don't know. We've gone for

173

longer periods without. I have a lot on my mind.' I am doing my best to sound calm but being forced to prevaricate is getting me angrier and angrier.'

'Yes, yes, Michael,' says Virginie patiently, 'you said identically that before. What is on your mind?'

'Oh, Bach, the "Art of Fugue", a possible recording.'

Virginie hardly reacts to this news. No congratulations, no astonishment, nothing. 'Really?' she asks. 'I want to see you this afternoon. Let's go to a matinée.'

'I can't, Virginie.'

'What are you doing?'

'Must you know everything?' I ask.

There is silence at the other end.

'If you must know,' I continue, 'I have to go to Eric Sanderson's to show him my violin. It buzzes sometimes, as you know, and that bothers me.'

'Are you going by yourself?'

'Well, no . . . as a matter of fact, I'm not. Helen has to see him about a viola.'

'Helen?' says Virginie rather mutedly—and a bit speculatively.

'Virginie, just stop this. It's getting on my nerves.'

'Why didn't you tell me you were going with Helen?'

'Because you didn't ask me. Because it isn't important. Because you don't have to know every detail of my life.'

'*Va te faire foutre!*' says Virginie, and bangs down the phone.

3.13

Helen is hopelessly lost the moment we cross the Thames. I navigate with the aid of an A-to-Z. She is unusually silent. I attribute her tension not only to being where the charts are marked with whales and elephants, but also because she does not really believe that there is a solution to her viola problem.

'What was that about the pottery wheel?' I say to distract her.

'Oh, Piers, Piers, Piers,' says Helen impatiently. 'He gets into a bad mood every time we're in my house, and picks on me in some way. He's nice everywhere else—at least with me. Usually, anyway. It's my aunt's fault really.'

'Try and get into the left lane now, Helen. How was it your aunt's fault?'

'Well, obviously, because she left her house to me—I don't mean fault exactly. She was quite right about women having a harder time in life than men and needing to support each other, etcetera. But in fact, I think the main thing was that she disapproved of Piers. Or rather, Piers's ways. His lifestyle. She was quite sweet really. I liked her and Piers liked her too. Perhaps we shouldn't rehearse in that house, but where else is there? The moment he stoops to enter he starts growling.'

'Well, I suppose if you live in a basement studio . . .'

Helen zips through an amber light and turns towards me. 'I wish the house were big enough for both of us, but it isn't. And Piers could, I suppose, afford a better place himself. But he's saving hard to get a better violin. And temperamentally he isn't

175

a saver. It's a struggle.'

After a few seconds I ask: 'Can your parents help him?'

'Can but won't. The moment my father suggests it my mother starts frothing at the mouth.'

'Oh.'

'I think she's gone quite batty these last ten years. You can never tell, when you have parents, how they're going to turn out. I brought up the subject at Christmas, and Mother went off into a mad tantrum: every violin was as good as every other, when they were dead Piers could do what he liked with his share of the money but while she had a say in it, etcetera.'

'Tough on Piers.'

'He was at Beare's last week, but everything he found there that he liked was far beyond his reach. Poor old Piers. I really feel bad for him. He's hoping to try his luck at the auctions later this year.'

'Well, your viola's lovely,' I say.

Helen nods. 'So's your violin. Though you love it more than makes any kind of sense.'

'Not mine, actually.'

'I know.'

'I've spent more time with it than with any living soul, but, well, it's still not mine. And I'm not its.'

'Oh, please,' says Helen.

'Incidentally, it hardly ever buzzes these days.'

'Hmm,' says Helen.

We are silent for a while.

'Did you know what being in a quartet would be like?' asks Helen. 'That we'd spend so much time with each other?'

'No.'

176

'Too much?'

'Sometimes when I'm on the road I think so. But I think it's hardest for Billy. After all, he's attached. Doubly attached.'

'And aren't you?' asks Helen somewhat tensely.

'I'm just semi-attached. Or semi-detached; comes to the same thing.'

'I was talking to Lydia the other day after the concert. She says that sometimes Billy's bag stands in the hall not even unpacked until it's time to pack again. I don't think it's easy on spouses either.'

'So what's the solution to the attachment problem? Casual affairs?' I ask uncomfortably.

'I don't know,' says Helen. 'Do you remember Kyoto?'

'Of course, but I don't try to.'

'I try to remember it,' says Helen, 'from time to time.' She smiles—to herself, not at me.

'Helen, it was a one-off thing. But I don't feel that way. And never will. Good thing too.'

'In the Quartetto Italiano the woman was serially married to all three of the men.'

'Well, in the Quartetto Maggiore that would involve bigamy and incest.'

'Not with you it wouldn't.'

'I, Helen, am no good to anyone. You should understand that once and for all.'

'Not to Virginie, certainly.'

'Perhaps it's because she's my student that I'm so sharp with her. I don't know. I wish I could help myself.'

'Nor to Julia?' Helen, getting no response, takes her eye off the road and looks at me carefully. 'You've been very preoccupied,' she says, 'ever since that night at the Wig.'

177

'Helen, we'd better concentrate. It gets a bit tricky here. Take the next right, and then a left about a hundred yards on. We're almost there.'

Helen nods. She knows better than to press her point.

3.14

Eric Sanderson is about forty, large and full-bearded with great owl-like spectacles.

His attic of a workshop is full of wood, in every stage of formation from mute logs to fully strung and tuned violins, violas and cellos. A couple of girls in aprons are tapping and chiselling away. The scent is ambrosial: the complex fragrance of many woods and oils, resins and varnishes.

'Now, that's a failure,' he says, introducing us to a perfectly decent-looking violin parked by the door. 'A rare failure, I hasten to add. But it's got a buyer. What am I to do? I've got to make a living. And someone picks it up and plays it and says, 'That's exactly what I want.' Well, what should I do? I want to say, I'm not selling that one. Soundwise, it's just a bad fiddle . . . but then along comes an overdraft letter from the bank manager . . . Still, even if I sell it, I'd rather the world didn't know about it. But of course a year or two down the line and a good fiddle could sound bad. Or vice versa, don't you think?'

'I'm sure,' says Helen, perplexed and disarmed.

'Is that natural?' he asks, looking at Helen's hair.

'Yes,' says Helen, blushing.

'Good. Good. A lot of henna around recently. Interesting pigment. Would Strad have used it if

178

he'd had it? Madder.'

'Madder?'

'Yes. Madder. Now that lovely red colouring, that deep red varnish. What a thing it must have been after those pale yellows. Stradivari uses it in Cremona and Gagliano in Naples and Tononi in Bologna, and . . . but you have a Tononi for me, don't you?' he asks, turning to me.

'Well, yes, but mine isn't red.'

'Oh,' says Eric Sanderson, looking somewhat put out. 'I can never understand it. Old Johannes has this lovely red in Bologna, but young Carlo goes off to Venice and reverts to the old yellow. Why? Why?'

He looks at me closely through his owl-glasses. The two apprentices continue to work, unfazed by their master's cries.

'I'm afraid I don't know,' I say. 'But, well, I suppose I'm used to it, and I really do like the colour. It's not just yellow. It's a sort of honey-amber.' I take it out of its case, and Eric Sanderson turns it around.

'Yes,' he says with approval. 'For a honey-amber it's a pretty passable sort of honey-amber. But it buzzes sometimes? Play something.'

I play about half a minute's worth of a Bach partita.

He looks dubious. 'Not much of a buzz. But I suppose it's shy in company. Leave it here.'

'I can't really,' I say. 'Not this week, anyway.'

'Well, how can I help you then? Anyway, what's the history of the problem?'

'It buzzed quite a bit on our American trip last year. I had it looked at some months ago, but it played up again a few weeks later. It's settled down

179

now, but I'm just worried it'll start up again.'

'Could be any of a number of things. So you went to Alaska and Hawaii in the same week?'

'Neither, actually.'

'L.A. and Chicago?'

'Yes, as it happens.'

'People travel too much nowadays,' says Eric Sanderson. 'And too fast. If they were made of wood they'd think twice about it. Hmm, shaved a bit,' he says, examining the interior with a sort of dentist's mirror. 'Not too bad, though. No obvious cracks. Could be anything. There was an exhibition of Venetian instruments a little while ago. Like a Gaudy, I suppose. Lots of gossiping among them. "Haven't seen you for centuries, my dear. Did you hear about the Fenice? I was there when it happened the first time around, but I managed to escape. Poor old Serenissima. Musically hopeless now, of course, but everything was born there— opera, antiphony . . . Now, who was disputing that the other day?" . . . Where did you pick this up?'

'Rochdale.'

'Rochdale, did you say?' Sanderson pats his beard, frowning.

'Yes.'

'There's no poetry in the name. No, no poetry there at all. Ashby-de-la-Zouch: now there's something. Listen: sandarac, dammar, mastic, colophony . . .' He incants the names with mystic reverence.

Helen sighs.

'Poetry is more to me than music,' says Eric Sanderson. 'Anyway, most musicians are on beta-blockers. This will cost you dearly,' he says, turning to Helen, who looks a bit alarmed.

'It will?' asks Helen, rattled by these swift leaps.

'And it isn't worth it. From your call I gather you want me to make you an instrument for one particular purpose. Scordatura . . . scordatura . . . now there's a delicious word. But how will it live out the rest of its life? Unplayed, un-honoured and unstrung.'

'Well,' says Helen, 'perhaps it could be tuned normally then, and I could play it like any other viola.'

This meets with silence, followed by further tangential musings.

'I believe in sycamore and the English woods,' says Eric Sanderson. 'Why should everyone use Italian maple? Wouldn't the Italians have used sycamore if they'd lived here?'

'I'm sure they would,' says Helen.

'They used beech, they used poplar, they used . . . why, even the purfling . . . pearwood here, ebony there, whatever was to hand. I was admiring a design the other day and someone said: "But that's mere purfling." "Purfling is never mere," I told him. "Never, never mere."' He turns to me. 'For all I know, that could be the cause of your buzzing.'

'But can you do it?' asks Helen plaintively.

Sanderson taps the plaster cast of a cello scroll. 'I've been thinking about it,' he says. 'My first reaction was, it's a challenge. But on consideration . . . this is how it is. Tuning down a second, no problem. You could probably do that on your own viola. A minor third, very tricky. A major third, impossible, I would say. Even if you could get a sound out of it, it would be a flabby sort of sound. A fourth—but why would anyone in their right mind ever want to tune a viola down a fourth? Oh yes, "Art of Fugue", "Art of Fugue", you mentioned it. My mind isn't very receptive at that time of day. And my daughters were demanding breakfast. I think, you know, that you should try the early music fraternity. They'll give you much better advice than me. They're more experienced in tunings and retunings. I'll give you a couple of numbers.'

'You can't do it, then?'

Eric Sanderson purses his lips. 'Do you really want to throw seven or eight thousand pounds away on something so specific? Well, it would be an interesting design problem. But it would have to be very big.'

'I played on a seventeen-inch viola once,' says Helen. 'After a while it stopped feeling unwieldy.'

'Was it a good instrument?'

'It was a wonderful instrument.'

'If I were you,' says Eric Sanderson, 'and I say this against my own interests, get hold of that viola again, and talk to the early birds. They're a rum lot, but they know how to twist a gut.'

Back in the car, Helen is silent. Then, just as we are crossing Albert Bridge, she says: 'He didn't tell me a single thing he couldn't have on the phone.'

'Well, I suppose not, but it's always good to . . .'

'I'm going to tell Piers it's fine. We've got to go ahead with the recording. I've got the viola I want.'

'But Helen, that's a barefaced lie. You don't.'

'I do,' says Helen. 'I can see it in my mind's eye. I can hear it in my mind's ear. It exists.'

Helen is driving through Chelsea in a carefree manner. 'You'll come with me to the early music people, won't you?' she asks.

'No, I won't.'

'Oh, Michael, don't be unreasonable. You've

182

always been so helpful. How could I have put up my shelves without you?'

'No, no, Helen, don't try to jolly me along. And I'm not going to be part of your plan to tell Piers you've solved the problem either. Don't you realise how bad it'll be for all of us if we have to pull out later?'

'But we won't have to,' says Helen calmly. 'Let's stop and have a coffee. It's such a relief to be back in London.'

3.15

A restless night, followed by a restless morning. At eleven—long after I have stopped expecting her, and without buzzing me from outside—Julia rings my doorbell. My delight must be evident. So must my surprise. For one thing, she is astonishingly well-dressed: long black cashmere coat, grey silk dress, opal pendants. Her hair is done up in some sort of bun. She holds out her hand to me—to forestall, I suppose, any attempt at a kiss.

'Your porter let me into the building. He must have remembered my struggles from the last time.'

'I'm not surprised.'

'But he didn't engage me in conversation this time.'

'I'm not surprised at that either. You look rather like a vision.'

'I'm so sorry—I got delayed.'

'Oh, don't worry about that,' I say, helping her off with her coat. 'But why all this finery at eleven a.m.?'

Julia says nothing, but wanders over to the huge

window. I don't press the question.

'How calm and beautiful it looks from here,' she says. 'The park, the lake, the far hills on both sides. And the entire valley in between taken up by people. This morning as I was dressing I asked myself, what is a Londoner? You're not, I'm not, James is not, Luke doesn't want to be. There's some kind of lunch in the City today and for some reason James wants me to go. You must be wondering about all this stuff I'm wearing.'

'When's the lunch?'

'Twelve thirty. I have a few errands to do before then, so I'm in a rush. I can't stay long. I haven't brought Bach, but I have brought someone else along. Is that all right?'

'But yes! Yes, of course.'

We enter the little soundproof music room. I adjust the lamp so that the light falls on the music-rack of the piano.

'Oh, that's all right, I haven't got the music. It's just one movement, and I know it well enough. You'll remember it, too.'

I sit to one side of her.

Julia begins playing without even testing the sound of the piano. With the first four notes, I am taken back to the student concert in Vienna where we first met. It is the slow movement of Mozart's Sonata in C major, K330.

There is something tender and indefinably strange and searching about her playing, as if she is attending to something beyond my hearing. I cannot put my finger on it, but it undoes me. I sit with my head in my hands, as Mozart drops note by note into my mind.

When it is over she turns towards me, looking at

me very attentively.

'I didn't expect that,' I say.

'Was it all right?' she asks.

I shake my head. 'No. It wasn't all right. It was a little better than that . . . Sometimes over these past years I've thought you were dead.'

Julia frowns, as if trying to comprehend what has brought about this remark, then murmurs: 'I must go.'

'Don't go at once. How about a quick coffee?' I say as we enter the corridor. 'Or tea. Did I say something wrong?'

'I really can't.' She looks at her watch.

'I'd like you to listen to a movement of something else,' I say, playing for time.

'What is it?'

'One trip down memory lane deserves another.'

'Don't be a tease, Michael. What is it?'

'You won't know if you won't listen. Forget your errands. I'll put it on. It's an old friend transfigured. But I won't tell you in advance what it is.'

'Do you have it on CD?' asks Julia, perplexed. 'May I borrow it? I really don't have time to listen to it now. And I don't—I really don't—want to burst into tears in front of you.'

'It's on an LP.'

'That's fine. We've got a turntable.'

I remove the jacket of the Beethoven string quintet and give it to her in its plain white sleeve. 'You mustn't look at the label on the disc itself,' I tell her. 'In fact, give it back to me for a second. It's difficult sometimes to resist reading things. I'm going to cover the label with a yellow sticker.'

'Why all this mystery?'

'So that you don't know what it is until you hear the first few notes.'

'Do you have the score as well?'

'Well, yes, as a matter of fact.'

'Give it to me in an envelope. I won't open it until later.'

As I help her on with her coat, I feel an almost irresistible urge to hold her, to kiss her. But I can read that this is just what she fears. I must keep to the innocent rules of these visits, so filled with anxiety for her. Even the intimacy of music is not guiltless. The record in her hand reminds me of our trio, and she is so close I can hear her breathe.

I wait for the lift with her, happier and uneasier for our few minutes together.

This time, when she is inside, I press my nose to the gridded glass, and as the inner door slides across I can see—and hear—her laugh.

3.16

Late at night, I receive a fax, in English, from Julia:

Dearest Michael,

I could not believe it. I've never heard it. I've never even heard of it. You know what that trio meant to me.

May I see you tomorrow morning, nine-ish? I assume from your earlier fax that you're free. If for some reason you're not, please fax me back.

Julia

I read and re-read the note. The first and last words, seen in that unchanged hand, contract the intervening years. She didn't write 'Love', but surely one can't be 'Dearest' without it.

At nine, again avoiding the intercom, Julia buzzes my doorbell directly. Rob must be charmed off his feet, I think, though this morning she is in jeans.

'What do you know by heart of Mozart?' she asks without preamble, leading me to my soundproof cell.

'Of his violin sonatas?'

'Yes.

'Why?'

'I don't want you standing behind me, looking over my shoulder.'

I stare at her in amazement. 'I could have my own music separately on that stand,' I say.

'Well, answer my question,' says Julia almost brusquely.

'You mean a whole sonata? None, I don't think. Not now.'

'A movement will do,' she says. 'Yes, in fact, a movement would be better. The second movement of the E minor?' She hums a phrase, dead on key.

'Yes!' I say, still a bit dazed with anticipation. 'I think that's one of the few I do know by heart—or almost. I've listened to it recently, but I don't think I've played it for a few years. I'll have to look at the music . . . Here it is. I'll keep my part open on that stand, but I'll only glance at it if I'm stuck. I'll stand here if you want. But why don't you want me looking over your shoulder?'

'Call it a whim.'

'All right. Let me tune up. Let's have an A.'

187

I pass my eye over the two facing pages of my music for a few seconds and tell her when I'm ready. Every joyful memory of Vienna comes flooding back to my mind.

We play the movement through. I get the sense that Julia is leading me. Her part is continuous—she has no entries as such where she has to take her cue from me. She fluffs—or is it I who fluffed it?—the point where we both strike up together after a rest. Her eyes are often on me. But again, as with yesterday, an intentness, an inwardness that goes beyond Vienna, a lovely subtle directness imbues her music; and, by conduction, mine.

In one zigzag descending line I play an A natural for an A sharp, rather a horrible mistake, but she doesn't say anything, then or later. Perhaps she has chosen not to be too exacting with me the first time around. Or perhaps she sees things more in the round, and feels it would be petty to cavil over a single note in a movement so intensely played.

'Should we do the other movement too?' I ask when it is over.

'Let's let it be,' she says. We look at each other.

'I love you, Julia. Pointless to say it, perhaps, but I do—still.'

She sighs, not from happiness. Her fingers massage an imaginary ring. Falling back in love with her, whom I had never forgotten, is inexpensive for me. For her, who had succeeded in putting me out of mind, whose very name has changed to another's, it could be costly indeed.

'I you,' she says at last in a voice so full of regret she could almost be saying the opposite.

We do not even touch to confirm what we have said. Then, gently, lightly, I kiss the side of her

188

neck. She breathes slowly, but says nothing.

'Well?' I ask.

She smiles, a little sadly. 'Making music and making love—it's a bit too easy an equation.'

'Have you told him about me?' I ask.

'No,' she says. 'I don't know what to do about all this subterfuge: faxes in German, coming up to see you here . . . but it's really Luke who I feel I'm . . .'

'Betraying?'

'I'm afraid of all these words. They're so blunt and fierce.'

'And of music?' I ask.

'Yes, of music too, in a way. But at least I can speak about it with you. I've been so hungry to speak of music—and to play it with someone who understands me as I was before I—before all these changes in my life.'

I hold her hand. She shakes her head, but lets it be.

'What should I say, Julia? What do you want me to say? It's easy enough for me to say love, love, love. I'm not married.'

'And does your friend from Lyon know?' she asks.

'Nyons. No. She doesn't . . . What were you reading that day when I saw you on the bus?'

'I can't remember. Isn't it odd—I can't remember at all. And it's the sort of thing one never forgets.'

'I've never really recovered from losing you. You must know that. But now I feel so afraid of talking to you—of putting a foot wrong and never seeing you again. Have things changed so much between us?'

'I don't know. I don't know. I've just dropped

189

Luke at school. He's not terribly musical, you know. Michael, this is terrible. We really can't.'

She closes her eyes. I kiss them open.

'Well?'

'I can see a couple of white hairs,' she says.

'They're unearned,' I say.

'I doubt that.'

She kisses me. I hold her in that soundless room, far from daylight and the traffic of Bayswater and all the webs of the world. She holds me as if she could never bear to let me desert her again.

3.17

The sun falls on our bodies. She does not want the blinds drawn. I run my hands through her hair, so much longer than it used to be. We make love not with tenderness but with ecstasy born of starvation—yet in her I sense a tension drop away. She does not want me to speak, nor does she speak herself, but her eyes are on my face as if to catch every expression of mine. The scent of her body, mixed with her faint perfume, drives me into a frenzy.

Afterwards, when I return to bed, she rests her head on my shoulder and drowses off. I cannot look at her face. I lightly place the palm of my free hand first on one eyelid, then the other. She is deep in some other world, far from my domain. Somewhere in the distance a helicopter clatters past, but she does not wake. A little later I get up again, gently disengaging my arm. For a while—it could not be more than half a minute—I watch her. Perhaps she senses this. Her eyes open; she looks at me as if she were reading my thoughts. In her face, clear first with passion, then with peace, I see ambivalence return.

'I had better go, hadn't I, Michael?'

I nod, though I can't agree. I try to smile reassuringly. We hardly ever made love in the daylight when we were together years ago, I don't know why. My thoughts are perplexed by many things: they wander over everything since I first saw her as a student to all the acts—of speech or music or love—of these last few days. I know there are things that disturb me, that I cannot reconcile, but I cannot even put my finger on them. But just the thought of what has happened burns through these light, unsettled mists.

3.18

Though she left hours ago, the room smells of her. A day passes; two. I do not hear from her: neither phone nor fax nor letter nor visit.

By day, by night, I sink my face into the sheets. I am in all the hours that we have ever spent. I am in all the rooms in which we have ever been.

3.19

Three days have passed. I can stand it no longer. I walk in the park to calm my thoughts.

The plane trees are all bare, but their flaked bark is lit by a slanting light. The fountains at the end of the Long Water, dry and surrounded by mud a couple of weeks ago, are playing again.

Snowdrops are coming through, and the odd crocus here and there. The weeping willows have come to life again, all lime-green by the Serpentine.

It is about three in the afternoon. School will soon be out. Will she pick Luke up from the door? My steps find me at the corner of the square. I watch the street, idle, alert. Was it then to seek her out that I left my building?

She appears on foot, walking quickly. She climbs the front steps and stands in a queue with the other women. In a few minutes the little boys in little green caps emerge and are hugged and kissed and taken away.

Julia and Luke walk hand in hand along the square, and then along a street just off it. They stop by a Range Rover and release a huge brown dog with a black face, who is so delighted to see them that it is difficult to put him on his leash.

They are on my street now. I view them with the eye of an outsider: a little boy with a cap; a well but casually dressed woman of medium height with a lovely unhurried gait—her hair is more gold than brown, but it is difficult to see her face from where I am, so many yards back, trailing them half-unwittingly; and a huge golden-brown dog with a funny shambling walk, whose presence makes the family inviolate.

I see her expression now, for she has passed my building. She glances to the right and upwards, searching, troubled. Then they walk on, towards the park.

They pause at a zebra crossing. The dog strains at the leash. The boy leans his face against his mother's hand.

And now I am back where I started: the park. I

follow them at a distance as they walk along the avenue of young limes, the boy and the dog making forays onto the grass. A couple of minutes later the dog, whose face resembles that of a grizzly bear, bounds past me, barking, then turns and wheels back towards his owner.

'Buzby! Buzby! Come back here. Good boy!' shouts Luke's treble voice.

Julia turns; stands still; and something in her stance tells me she's seen me. I hesitate, she hesitates, then we begin to walk towards each other. The boy and the dog orbit her like irregular, colliding planets.

'Well, hello,' I say.

'Hello.'

'So this is Luke?'

The boy looks enquiringly at his mother.

'Yes. Luke, this is Michael.'

'Hello,' I say.

'Hello,' says Luke, shaking my hand.

'Do you come here often?' I ask.

'Sometimes—after Mom picks me up from school.'

'Our dog likes it,' explains Julia. 'There's a communal garden—quite a large one—behind our house, but he prefers the park.'

'Buzby!' I say, patting the dog's head. 'Nice dog, nice name.'

Julia looks at me in astonishment. 'Luke was calling him,' I explain.

'Oh, yes, of course,' says Julia.

Buzby rushes off to bark up a tree. Luke follows him.

'It's been three days,' I say.

'Yes,' says Julia, smiling at me.

193

'I've been so happy. I *am* so happy. But why've you disappeared?'

'I haven't. Here I am.'

'Are you happy?'

'I—how can I answer that? But I'm happy to see you.'

'Do you really come here often? You mean I could have met you here by chance any time this past year?'

'Not often exactly. Once a fortnight or so. Less often in the winter. And—well—we *have* met here by chance, haven't we?'

I start to laugh. She joins in. Luke returns. He looks at us quite calmly, with a little frown, until we stop.

'Mom, let's take Buzby around the Round Pond,' suggests Luke, enunciating clearly—and with the residue of what must be a Boston accent. He looks at me with interest. And I look at him. He is a good-looking kid, with much darker hair than Julia—as he might have had if he'd been our son.

'I think we'd better get back,' says Julia. 'It'll be dark in a little while.'

'It was a squirrel,' says Luke to me by way of diversion. 'He goes wild around squirrels. We won't be five minutes. Promise, Mom.'

'Luke, I said no,' says Julia quite firmly. 'And I've had enough of a walk.'

'Michael can take us then,' says Luke, grabbing my hand. 'Buzby likes him.' As if to confirm this, Buzby returns and stands, attentive-eared, in front of us.

Julia looks at me, I at her, Luke at both of us, Buzby at all three.

'If you're not back in ten minutes, Luke, I shall

put an apple in your lunch-box tomorrow.'

'Oh, yuck, I'm so scared,' says Luke, grinning. 'What's worse than finding a worm in an apple?' he asks me.

'Now, Luke,' says Julia.

'Well, what?' I say.

'Finding only half a worm,' says Luke, and goes off into fits of delighted laughter.

His mother, who has probably heard this a hundred times before, makes a wry face. His mother . . . his mother . . . What is she thinking as I take charge of her son?

When Luke and I get to the Round Pond, he says, 'No, not clockwise, anti-clockwise. Buzby prefers it.'

'Shouldn't you Americans say counter-clockwise?'

'Yes, I guess so. My Dad said that once. But I'm English here. How do you know my Mom?'

'I've known her from Vienna.'

'That was before I was born.'

'That's right.'

Luke seems lost in thought. Buzby trots off, then returns to bark, quite good-naturedly, at the swans.

'My name is Lucius, actually,' volunteers Luke. 'Lucius Hansen. My grandfather is called Lucius too.'

'But everyone calls you Luke?'

'That's right. What's the difference between a dancer and a duck?'

'A duck, did you say? Or a dog?' Luke has started mumbling.

'A duck, stupid. Oops. Sorry. A duck.'

'Oh, I don't know. One's fat and flies, the other's thin and dies.'

'A dancer doesn't die.'

'In *Swan Lake* she does.'

'What's swan lake?'

'It's a ballet: you know, where people dance around on a stage. Not very interesting. The music's quite nice, though.'

'Anyway, it's the wrong answer,' says Luke, unimpressed.

'What's the right one, then?'

'One goes quick on her legs, the other goes quack on her eggs.'

We both laugh. Buzby runs up to us, shaking off water.

'Did you make that up?' I ask. 'It's good.'

'No, I read it in a riddle book. Dad gave me one for Christmas. He gave me three books: a riddle book, an airplane book and a book on stamps.'

'No dinosaur book?'

'Dinosaurs are dead,' pronounces Luke.

'What sort of dog is he?' I ask. 'Some kind of giant labrador?'

'Labrador?' exclaims Luke contemptuously. 'He's a Leonberger. And he's actually only a puppy. He's eleven months old.'

'A puppy?' I exclaim. 'But he's as big as a lion.'

'He's quite silly,' confides Luke. 'He ate grass with snails on it last month and got dyspepsia or something.' Luke has a vocabulary beyond his years.

'What's all this about apples in your lunch-box?' I ask him.

He makes a face. 'I don't like apples.'

'All kids like apples.'

'I don't. I prefer peaches. Or oranges. Or anything else.'

When we are halfway around, Luke says, 'Did you meet Mom before she met Dad?' He doesn't sound too pleased.

'What? Oh, yes. Well, we were students together. I'm a musician.' There is a short pause while Luke considers this. 'Mom makes me practise piano,' he says at last. 'I tell her I'm going to be a pilot so it's a waste of time, but she doesn't listen. At all.'

'Do you like it?'

'It's all right,' says Luke, staring at the water, then adds something inaudible about scales.

'I didn't get that. You're mumbling.'

'It's the way I speak,' says Luke with sudden sullenness.

'But you spoke so clearly just a little while ago.'

'That's because Mom finds it hard to hear me. She's deaf . . . Oops!' He claps his hands over his mouth.

I laugh. 'Why? Because she makes you practise scales?'

But Luke, his eyes open wide, looks utterly shocked at what he has just said. 'Don't tell her—' he blurts out.

'Tell her what?'

Luke's face has gone white. He looks horrified.

'What I said. It's not true. It's not true.'

'All right, Luke, all right. Take it easy now.'

He says nothing at all for the next few minutes. He looks guilty and alarmed, almost stricken. I put my hand on his head and he does not object. But I am filled with unease and desperate concern, and in the face of his words I can think of nothing to say.

197

3.20

We return to where we started. Buzby runs up to Julia, barking energetically, and circles around her a few times. Luke seems upset again.

If it is true, I cannot think it through. The light is fading. I remember how, in the Orangery, when she stood by the radiator, I spoke, and she did not respond, and all her non-responses—those I can remember—now begin to take on a haze of sense. Her avoidance, as I thought, of certain random subjects: can I remember now if my face was averted then—or hers—when I broached them? Am I reading too much into one remark of Luke's, and a few minutes of dismay?

She has not changed. She laughs, tells us we are almost a minute late. Buzby, after orbiting twice, leaves the solar system, and Luke chases after him.

'I hope he wasn't too much trouble,' says Julia. 'He's sometimes quite moody. He looked a bit subdued just now, as if he thought you might complain about his behaviour. Was he good?'

'Good as gold. But he doesn't know what *Swan Lake* is.'

'I'm sorry?' Julia looks puzzled.

'*Swan Lake*—the ballet,' I carefully and too articulately explain.

She frowns. 'Of course, but, Michael, he's not even seven yet. What did you talk about?'

'Books mainly. And riddles.'

Her face lights up. 'Yes, he's into those. Did you get the dancer and the duck?'

'Quick and quack. Yes.'

From far off I hear the sound of distant honking, of swans taking flight.

'Is something the matter? What is the matter?' asks Julia. 'What's bothering you?'

'Nothing.'

'Nothing?'

'Really, it's nothing. Just the swans. Will I see you tomorrow?' I hold her hand.

'Don't.'

'Sorry. I forgot.'

'I don't think we should meet for a while. I really don't.'

'I must see you. I've got to talk to you.'

'What is it, Michael—are you all right?' she asks, her voice charged with alarm.

'Yes, I am. Say you'll meet me—'

'All right, but—'

'Tomorrow morning?'

She nods warily.

The light is going. The boy and the dog are returning. If it is true, it will soon be too dark for her to see what I am saying. I claim I want to continue my walk, and the three of them turn to leave.

Luke holds her hand. She bends down to kiss his face. The noises around me are all nebulous now. Into the dusk the three forms move, merging with others wandering at this hour. Soon they are lost, and I too turn away.

PART FOUR

4.1

The next day brings a bright and clear dawn. There is a yellow-gold glow on the Round Pond far off beyond the trees. I love this season of wood: the branches going up on one tree in counterpoint to the down-hanging boughs of another. The whitebeams look like hedgehogs against the fresh green grass.

A huge old leafless chestnut tree, an anomaly beside the youthful avenue of silver limes, offers its down-hanging branches even though they have nothing in this season visibly to yield. But among its uppermost twigs a bird is singing—a robin, by the sound, though it is so high that even this bare lattice is enough to obscure the small bird.

I take a few steps backwards, attempting to distinguish it from its surroundings. A heavy pigeon flutters its way to the high branches, and now it is almost as if this absurd bird were singing so beautifully, pleased to accept credit for the performance of its invisible neighbour.

It was when I mentioned the nightingale that Julia's eyes filled so suddenly—surprisingly, but not unaccountably, as I thought then—with tears. Now I realise I assigned them to the wrong account.

In the sunken garden, a few yellow primroses are the only inklings of life; and in the ancient lime hedge around, twice my height and many times my age, there is a faint flush of reddish buds and twigs. This we could share, but what of the dawn chorus in full rowdy swing all around? The plane descending west towards Heathrow?

I walk where Luke and I walked yesterday. The gulls are silent so early in the morning. I count the swans: forty-one, including five young. One grubby black-footed cygnet gives me a canny sideways stare. Five adults take off from the far side of the pond. The wings of the huge ungainly birds make a slow, heavy ruckus as they steer overhead. Geese flee, honking.

What of this could she hear? How much am I imagining of what she can and cannot?

The cawing of a crow, the chacking of a magpie in a plane tree near the Bayswater Road, the buses roaring and sneezing—what can she hear?

4.2

She does not turn up as she promised, and I don't know what to do. I could fax her again, but then, if she had wanted to, she could have faxed me. I understand only too well now why she does not call me on the phone. The one time she did, she must have known she'd get my answering machine. Presumably she heard the bleep. Or did she just wait a few seconds before speaking? Does she have a hearing aid? I never felt any such thing when I touched her hair, her face.

But we have played together, violin and piano, in key, in time, in this room, and she played with an awareness so simple and clear that she must have heard the music we made.

In key, I said, but of course the piano, if in tune, would remain in key. And though she responded to my playing, it was as if the intimacy was almost personal to herself. She asked me to stand there, where she could see me. Now I ask myself: was it to see my bow and my fingers move?

She sang a phrase, in key, before she went to the piano. She had absolute pitch when I knew her, but would she have maintained this, unreinforced by external sound?

Some things become clearer, some more mystifying. The clues are fugitive. Lyon for Nyons: a slip of the tongue? a lapse of memory? an unheard consonant? I make such mistakes all the time.

How can she handle it as she does? Why did she not share it with me? How can she bear to play music, to think of music at all? When she came to hear us play at the Wigmore, what did she hear? The encore was not announced in the programme.

A day passes, and I feel unhinged, so anxious, so uncertain am I. There are no rehearsals, so I am not compelled to play. I can't even listen to music. I read a few poems from an old anthology. But I am gripped with a sense of horror that this should be true and a compelling, hopeless wish to protect her—for what can I do?—from the fact of it.

The next day I decide to write to her. But what can I say other than that I want to see her again? Does she want me to know? Has Luke told her anything? Am I deluding myself? Is there anything to know at all?

4.3

Into my perplexity falls a letter: blue envelope, dull golden stamp, yesterday's postmark, the familiar slanted hand. Once again I use the paper-knife she

205

gave me on an envelope sealed by her.

The morning light falls on several sheets of light blue paper on which, in dark blue ink, I read the longest letter she has ever written to me.

Dearest Michael,

Yes, it is true. You would have found out sooner or later, and, through our meeting in the park, it's turned out to be sooner. Luke was very upset, and it was clear that you too were shocked about something. When we got home he told me he had told you. He didn't mean to let it slip. Poor Luke: he was glum for a whole hour. He felt he'd betrayed me when really he'd taken the burden of divulgence off my shoulders. He's usually very protective of me in a James-James Morrison-Morrison sort of way, and when his friends come over he makes sure that everything is completely natural. He doesn't want anyone, least of all any of his friends, to have an inkling that anything at all is the matter with me. But a lot is the matter with me, I'm afraid—and I've been afraid to tell you, afraid that it would break things somehow, or break into things. If I had to come backstage and bring to life those dormant memories, I did not want you to feel that we were on anything but an equal footing. Certainly I didn't want what I saw in your eyes two days ago. That is also why I am writing to you, not speaking to you, about it.

But my situation is not quite pitiful—or is it pitiable? The fact is that, as deafness goes, mine at least gave me time to cope. It happened over months rather than minutes, and it had no horrendous side-effects.

I'm not trying to make light of it. I did not think at first that I could live through it. Music is the heart of my life. For me, of all people, to be betrayed by my ears was unbearable.

How did it all start? I won't be able to take your questioning me face to face and in detail, so I'd better knuckle down and tell you the whole story this once. It began about three years ago. At first I didn't realise anything was wrong, though people seemed to be mumbling a lot, especially on the phone, and I began to sense that I was using a heavier touch on the keyboard. I wondered once or twice why I didn't hear the birds so often, but assumed that that year in New England we were having a quieter spring. I wasn't playing with other musicians at the time, so catching my cues was not an issue. And when I listened to music I simply turned the volume up. A couple of times James did tell me that the sound level was a bit high, but I didn't think too much about it.

It probably was getting more difficult for me to hear the piano, but so much of what one hears is in the mind and the fingers anyway. The truth of it is that I don't think I understood what was happening. How could I imagine that I was going deaf in my twenties!

But then something really alarmed me. One night, when James was away, Luke had a nightmare. He was crying in his room and I didn't hear him until he stumbled into mine. Two days later, when I took him for a routine visit to the doctor, I mentioned what had happened. The doctor took it seriously and sent me to see someone else, who in turn told me

207

that I had a 50-decibel hearing loss in both ears, and asked why on earth I hadn't come to him earlier.

By the next week, the hearing loss was closer to 60 decibels, and the doctors were very worried and completely perplexed. There had been no history of this kind of thing happening to a young person in my family. Tante Katerina, who lives in Klosterneuburg, is quite hard of hearing, but then she's over 70. It's true, I had had an infection in both ears—probably from swimming—when I was about eight, and it had lasted almost a year. But that had been clearly diagnosed, while these symptoms seemed to be completely causeless. They defeated the first specialist we went to, and it was only a month later that a second specialist, a much younger man, came up with the probable diagnosis of 'auto-immune ear disease'—something I'd never heard of before. He kept explaining to James the value of a 'high index of suspicion' for recognising comparatively uncommon diseases, something that he had always possessed: a sort of Hitchcockian gift, it sounded like—but apparently this is standard phraseology.

The treatment was heavy doses of mixed steroids and immunosuppressants. If you'd seen me at the top of that double-decker bus then (not that you could have, since I was in Boston) I doubt you'd have recognised me. It was just horrible. I looked in the mirror and saw someone bloated with drugs and desperate with fear.

For a while my hearing stabilised, even got better. But when they tried to taper off the drugs, things not only reverted to what they'd been before but got worse. Finally they managed to get me off steroids, but my hearing was shattered—is shattered. I feel as if I'm muffled in cotton-wool, and without my hearing aid I can hear almost nothing clearly. Then suddenly things bang out at me or I hear an unearthly high whistling. That's how it's been these last two years. I have my good days and bad days, and sometimes this ear is better and sometimes that, but I no longer have any hope that my hearing will return.

The doctors have explained that the protective systems of my own body are treating parts of my inner ear—no one knows why or how—as hostile or dangerous, and destroying them. But don't read anything symbolic into this. I did, and it made things worse. I felt I was going out of my mind. I don't any longer. It is just another thing: a strange physiological fact, which no doubt will be curable a generation or two down the line, but not, alas, now.

It was a strange transition from the world of sound to the world of deafness—not soundlessness, really, because I do hear all sorts of noises, only usually they're the wrong ones. I was so afraid to lose my music, and I was so afraid for Luke, left with a mother who couldn't even hear him cry. If it hadn't been for him, I don't know if I would have had the will to cope. Poor baby, he was only four years old at the time. James was wonderful—when he was there. He shaved off his moustache so that I could lip-read him better! His bank kept him flying to and fro until he told them he wanted a posting with a

209

bit of stability. Hence London.

James said, quite rightly, that I couldn't withdraw from life—and from him and Luke. We could afford a sort of nanny. She would take a lot of the work off my hands, and be there for Luke when I couldn't be. I should concentrate both on my music and on trying to come to grips with my, well, my condition.

So I threw myself into the foreign world of the deaf: preventive speech therapy classes, lip-reading classes with hours of practice before a mirror; even a bit of sign language—which I've never really used. Learning anything takes so much time, so much effort—especially something you need just to be able to function as well—half as well—as you could before. It was difficult for me to summon up the will-power to do it. But, as I told myself, music is a language, German and English are languages, reading the hands and the lips are just languages—where one improves one's skills with time and effort. It could be interesting. It was, it is, exhausting, but I'm much better at it than I ever thought I would be. (The fact that I had that ear infection when I was eight years old may have helped, as I must have been lip-reading then.) At any rate, I took to it like a natural. But, as one of my teachers once pointed out, you will never be able to learn from the lips alone if someone has lost her glove or her love.

I use a hearing aid, but not as often as you might think. It's complicated—sometimes it prevents me from hearing the correct pitch. When I've been with you, I haven't used it at all, except at that concert. There's some sort of wire

210

loop at the Wigmore Hall which helps when I set my hearing aid to a certain position. It's all very boring until it becomes desperately crucial.

As for making music, since I do play chamber music still, I have learned to judge—from the bow, the fingers, the change of posture, the visible up-beat of breath, from everything and nothing—when to play and at what tempo. You heard my sad new virtuosity in action the other day with the Mozart. But it worked because I knew the sonata well, and I knew from the past how to read your hands, your eyes and your body. I couldn't hear much of what you played, yet I could tell that you played well—though I can hardly tell you how I know that. And when you lent me the Beethoven quintet based on 'our' trio, I didn't listen to it as in the past I would have. I put the bass on high, and half-heard the quintet, half-sensed it through vibration, as I read the score with my eyes. I got a great deal from it. But I know I will never truly hear what I have not already heard with these physical ears and can somehow revive in tune and texture from my memory.

But let's not talk of Beethoven. Do you remember our walks in Heiligenstadt? . . . But enough of that. No, but well, do you remember where he says: *'Aber welche Demütigung, wenn jemand neben mir stund und von weitem eine Flöte hörte and ich nichts hörte oder jemand den Hirten singen hörte and ich auch nichts hörte . . .'* Well, when you heard the robin sing in the Orangery the other day, that was what I felt, but it was not just humiliation, it was a sense of bitter injustice and deprivation and grief and loss

211

and self-pity all mixed up in a frightful lump. And then you went on to talk of blackbirds and nightingales. Really, Michael, now that you know I'm deaf you had better amend your remarks so that you don't pierce me so neatly to the heart.

It is a sunny morning as I write this. The house is empty. Luke is at school, James is at work, our mother's help is taking morning classes in French somewhere in South Ken. From where I sit, on the first floor, I can look down through a bow-window onto the communal garden with its first crocuses, white, saffron, purple, yellow. A ninety-year-old woman is sitting on a bench, reading, with her small white dog—some sort of short-haired terrier—near her. Directly below the window is our own little plot, and I will busy myself with a little work there late this afternoon, after I've practised.

I know where and how you live, but you know nothing of the geography of my days—the shape and colour of my rooms, the curve of the crescent garden, my cyclamens, the tone and touch of my piano, the light on the plain oak dining table. I've told James we've met a couple of times—professionally, that is. Luke and he do jigsaw puzzles together, so the fact that we've met was bound to emerge anyway. James wasn't disturbed; in fact he suggested that I have you around for a meal. (You will, I think, get on with each other.)

I do want to share my life and my music with you in some way. But, Michael, I don't see how our love can reach any sort of full expression. Years ago perhaps it could have, but how can it now? I can't live two lives. I am afraid of hurting everyone, all of us. I don't know how to proceed—or even retreat. Perhaps by trying to get you two to meet each other I'll be integrating nothing, since nothing can be integrated.

You connect me to the greatest happiness— and unhappiness—I have known. Perhaps that was why I avoided you. (Besides, how could I phone you even when I had your number?) Perhaps, again, that was why I stopped avoiding you, and came to meet you that rainy evening when your head—and mine—was swimming with all those fugues.

Write back soon. Does all this make a difference to anything between us? It must—but what sort of difference? I could have faxed this letter, I suppose, but it didn't seem right.

There was so much to tell you, Michael. I have probably said too much and too little.

With my love,
Julia

4.4

Dearest Julia,

I'm replying at once. You've asked me to, so I'm assuming that what's addressed to you can only be read by you. Why didn't you tell me earlier? How hard it must have been for you, knowing that I'd have to know and not knowing when or how to tell me. What can I say? If I say all this is horrendous—which it is—I am afraid of disheartening you. I had better stop; this will sound too much like pity. But if it had happened to me, and you had learned about it, would you not pity me? 'She loved me for the dangers I had passed . . .' And yet, when you played the Mozart that day alone, or the other day with me, none of this would have made any sense at all. I felt, well, just blessed to be in the periphery of that sound.

What can you hear? Can you hear your own speech? Your voice hasn't changed. Is there really nothing that can be done about all this? As you said once, I'm not good at seeing things through anyone else's eyes.

It wasn't Luke's fault at all. If I had to know, and indeed I had to, his remark and your letter were, you're right, the simplest way. Seeing your handwriting on a letter again—so many miles of it in your easy sloping hand, with only a few words crossed out in five pages—put something back again into the silence of these years.

No, I don't know your life now except those shards of it you spend with me or tell me about. I see you in your small room in the student hostel, or in my own rooms under the stairwell eye of Frau Meissl. I can't visit you where you live—I don't think I could handle that at the moment. But I must see you soon. I can't live without you; it's as simple as that. And, Julia, don't you need me too?—not just as a friend but as a fellow musician?

I have to talk to you. If you miss me, you must know how much I miss you. Come and see me, not tomorrow—you probably won't get this till tomorrow afternoon—but on Friday. Can you make it? If you can't, fax me. Or leave a message on my answering machine. If I pick up the phone, speak on regardless. I at least will have the pleasure of your voice.

I opened your letter with your letter-opener. So much has become clearer: your silences, the sudden tacking of our conversations. But all this is still so puzzling and, well, so frightening to me. Is there nothing I can do to help in any way? We must meet on Friday. This can't, this mustn't make a difference to us.

Love,
Michael

4.5

After a rehearsal with the quartet, I go to a large bookshop near the University and in the medical section downstairs buy a book about deafness. I feel compelled to know something about it. It is clearly if technically written—and so interestingly in fact that later, at night, when I am sitting up in bed with the book resting on my knees, for a few minutes at a time I lose sight of the fact that it is Julia's affliction that has spurred me to read it. I have put on a record of Schubert's string quintet and it is to the sounds of that music that I make my first acquaintance with the elaborate chaos that lies behind the tiny drumskins of my outer ears.

The new words sink in one by one: recruitment, tinnitus, stereocilia, the organ of Corti, the basilar membrane, tympanometry, degeneration of the stria vascularis, membrane ruptures, neurofibromatosis . . . The music finishes. I read on

215

without getting out of bed to change it. Structures, symptoms, causes, cures . . . not much about auto-immunity . . . a certain amount about idiopathic conditions—which by definition have no known cause.

She has faxed me to say she is going to come over tomorrow morning. I dread and long for this meeting. I want to leave it to her to speak; but what if she leaves it to me?

There are so many exact questions—but beyond all that, and before all that, there is the fearful, unsurmisable question—what does it mean to her? And selfishly: what do I mean to her? Why, when music is slipping away from her, has she chosen to re-involve her life with mine? Am I for her a static mark, a reversion to the days when music was for her an actual sense, not merely an imagined beauty?

4.6

Julia is laughing. She has been here for less than five minutes. This is not how it's supposed to go.

'What's so funny?'

'Michael, you're hopeless when you're being considerate, and it distorts your face.'

'What do you mean?' I say rather sharply.

'That's better.'

'What is?'

'What you just said.'

'You've lost me completely.'

'You spoke naturally just now—because you forgot to be considerate. It's much easier for me to read you when you speak naturally, so don't mouth things. Please! Unless you want to make me laugh. Now I've forgotten what you asked me.'

'I asked you about your music,' I say.

'Oh yes,' says Julia. 'Yes, I'm sorry.' She holds my hand, as if I were the one needing sympathy. 'I told you how I stopped playing after my exams in Vienna—well, after we were married, James persuaded me to take things up again, for my own pleasure, for no audience at all. After he'd left for work, I'd creep over to the piano. I was so nervous, I could hardly touch the keys. I was two or three months pregnant, and was getting sick all the time, and felt really fragile, as if a chord of more than two notes would shake me apart. In fact, I began with the 'Two-Part Inventions'. They had no associations with you at all, just with my early piano lessons with Mrs Shipster. I hadn't played for about a year and a half—yes, it was a year and a half—'

'Good for Mrs Shipster,' I remark. 'And good for your parents. And good for James. At least you didn't have to earn your living with your fingers.'

Julia says nothing. I notice how attentively she is looking at my face, my lips. What is holding me back? Can't I simply tell her how much I love her and want to help her?

'Your hearing aid: is that why you keep your hair long?'

Yes.'

'Long hair suits you.'

'Thank you. You've said that before, Michael, you know. You don't have to repeat it now, just because—'

'But it does . . . Have you got it on at the moment?' I ask. 'Or is it "in"?'

'No, I don't have it in. I thought about it. But

217

why change things?'

'How can you be so philosophical about it?' I say. 'I can't understand it.'

'Well, it's new to you, Michael, this whole weird world.'

'And it's getting worse all the time?'

'A little.'

'Day by day?'

'Well, month by month. I don't know how much longer I'll be able to play with other players. Luckily, with the piano, you can be more than one player all by yourself, so it won't be such a lonely world. I have a few solo concerts lined up, including one at the Wigmore this December. Schumann and Chopin. You can astonish me and come backstage for that one.'

'Oh no—I'm not coming to hear you play Schumann,' I say, attempting to be casual. 'He's the wrong Schu.' I can't for the moment remember where I've heard that before.

Julia laughs. 'You're so narrow-minded, Michael.'

'Narrow gorges run deep.'

Julia looks perplexed, then recovers. 'Narrow gorges run narrow.'

'All right, all right. But you haven't told me anything about your career. When did you begin to play in public again?'

'When Luke was a few months old. As a baby he loved listening to me play, and I'd alternate between playing for him and feeding him. Sometimes I'd be feeding him at the piano and playing with my free hand—a sort of one-part invention.' She smiles at the slightly ridiculous vision.

'And you played like that in public?'

'Very funny. Now you've made me—oh, yes, James asked me one day whether I'd play for a few people the next evening. He very rarely asks me to do anything he feels doubtful about, so I said yes without thinking. When they came, I discovered that they included the music critic of the *Boston Globe* and a couple of other high mucky-mucks in the musical world. I wasn't happy at his little trick, but I'd promised, so I played, and they liked it and things went on from there. Salon rather than stage at first, but after a year or so James and the others suggested I perform publicly—and I felt ready for it, so I did. But most people in the New England area knew me as Julia Hansen, so that was what I stuck to.'

'New name, fresh start, no old associations?'

'Yes. It was Julia McNicholl who had stopped playing.'

'You played for months after I left.'

'I had my studies. I kept to them.'

I say nothing.

'But I never knew how fortunate I was, despite all that,' says Julia. After a while she continues: 'No one knows how this thing came about. I get so *exhausted* lip-reading. Our ears are strange things. We can't hear dog-whistles. Did you know that bats begin beyond Bach?'

'You've lost me,' I say.

'Their entire range of hearing lies beyond Bach's four octaves.'

'Well,' I say, 'I suppose one could transpose everything up four octaves for the benefit of bats.'

'Michael, you turned away. I missed that.'

'Oh, it's not worth repeating.'

219

'Repeat it,' says Julia very quietly.

'It was a pathetic joke.'

'Let me decide that,' says Julia quite sharply.

'I said that perhaps one ought to transpose Bach four octaves up for the edification of baroque bats.'

Julia stares at me, then begins laughing. Soon tears are rolling down her cheeks: the only tears she's shed so far, and not the right ones at all.

'Yes, you're right, Michael,' she says, giving me a hug, the first for a week. 'You're right. That was pretty pathetic.'

4.7

Helen phones me in high excitement.

'Lunch. Yes. Today. No, Michael, no excuses. I'm paying. It's the viola. I've got it!'

We meet at the Santorini Taverna. Helen, not willing to waste time with irrelevancies, orders for both of us.

'I went to the opening of this marvellous ceramics exhibition yesterday,' says Helen. 'Very Chinesey, very quirky, very deep. But some disgusting collector marched in before anyone else had the chance to see anything, and put red dots under every single item. Everyone who came went around looking totally disconsolate, turning the pots upside down and scowling.'

'Why didn't you let me have a look at the menu?'

'What would you want to look at the menu for?'

'Just in case there was something I might have liked better.'

'Oh, don't be silly, Michael, the kleftikon is

absolutely delicious. You do like lamb, don't you? I can never remember. And let's have a bottle of the house red. I'm in the mood for a celebration.'

'We're rehearsing in an hour and a half.'

'Oh—' Helen waves her hand about. 'Don't be such a damp squib.'

'It's you who'll get tipsy, not me. Or sleepy. Or both. Women get too high on too little at lunch.'

'Oh, is that so, Michael?'

'Believe me. And I want some spinach.'

'Why spinach?'

'I like spinach.'

'Spinach is bad for you. It makes your eyes pop.'

'What nonsense, Helen.'

'I've never liked spinach,' says Helen. 'Nor has Piers. So there is something we agree on. I sometimes wonder why he ever asked me to join the quartet. And I wonder why I ever did. I'm sure we'd get along better if we weren't yoked together like this. Or if we weren't both musicians. Or if he hadn't bagged the violin first. Not that I mind— every decent composer preferred to play the viola . . . Ah, good.' She has just noticed that our waiter is standing near her. 'We'll have a bottle of the house red. And my friend here wants some horrible spinach,' says Helen.

'We only serve excellent spinach, madam.'

'Well, he'll have to have some of that, then.'

The waiter bows and disappears. Helen is obviously a much-loved regular.

After a quick glass, Helen tells me that she has found someone in the early-music twilight zone who has solved her problem.

'The real difficulty wasn't getting one of those huge violas—there're quite a few lying around here

221

and there—it was the rigging. How do you rig it down a fourth? Hugo—he's absolutely brilliant, I've never met anyone like him, he looks rather like a hairy embryo, but he's an absolute darling—he strung the lower two with thick silver-covered gut and the top two with plain gut, and we rushed off to some fiddle-shop—in Stoke Newington, can you believe it?—to work out the tension. It was opposite a jazz bar and Hugo wants us to go there sometime, but I just don't feel it *here*—'

Helen thumps her left breast and gulps down a glass with an alacrity reminiscent of Captain Haddock.

I pour myself a second glass. If I don't share the bottle, Helen will be legless by the time we play our scale.

'Well,' continues Helen, 'the first try at rigging it down a fourth was absolutely hopeless. The strings needed a huge amount of tension, and the plates stopped vibrating. It completely clammed up . . . No: that's for him . . . I really don't see how you can eat it, Michael. I really detest it. When I was six I had to sit in the corner for a whole hour because I refused to eat it. I never did. And I didn't say sorry either.'

'So, Helen. It clammed up. And then?'

'We were talking about spinach—'

'We were talking about your viola.'

'So we were. Clammed up. Etcetera. And then. Where was I?'

'Right, Helen, no more wine until story-time's over.'

'And then—then, oh, yes, then he went up to Birmingham or Manchester or somewhere and found a man who's the Tsar of strings. He gets the guts straight from the slaughter-house, and they lie about steaming in tubs all over the place. Apparently his house smells like an absolute abattoir.' Helen pushes her kleftikon aside with her fork. 'Do you know, if it weren't for the fact that I don't like vegetables, I would certainly be a vegetarian.'

'Everything all right, madam?' asks our waiter.

'Oh, yes, perfect,' says Helen a little absently. 'So then Hugo came down reeking of strings—huge fat strings—and we tried a few of those. We got the right tuning without using too much tension, but of course when he applied the bow, the strings were so slack you could literally see them vibrating from side to side.'

Helen waves her hand about by way of illustration, and upsets her glass which, however, is empty. When she puts it down, I move it to safety.

'I do try not to think of the poor cows. Or is it sheep?' asks Helen.

'Your strings . . .' I say.

'Yes. It sounded weird, and you just had to coax the sound out. It took hours from the time the bow was in motion till you heard the note.'

'That's always a bit of a problem with the viola, though, isn't it?' I say, while several viola jokes amble through my head.

'This was several hundred thousand times worse,' says Helen. 'But a bit of trial and error, and re-stringing with those northern guts, and Hugo got it going well enough. He used a very very very heavy bow which he borrowed from a friend of his, and it's still slow, but it sounds just wonderful. I just have to practise to get the time-lag right. I don't know how to thank him. He suggests . . .'

'That's marvellous, Helen,' I say. 'Now eat up. This calls for a celebratory glass of mineral water.'

'Water?' says Helen, blinking. 'Water? Is that all your enthusiasm amounts to?'

'Water,' I say firmly, looking at my watch. 'And perhaps a coffee if we've still got time.'

'Wine,' says Helen. 'Wine. Without life, wine isn't worth living.'

4.8

Billy has the habit of making expansive gestures on the open string: a disease common to cellists. When he hits one, especially at the end of a phrase, he raises his left hand from the neck of the cello in a gesture of ostentatious relaxation—look, Mum, no hand. When this happens with the C-string, it is almost a gesture of farewell.

I have never taken to it. It's a bit like those pianists who describe grand parabolas with their hands, or lieder-singers whose heads sway like daffodils on the stalks of their necks.

There is a rather dangerous glaze of intentness in Helen's eyes. Considering how much she put away at lunch, she is playing surprisingly well. What is odd today, though, is what she does whenever she has an imitative phrase: she responds with a phrase that is almost a clone of the previous player's. At first this is limited to the sound of it, and this is bothersome enough: Piers stumbles at an arpeggio in staccato triplets, and Helen stumbles at exactly the same point in exactly the same way, as if some goblin had jumped out of him and into her. I should have helped her out more

224

with that wine.

We are playing one of the quartets in Haydn's opus 64, and zipping along quite happily as we often do with him, even though all this is a bit distracting. Billy's gestures, with so many delectable open Cs, have become even broader, and Helen's imitation has extended towards facial expressions. But now I notice she is doing something even odder. Whenever she has an open string followed by a rest, she takes her hand off the viola.

So fascinated am I by this that I do not notice that I have begun to do the same. But it comes to me as a bit of a shock when I see Piers staring at Helen and me, and beginning, with a broad grin, to raise his hand off the fingerboard too. All of us are playing with Billy-like abandon on our miniature cellos, making extravagant gesticulations whenever our left hands have nothing better to do.

Billy's face becomes redder and redder, and his gestures smaller and smaller. And his playing itself becomes more and more cramped and pinched until, in the middle of a phrase, he sneezes twice and suddenly stops. He gets up, leans his cello against his chair, and starts to loosen the hairs on his bow.

'What's the matter, Billy?' asks Helen.

'I've had enough,' says Billy. He glares at us.

Piers and I both look contrite, but Helen merely looks puzzled. 'Enough of what?' she asks.

'You know what,' says Billy. 'All of you. When did you plan this?'

'We didn't plan anything, Billy,' says Piers.

'It just sort of happened,' I say.

'What happened?' asks Helen. She smiles at

Billy in a haze of benevolence.

'You began it,' says Billy accusingly. 'You—you began it. Don't play the innocent.'

Helen glances at the chocolate biscuits, but decides that they might be more exacerbating than emollient.

'I'm sorry, Billy,' I murmur. 'I don't think Helen even noticed. Piers and I shouldn't have joined her.'

'If you don't like what I do on the open string, it's a very nasty way to let me know.'

Helen, comprehension dawning, stares at her left hand. 'Oh, Billy, Billy,' she says, standing up and kissing him on the cheek, 'sit down, sit down, I had no idea what I was doing. Why are you so sensitive all of a sudden?'

Billy, looking rather like a bear with a sore paw, consents to sit down, and tightens his bow. 'I hate it when you gang up on me,' he says with a hurt expression in his eyes. 'I hate it.'

'But, Billy, we don't,' says Piers.

Billy looks at us darkly. 'Oh, yes, you do. I know that you don't want to play the quartet I've written.'

Piers and I glance at each other, but before either of us can speak Helen blurts out: 'But we do, Billy, of course we do, we'd love to play it.'

'To play it through,' I add quickly.

'Once,' adds Piers.

'Just for the heck of it, you know, sometime,' I mumble guiltily.

'Well, it's not finished yet,' says Billy.

'Ah,' says Piers with evident relief.

'Perhaps we should wait till after Vienna,' I suggest.

'And after we've begun working on the Bach,'

226

adds Piers.

Helen looks at Piers rather curiously but doesn't say a word. Billy, his fears confirmed, doesn't look at any of us. I busy myself examining the music for the next movement. Helen's fridge hums on, emitting a note stuck rather irksomely somewhere between G and G sharp.

4.9

Almost all the time—through spinach and open strings and all—my mind keeps drifting back to Julia, so I am ill-prepared for a call from Virginie.

'Michael, this is Virginie speaking. If you are there, please answer, and do not hide behind your answering machine. Hello, Michael, can you hear me, please pick up the phone now, please, Michael, stop playing games with me, I am not going to . . .'

'Hello.'

'Why didn't you pick it up earlier?'

'Virginie, do you know what time it is?'

'It's eleven thirty. So what? You haven't spoken to me in two weeks. Do you think I can sleep easily?'

'Virginie, I can't talk now.'

'Why not? Have you had a hard day?'

'Well, yes, sort of.'

'Poor Michael, poor Michael, and you're quite in a hurry to get back to sleep.'

'In quite a hurry.'

'*Oh, qu'est-ce que tu m'énerves* I'll speak any way I like. Who are you sleeping with? Who is she?'

'Just stop this, Virginie.'

'Don't lie to me again. I know it, I know it. Are

you sleeping with someone?'

'Yes.'

'I knew. I knew!' exclaims Virginie. 'And you lied to me. You lied and lied and said you weren't seeing anyone. And I believed you. How disgusting you are, Michael. Let me speak to her.'

'Virginie, calm down—be reasonable—'

'Oh, I hate you English. Be reasonable, be reasonable. You have hearts like cement.'

'Virginie, listen, I'm fond of you, but—'

'Fond. Fond. Put her on the phone. I'll tell her how fond you were of me.'

'She's not here.'

'I am not a cretin, Michael.'

'She's not here, Virginie, she's not here, OK? Don't make yourself miserable. I feel bad about all this. But I don't know what to do. What would you do if you were me?'

'How dare you?' asks Virginie. 'How dare you ask me that? Do you love her?'

'Yes,' I say quietly after a second's pause. 'Yes. I do.'

'I don't want to see you again, Michael,' says Virginie, her voice veering between tears and anger. 'I never want to see you again. Not as a teacher or anything. I'm young, and I'm going to have a good time. You'll see. And you'll regret it. You'll regret everything. I hope she makes you miserable. So that you can't sleep or anything. You always took me lightly because I loved you.'

'Goodnight, Virginie. I don't know what to say. I'm sorry. I really am. Goodnight.'

Before she can say anything, I put down the phone. She does not ring back.

I am behaving dreadfully and I know it. But I

228

have no room to manoeuvre. I never thought I was using her when I was with her. It was an arrangement I thought she was content with. But now I can see us becoming strangers, thinking of each other less and less as the weeks pass, and with time drifting entirely out of each other's lives. Poor Virginie, I say to myself, and feel a little ashamed even as I think the thought. I hope she finds someone unlike me: unexacting, happy of spirit and, most of all, not irreparably imprinted with the die of someone else's being.

4.10

One Saturday morning just before eight, Julia, to my astonishment, turns up at the Serpentine. Normally I would never see her on a weekend, but James is away and Luke is staying over at a friend's. She looks at the proceedings, amazed. She didn't believe I actually did this, and now she can see it she still doesn't understand why I do. After all, I'm not particularly sporty. I tell her that her job is not to speculate but to cheer me on. However, her presence makes me swim diagonally across the course, and I finish last. The rowdiest of the others make lewd enquiries as to who she is. I tell them she's my charlady.

After we get back to my flat we make love. The tension falls away from her; and her tortured ambivalence. She closes her eyes. She sighs, she tells me what to do. The things I say to her she cannot hear.

'I feel like a kept man,' I tell her afterwards. 'You visit me; I can never be sure exactly when.

229

Then I can never tell whether you'll want to make love or not. When you're here I'm ecstatic, and the rest of the time I go around wondering exactly when you'll turn up. And you bring me goodies, which I like—but when will I ever wear your cuff-links except on stage?'

'And Virginie, does she—did she—pay you?'

'You're changing the subject.'

'No, I'm not. *Did* she?'

'Yes, for lessons, of course.'

'And did she stop when you began making love?'

I look at Julia, surprised. This is blunt, coming from her. 'No,' I reply. 'I did suggest it once, but she said that that would mean that I was in effect paying her.'

'She sounds formidable. Perhaps you don't value her enough.'

'Really?' I say, and kiss her. 'Why don't we take a shower together?'

'Good heavens, Michael, what's happened to you in the last ten years?'

'Come on. I'll soap the Serpentine out of you.'

But this is abortive, because in the middle of it, the erratic water pressure of Archangel Court strikes once again, and she is left soaped and shampooed with only a tepid trickle coming down.

'Don't panic,' I say. 'I'll get some water from the tap. That usually works.'

She squints to read me through the soap. 'Hurry, Michael,' she says.

'You look gorgeous. I'll see if there's any film in my camera.' I make a clicking gesture.

'That isn't funny.' She sounds upset.

The buzzer rings. Young Jamie Powell, one of my students, appears in the little blue screen. I tell him to walk around the block and come back in ten minutes. He is the most reluctant of my students, so he sounds more pleased than surprised.

Julia is dressed by the time he enters. Jamie is a useless little adolescent brat, quite musical, guitar-obsessed, hopeless on the violin. Why his parents insist on his continuing his lessons with me I don't know, but at least it's income. He looks at the two of us with knowing amusement. There are quick introductions, 'Jessica, this is Jamie; Jamie, Jessica,' before she leaves, unkissed and unkissing. But Jamie snickers on throughout his lesson.

Even though it's been interrupted, even though she's gone and I may not see her for a while, her visit has made me happy for the rest of the day. I hardly think of the future of our relationship, so dazed am I by the intimacy and disbelief and excitement of its renewal. When we are together we talk of almost everything—about those times in Vienna when we were happy, and about music, and about our years apart—years not lost now, but missing. But though I talk about the shape of my life during this period, I do not touch upon the darkness, still almost inexplicable to me, that came over me and caused or forced the breach between us.

I tell her now of the time, listening to the radio in the taxi, that I felt certain I had heard her play. I felt it in my spirit, I say; I could not have been mistaken. She thinks for only a second, and tells me that I must have been. Neither was she in England at the time nor has she ever played Bach in public. It could not have been her, she says, but some other woman.

'Woman?' I ask.

231

'Yes,' she says. 'Since you say you mistook it for me.'

4.11

Though she talks about her family, she never touches on how exactly or where exactly she met James, and how he wooed and won her. Nor do I want to know.

Our endearments are not the same. Rebuked once, I do not call her what used to be so natural. There is room for only one darling, and I don't wish, even if it didn't disturb her, to remind her of her crescent, her dining table, her child, her husband. But I feel I know her uniquely—as this man who lives with her cannot—in the core of her being: the great, fraying cord that links her to her music. I knew her when she was in love for the first and—but what do I know of this?—perhaps the only time.

Things are well between us, and my hours, even when I am alone, revolve around this varying brightness. But she inhabits dual worlds, which chafe each other. She has a life beyond me, places and people that are closed to me. In Vienna my friends like Wolf and hers like Maria enriched our sense of each other, even became each other's friends. Now we are in a bubble, and the beings of others are figments of our speech. We are narrowed into amours. But we have anyway become less sociable over these years apart: she cannot cope in a crowd, and I have merely reverted to the solitariness of my earlier life.

Even when there is a concert that we would both

love, in a hall equipped with an induction loop, we do not go. Who knows whom we may meet, or who may see us. Besides, her hearing aid, even adjusted to the loop, sometimes prevents her from hearing the right pitch. When she's been with me she hasn't worn it at all.

I would have expected more protest, more despair, more rage. When I say so, Julia tells me about people she has met in her lip-reading classes. One suffers from a disease that gives him dreadful, nauseating attacks of dizziness while progressively stripping him of his hearing. One became deaf after a serious stroke; he bumps into people on the street and they shake him off as a drunk. One, a woman of about fifty, lost all her hearing overnight as the result of a bungled operation. 'They get by,' she says. 'I'm much better off than them.'

'But you're a musician. That must make it hardest of all.'

'Well—I have you now to share it with.'

'You're taking it too lightly.'

'Well, Michael, it's for me to take. You would have managed somehow if this had happened to you. You might not think so, but you would have.'

'I doubt it, Julia. I don't know what I'd have done to myself . . . I . . . You have more grit than me.'

'I don't. I just remind myself that a deaf mother's better than none.'

I can't think what to say to this.

'At least,' she says after a while, 'at least I wasn't born deaf. At least my memory can tell me what Schubert's string quintet sounds like. I'm luckier there than Mozart—who never heard a note of it— or Bach—who never heard a note of Mozart . . .'

Sometimes the mask slips and I sense her wretchedness.

I ask her how she still makes music with her hands, how she plays as finely, as feelingly as she still does. It is beyond my comprehension. She, who is so eager to talk of music in general, retracts herself into brevity. All she tells me is that she finds a mental analogue to the way she hears a phrase, and then lets her body portray it. For me her deafness has broken some ideal dream, but how can I question her more aggressively? What does she even mean by 'portray'? What do her ears feed back to her? How does she now sense exactly what the pedal sustains?

She is still fond of the small graspable pleasures of life. One of these is the view from the buses, and we ride them sometimes, sitting upstairs on opposite sides of the aisle. This must remind her, like me, of the time we first sighted each other. 'I don't feel proud of these trysts,' she says today. 'If someone else were doing what I am, I wouldn't know what to think of them.'

'But that makes them sound so grubby, Julia. You can't mean that. You're not unhappy to be with me, are you?'

'No, how could I be?' she says, reaching out to hold my hand before she sees the conductor and thinks better of it.

What is it like for her? How can she sustain these visits to me while being wife and mother at home? Since she believes in trust, I see her pain, and yet I dare not probe for fear that it will spill that world into our own. I don't ask her, nor does she tell me whether she has been to church these last two weeks, and if so what thoughts passed through her mind.

Adultery and sin: ludicrously, there are no gentler words. But Julia cannot accept all this brimstone: gentle herself, she must believe in an understanding God. All this is foreign to me, incomprehensible even. But have I forced her into more than what she wanted? Should we have continued making music together, nothing else, to re-create the bonds of stimulation and companionship so long lost? Would there then have been no guilt? Could she have reconciled herself to having two husbands, each for a different world? Could I have stood it and not singed and warped?

Pointless to think of it, now that it has begun. But what if it had not begun? What if we were not making love together, we whose blood beats in one pulse? How touching it would be, how chaste, sad, poignant, beautiful—how self-congratulatory, how false, how agonising, how comfortless.

4.12

Erica and the four of us are sitting in a black cab on our way to Stratus Records. Erica has just told us that the new girl in her office has booked us for four, rather than five tickets to Vienna and Venice. She didn't realise that Billy's cello always gets a seat of its own.

'That's absurd, Erica,' says Piers. 'Get rid of her.'

'Well, she's new, she's young, she's just out of college, she didn't know.'

'So what do we do about the last ticket—or do we go on separate flights?'

'The travel agents said they'd get back in touch with us by the end of the week. I'm quite optimistic.'

'When aren't you?' exclaims Piers.

'Anyway,' says Billy, staring rather morosely out of the window of the taxi, 'I'm not so hot on Vienna.'

'Oh, what is it now, Billy?' says Piers impatiently. 'You've never complained about Schubert before.'

'Well, for a start, I think our programme's unbalanced,' says Billy. 'We can't play both the string quintet and the Trout.'

'What is it this time, Billy? Chronological stress? One's too early, one's too late?'

'Well, yes, and they're both quintets and they're both massive.'

'We're going to play them,' says Piers. 'All Schubert goes together fine. And anyway, if he'd lived to be seventy, all this would be early Schubert. If you had any objections, why didn't you bring them up earlier?'

'And I'd really much rather play second cello in the string quintet,' adds Billy.

'But why?' I ask. 'The first cello has all the loveliest tunes.'

'I've got all the loveliness I can handle in the Trout,' says Billy recalcitrantly. 'And I like all those stormy bits in the string quintet: Duh-duh-duh Duh-duh-duh Duh-duh-duh Dum! I should be the one to play them. I'm the anchor of the quartet. Why should the outside cellist always play second cello?'

Helen, who has contrived to put her arms around both Billy and me, squeezes his shoulders and, incidentally, mine. 'You'll get to play second cello with some other quartet sometime,' she says.

'I don't know,' says Billy after a while. 'Anyway, that isn't the same thing at all.'

'What is the matter with everyone today?' asks Helen in exasperation. 'Everyone seems to be tense about something.'

'I'm not,' I say.

'Oh, yes, you are. And you've been that way for the last God knows how long.'

'And you're not?' Piers demands of Helen.

'No, why should I be?' says Helen. 'Look!' She points out of the window at a bit of St James's Park. 'It's spring.'

'Helen's in love with a horrible fellow called Hugo,' says Piers for our benefit. 'He's part of an outfit called something Antiqua, he plays a baroque fiddle and wears sandals and sports a beard: you get the idea.'

'I'm not in love,' says Helen. 'And he's not horrible.'

'Of course he is,' says Piers. 'You must be blind.'

'He's not in the least horrible, Piers. I was in a perfectly good mood just now.'

'He looks like a hairy slug,' says Piers.

'I won't have my friends talked about in this way,' says Helen hotly. 'You've only met him once so you don't know how nice he is. And it's thanks to him that I've managed to get a deeper viola, and it's only because of that that we can make this recording at all. Don't forget that.'

'As if I could,' says Piers.

'Don't you want to make this recording?' asks Helen. 'I thought we'd convinced you at long last.'

'Well, it's three to one,' says Piers, almost to himself.

'Piers,' says Helen, 'everyone feels it's three to one against them at some time or other. And no one's forcing you to do anything. When Tobias was—'

Her brother fixes her with a piercing look, and she stops in midsentence.

'All right, all right,' says Helen. 'Sorry. Sorry. I didn't mean to bring that up. But it's absurd. One can't talk about Alex. One can't talk about Tobias. One can't talk about anyone.'

Piers, jaw tight, says nothing, and avoids looking at any of us.

'Negative, negative, negative, everyone's so negative today,' says Helen brightly. 'This morning when I was making coffee I suddenly realised how boring musicians are. All our friends are musicians and we aren't interested in anything except music. We're stunted. Totally stunted. Like athletes.'

'Right, troops,' says Erica. 'Here we are. Now remember. What we need is a united front.'

4.13

Ysobel Shingle plumps us up with passionate praise, and is not at all rigid about time-tables, style of playing, the ordering of those parts of the 'Art of Fugue' where different orderings are possible. She is delighted with the thought that, owing to Billy's insistence and Helen's explorations, it will be possible to play the whole thing without transposing anything.

She asks us if we would prefer to record in a regular studio or somewhere with a more natural atmosphere—she mentions a church they sometimes use. Erica tells her we can't decide so early on, and this, like everything else, doesn't seem to bother her.

She is extremely intense and nervous throughout the discussion, and we end up in the strange position of trying to put her at ease. There is something spectral to her tremulous pallor, as if she has just landed from another planet and is trying to come to terms with her displacement and to perform her transgalactic mission simultaneously.

She appears to be terrified of Erica, of the telephone, even of her own secretary, but Erica has told us already that in fact Ysobel Shingle is not terrified of anyone, including the financial figures who ostensibly own and control Stratus Records. She goes to their meetings, and whenever they criticise or question anything, she lowers her voice to a whisper and mumbles so intensely that they drop their objections. Everyone is afraid of losing her, since she is the constructive force behind what Erica calls their 'A and R', shorthand, apparently, for 'Artists and Repertoire'.

From time to time, even in the course of our meeting, her voice almost disappears, and only her lips appear to move. Though it has us completely perplexed, I reflect that Julia would be fine in a situation like this. I am rather startled at the thought, and even at myself for thinking it. But suddenly Ysobel Shingle smiles in a wintry manner, and appears to gain some tentative confidence, and the train of her voice emerges from its tunnel to say, 'So we could, you know, go ahead with that too—if it's acceptable to you, of course. Publicity and Promotion will skin me alive if you don't agree, but it's entirely up to you.' Her smile becomes wanner at the thought of her impending martyrdom, and we swiftly agree to whatever it was she requested under her breath.

Piers keeps his reservations to himself and is outwardly almost enthusiastic about the project. Helen tries to disguise her surprise and gratitude. After it is over, Erica, full of delight at how things have gone, and finding she is late for her meeting with a Spanish diva, dispenses 'mwah-mwah!' kisses to each of us, hugs the flinching Piers, and rushes halfway across the street to grab a taxi which has halted at a set of traffic-lights.

4.14

'Michael, is that you, Michael?'

'Yes, hello, Dad. What's up?'

'Oh, not a lot, Zsa-Zsa's sick. We're taking her down to the vet tomorrow.'

'Nothing serious, I hope.'

'She's throwing up all over the place, and she doesn't, you know, she doesn't seem to have any, any . . .'

'Energy?'

'Energy.' My father sounds relieved.

But I can't contrive to be worried about Zsa-Zsa, who once every year or so frightens everyone and in due course emerges in hardier health. She has exceeded her nine lives already and appears to be neither conscious of it nor grateful for it.

'Are you all right, Dad?' I ask.

'Fine, fine . . . haven't heard from you in a while.'

'Oh, I've been pretty busy.'

'I can imagine. Vienna, wasn't it?'

'No, Dad, that's coming up.'

'How you do it, I don't know.'

'Do what?'

'You know, keep things up, Joan and I were saying how proud we were of you. Who would have thought you'd be doing all these things . . . oh, I know what I had to say. Has Mrs Formby called you?'

'No, no, Dad, she hasn't.'

'Oh. Well, she wanted your telephone number and I couldn't see any reason not to give it to her.'

'That's fine, Dad.'

'I don't want to give your number to a whole ruck of folk. I don't want them disturbing you if you'd rather not.'

'You just use your judgment, Dad. If you give it to someone, it's fine by me. What did she want? Did she say?'

'No, she didn't. Should I have asked?'

'That's all right. I just wondered.'

'Oh, she said she loved the Christmas pudding you took around. Nice lady she is. Always has been.'

'Auntie Joan all right?'

'She's all right, except for her, you know, the hands . . .'

'Arthritis.'

'That's it.'

'Give her my love.'

'I will.'

'Well, bye, Dad. Talk to you soon.'

I re-play the conversation in my mind. I suppose I can expect a call from Mrs Formby soon. I go to my small music room—more music cell than music room—and open my violin case. I lift the olive-green velvet covering and take out the Tononi. Gently, very gently, with the back of my hand I touch its back, its belly. How long we have lived together, the two of us: my time in Vienna, the solitary years that followed, these years with the Maggiore. It came into my life the same year as Julia. How long we have sung in one voice. How much we have grown into each other. How could anything part us now?

4.15

I fear the phone. Nothing good can come to me over it. Julia cannot speak to me. All it can yield are the upbraidings of a young woman who sees herself as wronged, or a request from an old woman who, though she has done nothing but good to me, has it in her power to part me from what I love.

Virginie does not call. Mrs Formby does not call. Often there are no messages on my answering machine, and I am thankful. Sometimes there are several. Occasionally I am pestered by the customers of the London Bait Company. I should do something about this, I suppose.

I look at myself in the mirror. A fortnight past the equinox, I will be 38. At my temples, near the edge of my ears, there are flecks of white. Where am I now, with my life half gone? Where will I be when I am my father's age?

Who ever saw a banker with a moustache? What was so remarkable about his shaving it off?

Julia and I cannot spend much time together.

What we have is snatched from the day. We have not—except for that first meeting—met in the evening, nor can we hope to. Thus the night is given to me unshared: to my work, to my reading, to walking with no aim around the neighbourhood. Once I walk past her street. There are cracks of light at the edges of drawn blinds. Are they in those rooms or the rooms facing the gardens of the crescent?

She has told me of her evenings. They are a template of domesticity: Luke, James, the piano, books, television with the subtitles turned on, Buzby. They do not often go out.

Though I know what it is she does, I have no sense of the pace of it, the rhythm of it. That is beyond my reach. Yet what we share in daylight is more than I could have foreseen, in the drizzle of winter, as ever being part of my life at all.

Magnolia; forsythia; clematis. It is as if the weather has gone awry these last few years, and everything has jumbled and merged.

I wonder if I should call Mrs Formby, but do not. Our instruments are the other quartet; each has its parallel life. Helen has been getting used to the restrung viola she has borrowed. On it she wanders over the lower reaches of the tenor voice of the 'Art of Fugue', while playing everything else on her own viola. Does the huge, borrowed instrument rebel at its curious tuning? What does it think of the low, slow tones of its remade voice? Does it look at its smaller, often-played colleague with envy of its repertoire or disdain at its puniness?

Piers's violin, I suppose, is insecure. It knows he is looking for another one, that he plans to sell it off.

Billy's cello, well-loved, has an interesting existence. Apart from playing his own unperformed creations, it gets experimented on stylistically and technically. Lately Billy has taken to a slightly greater flexibility in timing. Without increasing the volume of his sound or detracting from his rhythm-setting beat, this brings out his own voice to subtler effect and enlivens whatever we are playing. His cello has, after all the confusion, managed to get a seat on the same flight as us to Vienna.

I think of my old life in that city and this unimagined recapitulation. I sense in Julia, now that she has nothing to hide, an ease that I can hardly credit or understand. When what is happening has run its course, will all she hears be in her mind?

We play a couple of Vivaldi's Manchester Sonatas together. My Tononi sings them ecstatically, as if to say it remembers these well from the days when it played in Vivaldi's own concerts. What she plays at the keyboard she plays clearly and finely. Only now I do notice that very rarely, at the end of the arc of a phrase, her finger touches a key visibly enough but so softly that I cannot hear the sound she doubtless hears.

The daylight we now share merges with the evenings we shared once in that city, half dreaded, half loved. I will be there soon: lilac in bloom, chestnut in noisy leaf. Strange to think of her mother living there now, and she herself in London.

The Maggiore runs through the Schubert string quintet without the fifth player: full rehearsals will have to wait till we meet our second cellist in Vienna. It is a curious exercise but a necessary one;

we often have to rehearse with an imagined partner. Billy is subdued at first, then plays the first cello in his usual masterly way. At one point he makes us laugh by hamming out one particularly lush tune to show us he is not aggrieved.

The Austrian pianist who will be playing the Trout with us was due to come to London last week for a concert. We were supposed to fit in a pre-Vienna rehearsal, but it did not work out. For some reason his concert was cancelled, and he did not come to London at all.

This coming trip to Vienna would have been a hard one. I would have wanted to lock myself in the hotel, but my mind would have taken me round the city: the parks, the cafes, the reaches of the Danube, the hills of the northern districts. Now we have met again, I fear no grief in that spent habitat.

Lilacs, certainly, in May. And that white flower that I have seen only in Vienna, on all those acacia-like trees.

4.16

The doorbell rings. I pull on my dressing gown, and get to the door.

'Who is it?'

Silence.

I look through the peep-hole. It is Julia, standing in the corridor with an amused expression. I suppose Rob let her in. She would only have had to smile at him.

'Oh, how dingy!' says Julia as she enters. 'It's too dark. Roll up the blinds. I can't see anything. And I can't hear anything. Not that it's such a nice day anyway. Michael, it's past nine o'clock. You can't just have got out of bed. We're going shopping.'

'Don't bully me,' I protest. 'We got back late from Norwich last night. I'm catching up on sleep.'

But Julia is drawing up the blinds and does not respond. 'Ah, that's better,' she says.

'Let's go to bed. Back to bed,' I say.

'No time for that. Don't bother about shaving. Have a shower. I'll make the coffee. Stop yawning. Seize the day.'

Still yawning, I try to do as she says. In the shower a question occurs to me, and I shout, 'Why shopping?' though even as I do so, I realise that her answer will be garbled by the sound of running water. Then it strikes me that there won't be an answer at all. But why shopping? I'd rather just stay home with her.

'Because it's your birthday in a week,' says Julia over coffee.

'Oh,' I say, pleased.

'So you're in my hands.'

'Yes, I see I am.'

'You have horrible dowdy sweaters, Michael.'

'But it's almost April. I don't need another sweater.'

'You need a light summer sweater. Let's see what you have . . . What were you doing last night? You look tired.'

'I went up to Norwich for a concert with the Camerata Anglica and only got back at three.'

'At three?'

'I got a lift with someone—his car-key snapped, and we had to call the AA . . . you don't want to hear the details. It's good to see you.'

'Likewise.'

'Likewise—is that a Jamesism?'

'A Jamesism, did you say? It is not!'

'I'm sure it is. You never used to say "likewise".'

'Well, I must have picked that up in the States . . . Finish up now, Michael. We haven't got all day.'

'What a day! I just want to lie in bed with a teddy-bear and a thriller.' Julia looks out of the window. It's drizzling. The clouds, covering the entire sky, are smoky cotton-wool, and grey buildings mark the skyline. Even the raindrops trickle sluggishly down the window-panes.

'It's a rather Viennese day,' says Julia. 'I like it.'

'Where are we going?'

'To Harvey Nichols.'

'That's not my sort of place.'

'It isn't mine either. But that's where we're going.'

'Why?'

'A friend's husband was wearing a sweater the other day. I coveted it, and I want to buy one for you. That's where he got it from.'

Half an hour later we are in the basement, in the men's section, looking not just at sweaters but at ties and shirts as well. A girl from the shop smiles at us: a couple out shopping together. I feel a momentary elation and then anxiety.

'We're going to bump into one of your husband's colleagues,' I say to Julia.

'Of course not, Michael, they're all sitting in Canary Wharf advising the world about pharmaceutical mergers. What do you think of this one?'

'It's really nice.'

She holds a maroon sweater up against me and looks serious. 'No, it's not. No, you want something

247

more in green or blue. Russets and reds and pinks and so on have never suited you.'

She extracts something in dark green with a polo neck. 'I don't know,' I say. 'It reminds me of the carpet in the green room of the Wigmore Hall.'

Julia laughs. 'So it does. And it isn't all that summery. But I like the feel of it. It's chenille.'

'I'll take your word for it.'

'You're hopeless.'

'Actually, I'm feeling a bit strange, Julia, a bit dizzy.'

'I'm sure you are. You've never liked shopping for clothes.'

'No, Julia, really.'

I do feel uneasy, oppressed, dizzy: the bright lights, the large number of people all around, the heat, the colours, the sense of being underground, perhaps even my lack of sleep . . . I don't know what it is, but I want to sit down. I feel as if I am in two worlds. This is the ultimate intimacy—we are shopping together, and salesgirls smile at us.

I sit down against a wall and cover my eyes with my palms.

'Michael—Michael—what's the matter?'

Somewhere I sense a door closing on me. The sounds merge: customers in several languages, frozen turkeys silent in a morgue, the whirring of the motor that runs the meat fridge, a desperate need to escape from everything around me.

'Julia—'

'Are you all right?' she whispers.

'Yes, yes—just help me up.'

'Michael, take your hands away from your mouth—I can't hear what you're saying.'

'Julia, help me up.'

She sets her bag down on the floor, and somehow, with her help, I manage to stand upright. I am still leaning against the wall.

'I'll be all right. I'll be all right. I just have to get out.'

'I'll get someone to help us.'

'No, no, let's just get out of here.'

We get to the escalator, then to the door. Julia says: 'Oh no—my bag. Michael, just lean here. I'll be back in a second.'

She is back in half a minute; her bag is safe. But I can read in her eyes how terrible I must look. Sweat is trickling down my forehead. Someone from the store is rushing over towards me.

'I'll be all right.' I manage a smile. 'I hope it's drizzling. I need some fresh air. I need a coffee.'

'There's a place upstairs . . .' says Julia.

'No. Please. Somewhere else.'

'Yes, you poor darling, of course. Somewhere else.'

I nod and lean against her. 'I'm so sorry . . .'

'Shh,' says Julia, taking me out into the rain. She cannot use her umbrella, and the rain drenches her hair and spots and stains her dress.

4.17

We are sitting upstairs in a cafe in a small passage a hundred yards away. Julia has seated me facing the window. We have ordered coffee. I look out in silence for a while.

'That hasn't happened to me for years,' I say.

'How are you feeling now?' she asks.

'Things seemed to be closing in on me,' I say,

249

and bow my head.

Julia reaches out to stroke my cheek gently.

I am quiet for a few minutes. She allows me to recover my breathing.

'That's why I live where I live,' I say, '—way up there in my eyrie. Do you remember how I used to unwind as soon as I got out of the city?'

'Yes. I remember.'

But the way she says it tells me what she is remembering: the scene of our parting. That too was at the outskirts of that city. It was at Lier's: a jug of white wine on a table beneath chestnut trees, and an exhausted bitterness. She walked down the hill alone. I was not to follow.

'You've never been up north with me—to Rochdale. I promised, didn't I, to take you to hear the larks on the moor.'

'Yes,' says Julia, looking at her hands. Her slender fingers rest on the ketchup-flecked tablecloth near her stubby coffee cup. Now, as then, she wears no wedding ring.

'How stupid of me,' I say.

'Well, I could see them,' she says.

'Larks aren't much to look at.'

'I can't come north with you,' says Julia. She half smiles. 'But I am going to Vienna with you,' she adds offhandedly.

All I can do is stare at her.

'I thought I was the one with the hearing problem,' she murmurs.

'You're having me on. You can't be—you *are* serious.'

A minute ago I was in darkness. What is this mad change?

'Ask Piers,' she says.

'Piers?'

'And your agent Alicia Cowan.'

'Erica. No! I would have known about this.'

'It all happened yesterday. I'm playing the Trout with you.'

I can feel the blood leaving my face. 'You're not.'

'Well, which is more unlikely: that it's true, or that I'd invent something so implausible and expect to be believed?'

Julia is behaving intolerably coolly: a clear sign of enjoyment.

'Stay right here,' I say. 'Don't move.'

'Where are you off to?'

'To the loo.'

'Well, are you pleased?'

'I'm stunned.'

I go downstairs, and walk to a phone-box. Piers will not be in, I am convinced of it; but he is.

'What the hell's going on, Piers?'

'Hey, hey, steady on, what's the matter, Michael?'

'What's this about the Trout and Vienna and Julia? Is it true?'

'Oh, yes, perfectly true. It all boiled up yesterday. I tried to get in touch with you but you weren't in. Where were you?'

'Norwich.'

'Ah, good. I like that part of the world. Did you go via Newmarket or Ipswich? . . . Oh, I know what I wanted to tell you. I don't know why you had such difficulty getting the music for the C minor quintet we played. There's a perfectly good Henle edition. I was in Chappell's yesterday, and—'

'Piers,' I say threateningly, 'I'm talking about Vienna, not about Chappell's.'

'Didn't you get my message?' he asks.

'I haven't listened to my messages. We got back at three. What was your message?'

'That I had to speak to you urgently. That's all. Anyway, it's no big deal. You're not playing in the Trout.'

That, I reflect, is all too true. It has a piano and four strings all right, but a second fiddle isn't one of them.

'Do you know Julia Hansen?'

'Do I know her?'

'Well, you referred to her as Julia, so I assumed you did. Does she play well?'

'Are you crazy, Piers?'

'Look, Michael, if you can't be civil . . .' says Piers, sounding more tired than counter-aggressive.

'OK, OK,' I say. 'I'm sorry. Just give me the facts.'

'It was a crisis. Otto Prachner has had a minor heart attack, and can't play for the next few months. That's why he couldn't be in London for his concert. For some unaccountable reason, his agent contacted Lothar only yesterday. And Lothar immediately got in touch with Erica and with the management of the *Musikverein* and also—rather decently, and I suppose to save time—directly with me, the 'primarius' of the quartet, as he likes to call it. He suggested Julia Hansen, whom he also represents. Apparently she's good, there's a Viennese connection, as with poor old Otto, and she's agreeable. Faxes were flying all over the place yesterday. Are you still there, Michael?'

'Yes, I'm here all right.'

'Well, I got in touch with the others before I agreed, because they're playing in the Trout. And I

252

did try to get in touch with you. But since you're not directly concerned, I can't see why you're so het up about it. Do you know her personally? I hope to God she's all right. Surely Lothar wouldn't put up someone half-baked to play Schubert before the Viennese.'

I can't take all this in. 'Aren't the programmes printed?' I blurt out. 'It's only a few weeks before the concert.'

'Oh, no,' says Piers in a more relaxed voice. 'Apparently, the actual programme is printed just a couple of days before the performance. Anyway, what can you do if someone falls ill? But you haven't answered my question.'

'Yes, that seems to be my problem today. Not answering stupid questions.'

'I'm sorry?'

'You know bloody well, Piers, that I know Julia.'

'And how would I know that?' retorts Piers angrily.

'*You* know Julia. Julia is Julia. Banff, remember? The Wigmore Hall? My trio in Vienna. Christ, Piers!'

'Oh!' says Piers. 'You're not saying it's her.'

'Who else?'

'But wasn't she Julia Mackenzie or something?'

'You mean you really didn't know?'

'That's what I've been saying all along.'

I begin to laugh, a bit maniacally, I suppose. 'Michael?' says Piers anxiously.

'I just can't believe it.'

'Well, if it is that Julia, I seem to recall from Banff that she's pretty good.'

'She's that all right,' I reply.

'So it's OK with you?'

253

'More than!'

'Then why were you so annoyed about all this?'

'I just thought you knew who she was, and didn't bother to talk to me about it.'

'Oh, I see. Good. Good. You had me worried there.'

'Did Lothar say anything else to you and Erica?' I ask.

'Like what?'

'Well, that she doesn't play much in ensemble these days.'

'Oh, why's that?'

'I'm not sure . . . I think she likes the solo repertoire more.'

'Oh, well, that's not too important . . . Incidentally, Lothar said something about her living in London. We should have a couple of rehearsals before Vienna.'

'Yes . . . yes.'

'And, Michael, talking of rehearsals, Helen says that next Wednesday's venue might have to be changed. She's got builders in, and—'

'Sorry, Piers. My money's about to run out. I'll call you later.'

I step out of the booth. I stand in the rain and laugh. I let it mat my hair and cool my skull.

4.18

Julia has ordered another coffee, and is sipping it with a worried expression. A young woman armed with a couple of Harrods shopping bags is standing by her table chatting away. Julia's replies are monosyllabic.

Her face lights up when she sees me. She makes no attempt to disguise it.

'Sonia; Michael,' says Julia perfunctorily. 'I'm so sorry, Sonia, we've got a bit of musical business to talk about, which you'd find very boring.'

The woman takes the hint and parts effusively: 'I really have to be off, anyway, Julia darling. Lovely to have bumped into you, and in a place like this. Rain really does force one into taking refuge wherever one can. We must have you and James over soon.' She smiles at me, more with her mouth than her eyes, and goes downstairs.

'Who was that?'

'Oh, the mother of a friend of Luke's,' says Julia. 'Bossy woman. Pesters the teachers to give her son a good part in the nativity play. Your hair's wet. Where have you been?'

'It's amazing,' I say, holding her hand tightly. 'I can hardly believe it. *Mohnstrudel! Guglhupf! Palatschinken!'*

'Mmm!' says Julia, her face lighting up at the thought of her favourite confections. 'Ouch! Let go my hand.'

'I've been talking to Piers.'

'Ah,' says Julia, raising her eyebrows.

'I can't believe it. I just can't believe it.'

'That was my reaction when I saw the fax from my agent yesterday.'

'How did you know I didn't know?'

'It was perfectly obvious. You couldn't have remained so cool for so long,' she says, laughing.

'And you could?'

'Well, didn't I succeed?' she says, looking radiant.

I am about to kiss her, then think better of it.

255

Who knows what Sonias are lurking around? 'I don't need a birthday present now,' I tell her.

'Well, I can see I'll have to choose one on my own.'

'Julia, Piers doesn't know about the hearing thing.'

'No,' says Julia, the radiance dimming. 'No. Of course not.'

'Does your agent know?' I ask.

'Yes. But he thinks it could be disastrous if it got to be common knowledge in the musical world. If I can manage to play well enough, what does it matter?'

'That's true,' I say. 'But how long can something like this be kept hidden?'

'I don't know,' says Julia.

'How have you managed?'

'It's an impossible effort,' she says. 'I don't know if I've succeeded completely. But if anyone suspects, it hasn't come back to haunt me so far.'

I nod, distracted. My earlier unease is now a far haze. It is a weird and jarring joy, this sensation of my two worlds coming together: rehearsals here in London, and then Vienna a decade on. Julia and my colleagues will play together, and I will be only an observer, an auditor. But I must attend these rehearsals. They will be filled with hazard for her. And apart from that, what would I not give to hear her bring the Trout to life?

4.19

But meanwhile, I have been invited to an evening out with Julia, the first time since we parted.

It is my birthday. James is not in town. We are in a restaurant not far from where she lives. It is spacious, with no music and good lighting. The walls are white, with variously shaped alcoves in deep green and indigo. White orchids in celadon vases are scattered here and there. She has made the reservation, though it is in my name. I arrive a little early, she a little late. She sees me, smiles, and looks quickly around the restaurant before sitting down.

'Would you rather sit here?' I ask. 'I mean, for the light?'

'I'm fine,' she says.

'There's no one here that you know, is there?' I ask.

'No. And if there is, I'm just having dinner with a friend.'

'You'll let me take you out, won't you, on your birthday?'

'Well—'

'I don't mean on your birthday exactly, but thereabouts.'

'Maybe,' says Julia, smiling, 'but you'll have to dress better if we're to go out again. You're good-looking, Michael—how do you manage to dress so horribly? Don't you have a decent suit?'

'I think I dress fine,' I protest. 'And I'm wearing your cuff-links.'

'It's that shirt—'

'Well, you haven't been here to train me. Anyway, there's no point in my dressing well. When there's a do while we're on tour, it's usually just before or just after a performance, and we have our standard penguin garb.'

'Michael,' says Julia, looking suddenly serious,

257

'tell me all about the others in the quartet.'

'But you know them.'

'Hardly. What are rehearsals with them like? I've been worrying about it these last few days. Give me a sense of what to expect.'

'Well, I don't know where to begin. Rehearsals are pretty intense. Piers tries to run a tight ship. Billy has his own ideas about things. Once he gets something into his head it's difficult to dislodge it. And Helen, well, she's a wonderful player, but she's quite distractable. By the way, you'll be happy to know that Billy's always late for everything, so you'll have company. Oh, and also, Billy prefers to rehearse than to perform, or so he says. Rehearsals let him explore, performances just make him nervous.

'But everyone's friendly with everyone else?' asks Julia.

'Yes, basically—at the moment.'

'That's a relief. It'll be complicated enough as it is.'

The waiter has been hovering; we order.

'Any vegetables?' he asks.

'What do you have?' asks Julia.

The waiter breathes deeply. Clearly we have not studied our menus with the respect they deserve. 'Broccoli, courgettes, beans, leeks, spinach,' he says.

'I'd like peas,' says Julia.

The waiter looks at her with obvious puzzlement. Julia, noticing this, looks anxious.

'I'm afraid, madam,' says the waiter, 'we do not have peas on the menu.'

A look of momentary bafflement passes over her face. 'I meant beans—French beans,' she says quickly.

He nods. 'And what would you like to drink? Have you seen the wine list? Or would you like to have a word with the sommelier?'

I quickly pick out something at random from the wine list.

Julia is upset by her slip and seems a bit defeated.

'We don't have to eat here, you know,' I say when he has disappeared.

'Oh, lets forget it,' she says. 'At the end of the day I sometimes run out of energy. Actually, I prefer beans. What's the matter?'

'Well, I don't like this fellow who's waiting on. He looks like an out-of-work actor who's trying to take it out on us.'

'Waiting on,' says Julia, amused.

This irritates me a bit. Julia, whose German never affected her English, was always pointing out little bits of dialect that occasionally surfaced in my speech.

'What are you thinking about?' asks Julia. 'You have a far-away look.'

'Nothing . . .' I say, reverting to what I was thinking about earlier. 'I wish *I* were playing the Trout with you.'

'It is amazing, isn't it,' she says, 'that Schubert isn't among the composers on the frieze of the Albert Memorial. I read that just the other day. It makes me want to take a chisel and carve his name in with the others.'

I laugh. 'Let's go and do it tonight,' I say.

'Is it worth getting arrested for?'

'Yes. James can bail us out.'

The moment I say it, I wish I hadn't. But to my

surprise the remark passes without shadowing her mood. Nor does she bring up the question of my meeting him. Untenable—untenable—how could she think we could meet? . . . How often do they sleep together? . . . Had they met before she went to Venice with Maria? . . . Why has she chosen to play with the Maggiore now? For Vienna? For the chance to play the glorious Trout? For me? . . . What is wrong with my conscience, that I can feel worried for her but not guilty?

Perhaps he has had to care so much for her these last three years that all that's left is tenderness. Perhaps the romance, if there ever was one, has waned. Is it his *life* with her I'm jealous of? She must wonder about me and other women, but she's never asked if there was anyone apart from Virginie these many years. Is that off-limits too, like why she married James: a reciprocal discretion between us?

Yes, she can read my lips, but no, not yet my thoughts. We talk of this and that. The wine comes, and the food. Around us is an unimpinging blur of conversation. Julia is not looking at my face. She seems preoccupied.

'Hearing is wasted on some people,' she says suddenly with a sharp flare of bitterness. 'A few days ago I was talking to a really hardboiled cellist from the Philharmonia, and it was obvious that he was utterly jaded by his work and bored with music—he almost seemed to hate it. And I gather he must have been a good musician. Perhaps he still is.'

'Well, there's a lot of that,' I say.

'I can understand a banker or a waiter hating his work, but not a musician.

260

'Oh, come on, Julia. Years of training, long hours, pathetic pay—and being no good for anything else—and having no choice in what you play—you could feel trapped, even if you loved it once. I felt like that a bit, when I was freelancing in London. Even now things aren't that easy. And, after all, you too gave up playing for a while. The only difference, I suppose, is that you could afford it.'

She frowns, then unknits her forehead. She says nothing, sipping her wine with determined serenity. My eyes move from her face to her little gold watch, and back again.

'That wasn't the only difference,' she says at last.

'I shouldn't have brought that up.'

'I can't imagine you hating music,' she says.

'No, I suppose not,' I reply. 'Actually, Helen teases me for waxing too rapturous about it. And she thinks my relationship with my violin's a bit over the top.'

'Well, I'm very attached to my piano.'

'But you can't lug it around with you on tour.'

'So?'

'Well, I don't think the relationship's the same if you practise on one instrument at home, and then go out and perform on another.'

Julia frowns.

'Not that Helen is such a pragmatic soul,' I quickly add. 'Last week she was quite upset by a programme she saw about the universe and how it could all run down in God knows how many billion years. Why get upset about where the universe is headed?'

'When there's so much to get upset about closer to hand?' asks Julia, amused again.

261

'Well, there is, isn't there?'

'By the way, what's happened to your Mrs Formby?' asks Julia out of the blue.

'Mrs Formby? Why Mrs Formby all of a sudden?'

'I don't know,' she replies.

'But you haven't even met her, Julia.'

'I don't know what made me ask about her. I was thinking of Carl—or maybe I was thinking about your violin—and then she came to mind. For some reason I've often thought about Mrs Formby these last few years.'

'More often than you've thought about me, I'm sure,' I remark flippantly.

'Michael, I thought of you as if you'd committed suicide—without leaving a note.'

She looks down at her plate. I am not permitted to respond. For a while I sit still, too stunned to do anything. I press my foot against hers, and she looks up.

'Mrs Formby is fine,' I say. 'How's your duck?'

'Delicious,' says Julia, who hasn't touched it for the last couple of minutes. 'Do you really not care about the universe—and all that?'

'Oh, no, you're not going to draw me into a religious argument,' I say warily.

'But you like reading Donne. 'Donne the Apostate', our nuns used to call him.'

'It doesn't mean anything, Julia. I like reading him precisely because I don't care about what's behind him. I find him relaxing late at night.'

'Relaxing!' says Julia, shocked.

'I like his language. I mull over his ideas. I don't care about his scriptural arguments . . . I can never understand why people make such a fuss about the

God thing,' I add brutally.

'You just can't stand authority, Michael, in any form,' says Julia. 'You hero-worship, but you can't stand authority. And God save your heroes if they turn out to have feet of clay.'

'For heaven's sake,' I say, annoyed by this analysis of my character—something Julia has always been prone to.

'My father wasn't himself towards the end,' she says. 'I remember praying that he'd die quickly. Every time we visited him he seemed to be more hostile, more unclear. At the end he didn't even care about Luke. At least he died before I lost my hearing. It would have made quite a good comic turn: he not understanding me, and I not understanding him.'

I put my hand across the table and rest it on her wrist. She seems pleased, but then withdraws her hand.

'Perhaps we should have dined somewhere else, further from home,' I say. 'I'll keep my hands to myself.'

'It's not that, Michael. It's too clear that we're not just friends.'

While our plates are removed, I try to change the subject. 'You mustn't worry about the rehearsal,' I say.

'You'll be there, won't you?' she asks.

'Of course.'

'Not that you need to be.'

'I'll be there because I want to hear you.'

'It's such an amazing part for the piano.'

'And for the violin,' I say regretfully.

'And the cello,' she adds. She hums a bit of the cello part from one of the variations.

263

The waiter enquires whether we would like coffee or dessert, but she continues to hum. He is standing behind her, and it is only when she notices me looking at him that she is aware that we are being addressed. She turns towards him, sees him poised to take her order, and says quickly: 'Yes, that's fine. Yes, that's what I'll have.'

An almost imperceptible ceilingward flick of the eyes is followed by emphatic patience. 'Which, madam?'

'Which? Oh, I'm sorry, could you repeat what you were saying?'

'Espresso, cappuccino, latte, filter; decaffeinated or regular,' he says, with exaggerated pauses between the words.

Julia colours, but says nothing.

'Well, madam?'

'Nothing, thank you.'

'And dessert? We have—'

'No, thank you. If you could just bring the bill.' Flustered, she pushes her chair back slightly.

'I'm sorry,' I say. 'I'm really sorry. I should have said something to him. He was rude.'

She shakes her head.

'He couldn't know what was going on,' she says. 'I should have told him that I have a hearing problem and asked him to repeat the order. That's the first thing we're taught: not to be embarrassed about it. Why do I find it impossible? Is it because I can't afford to let people in general know about me? Or is it that I'm just a coward?'

He brings the bill. She pays, leaving, I notice, a generous tip, and we get up to go. But she still seems ill at ease.

The evening is ending on an unhappy note. I ask

her to come to my place with me, knowing what her answer must be even before she tells me she must go home to Luke. But she consents at least to go to Julie's Bar, not far away. It is a clear, warm night, and we sit outside and allow our happiness in each other's company to flow through us again. We dawdle over coffee and liqueur, and share a dessert. Afterwards I thank her but do not kiss her. I walk her most of the way home but, at her request, not to her door.

4.20

'I didn't realise,' says Julia, 'that we'd be rehearsing without a bass player.'

Piers, Helen, Billy and Julia have gathered for their first rehearsal of Schubert's Trout Quintet. We have managed to secure a practice room with a reasonable piano at the Royal College of Music. I am, for this part, an onlooker, but a short rehearsal of our quartet is to follow.

If I had thought about it, I would have seen how the absence of the double-bass might affect Julia: its deep rhythmic pulse throughout the piece would have helped her immeasurably. If only I had warned her in advance, or done something about it.

'Well, the problem is that the bass player is in Vienna,' says Helen.

'Nothing to be done about it. We'll have a couple of rehearsals with her when we get there.'

'Her?' says Julia, a bit surprised.

'Yes. Petra Daut,' says Piers.

'I'm sorry, I didn't quite get her last name. How's it spelt?'

I remain silent, and let Piers reply. The fewer faces she has to look at the better.

'D, A, U, T. Do you know her? I mean, with your Viennese connections—'

'Not really,' says Julia. 'But then, I don't move in the orchestral world, so I'm a bit out of touch with bass players.'

'Shall we begin?' asks Piers.

'Piers,' says Julia. 'Before we begin, just a couple of things—'

'Yup?'

'We do have another rehearsal before we leave for Vienna, don't we?' she asks in a deliberately relaxed voice. 'I'd like us to—I'd really like us to have a bass player for it. I don't think we'll get the true feel of the piece without it.'

'Would you like us to provide a female bass player?' asks Helen. Billy looks up from his cello for a second.

Julia refuses to be drawn. 'I'm not particular,' she says.

Billy pipes up: 'I think we should practise with a bass as well. This is one of the few pieces where someone's supporting me from below, and I like that. I can ask Ben Flath if he'll rehearse with us.'

'Won't he mind rehearsing with us when he's not going to be playing in the concert?' asks Piers.

'He's a buddy,' says Billy. 'He'll do it to help out, and for the heck of it, and on condition that I don't outgrowl him in the Scherzo, and for a few drinks afterwards. A good few,' adds Billy.

'That sounds fine, Billy,' says Julia. 'Thank you, everyone.'

'I'm an extra in the Philharmonia tomorrow night, so I'll be meeting him,' continues Billy.

'Should I ask him if he's willing and when he'll be free?'

Everyone nods.

'Shall I turn the pages for you?' I ask Julia.

'That's all right, thanks, Michael, I'm not using the music, so it'll be distracting to have it up here. But would you keep my score on your lap and follow it so that if we stop in the middle of a movement, you can point out the place where we want to start from again?'

'You're sure you don't want the music?' I ask.

'Quite sure. I know it so well. I hope we're going to run through it without interruption the first time through. Let's plan to do that—if it's all right by everyone.'

Piers raises his eyebrows. Her statement is more than a request. We string players are used to communicating among ourselves while playing, and are happiest giving all the leads and cues, leaving anyone else to fend for themselves—especially if, as in this piece, the three strings form a curve with the pianist tucked almost invisibly behind.

'Well, all right, that's fine by us,' says Piers graciously enough, though I know he's not delighted to accept directions from an outsider.

I glance down at the score. I see lots of rests in the piano part, and am worried about Julia's re-entries. By going through without stopping at least the first time around, perhaps she can sense the rhythm better.

'Is this OK?' asks Piers, beating time: 'TUM-mmm-umtata-tatata-TUM?'

'Seems a bit slow to me,' says Billy. 'But what do you think, Julia? It's your phrase.'

'It's Allegro Vivace—so a bit more vivace,

267

perhaps?' says Julia, demonstrating what she wants on the piano by way of tempo.

Piers nods. 'Right. I'll give one upbeat. Ready?'

I look at Julia, my heart pounding. She appears relaxed, alert, her eyes on the other players, not on either the keyboard or the score. Now I see why it is so crucial for her to have learned the piece—and not just her own part—by heart.

While her fingers draw music from the keys, her eyes move from Piers to Billy with the alertness of someone reading from the page. Their fingers, their bows, their breaths give her her cues. At the beginning, where all the double-bass would have uttered would have been a low continuous undemarcated growl, this is what she would have had to do anyway. But elsewhere I can see how much harder she has to work in its absence. And the visual cues that she would have got from the fingers of the bass player . . . but it is pointless to speculate about all this, when I feel that I am on a tightrope over a chasm listening to a bird rising from below and singing high above me, higher and higher: an odd image for a piece named after a fish.

In her solo theme, she dots a couple of quavers that are often played undotted. I imagine this is a variant reading, but Helen looks up rather sharply.

'Repeat?' asks Julia as they approach the first point of decision.

'Straight on!' says Piers exultantly.

They get through the first movement. 'Get through', in fact, is unfair; they play it wonderfully. But I can hardly enjoy its beauty for my tension. At some places where I do not expect it, Julia takes the lead, so as not to be forced to follow intricate cues; at others, she looks down at her hands, and I cannot see at all how she manages to remain in sync with the others. When they get to the final twelve-note chord—eleven sans bass—that mirrors the twelve-note chord at the beginning of the movement, my left hand, resting on the score, is trembling.

'Should we skip all the repeats?' asks Piers.

'Except in the Scherzo,' says Billy.

After determining the tempo, they play the Adagio; there are a few problems, but not enough to make them grind to a halt. Then comes the third movement, the Scherzo, and a complete impasse.

The problem lies in the very first phrase. Piers and Helen have three presto quavers followed by a downbeat crotchet, on which everyone else crashes in.

They try it again and again, but it is never exactly co-ordinated. There is no point in rushing through as before. The problem needs to be resolved. Julia, I can tell, is getting more and more distraught, the others more and more puzzled. Since she has been playing so well before, the problem cannot be one of musical ability.

'It's always difficult to play with a new group the first time,' says Billy.

'Let's take a five-minute break,' suggests Piers. 'I need a cigarette.'

'Is it OK to smoke in here?' asks Billy.

'Why not? Oh well, perhaps I'd better go outside.'

'I'm going to stretch my legs,' says Helen in a somewhat preoccupied manner. 'Coming?'

'Sure,' says Billy. 'Good idea. Sure.'

'I'll hang around here,' I say.

Julia says nothing. She seems to have sunk into a

world of her own, to be remote from me, from all of us.

My own anxieties melt away. Left to ourselves, I say: 'Are you wearing a hearing aid?'

'Yes; in one ear. It did help at the beginning, but it began to get to me, Michael, the way it distorted the pitch. I couldn't adjust it without giving myself away, so I just turned it off after the first movement. Then in the second movement I found I wasn't coping too well, so when I came to a rest I turned it on again. Now it's got me completely confused. I'm sure, if there was a double-bass . . .'

'That won't solve the problem at the beginning of the Scherzo,' I say quietly. 'Or wherever that phrase occurs.'

'That's true. Perhaps I'll just have to come clean . . .'

'Don't do that for the moment. Don't even think about it. It won't help with this, and it'll open up a whole new can of worms. Just relax.'

Julia smiles, but sadly. 'That's like saying, "Don't think of a giraffe." It's guaranteed to have the opposite effect.'

'And you mustn't mind Helen.'

'I don't.'

'Look, Julia, if you're getting your cues from the tempo and the upbeat—that is, visual cues—maybe you should simply take out your hearing aid. I don't see how you have time to react to the sound anyway, especially if it's distorted.'

'Maybe.' Julia sounds completely unconvinced by this advice from someone who cannot begin to understand what she can and can't hear.

I kiss her. 'Here. Try it with me. You've nothing to lose.' I take out my violin, tighten the bow

270

quickly and, without bothering to tune up properly, give her the beat, nod my head a couple of times and play the first phrase.

After a few tries it works—or at least works much better than it has so far.

Julia does not smile. She simply says: 'Any other suggestions?'

'Yes. In the Andante, where everyone else is playing six notes per bar and you're playing three notes for every one of theirs, you're slowing things down quite a bit. Everyone else was trying to push it along, but for once, you weren't following them with your eyes.'

'Well, I was leading,' says Julia.

'From behind.' I laugh, and she laughs too. 'Here, try it with me,' I suggest, taking up the bow again; and we do.

'That's good,' says Piers.

I jump, and then Julia too is startled. I didn't notice him coming back in.

'Just carry on,' says Piers.

'Left your lighter behind?' I ask, annoyed.

'Something like that,' says Piers evenly as he goes out.

The rehearsal continues when everyone returns. They play straight through the Scherzo without crisis, and follow through with the fourth and fifth movements.

At the end, Piers says: 'That was good, that was good. But somehow, you know, I think I'd prefer to keep the detailed work for a rehearsal with a bass player. So let's call it a day with the Trout. I hope you don't mind, Julia. The quartet needs to go through a couple of pieces now, and we're a bit pressed for time. When Billy gets some dates from

271

Ben Flath—assuming he's willing in the first place—I'll be in touch with everyone about the next rehearsal. I don't think I have your phone number,' he says, turning to Julia.

'Could you fax me?' asks Julia. 'The phone ruins my concentration when I'm practising—which is much of the time these days.'

'Don't you have an answering machine?' asks Piers.

'A fax would be better,' says Julia with a calm nod, and she gives him her number.

4.21

Piers lives on Westbourne Park Road, at the edges of gentrification, in a basement flat consisting of a single room. The ceiling is high for a basement—which, given Piers's own height, is a good thing. Above him is a travel agent which advertises for the most part cheap tours to Portugal; on one side of the travel agent is a take-away pizza place, on the other a newsagent. Opposite is a massive tower block, and close by is a brown-bricked housing estate.

Having asked me over for a drink, he now opens a bottle of red wine. He is hospitable, but looks troubled. It is the day after the rehearsal.

'You get a bit of late light on that wall in the summer,' he says.

'Aren't we facing north?' I ask.

'Sort of,' says Piers absently. 'I bought this from an artist.' Then, following my train of thought he adds: 'You're right, it's a bit odd. It comes from that direction for a few minutes at sunset in high summer. Maybe it's reflected off something. Lovely reddish patch. Last year the newsagent chained a huge metal bin to the railings, and that's reduced it. It's annoying.'

'Why don't you talk to him?'

'I have. He says that people have started stealing the newspapers and magazines deposited outside his door, and he's had no choice but to do what he's done. I'm sure I should follow it up, ask him at least to move it outside my line of light, but . . .' Piers shrugs. 'You know what I want to talk to you about?'

'No, I thought this was just a date! . . . Yes, I do. I'm pretty sure I do.'

Piers nods. 'Tell me, I don't understand it. What exactly is the matter with Julia? She's a wonderful player, she's so, well, musical in her playing; you know what I mean. It's a real pleasure to play with her, but we're all puzzled . . . We're not freaked out or anything, but, well, can you explain that problem with the opening of the Scherzo? Is it just a tic that happens sometimes?'

I take a sip of my wine. 'It got solved, didn't it?'

'Yes,' says Piers warily.

'I guarantee that when Ben Flath joins us, most of the other problems will disappear.'

'Us?' says Piers with a smile.

'You, to be exact.'

Perhaps Piers notices the tinge of regret. At any rate, I am floored by his next remark.

'I want you to play the violin in the Trout.'

'No!'

The word escapes from me involuntarily, but it patently means 'Yes!'

Piers is tapping a slim silver lighter with the

273

index finger of his right hand. 'I meant that,' he says.

'But you love it, Piers,' I exclaim, recalling what took place when Nicholas Spare maligned the Trout.

'What exactly happened in the interval?' asks Piers, thus avoiding a response.

'The interval?'

'Well, you know, when we went out of the room.'

I shrug. 'Oh, we just played a little, tried out some of the difficult bits with a slightly different approach . . .'

'There was something there,' says Piers quietly. After a while he says: 'Look, don't mind my asking you this, but—'

'Ask away.'

'You're not worried that you won't be able to do it? Don't get me wrong. What I mean is, you know, playing in the register you usually do . . .'

'Do you mean, can I handle the squeal variation in the fourth movement?'

Piers nods, a bit embarrassed. 'Yes, that, and other bits too. It's so exposed.'

'I'll manage,' I say, unoffended. 'I've played it before—at college. It was ages ago, but it should come back to me. But look, Piers, I know you'd love to play the Trout. Are you sure you want to be so generous?'

'I'm not being generous,' says Piers in rather a prickly tone. 'It's a piece that tends to be done brilliantly or to fall completely flat. And the real interplay is between the violin and the piano. At the moment, I may as well tell you, it'll be a relief not to do it. I've got a lot on my plate—too much. And I assume that if the *Musikverein* can accept

274

one change of player, they can accept two.'

'What precisely do you have on your plate?' I ask with a smile.

'Oh,' says Piers vaguely, 'this and that.'

'And the other?' I say without thinking.

'What?'

'Sorry—sorry—just something that came into my head. An automatic response. Forget it.'

'You're a strange fellow, Michael.'

'Well?'

'Well, what?'

'What else do you have on your plate?'

'I'm doing the Sinfonia Concertante with St Martin-in-the-Fields, and I've got a solo concert coming up just after Vienna, and there's this Bach thing, which you and the others seem to be determined on.'

'And you're not?'

Piers spreads his hands. 'I'm only just beginning to feel as if it hasn't been foisted on me. Last night, for some reason, I was practising it at two in the morning. It's peculiarly addictive.'

'Your neighbours would probably choose another word.'

'What neighbours?' says Piers with a slightly twisted smile. 'I don't have neighbours in this burrow. That's a travel agency above our heads.'

'Yes, of course.'

'At any rate,' says Piers, 'it's not the first time—as you know—that I've felt at odds with my colleagues, or partners, or cohorts or whatever you are. There must be a word for it.'

'Co-quarts?'

Piers continues, not so much unamused by my remark as oblivious to it: 'It's the weirdest thing, a

275

quartet. I don't know what to compare it to. A marriage? a firm? a platoon under fire? a self-regarding, self-destructive priesthood? It has so many different tensions mixed in with its pleasures.'

I pour both of us some more wine from his bottle.

'I don't think I really knew what pain was involved in all this,' he says, half to himself. 'First Alex; then that whole thing with Tobias. Every few years something shattering happens—and is bound to happen.'

'Alex was before my time,' I say, trying to avoid discussing what affected all four of us when Tobias was in charge of Piers's soul.

'The one good thing about that monster of a tower block is the morning light that reflects off it from about eleven o'clock,' says Piers. 'This place would be even dingier without it.'

I nod, and say nothing.

'It was the light in Venice, you know,' says Piers, almost to himself. 'We spent a month there. At first it gave him dreadful headaches, then they suddenly stopped and he began to love it. It was just a few days afterwards that we had our great idea of forming the quartet. Alex had it, actually.' He looks down at the lighter again, then says, as if impatient with himself, 'Why am I going on about that?'

'I wonder if the Maggiore will continue even when we've all disappeared one by one,' I say. 'After we're grizzled and distinguished, of course.'

'I hope so,' says Piers. 'A dozen years isn't all that long in the life of a quartet, I suppose, though it sometimes feels like a century. Well, the Takacs has two new members, the Borodin's only got its

276

original cello left, the Juilliard's got none of its original members. But they're still what they are.'

'Like George Washington's hatchet?' I suggest.

Piers frowns, waiting for an explanation.

'It's changed its head twice and its handle three times, but it's still his hatchet.'

'Ah, yes, I see . . . Oh, and another thing: you remember about the Beethoven quintet, and your wanting to play first violin?'

'It's not likely I'd have forgotten, is it?' I say guardedly.

'I suppose not. Well, I've been considering things. Or, rather, reconsidering them. I don't want the kind of tensions that arose when Alex and I alternated between being first and second violin.'

'No. I agree.'

'But you might find being second violin all the time a bit oppressive. Or frustrating.' Piers takes a sip and glances at me, making this into a question.

'I don't, actually,' I say, wondering if I truly believe it. 'It's, well, it's a different instrument from the first. It's a sort of chameleon, shifting from tune to accompaniment and back again. It's more—well, I find it interesting.' I suppose, after all, I do believe it on the whole.

'But you did want to play first fiddle in that string quintet?' presses Piers.

'That was for a particular reason, Piers, and I told you so. That quintet means something quite specific to me.'

'Well,' says Piers, 'my question is simply this: would you consider, would you want to, would you mind playing first violin or the only violin when we don't play strictly as a quartet?' Noticing my look of surprise, he continues: 'For instance, in a string

277

sextet or a flute quartet or a clarinet quintet or something of that nature.'

'Piers,' I say, quite astonished, 'this wine is going to your head. Or have you been seeing a shrink?'

'Neither, I assure you,' says Piers a bit coldly.

'Well, I certainly wouldn't mind, and I could consider it, but I'm not sure I want to.'

'That's rather a complicated answer, and a bit contradictory.'

'I'm sure it is. What I mean is this—and it's something you touched on yourself. It's not just for the two of us to decide this sort of thing. Billy and Helen won't like it. They felt unsettled by you and Alex alternating. And in anything like a string quintet or a string sextet it's bound to have the same effect on them.'

'And in something like a flute quartet? Or a piano quintet—like the Trout?'

'It might be a bit different, you're right. Well, I'll consider it, and—no, actually, I won't consider it. I'm happy where I am.'

'So you won't do the Trout?'

'I will!' I say quickly.

'Why? Another specific association?'

'No, it's more ad hoc than that. I want to play with Julia. It may be one of the last times she—'

'She what?'

'She plays with other players.'

'What precisely do you mean?' Piers is looking at me carefully, with all his forensic feelers out. 'Does she really have serious problems playing with others?'

'No, not really.'

'Michael, I don't think you're being completely straight with me.'

278

'I am. I'm just telling you that she wants to develop her solo career. And that means gradually cutting down on ensemble playing. But I don't know exactly when she's going to decide to stop. I don't even really know whether she's going to.'

'So she doesn't enjoy playing chamber music?' says Piers.

'I didn't mean that,' I say heatedly.

'Well, what did you mean? What is the matter with her exactly? What happened at the rehearsal? I mean, does her concentration lapse suddenly? Is it a problem with that particular piece? Or is it your, well, your friendship? You must know. Or you must at least have an idea.'

I try to evade this nervous and aggressive salvo. 'I don't know, Piers,' I say. 'Anyway, in the future it won't be a problem.'

'But it is a problem,' says Piers. 'I'm beginning to wish I had managed to get in touch with you before we agreed to her playing with us. You obviously know something that the rest of us don't. We're in a quartet. It's based on trust. Now what is it? Spit it out.'

I am cornered. I have lied under compulsion, but I have lied, and Piers knows it. 'I can't tell you until I speak to Julia,' I say at last.

Piers fixes me with an inquisitorial stare. 'Michael, I haven't the least fucking idea what it is, but I do know it's got me worried. And it's obviously got you worried. Now, whatever it is, you've got to tell me—and you've got to tell me now.'

'It's a hearing problem,' I say, almost inaudibly, looking at the floor.

'A hearing problem? What sort of hearing

problem?'

I don't say anything. I am overcome by what I have been compelled to divulge. But wasn't it I who opened the crack that let him prise the matter out?

'Well?' says Piers. 'Let's have it, Michael. Or I'll phone Lothar right now and find out from him. I'm serious. I'm going to phone him right now.'

'She's going deaf, Piers,' I say helplessly. 'But for God's sake don't tell anyone.'

'Oh, is that all?' says Piers. His face has lost all colour.

'Yes, that's all.' I am shaking my head from side to side.

Piers may be perplexed but I know he believes me. 'This is true, isn't it? Yes or no. Just one word.'

'Yes.

'We'd better phone Lothar,' he says quietly. 'This is a disaster.'

He half gets up. I grab his arm and almost force him to sit down.

'Don't,' I say, looking him in the eye. 'Don't even think of it. It is not a disaster.'

'Does Billy know? Does Helen?'

'Of course not. I haven't told them. I should never have told you.'

'You should have told us before,' says Piers with a touch of contempt in his voice. 'How could you have kept this from us? You owe it to us—and to yourself.'

'Don't tell me what I owe you,' I say fiercely. 'I've broken a confidence by saying what I've said. God knows I might never be forgiven for it. I never meant to tell you. I only hope it'll help her in some way—I mean, if all of us understand what cues we need to give her, and where to let her lead—'

'So we're to stumble along, are we?'

'She'll give a great performance. She will stun you and the good burghers of Vienna, and Billy will call on the spirit of Schubert to bless us, every one.

'Including me, the silent observer?'

'Including you, since he'll know what you've sacrificed.'

'It doesn't seem much of a sacrifice now,' says Piers wryly.

'You'll see it is,' I say fervently.

I am waiting for him to say something cutting about Julia but he surprises me.

'Well, I hope so,' he says. 'For our sake and for the spirit of Schubert.' He muses for a few seconds in an almost unsettlingly calm manner. 'Perhaps I was annoyed by Nicholas's remarks because I have mixed feelings about the Trout. It's a funny old piece. It stops and starts and has so many repeats and, you're right, its last movement sometimes feels as if it's just been tacked on—which it has— but I truly love it. It seems absurd that he was twenty-two.'

'We may as well just give up,' I say.

After another longish pause, Piers says: 'Well, yes, that's what I thought for a long time. But now I've stopped thinking that anything short of creating a masterpiece is pointless. I just ask myself two questions about what I'm doing here in my niche in the galaxy. Is it better done or not? And is it better that I do this than something else?' He pauses, then says: 'And I suppose I've just added another one: is it better that someone else does this than me?'

'I see, Piers. Thank you for that. From the bottom of my heart.'

Piers raises his glass rather seriously. 'And from the bottom of your glass?'

I nod, and toast him gravely.

'I suppose you're surprised I haven't said how sorry I am for Julia.'

'No, I'm not surprised,' I reply, after considering the matter for a moment.

But I am surprised at myself, that I should so suddenly have broken faith with her, that I should have, even if without premeditation, almost conspired by my responses to disburden myself— and her, I keep telling myself, hoping it is true—of the weight of this secret. But unpermitted, unlicensed, how could I have done it? I make Piers promise that he won't tell Helen and Billy on condition that I do so myself tomorrow.

4.22

I fax her as soon as I get back home. No facetious parody of bureaucratic style this time, just the bare statement that as a matter of urgency we must meet tomorrow morning. Even if she can only spare ten minutes, she must come over to my flat.

She does. I presume she has just dropped Luke off at school. This time when we kiss, she knows something is wrong, because she stops suddenly to ask what's worrying me. She has an hour to spare, but suggests we get the ten minutes of urgency over with at once.

'Julia, he knows. I had to tell him.'

She looks at me with something akin to terror.

'I told him last night—I couldn't get out of it. I'm so sorry.'

'But I was with him last night,' says Julia.

'With whom?'

'With James.'

'No, no—I meant Piers. He sensed something was up.'

'But—what are you talking about, Michael? If Piers knows, does that matter so very much? What's the urgency?' She begins to relax, though she is still puzzled.

'I have to tell Billy and Helen today. That's why I had to talk to you first,' I say.

'But, Michael—I don't understand—what exactly did you tell him?'

'Well, about you, your problem.'

She closes her eyes in all too evident shock.

'Julia, I don't know what I can say—'

But her eyes are still closed. I hold her hand and put it to my forehead. After a while she opens her eyes—but now she is not looking at me but at something through and beyond me. I wait for her to speak.

'Couldn't you have talked to me about it beforehand?' she says at last.

'I couldn't. He asked me point blank. It was a question of trust.'

'Of trust? Of trust?'

'I couldn't look at him and keep lying.'

'What do you think I have to do at home about you? It doesn't come easily to me. It's just that the alternative's worse.'

I explain what happened and how it happened. I tell her that it could possibly even help—if it results in cues, sympathy, assistance. I know all this is pathetically self-exculpatory.

'Perhaps,' says Julia quietly. 'But in the long run,

why would anyone who knows this take me on?'

Her question is unanswerable.

'I've harmed you,' I say. 'I know it. I'm so sorry.'

'I'm not foolish, Michael,' she says after a few moments. 'It had to get around sometime. My father used to talk about the academic world being leaky, but the musical world is worse. Maybe some people apart from Lothar know or suspect already. I've given myself a reputation for eccentricity, just to disguise things somewhat. But all that's pointless now.

'I'll swear them to secrecy.'

'Yes,' she says in a tired voice. 'Yes. Do that. I must go now.'

If no one wants to perform with her, I will have hastened what I most feared. How do I tell her now that I'm playing with her in the Trout? This cannot be the time. But if not now, when?

'Stay a little longer. Let me talk to you, Julia.'

'And the bass player—Billy's friend?' she says.

'I don't know.'

'I must go.'

'What are you going to do?' I ask.

'I don't know. Take a walk.'

'In the park?'

'I suppose so.'

'You don't want me to come with you?'

She shakes her head. She does not even wait for the lift this time, but begins to walk down the many flights of stairs.

4.23

Helen, Billy and I meet in a cafe nearby. Helen has

284

builders in, and I don't suggest we meet in my flat, which, for the moment, is haunted by this last encounter. I have decided to tell both of them together. I apologise to Billy for the place and the suddenness of the meeting, but he says he was coming into town anyway. To tell them separately would have been unbearable: I just want to get it over with.

As soon as our coffee arrives I say what I have to say. At first, neither can believe it. Helen looks almost guilty. Billy questions me closely about the practical music-making side of it. I tell them I have told Piers, but that no one else must know. Helen nods. Her shock and sympathy are obvious. Billy says he'll tell Lydia but no one else.

'Please, Billy,' I say. 'Not even Lydia.'

'But there are no secrets between us,' he says, adding blandly, 'That's what marriage is about.'

'Jesus, Billy, I don't want to know what marriage is about. This is not a secret between you. I'm trusting you with her musical life. Don't you think Lydia would understand?'

Billy says nothing but looks astonished.

'And the bass player, your friend Ben—'

'It'll be impossible to keep it hidden from him,' says Billy, recovering to address the matter at hand. 'He's smart. It's not so much how Julia plays as the way all of us are likely to behave. Leave him to me. And no, I won't tell Lydia. I'll try to avoid it anyway.'

'Of all concerts it had to be this one,' says Helen. 'And the *Musikverein* of all places. What should we do? What can we do? It's not that I don't feel desperately sorry for her.'

Billy says, 'Well, there are only four choices. We

285

can withdraw from the concert. We can try to find someone else immediately. We can just go ahead with her and not tell anybody. Or we can cut out the Trout and try doing something else with the hall's permission. I myself think we should have another rehearsal and see how it goes. It went well enough the last time except for that funny glitch in the Scherzo. Still, that's certainly a mystery cleared up. What does Piers think?'

'Piers isn't playing in the Trout,' I say. 'I am.'

Helen and Billy both stare at me in stupefaction.

'And I say we should go ahead,' I continue. 'In fact, we must go ahead. I have an incredible feeling about this. It'll be a superb performance. Believe me, we'll astound the Viennese. I know that nothing at all will go wrong on the night.'

4.24

I fax Julia the news about the Trout. This is the only way to tell her before the rehearsal. There is no time to arrange a meeting, even if she still wants to meet me. I receive no answering fax.

We meet at the rehearsal. I have been practising for days and have the external calm of someone numb with nervousness. She nods at me with no singular warmth. Perhaps she is trying to place an equal, a balanced distance between herself and each of us. Ben Flath—presumably on Billy's advice—has turned his double-bass slightly towards the piano, so that she can get a better sense of the movement of his hands. The profound pulse of the bass helps enormously. So too do the exaggerated upbeats of Billy's head, and his open string gestures,

286

which he now feels entirely justified in making. All this visual drama will have to be toned down when we rehearse in Vienna, but it helps us here.

To play with her, indeed, just to play the Trout, which I have only played once before—and that in Manchester, years ago—is the fulfilment of an unsensed expectation. Yet for all the happiness of the piece, there is something in our playing that is tense and strange. Where we work on it in huge arcs, there are fewer problems. Where we work on it almost bar by bar, Piers, as the looker-on, with tact and analysis and very little by way of exaggerated mouthings and pointings, helps to explain what she might not have caught through that residue of sound which still beats against her nerves.

At first it surprises me that Piers is sitting through this rehearsal. After all, he has just abdicated his part in this piece. But he is acting not as a control freak but a sort of outside adviser in a situation unprecedented both for our quartet and for Julia—one of clear mutual knowledge of this physical deficit.

For all her coolness towards me, by the end of the rehearsal I feel that we have withdrawn from a precipice.

But when Piers says, 'I think you should all have another rehearsal before Vienna,' everyone nods, including the obliging Ben Flath.

4.25

Once more we meet. This time it works out fine. The thrum of the bass is well bound to her pulse.

But as soon as we have played, she leaves, with just one word or two to me—no more than she says to all the rest.

I do not know what to fear in all this. Has her trust shrunk or does she need time on her own to grasp this piece? I have not heard from her for days. The bell does not ring; she does not write. It eats through the calm that I had gained. I think of her all the time.

These nights are cool, these days are bright with spring. The low green on the trees has spread right to their tops, and in the park the wide, clear sight that I so much loved of lake and low knoll through nets of bare twigs has been leafed out and curbed. The world is in bloom, and if I am irked or sad it is due to the sense, more strained with the drift of each day, that it is not mine to share. In a few days it will be May, and we will all be on that plane.

At last she sends a note: will I come to lunch in two days' time? It suits James: the end of the week, the day of rest, a brief snooze for stocks and shares. But she does say that she has missed me. Lunch makes sense, as Luke will not have gone to sleep, and he would like to meet me too. They all send their best.

These are her first real words, yet what do they mean? Why must I meet him now? Why take this risk—could this be what she wants? Need I be bound and lashed for what I've done? I don't know James, yet they all send their best. What then have I to say?

All of them: man, wife, child, dog. From my high lair I view the world. I will say yes, of course; and try to feign, as best I can, the calm I do not feel. Those whom she loves must not be hurt. But I know I am no good at this: if I had my way I would not go at all. I would find some means, some sleight of time or work to put things off. But I have not seen her for so long. If it is a risk, it is one that has been made for me, one on which my grasp, like it or not, has closed. I write back, ill at ease, to say I will be pleased to come.

4.26

I have an ache that pulses behind my left eye. The bells ring, the one from the church near me tolling G. It is the day of my lunch at Julia's. I shave with care. These eyes are full of doubt.

What does James Hansen know? How much would she have told him, for her sake, for his? She was bitter about our parting in Vienna all those years ago. If there was no solution, no resolution, to all that her heart had to bear, would she have spoken of it? Would she have spoken of it to him, with all he may have felt of not being the first one chosen—or the first of choice?

But why should he know about our past? I am one of her musical friends, no more; a colleague from long ago, from the city where he met her. She would not tell me of his courtship, whether they went to Mnozil's together, or Lier's, or Café Museum, whether these zones, intimate to us, admitted an intruder, or whether these were places she most particularly shunned. Why should she have told him of me, of our meetings in grey rooms, of our parting at a table under chestnut trees?

What secrets survive nine years of marriage, or

nine times that time? What if James and I dislike each other, what then? What if I like him?

It was he who got her to play again, for which anyone who has heard her will thank him. I thank him. I cannot wish to meet him. Does she not sense any danger?

Why does she want me to meet her there? Her first, long letter talked of windows, pianos, gardens: she knew my style and space; should I not know hers? But why unify disparate existences: her life with me, her life with him? Or will my coming assuage our guilt? Or head off doubts when Luke speaks of me? Or does she know it cannot work between us? Am I myself one of those letters, to be left intentionally-unintentionally in view, so that things can, unstated, be understood?

Can I not be ill? But not to see her then?—to smell that light scent she wears, or dredge the memory of that darker musk. She says she misses me. It must be true. I walk along the white-housed squares and streets that lead me to her home.

4.27

He opens the door, not she.

'Hello, I'm James. You're Michael?' He shakes my hand, smiles easily.

I nod. 'Yes. Pleased to meet you.'

He is shorter than I am, and broader. Clean-shaven, blue-eyed like her, pale-haired. Luke's dark hair must be a throwback. His accent is Bostonian, unconcerned to anglicise itself.

'Come in. Julia's in the kitchen. Luke's out in the garden. He tells me you've met him.'

290

'Yes.'

'Well, he wants to ask you a few riddles . . . Are you all right?'

'It's just a bit of a headache. It'll go away.'

'Tylenol? Nurofen? Paracetamol?'

'No, thanks.' I follow him into the drawing room.

'Well, what will you have to drink? Don't say you're going to have orange juice. A glass of wine? A martini? I'll mix one that'll get rid of your headache just like that.'

'Why not a martini then?'

'Good. I like them, but Julia doesn't. Nor do any of her friends. Nor does anyone in this country.'

'Why did you offer me one?'

'I never give up hope of finding someone who does. Have you been to the States?'

'Yes. On tour.'

'And you're taking Julia off to Vienna in a week.'

'I am. We are.'

'Good. She needs a break.'

'Well, it's not exactly a break,' I say, feeling—and struggling not to express—a strange sense of outrage at this remark. 'It's a lot of work for her. It would be for anyone. But with her deafness—'

'Yes,' is all he comes up with. He busies himself fixing my drink. Then, after a pause, 'She is amazing.'

'We all think so.'

'How's her playing?'

'More beautiful than it was even then.'

'Even when?'

'Even in Vienna,' I say, looking out of the bay window of the drawing room at a leafless plane tree that doesn't seem to have woken up to the fact that it's April.

'Of course,' says James Hansen. 'Now, this is stirred, not shaken. I'm not very particular, I'm afraid.'

'Nor am I,' I say, taking the drink. 'That's the advantage of not being much of an expert. For me the excitement lies in the olive.' What am I blathering on about? My eye falls on a wedding photograph, a picture of Julia's father holding (I suppose) the infant Luke. Photographs, paintings, books, carpets, curtains, cushions—a populated room, a life as solid as a rock.

James Hansen laughs. 'Now that's interesting,' he says. 'I can see why expertise pays off in banking. But in the arts it could be a disadvantage. If you don't have any sense of discrimination, you enjoy many more things.'

'You don't really believe that,' I say.

'No, I don't,' he says evenly.

Is this the man who is married to Julia? Is it this man who sleeps with her every night? What am I doing exchanging pleasantries with him?

'Well,' he says, 'should we wait till Julia comes up, or should we go and see what she's doing? Caroline—that's our help—has the day off, so Julia decided to make some sort of casserole, which usually means she doesn't have to hang around the kitchen. But maybe she didn't hear the doorbell.'

The kitchen is in the basement, as seen from the street, but it opens out onto the garden. Luke is just rushing in, and Julia is turning a knob on the oven when, clutching our glasses, we get to the foot of the stairs.

'Luke!'

'Dad! Buzby's been chasing Mrs Newton's cat, and she's . . . Oh, hi!'

292

'Hello, Luke . . . Hello, Julia,' I say, for Julia has turned and is smiling at us all.

I have never seen Julia the hausfrau before. Son; husband; a huge, heavy stove; a glimpse of cream-coloured camellias from the garden; copper pots hanging from the ceiling; apron; ladle. I am disturbed by this radiance.

'Where's Buzby?' I ask Luke, feeling a sudden, shocked vacancy in my mind.

'In the garden, of course,' says Luke.

'Well, it's ready,' says Julia. 'But before we eat, let me take Michael on a tour of the garden. Would you lay the table, darling?'

She unties her apron, opens the door, and leads me into the little private plot that precedes the undivided crescent garden. We are alone.

She talks of her plants for a while: tulips, red and gold, some already blown; rich brown-and-yellow wallflowers; a few pansies, maroon and purple, still soldiering on; and, oh, of course, these astonishing tardy camellias.

He, then, is 'darling'. I am a guest: suffered or honoured, it makes little odds. My hostess is the exquisite Julia . . . Julia and James, a delightful couple . . . made for each other, yes, even their monograms match . . . a charming addition to our little community here—though he's American, as you probably know.

Julia follows my gaze to the old wistaria against the wall, its clusters in every stage of life from emergence to fulness to decay, bees busying themselves around. How much of a garden is its sound, dead to the deaf?—our footsteps on the gravel, the plop of water from that small fountain, birdsong and bee-buzz? How much of a conversation must be read in the eyes?

'I never really met them,' Julia is saying. 'James came over and arranged all that; I was going through a hard patch. It was a family who'd lived here for twenty years.'

I nod. I do not trust myself to speak. I feel half insane. Twenty years. Let us measure it in stacks of photographs, in school fees, in shared meals, in the mellow delights of the connubial bed, in hard times shared, in the gnarledness of wistaria. Let us measure it in trust, too heavy to weigh an ounce.

'That lemony-jasmine fragrance that's so dizzying comes from these little white blossoms here. You'd hardly think it, would you?'

'Oh, I thought it was you.'

Julia blushes. 'Aren't they lovely?' she asks, pointing now at the cream-coloured camellias. 'They're called Jury's Yellow.'

'Yes,' I say. 'Delectable.'

She frowns. 'The thing about camellias, you know, is that when they're about to die, they won't tell you in time. If they lack water, they don't look unhappy for a while, and show you they're suffering; they just die.'

'Why have you got me here? Why?'

'But, Michael—'

'I'm going crazy. Why did I have to meet him? Couldn't you see what would happen?'

'Why did you accept if you feel this way?'

'How else could I see you?'

'Michael, please—please don't make a scene. Don't let me down again.'

'Again?'

'James is walking towards us . . . Please, Michael.'

'Lunch is on the table, sweetie,' says James Hansen, walking up. 'Sorry to cut the tour short, but I'm starving.'

Lunch passes in a blur. What do we talk about? That they don't usually have more than a couple of guests because it's difficult to follow a conversation. That celery has been banished because Julia can't hear anyone when she or they are crunching it. The hailstorm two weeks ago. Luke's music lessons. His least favourite subject at school. The state of Britain and the state of the States. The difference between American and German Steinways. Something about banking practices: I can't even remember what my question was, or why, having no interest in the matter, I asked it. Yes, lamb casserole. Yes, delicious. Oh, project finance? Couscous—my favourite, yes.

Her husband is a perceptive man, a man of wit and substance, not my presumed image of an East Coast banker. I cannot see how he cannot see; but would he be so calm and *friendly* if he could? Rice pudding, bespattered with raisins. Mother bear, father bear and baby bear all attend to their porridge. I feel numb hatred for this decent man.

'Gran will be coming in a week. She makes an even better rice pudding,' says Luke. 'She puts in even more raisins.'

'Oh, does she!' says Julia.

'I thought she was going to be in Vienna for our concert,' I say.

Luke starts to laugh. 'That's Oma,' he says, 'not Gran.'

What am I doing here? Is this not rash? Or was her true rashness then, when she came to the green room of the Wigmore? Am I a sort of algae on this rock?

'I understand you're all flying out together,' says James.

'Well, on the same plane,' I reply. 'Our agent managed to get a sixth ticket after there was a cancellation.'

'Does he accompany you on all your tours?'

'She—no, she doesn't.'

'It's a great hall you'll be playing in,' says James. 'Julia says it's got the best acoustics in the world. We've been there several times. It sounded pretty good to me.'

I say nothing.

'We'll be playing in the smaller hall, darling, the Brahms-Saal,' says Julia to her husband. 'I don't think we've ever been there for a concert.'

'So who's the sixth ticket for?' asks James.

'Billy's cello,' I say. How admirably level I keep my voice.

'You mean, it sits there with all the passengers?'

'Yes.

'And gets fed caviare?'

Julia laughs. Luke joins uncertainly in. 'Not in economy class,' I say.

No, Julia, I have not made a scene. But why am I here? Is it to boil my heart for what I did? I am not far from hating you in this.

'Does it put on a seat-belt for take-off ?' asks Luke.

'Yes, I think it does . . . You know, I'm sorry, but I must go.'

'But you haven't seen the rest of the house,' says Julia. 'You haven't seen my music room—'

'And I haven't asked my riddles.'

'I'm sorry, Luke, really sorry. Next time.

Wonderful meal. Thank you very much for having me over.'

'Finish your coffee at least,' says James with a smile.

I do. For all I know it could be bleach.

'Well, it's been a pleasure,' he says at last. He turns away from her to add: 'That's not the case with all of Julia's friends. Rather rude of me, I suppose, to say so. Well, I hope we meet again soon.'

'Yes . . . yes . . .'

As we approach the door, the doorbell rings, a longish insistent buzz—a chord of two notes, one high, one low. Julia does seem to notice it.

'We're not expecting anyone, are we?' asks James.

An overdressed woman and a small boy stand on the doorstep.

' . . . just driving past, and he insisted, and of course since we were so close anyway it seemed pointless to call you on the mobile, and they say that it's so dangerous to use them in the car anyway . . . oh, hello,' she says, looking at me.

'Hello,' I say. She looks familiar, but I cannot concentrate on anything the way things are pulsing behind my eyes.

The crescent curves across a busy road. Who can travel both at once? It is unravelling, things are flowering too late, or too early, and the bank has stepped in and taken possession. Luke will count twenty years, forty, sixty in rice-pudding raisins. Who must follow these prerogatives, these hidden histories of this chameleon word *love*? What has this man to do with Vienna? There at least we too have had a past. No stranger there could fully beat

297

the bounds. He passed through, that was all, but the city belongs to us.

PART FIVE

5.1

Billy and his cello sit next to each other on the late afternoon flight. Piers and Helen have seats nearby. Four rows further back, Julia and I sit, she next to the window, I on the aisle. A little earlier she was reading. Now she has drowsed off.

An Austrian Airlines flight attendant passes by with a tray of sandwiches wrapped in coloured paper napkins. 'The cream ones are cheese, the others salmon,' she says, offering them to me.

'I'm sorry?' I say, straining to hear her above the noise of the plane. I can see nothing even vaguely resembling cream.

'The cream ones are cheese, the others salmon,' she repeats in a God-save-me-from-this-idiot voice.

'I'm not a nitwit, you know,' I tell her. 'I do speak English. Which are the cream ones?'

'These,' she says, looking baffled, but pointing.

'What's cream about them? The filling?'

She looks at me incredulously. 'The paper, of course . . . oh, I'm sorry, sir, I didn't realise you were colour-blind.'

'I'm not. You must be the one who is colour-blind. These are green.'

Her eyes open wide in astonishment and, after I have taken my sandwiches, she continues to hold out the tray. Then she suddenly scurries off to recover without serving anyone else.

'She was saying 'green' all along,' says Julia, who must have woken up in time to see most of this exchange.

'In that case why on earth didn't you stop me

from making a fool of myself?'

'Usually the shoe's on the other foot. "Cream" and "green" look quite different. Anyway, why were you rude to her?'

'*I* rude to her?'

'Whenever you see someone in authority your hackles go up. All it takes is a uniform.'

'Since when have stewardesses been authorities?'

'Tortoises?'

I begin to laugh.

'Well, laugh away,' says Julia. 'But it's difficult to lip-read at this angle and distance. It's easier in business class.'

'I'm sure,' I say. 'And easier still in first. I'll take your word for it.'

We have not met since that lunch at her place. Julia almost missed the flight, getting to the departure lounge just as we were boarding. After the seat-belt sign went off, I found her seated next to a grey-haired man who was deep into the duty-free mysteries of the in-flight magazine. I asked him if he would mind terribly changing places with me. My wife and I had checked in too late to get seats next to each other. I addressed her as 'darling' a couple of times. He was very obliging and, when he left, Julia made out that she was annoyed.

But I have decided that what is behind us is behind us. Now we are on our way to Vienna. I will not think of that first evening I saw her, or of the late light of our parting. The quiet of the cafes will restore us. But we are here as performers, not as lovers.

We do not talk about the lunch she forced on

302

me. She tells me she will stay on in Vienna with her mother for a little over a week after we have left. Her mother-in-law is in London and will take care of Luke. She tells me Maria has invited us to lunch tomorrow.

'Nervous?' I ask.

'Yes.'

'Strange, isn't it?' I say. 'Remember how we almost got a viola and bass and played the Trout with our trio?'

'Maria wants me to go to Kärnten with her.'

'Can you?'

'Not really.'

'Can't you tell your mother you'll be staying with us in our hotel just for these four days? After all, you'll have a week or more with her later.'

She shakes her head. Her eyes close again. She looks tired.

Could London ever have restored what we lost in Vienna? Can Vienna restore what we have lost in London? I sink my thoughts into the soft roar of the plane and look across her face into the evening sky.

5.2

The clouds have gone; sunset and night are on us. The night is black. Hugged by a zone of forest as black as a lake, Vienna comes into view—the great ferris wheel, a tower, grids of gold, here a white spur of silver, and there a lightless zone I cannot identify. In due course we land.

We talk little, Julia and I, as the carousel goes round and round with its accumulation and de-accumulation of baggage. It is all too strange and familiar. I talk to Billy while I keep an eye on her. Her suitcase comes quickly.

Mrs McNicholl is here to gather up her daughter and take her off to Klosterneuburg. Lothar turns up a few minutes later to welcome us and take us to the *Hotel am Schubertring*. He talks of a hundred things, none of which I register.

I am too restless to sleep. At midnight I get out of bed and put on some clothes. I cross the tramlines and enter the heart of the city. I walk for hours, here and there: here where this happened, there where that was said.

I cannot see the city as once I saw it: freshly, with enchanted surprise. These shapes to me are states of mind. Tall, cool and heavy with stone, half ghostly, half *gemütlich*, outsize heart of a truncated body, Vienna now is still.

Still ist die Nacht, es ruhen die Gassen. My footsteps tramp the depopulated streets. My thoughts burn out one by one. Around three I go to bed once more, and sleep dreamlessly—or at least with unremembered dreams. *Gute Ruh, gute Ruh, tu die Augen zu.*

5.3

Julia comes to the hotel after breakfast the next morning, and the five of us, plus Lothar, drive over to the long building in the 4th district that houses the old Bosendorfer piano factory, together with some of their business premises, a small concert hall and a number of rehearsal rooms, one of which we will use. Normally this building would be closed

304

on a Sunday, but Lothar has pulled a few strings. Our concert is on Tuesday, so there isn't much time to rehearse.

Petra Daut and Kurt Weigl, who are to perform with us, are already there when we arrive. None of us knows either of them, except by reputation, so Lothar, tubby and genial, performs the introductions.

Petra, the bass player in the Trout, has a round face, dark ringleted hair and a ready smile that makes her unremarkable features look surprisingly attractive. She disappears into the Bermuda Triangle after hours, since she makes most of her living by playing jazz in a nightclub there. Lothar has reassured us, however, that she has an excellent reputation, as a classical musician, and has in fact performed the Trout quite a few times before.

Kurt, the second cellist in the string quintet, is pale, tall, polite, diffident, quietly considered in his opinions. He has a small, fair moustache. His English is excellent, with occasional archaic formations, such as when he states his firm disagreement with those critics who find the Trout a 'neglectable' piece. This is nice of him, since he is not playing it. He knew that we were going to rehearse it first, but decided to come along from the start in order to get used to our style. As a result, however, Lothar has had to tell him about Julia's hearing problem.

Petra has been told about it weeks ago. Piers and Erica insisted she should know as far beforehand as possible. According to Lothar, she paused for a second on the phone, then said: 'All the better. She won't hear the hash I make of things.' But Julia now tells her that the double-bass is in fact what she will hear most clearly. The three of us stand to one side and discuss ways of making things work in terms of sight and sound. I can see this conversation is a strain on Julia, who has had very little opportunity to lip-read German for the last few months. The problem is that Petra keeps slipping back into it from English whenever she is afraid of not getting some nuance right.

The place is cavernous and deserted. When we enter our rehearsal room, we find that it contains an astonishing red grand piano decorated with abstract patterns in gold leaf. Even the edge of the lid and the wings are red-lined, and the brass legs have been designed to resemble the pedals. Julia stares at it with fascinated repulsion.

'It's chic,' says Petra.

'I can't play on this,' says Julia, a bit to my surprise.

'How do you know? You haven't heard it yet,' says Petra.

Julia laughs, and Petra looks embarrassed.

'Well,' says Julia, 'it's as if my old aunt had suddenly decided to put on a red-and-gold miniskirt and go to her favourite café. It's difficult to hold an ordinary conversation with her while she's dressed that way.'

'You don't like the colour red, I think,' says Petra tentatively.

'It looks fine on that Coke machine there by the lift,' says Julia, pointing to the foyer.

'Yes,' says Helen suddenly. 'Let's find something else. Horrible, garish beast. I wouldn't want to play Schubert on a polka-dotted viola.'

Luckily we find a large, empty, grey-carpeted practice room with an ordinary funereal piano.

Petra has brought along her own collapsible stool, which she now sets up and adjusts so that Julia can get a better view of her. The rehearsal begins. We run through the piece almost without interruption.

Petra, leaning forward, eyes closed, swaying, gives enormous emphasis to the syncopations in the last movement and then belts out the delayed quavers.

Helen, who is sitting just in front of her, stops playing, and turns to her. 'Petra, I think we should cool it here.'

'But that is what I do,' says Petra. 'This is supposed to be cool. Ur-cool.'

'I like jazz,' says Helen. 'And I'm sure Schubert would have liked jazz. But it wasn't jazz he was writing.'

'Oh,' says Petra, 'I wish we were playing in the *Konzerthaus*. They are so bourgeois, the audiences in the *Musikverein*. They need to be woke up.'

'Please, Petra,' says Helen. 'This isn't crossover music. It's just the Trout.'

Petra sighs; we agree to try it less 'innovatively', and the movement continues.

Despite Julia's great nervousness and my own, the first run-through has gone well. What is amazing to me is the way she picks up the rhythm from Petra, who by no means provides a strict mechanical beat. Especially in the last movement, where the triplets of the double-bass create a rolling, low, almost non-specific growl, the piano doesn't lose its pulse, but sails exactly and easily above it all.

I glance at her and almost cease to play. How well she plays; how well she plays with us. By what strange ways have we been led back here? The

Trout and Vienna itself: are they not unfinished business for us? From time to time my doubts disperse, and I seem to appraise the scene from a perspective where, against its custom, the past rises to bless, not haunt, and where every impossibility seems possible again.

5.4

After going through the Trout once more, we rehearse the string quintet. Later, having returned the keys to the building, we walk outside into the sunlight.

On the quiet, almost empty street, just opposite the Bosendorfer building is an empty lot, covered in grass and the puffy heads of blown dandelions. In the middle of it, under an acacia tree full of white blossom, stands the improbable white statue of a bear. He stands life-size on all fours, his shoulders high, his head lowered, rather like a large and lovable dog.

The others leave. Julia and I remain. Each holding an ear of the bear, we talk about how things went.

'I know how much of a strain all this must be,' I say. 'But you did really well.'

'It was one of my bad days,' she says.

'I'd never have guessed that.'

'The bass helps.'

'She's a good player. Though I agree with Helen . . .'

'I didn't mean that,' says Julia. 'I meant, I don't think I could manage without the bass. Things are getting worse. How much chamber music for piano contains a bass?'

I say nothing for a moment; then blurt out, 'Well, there's the Dvořák . . . no, I'm thinking of his string quintet.'

Julia turns away. Not looking at me, she says: 'This concert will be the last time I play with others.'

'You can't mean that!'

She does not respond, having blinded herself to my response.

I place my hand over hers, and she turns towards me. 'You can't mean that,' I say. 'You can't.'

'You know I do, Michael. My ears are wrecked. If I keep at this, it'll wreck my mind.'

'No, no!' I cannot hear this. I begin to hit my head against the hump of the stone bear.

'Michael—are you crazy? Stop that.'

I stop. She puts her hand to my forehead.

'I didn't hit it hard. I just wanted you to stop saying that. I can't stand it.'

'*You* can't stand it,' says Julia, with a touch of scorn.

'I . . . can't.'

'We'd better get to Maria's or we'll be late,' says Julia.

She avoids my gaze till we get into the car. While she drives, I cannot speak to her at all.

5.5

At Maria's door our trio, together again, can find nothing to say for a couple of seconds. Then there are the embraces, the 'how long it's been's, the 'you look just the same's. But underneath all this are the

309

swift ellipses of the earth, and the awkward knowledge that it is all quite different.

Though Julia and she have met off and on in the intervening years, I have not seen Maria since I left Vienna.

A small boy with curly brown hair pulls her back in. *'Mutti,'* he cries, *'Pitou hat mich gebissen.'*

'Beiss ihn,' says Maria shortly. But little Peter is insistent, so his mother examines his hand, declares him to be extremely brave, and tells him not to tease the cat because it will turn into a tiger.

Peter looks sceptical. Then, noticing that we are looking at him, he first hides behind his mother, then runs back in.

Maria apologises that Markus, her husband, is out of town, but says that she has a surprise for me. We walk into the kitchen to find Wolf, my buddy from my first year in Vienna, making himself useful mixing a large salad. He grins and we hug. We kept in touch for a few years—he left before me—but haven't heard from each other for the last three or four. He too joined a quartet, though in his case Carl Käll did not object to his turning away from a solo career.

'And what are you doing here?' I ask him. 'You've come all the way to hear us play, of course.'

'You've got a red mark on your forehead,' says Wolf.

'Yes,' says Julia. 'A bear attacked him. Or rather, he attacked a bear.'

'I walked into a door,' I say. 'Or rather, it walked into me. It'll disappear in an hour.'

'I hope you're not speaking from experience,' says Julia to me before drawing Maria apart.

'I can't come to your concert,' says Wolf. 'I'm

310

going back to Munich tomorrow.'

'That's a pity,' I say. 'So what are you doing here? A concert with your quartet?'

'Actually, they don't know I'm here, but they'll find out soon enough,' says Wolf. 'It's sort of hush-hush at the moment. I've been invited to try out as the second violinist of the Traun.'

'That's amazing!' I exclaim.

The Traun is one of the most famous quartets in the world; they are all in their fifties, and were already very well established in Vienna when we were students. I can hardly imagine my good friend Wolf among them. I remember their cellist, a fine player but a peculiar character, so shy he couldn't look anyone in the face. When we met after a concert, he acted as if he were expecting some devastating opinion from me, a humble student, about his playing—behaviour so unbelievable that at first I thought he was having me on.

'It was really odd,' says Wolf. 'My own outfit is falling apart. Two of us just can't stand the other two, and that's it. Well, I'd heard on the grapevine that the Traun were looking for a second violinist after Gunther Hassler had decided to retire, so I just wrote to them. They tried me out for an hour or two with different bits and pieces—and here I am. They want me to play a couple of concerts with them on a trial basis in a few weeks. I don't have any expectations, I'm completely in awe of all of them, I know they're trying out other people, but, well, you never know . . . Now tell me, what's on the programme apart from the Trout?—Maria told me about that.'

'The *Quartettsatz* to start off with; and the string quintet after the interval.'

311

'All Schubert, eh? Big programme.'

'Too big?'

'No, no, no, not at all. How come you're the one who's playing in the Trout?'

I tell him about Piers's suggestion.

'How different from our first violinist,' Wolf says, impressed. 'That's a noble gesture. Really. You know what you should have done in response?'

'What?'

'Suggested that you replace the *Quartettsatz* with the longer of the two string trios. It's just about the same length, and your first violinist would have appeared in it without you. That would have evened things out.'

I consider this for a few seconds. 'I wish I'd thought of that,' I say. 'But you know, he'd probably have said that we should appear at least once on stage as a quartet.'

'Nice fellow.'

'Not nice exactly,' I say. 'But good, maybe.'

'What's all this about Julia?' asks Wolf conspiratorially.

'What's all what?'

'Maria's being all tactful and evasive, so there's got to be something there.'

'You mean, between Julia and me?'

'Oh, is that all?' asks Wolf, disappointed. 'Anyone can see that. I thought there was something else. Well, is there? I mean, something mysterious?'

'No—not that I know.'

'She's quite a big name in Germany, you know, though she doesn't play that often: just a few solo concerts a year. She played in Munich a couple of years ago. Someone took me along, and I discovered it was her . . . Is this your first time playing in the *Musikverein*?'

'Yes.'

'Nervous?'

'Well . . .'

'Don't be. There's nothing you can do about it, so why worry? Are you going to do all the octavos in the first variation?' Wolf does a ludicrously exaggerated imitation of a desperate violinist squealing up and down the E-string, missing most of his high notes.

'What do you mean, am I going to do them? Do I have a choice?'

'Of course you do. One of the sources doesn't have those octavos. They sound bloody silly anyway.'

'It's too late; they're in my head and my hands.'

'I heard it played that way once,' says Wolf. 'It sounded much better—but of course everyone thought the violinist had simply chickened out . . . How's your sustaining going? Sustain, sustain, sustain,' says Wolf. 'You know he's ill, don't you? Have you made up with him? Don't leave it till he's dead.'

'I was thinking about him last night, walking about the city.'

'From bar to bar.'

'I wasn't with you.'

'Well . . . and?'

'And nothing; I just thought about him. Among a hundred other things.'

'We were performing in Stockholm a few months ago, and Carl came backstage afterwards,' says Wolf. 'He looked pretty dreadful . . . You were too impatient with him.'

313

'*I* was too impatient with *him*?'

'Exactly,' says Wolf, who never could decide whether he was a clown or a sage.

He doesn't elaborate and I don't ask him to. Years ago, Julia implied something similar. But how can one battle the compulsions in one's head? I could no more have played my fiddle under Carl Käll's view than if my fingers had been smashed. A horrible incapacity had taken me over. I felt helpless at the time—as she herself must have felt today. But at least my condition could be allayed or reversed with time.

5.6

Over lunch, Maria talks more—and more nervously—than I remember she used to, but whether this is to prevent Julia from speaking and giving herself away to Wolf or whether marriage, family and time have changed her in this respect I don't know. She, like Julia, has married 'out of music', but she has retained Maria Novotny as her professional name. She moves rapidly from topic to topic: the gloomy grey winter this year without any touch of sun, the sudden early arrival of summer almost without an intervening spring, the vast bushes of lilac in the large back garden which we must see after lunch, the family's plans for spending Pentecost at her husband's hometown in Kärnten, which she assumes Julia will come along for, Peter's relationship with their kitten Pitou, who is only a year old and likes sleeping in her cello case when she is practising, her regret that she isn't the extra cellist playing with us in the string quintet . . .

Wolf has to leave, and we see him to the door.

'We have to escape from Vienna at Pentecost,' says Maria over coffee. 'There are hundreds of buses parked in the Stadtpark, and thousands of Italians, happy, happy geese. And Japanese, serious, polite geese.

'Why would the Japanese celebrate Pentecost?' I ask.

Maria looks at me for a second, then continues, turning to Julia: 'So have you decided what you'll do after the concert? Will you come to Kärnten with us or stay here in Vienna with your mother? You spend no time at all with me ever since she's come to live in Vienna.'

Julia hesitates. 'I'm not sure yet, Maria. She's being very possessive. And my aunt's coming around today, so how I'm going to find time to work on my music I don't know.'

'But Kärnten?'

'I don't know, I don't know yet. Let's go out and see the lilacs. This is such wonderful weather.'

'I'll go and wake Peter first,' says Maria.

Peter is a bit cranky after his nap, but cheers up when he sees the kitten crouched beneath a lilac bush. He runs after it, stumbles and falls. After assessing the concern on his mother's face, he begins to cry. Maria takes him inside again, and Julia and I are alone.

A wonderful scent pervades the garden.

'Does Maria know about us?'

'Well, it would have helped if you'd looked at me a little less at lunch.'

'I was storing your image in my mind, for later referral . . . So you're going to your mother's this evening?'

'Yes.'

'Then come to the hotel now. We can at least spend an hour or two together.'

Julia shakes her head. 'It's three. I've got to get home and practise before my aunt turns up. Also, well, I haven't had time to go to church.'

She touches my forehead, where a small bump has formed.

'It's been such a long time,' I say.

'It's true,' she says, misreading me. 'It feels so odd, the three of us here together. I almost feel like saying, 'Maria, get out Beethoven's C minor trio . . .' I was about to say we should go to Mnozil's for lunch tomorrow—but, you know, Mnozil's doesn't exist any more.'

'Doesn't exist?' I say. It is as if Schönbrunn had evaporated. I shake my head in disbelief—more than disbelief: dismay. It feels strange that my wanderings last night didn't take my footsteps past it.

'No,' says Julia. 'It's gone. There's something else there instead—one of those impersonal heartless places, bright and sad.'

'But how come you've never mentioned this before? In London, I mean. What happened? Is he alive still?'

'I think so. I think he just sold up.'

I shake my head again.

'Well, is Asia still there?' When the heart of the city used to die at the weekends, the local Chinese was almost the only place where we students could get a decent bite.

'Yes,' she says. 'At least, it was a year ago.'

'Julia, did you mean—did you really mean—what you said about not playing with others again?'

316

'It's getting worse, Michael. I don't think I can.' Her eyes fill with pain.

Maria has come up to us. She looks at us with uncertainty and, I sense, something of disapproval, aimed mainly at me.

'We must go,' says Julia.

'All right,' says Maria, not asking any questions. 'I know you're busy these next few days. But the day after the concert we should spend an afternoon by the Danube, just like old times. Markus has been working late most evenings and even on the weekends, so I'm sure he'll be able to take a couple of hours off and come with us. A nice family outing. Agreed?'

'That's fine,' says Julia at once. 'Isn't it?'

'Excellent idea,' I say, trying to expunge from my voice all the regret I feel.

The day after the concert is a free day for the Maggiore; the day after that we are due to fly to Venice. It is precious time, time that the two of us could have spent alone.

5.7

I practise in my hotel room, using my mute. At first inexplicably rebellious, in an hour or so my fingers and brain and heart fall into a rhythm of calm.

My room is on the top floor. It is quiet. High on the wall is a window through which I can see the tower of St Stephen's cathedral.

Helen phones to ask me if I will have dinner with them: they haven't seen much of me; and as the only one in the quartet who speaks German and who knows this city, I'd be the best guide. I make some weak excuse, and assure them they can get by with English. At night, in this city, group-jollity will drive me mad.

At eight o'clock I think of ordering a snack and having an early night; but, as the light fades, I leave my room, traverse the labyrinth of corridors to the lift, and descend to the lobby. Lilies, ferns, chandelier, mirrors, umbrella-stand; the eyes of Schubert gaze at me from the reception counter. The clerk is tearing up paper forms.

I lean against the counter and close my eyes. The world is mad with sound: forms rip; trams rumble past, vibrating underfoot; coffee-cups clink, and over the murmur from the busy bar I can hear the peristaltic cranking of—is it a fax machine or a teleprinter? What does Schubert make of these noises?

'What can I do for you, sir?' No, he is not Viennese. What is his accent? Serbian? Slovenian?

'Nothing; nothing. I'm just waiting for someone.'

'Is the room satisfactory?' he asks, reaching for the telephone, which has begun to ring.

'Perfectly . . . I might have a drink in the bar. Or could I have it here in the foyer?'

'Certainly. I'll tell the waiter. Please have a seat wherever you wish . . . *Hallo? Hotel am Schubertring.*'

In a corner of the lobby, away from the smoke of the bar, I drink a cold glass of Kremser wine. Helen, Billy and Piers pass by in front of me. I look down at the peonies and roses arranged in a basket on my table.

' . . . and you aren't to take your Spartacus guide and disappear into the Bermuda Triangle,' says Helen.

'Until the performance I'll conserve my energy,'

says Piers calmly.

'What are you talking about, you two?' asks Billy, as they pass out of earshot.

A second glass of wine; and now it is dark. Time to walk; but it is three hours earlier than I set out last night, and the city is livelier. Memory and despair close in on me—pulsations of intolerable pressure, followed by relaxation, almost elation. By the *Musikhochschule* I feel that I can re-create the past, that any wrong turn can be righted, that I can just walk into Mnozil's and see the old man there, like some ancient Caesar, staring ahead of him, replying in brief, noncommittal remarks with no eye contact at all to the questions of some regular customer sitting in an unseen corner—family problems, the loss of a job, money worries. The strangest questions and confessions: but why would anyone bare his heart to rough old Mnozil, who almost made an art of abruptness?

I cannot recall having a proper conversation with him; a year and a half of frequenting his establishment, first by myself, then with Julia, was probably not long enough for that, though a bottle of wine, festively wrapped, stood on our table around Christmas my first, grey, happy winter. Frau Mnozil seldom emerged from the kitchen, but her Bohemian-Viennese presence was amply represented in the fare: *Knödelsuppe* or *Krenfleisch* or *Schokonuss-Palatschinken* . . . a litany of treats. Not that we could often afford them. Usually, when we couldn't stand the food at the student mess, it was potatoes in a vegetable soup for forty schillings, and unresented dawdling in the smoky, garlicky, coffee-scented fug.

He never deigned to serve. The waiter went to

the counter, and Herr Mnozil, who had already overheard the order, handed him the drinks. He was not tolerant of newfangled tastes. When one unlucky tourist wandered in and asked for mineral water, he was asked, in broad, indignant Viennese, whether he wanted to wash his feet: *'Wüsta die Füss' bod'n?'* To the timorous response, 'What would you recommend instead?', mine host's answer was dismissive: *'A andres Lokal!'*

I was happy here once. But what kind of life could I have given her? And how could I have stayed longer under the regime of my mentor? He too came here, but we sat at far tables. At the end we barely spoke. I walk past it now; all changed, changed utterly: glossy, unwelcoming tables, indistinguishable from a hundred other places. So is my memory consigned to history.

Attached to the counter was a glass cabinet containing vegetables—radishes, peppers and so forth—and sausages and wrapped cheeses. The funny thing was that no one ever ordered from it. Julia and I had a standing wager: whoever saw a purchase from that counter would be stood the next meal by the other. More than a year went by between our bet and our final parting, but neither of us ever claimed on it.

5.8

Late at night rain begins to fall. Heavy salvos against my window keep me awake and, when I have fallen asleep from exhaustion, wake me up.

While shaving, I notice that the bump on my forehead has almost disappeared.

320

The rehearsal is in the *Musikverein* this morning. They cannot spare the Brahms-Saal where we will perform tomorrow, so we practise in a long, narrow, beautiful room with a view of the Karlskirche. The rehearsal goes well enough, but after it is over, I am overcome by a sense of foreboding.

I look out at the strange, majestic church beyond the full-leafed linden trees: its blue dome, and one of its two mosque-like minarets. They remind me, in their aptness and their oddness, of the minarets of the synagogue in Bayswater, not far from my flat. London and Vienna project themselves upon each other. Something is going to go wrong tomorrow, badly wrong. I fear for myself, and I fear for Julia.

At the Asia, where Julia and I have lunch on our own, I say hardly a word. Afterwards I suggest we go to the hotel.

'Michael, I must go home.'

'Oh no—not again!'

'I can't. I must practise. I want to work on a few things that came up this morning.'

'How can you be so pragmatic?'

She laughs, and reaches out for my hand across the table. I can sense it trembling.

'What's the matter?' she asks gently.

'I'm anxious about tomorrow. It's as if I can see Carl in the audience, judging, disapproving, marking me down—I'm just worried, Julia. I shouldn't be saying this to you.'

'Don't be.'

'Come to Venice with me.'

'Michael—' She releases my hand.

'I don't know how I've lived without you all these

years.'

How feeble and trite my words sound to me, as if they have been plucked out of some housewife fantasy.

'I can't,' she says. 'I simply can't.'

'Neither your mother nor Maria knows for sure you're going to stay with them. So why must you stay with either?'

'I can't . . . Michael, how can I go to Venice with you? Just think what you're asking me to do . . . Please don't look so unhappy. If you want, we could go to my mother's place now, and we could both practise. And later go out for dinner.'

'I don't particularly want to meet your mother.'

'Michael, stop bending that fork.'

I put it down. 'What piano does she have?' I ask, seizing on the first thing I can think of.

'A Blüthner. It's been in the family for a hundred years. Why? You did say "piano", didn't you?'

'Yes. And does she still have a small dachshund?'

'Michael!'

'A coffee? At Wolfbauer?'

'I'd better get back. Don't put me under still more pressure. Please, don't.'

'All right. I'll come over to your place,' I say.

Shared time is better than none. Why taint such sporadic joy with long views before and after? We drive north. Her mother, introduced to me, starts visibly. Though we didn't meet at the airport, she must recognise me from photographs, surely. For years I have visualised her as a large woman being pulled along by a small dog. Julia is calm, refusing to ratify our antipathy.

I practise in the attic, she in the music room

leading to the garden. At four she brings me tea and tells me we won't, after all, be able to go out for dinner. We meet at seven for a silent meal presided over by her mother, interrupted mainly by jittery yaps from a far room. One of Mrs McNicholl's main objections to remaining in England was the absurdity of our quarantine laws. The other, according to Julia, was her wish to live once again in a Catholic country. After dinner I tell Julia I've had enough and am going back.

'I'm not practising any more either,' says Julia quickly. 'Let's call it a day. Let's drive around.'

Frigid thanks to Frau McNicholl are rewarded by frigid expressions of pleasure at our meeting. She stands under a copper beech in the garden—a blood beech, as she would call it in German—telling Julia to drive carefully, and to be careful.

In the car I ask: 'Did you have to tell Maria you'd spend our last day together with her?'

'I wasn't thinking at the time. I wish now I hadn't.'

Tall poplars parallel the train-tracks along the Danube and a lovely light touches the tops of the long stands of chestnut. On the other side of the road, light lingers on the walls of the houses and the monastery of Klosterneuburg.

'Why is Pentecost such a big deal here?' I wonder aloud, still annoyed with Maria.

'What did you say?' says Julia, glancing my way.

'Why is Pentecost such a big deal here?'

'I don't know. Perhaps because the Austro-Hungarian empire was so polyglot.'

'What do you mean by that?'

'Michael, it's best not to talk to me when I'm driving unless it's absolutely necessary. I need to keep my eyes on the road.'

She turns off at Nussdorf, and drives along the winding Kahlenberg Road.

'But—Julia!'

She stops and pulls over.

'Where do you think you're going?' I ask.

'Exactly where you think I'm going.'

'Julia, don't. Of all places, why there?'

'Of all places, why not?'

We are headed for the scene of our last meeting, years ago; though it was by tram and on foot that we came here that day.

Vienna stretches out before us beyond the vine-blanketed slopes: a pop-up map of memories. We drive on; we stop; we park a little distance away, and walk to the place. Perhaps, like Mnozil's, it too will have disappeared or changed. But no.

By the house stand two large chestnut trees, rich-branched in foliage. Smaller leaves cluster directly round their trunks. Geraniums bloom by the water-pump. On the long tables outside, young couples, friends, groups of students sit, drink, eat and talk in the late light.

A jug of wine from a vineyard beyond. The fall of night. We drink in companionable silence, not embitterment. My violin, uninsured against theft from a car, sits in its case at my side. Once again she touches my forehead, where it hit the stone bear.

Against the lamps, I note the veins of translucent leaves. A lit twig shines white against the sky. Beyond that, the night is black.

We talk little, perhaps because the candle on the table distorts my words.

I am pouring her a glass when she says: 'I'll come

324

with you to Venice.'

I say nothing. I never expected this. Somewhere in the dark I thank something, but I say nothing to her. Not a drop splashes. My hand does not tremble. I fill my own glass now, and raise it, unspeaking: to her? to us? to the spirit of fugitive love? Whatever it is I mean, she nods as if to say she understands.

5.9

The morning of the performance is blue and hot.

I send the fax that Julia wrote last night to a friend of hers in Venice —on the back of a sheet of music from my violin case—and wait till the hotel receptionist hands it back.

The Maggiore meets in the lobby. We are all tense and expectant but the sense of foreboding I felt yesterday has disappeared. We walk over to the *Musikverein*, a couple of minutes away. This morning's final rehearsal is in the Brahms-Saal itself.

The piano rests on the raised stage between two dull red pillars. Julia tried out several yesterday, and decided she liked the action of this one most of all. As for the sound, they are all well-tried, and Julia feels that if someone like Claudio Arrau could go onto the stage without ever having played a note on the piano allotted to him, she is in good company.

She has asked Piers, as onlooker, to do two things: first, to advise her about the balance of her sound in this hall, both absolutely and in relation to the rest of us. Second, she has asked him to follow the score closely when she plays piano or pianissimo, to make sure that she is not playing notes that only she, abstractly, can hear.

The hall has changed since I saw it last, sitting in the audience years ago. The colours are different: there was a lot more white and gold then, and a lot more dark red and marbled green now. But the white bust of old Brahms presides as always over the room where he once reigned, and I am glad that, unlike Helen and Billy, I will not be able to see him from where I am to sit.

The grumpy caretaker who took us to our practice room yesterday is less grumpy because I tipped him. I recall how, as students, Julia and I often managed to get into concerts in the main hall, the Grosser Saal, by tipping the programme-sellers we had got to know. Besides, in a building so riddled with staircases and corridors it was almost always possible to find one that was unpoliced. In the interval—and Julia, for all her shyness, was the more brazen in this respect—we would move forward into seats that were unfilled, nod at our neighbours, and sit down. She justified this by saying that artists felt much happier if at least the front rows were completely filled.

Julia and Petra are discussing what to wear this evening to avoid a clash. Julia will wear a green silk dress, and Petra a dark blue one. Kurt is talking to Piers about similar matters of peacockry: do we prefer tail-coats or dinner jackets? Piers tells him we do not have tail-coats. And cummerbunds? asks Kurt; do we consider them, in his words, 'of the essence'? No, says Piers, we do not consider them to be so.

Helen stands apart from all this, resting her head

326

first on one shoulder, then on the other, then stretching it upwards. She is worried, has always been worried, about the string quintet. Her viola is mercurial in its coalitions: a trio with both violins, with the other two middle voices, with both cellos . . . In all this beauty there is for her no stable role, only quicksands of delight.

Billy and I are looking over the slim golden programme for this evening, enjoying its elegance and amused by the *Musikverein*'s happy consciousness of itself. Under 'Franz Schubert' and before the dates of his birth and death and the music we are to play, is the legend *'Mitglied des Repräsentantenkörpers der Gesellschaft der Musikfreunde in Wien'.* The only reason, of course, why poor Schubert could become a member of the *Musikverein* at all was that he was, strictly speaking, an amateur, with no official musical post anywhere in the city of Vienna.

Nothing too surprising springs out at us for most of the rehearsal, except that at one stage, à propos of I don't know what, Petra suddenly says of our composer: 'But he is a psycho-terrorist!' Helen, Billy and I look at each other, and continue playing. It is joyful music and we play it joyfully. From time to time I think of what Julia said yesterday about not being capable of playing in ensemble again. How can that be true, when it runs so counter to what my ears tell me today?

A small cloud must have passed between us and the sun. For a few minutes the bright skylight grows dull, the hall dim. But then sunlight pours in again, and the slight, sombre interlude is swallowed up in the intensity of this final rehearsal.

In the last movement of the Trout something

odd happens—something that hasn't come up in earlier rehearsals: Helen and I have played the first motif in two phrases of two bars each, but Julia, to our astonishment, replies to it as if it were a single four-bar phrase with a continuous diminuendo. Has she rethought things, or is it the impulse of the moment? In any case, this results in a bit of a discussion, and we decide that the first time we introduce the motif it probably would work better her way. Thus, when the accents—and, still later, the syncopation—crash in, the contrast will be even more effective.

If she could have heard exactly what we played, would she have done what she did? And would we have amended things retrospectively? It is all to the good. But once again I feel a sense of unease, lest something of this sort should happen on stage a few hours from now: something unsettling, that we could not, in advance, have settled.

5.10

The statue of Beethoven in the arcade of the *Musikverein* building looks as if it is shivering from cold on this warm night.

A slightly smooth young man from the administration tells us that since our concert is part of a chamber-music cycle sold largely by subscription, we can expect a good audience. He takes us to the green rooms. The room for us men is bright but somehow also drab, with a red candy-striped wall, a grey floor, a mirror, and framed facsimiles of yellowed scores. Julia, Petra and Helen are next door in a room with a piano, a lurid

328

red-lipped portrait of Fritz Kreisler, and a huge coat-stand with a water stain on the carpet below. They emerge like rich moths, green and blue and gold: Petra in blue, bare-shouldered, smiling; Helen in pale gold, pressing a hand against the side of her neck as if in nervous pain; and Julia, wearing the same green dress she wore that evening at the Wigmore Hall, looking at me with what I think is concern—the gentlest, most speculative touch of concern. But am I not calm now? All will be well, though it is like a parting.

Mineral water rests on the table, and I drink; and Piers has a swig of whisky from Helen's little flask. Billy is preoccupied with a fit of sneezing. All of us are aware that the exacting Viennese can be trusted to know every note of their Schubert. Now Helen is tuning up quietly to the piano. So green, so gold, so blue. How staid Billy and I will look among such gorgeous beings.

Across the corridor, they wait, the ears for whom we play. Piers puts his eye to the peep-hole in the grand doors.

'Full house.'

'It's seven twenty-eight;' this from Billy.

'The scale,' says Piers, bringing his violin to his chin; 'C minor.' And slowly we four rise through it and slowly, degree by degree, return to our tonic. My eyes are closed; but I imagine Julia and Petra and Kurt, a little startled at our ritual, glancing at each other.

The young manager on duty nods, and the Maggiore gather at the doors. As the four of us enter, climbing the shallow wooden steps to the podium, the bustle of voices resolves to applause. Through all this I can hear the creak of old wood underfoot. I look beyond me: to my right, buff-sheened curtains drawn against the late daylight, and a chandelier casting its light on the bust of Brahms, not quite directly below; far ahead of me, at the end of the rectangular hall, high caryatids in gold and unresolved faces on the balcony; and to either side of me, on both walls, long thin balconies, all filled except for a few seats in the director's box. The dark stalls are almost all full; and in the second row I see Julia's mother and aunt, an empty seat next to them. If I must partly view the audience now, I will not have to when we play the Trout.

Silence now. Here too a gash in the ceiling lets in sunlight from above; and at this hour, as much pours down from the sky as radiates from the lamps. We bow; we sit; we tune once more for a few seconds; and Piers, even before I have time to register it, has suddenly begun; and now I have; and now Helen; and now Billy: we are shimmering away like manic bees at the start of the *Quartettsatz*.

A quick, full chord; and now, for the most part, Helen and I are calm, while Piers and Billy sizzle and grumble above and below. The author of perfectly unfinished masterpieces presents us with this, a first movement so symmetrical and full it need not long to link itself with any other. And what else lies ahead tonight? A piece almost over-finished at the request of a patron; and then the work that marked the close of his own unfinished life. If only he had lived, most generous Schubert, to be as ancient as Mozart.

The bees return, buzzing furiously, and with three sharp, sweet stings it is over. Heavenly concision! We stand, we bow gratefully to grateful

330

applause. We go off, we come on, off, on, and with Billy still passing through the stage door to the corridor beyond, the last of the clapping dies.

'Your mother's in the second row,' I tell Julia. 'And your aunt.'

'I'm joining them there after the interval.'

'But there's no loop in the hall. How will you manage to hear anything?'

'I'll watch.'

'Piers?' I say, turning away from Julia.

'Yes?' he replies.

I tap my bow on his shoulder, leaving two regimental stripes of rosin on his jacket. He does not bother to brush them off but smiles his usual half-smile: 'Good luck, then, Michael,' he says. 'It went well; and it will.'

But I feel a buzz of nerves now that the Trout is directly ahead. The tips of the fingers of my left hand begin to tingle slightly—as if they were touching a low-voltage wire.

The feeling goes. I am myself again. Piers steps back. Julia and Petra join us. We enter, we bow, we dispose ourselves about the stage, and from all five of us the first glorious chord of the Trout Quintet sounds out into the hall.

5.11

It is still light above; someone is fanning herself with the gold programme there in front; our sounds are all one, as are the faces there; Helen leads now, for she cannot crane her neck backwards to see what Julia is doing; but it all merges and goes forward. The bass is the motor. Whose is this lovely

331

light touch? It is the cello; he has closed his eyes. My ears cut out on me, I cannot hear, but I know these agile fingers have possession of the piece. Their intonation is perfect. The fingers are mine, the board on which they dance is of ebony. This silence I hear, is this what she is confined to? The attendant ghosts press down on me: out of my eye, to my right somewhere, is the statue of Carl Käll, who once reigned in my life; and on the balcony is Mrs Formby sitting next to my old German teacher. Schubert is here, and Julia's mother. They attend because of the beauty of what we are re-making.

The herringboned floor of the hall turns to tarmac: black ebony, white ivory; it is a carpark covered with snow, melting into the Serpentine. A slim fish leaps in silver scales from its murky shallows. Each time it emerges it is a variant colour: gold, copper, steel-grey, silver-blue, emerald.

And now this last movement, which Billy says can only work through frenzy. I never warmed to it, yet now I bless Paumgartner who begged Schubert to tag it on, for if it is the last piece she plays in ensemble, a few minutes more means everything; a repeat is everything; the last phrase must then be imprinted for ever; and the last note. It is a death, a passing; for will she ever?—she will not ever—play with anyone again. I glimpse her at the piano, a shimmering vision in green. I am not an agent but a means, impermanent as the gold in her hair, the blue in her eyes, the electrical impulses that once involved the serpentine cochlea, where the body has attacked itself. Is she never to play again with other hands? The Member of the Board of Representatives of the Society of Friends of Music in Vienna was cold, then hungry, then ill; and, for a happy man, full of sorrow and haste. Thank you, then, my fellow citizens, for listening to this here, for your acute attentiveness to what is the mere elaboration of a song; my one concert was also under these auspices, and I am sure there would have been others if there had been time. But do not flee; applaud these players, then drink your Sekt, good burghers and return, for after the interval you will hear what I would myself have been pleased to hear through gut and hair and wood, not merely through the music of my mind. But it was the year I walked to Haydn's grave; it was the year I died; and the earth took my syphilis-riddled flesh, my typhoid-ravaged guts, my vainly loving heart many times around the sun before my quintet for strings was heard by human ears.

Applause rings out for the Trout. Applause and even cheers. This from staid Vienna. Perhaps some students? But where am I now?

'Michael.' I start at her voice, troubled, urgent.

They are standing, they have been standing for a while. I am still sitting. I stand.

Now we are in the corridor. I cannot return.

Julia's voice: 'Piers, would you keep his violin aside? Michael, hold on to my arm. We've got to take another bow.'

The creaking steps, the applause. Everyone is smiling. I cannot stand straight. I turn and make for the corridor, alone.

Her arm around my shoulders. Piers's voice, frightened, taking charge.

'I think that's enough. He's ill. Let him sit down. Don't take another bow. Let them clap on, it doesn't matter . . . What is it, Michael? What is it, for heaven's sake? Helen, give him a glass of water. Petra, it was great—well done! But look, we need someone from the management quickly. Where has Wilder gone? How long is this damned interval?'

5.12

I can manage no more than a whisper. 'The bathroom—Piers—Billy.'

'I'll take you,' says Billy. 'Here, Michael, hold on to me.'

'I'll be fine in a couple of minutes. I'm sorry, Billy.'

'Don't be. Just breathe deeply. Relax. It'll be a while yet. Helen has a bit of whisky.'

'I can't go on again.'

'You can. You will. Don't be afraid.'

'I just can't.'

The grey walls; grey tiles; on the floor small matt grey tiles. A grey metal square on the wall: I bend down to look at my face. It is like death.

Billy's voice outside. 'Michael, there's not much time. You'd better come out.'

'Billy—please.'

'No one will make you do anything.'

I let him lead me to the green room.

Piers and Kurt are talking to someone on duty, who is holding a large leather book open for us to sign. He also has a number of envelopes in his hand.

'Was ist denn los, Herr Weigl, was ist denn los, Herr Tavistock?'

'If you don't mind, Herr Wilder, can this wait till after the concert? One of our colleagues, Michael

334

Holme, yes, our second violinist—and he is playing in the quintet . . . no, it hasn't happened before . . .'

But it has happened, it is happening, it will happen.

A hubbub: a dozen people. Someone else I do not know: an older woman, kind, used to crises, someone higher up in the hierarchy. So many people. My repeated, floating name.

I am in a chair. My head is in my hands. Julia is speaking to me: words of comfort, I know, but incomprehensible to me. I look up at her face.

Herr Wilder is looking at his watch. *'Wenn ich die Herrschaften bitten darf . . .'*

Kurt looks panic-stricken. He rests his head against the neck of his cello. Billy, Piers, Helen . . .

'Bitte, meine Herren . . .' Herr Wilder says. 'Gentlemen, please, if you would be so good . . . Mr Holme . . . we are already somewhat late . . .'

Someone is putting my violin into my hands. What should I do with it?

Julia is staring at the wall, at one of the framed manuscripts. 'Look at this, Michael.'

I look at it. I can make out that it is a song by Schubert: *'Die Liebe'.*

'Let's play it—' I say.

'Michael, this is no time—' she begins.

'Do it,' says Billy, taking it quickly off the wall and placing it on the music-desk of the piano.

Julia begins to play both of her lines, then just the bass together with the vocal line. It is short, not sweet: urgent, unlyrical, agitated, uncertain.

'Tune up, Michael, quick; stand here; it's within your range,' says Billy.

I tune the violin swiftly; I play the line of the voice. No one interrupts us.

'I thought you'd never play with anyone again,' I say to her.

'Go onto the stage now,' she says, pressing my hand.

I have joined the others in the corridor. The haze drifts apart into a moment of terror. 'My music—my music—I don't have my music.'

'It's on the stand already,' says Helen, her voice white, drained.

The doors open. Calmly, unhurriedly, to welcoming applause, we move to the semicircle of five chairs on the stage.

5.13

It darkens above us during the quintet, as if the cells of life were dying. In the skylight above, the grey grows duller, darker. The last glimmer of the day is extinguished with the slow, grave trio. Noble, brooding, sorrowful, it helps one bear the world, and all fear of what may come in the sunless night.

These hands move as those hands moved on paper. This heart beats and rests as that heart beat and rested. And these my ears. But did he never hear this played: not once, ever?

Beloved Schubert, in your city I am adrift. I am consumed by past love; its germs long-embedded, half-contained, have grown virulent again. There is no hope for me. I turned away four thousand nights ago, and the path was closed in by trees and brambles.

I am eaten by futile pity. I make too much of much.

From one city of shrunken power and lapsing

music I travel now to another. Let there be some change in my state. Or let me live in a zone where hope is not a word. How can I long for what I do not grasp?

5.14

At eight in the morning I see a fax slipped under my door. It is from Julia's Venetian friend. Rather than asking us to stay with her, she has placed a small apartment she owns at our disposal. I go to the station and buy two tickets. When I return I ring Piers's room, but he is out. Helen, though, is in. Before she can say anything about last night, I tell her that I will not be flying with them to Venice tomorrow but going by train.

I do not want to talk about, to think about last night. To the audience, to anyone on that side of the stage, it was a success; more than a success. For my part, I survived it: it was not what happened ten—eleven—years ago. But without 'Die Liebe', without the help of my friends, how would I have recollected myself? During the string quintet, as I felt the storm of the second movement pass through me, I stared at the seat in the audience where she should have been sitting, and that dizziness almost undermined me again.

What must they think of me? What will Julia say when we meet?

Last night, before anyone else could come backstage, I fled—first to the hotel, then, fearing I might be sought out, into the streets.

'You want to be by yourself?' asks Helen now.

'I just want to go by train.'

'But your plane ticket is paid for. It's non-refundable. Do come with us, Michael. I'll sit next to you.'

'These train tickets won't come from quartet funds.'

'Tickets?'

'Julia's coming too.'

'And staying at the palazzo with us?'

'No, in Sant'Elena.'

'But that's—isn't that—that's at the end of the world!'

'She has a friend who has a spare apartment there; that's where we'll be staying.'

'Michael, you can't stay there. We should stay together, the four of us. We always have. And—well—we can't scorn hospitality we've accepted. I'm sure the Tradonicos could fit in an extra person.'

'Helen, that's not what I have in mind.'

Helen's face colours. She is about to say something, then stops herself. She glances at herself in the mirror, and this seems to increase her annoyance.

'You were fine before you met her again,' she says, not looking at me.

I consider this for a moment. 'No, in fact, I wasn't.'

'Well, I'd better tell the others. They were wondering how you were. We knocked at your door, but you weren't in earlier.'

I nod. 'Thanks, Helen. I don't know what happened. I've got to sort it out in my own mind. I'd rather not make it a quartet issue.'

This last, apparently obtuse remark of mine provokes an angry glance.

338

'And lunch today?' says Helen. 'And dinner? Or need I ask?'

'No. I'll be out.'

She takes a breath. 'You have the phone number and details of the palazzo, don't you?'

'Yes. I'll get in touch tomorrow evening. And here's the address and telephone number of the apartment.'

'A street name and street number! It really is the end of the known universe.'

'Yes, far from tourists like you lot,' I say, hoping to lighten the tension with banter.

'Tourists?' says Helen. 'We will be working in Venice, don't forget. Life doesn't end with the *Musikverein.*'

Whatever I think, I do not contradict this aloud.

5.15

I walk over to the administrative wing of the *Musikverein* to apologise for last night and to sign the page of the great guest-book, which contains all the performers' signatures bar mine. Seeing me with one of the staff, the urbane and genial secretary-general, dressed in a fawn-coloured suit, ushers me into his office and offers me a chair. He reassures me that this kind of thing happens 'even with the greatest of artists'; that he hopes they themselves were not at fault in the arrangements; that the concert was a great success; and that the *'Londoner Klang'*, as exemplified by us, will soon be as famous as the Viennese.

A portrait of Monteverdi looks down rather sceptically at us. 'So much for Vienna,' he murmurs through ancient lips. 'You see, I am stuck here among all these charming German-speakers, and never hear a word of Italian spoken for months at a time. At least your Tononi can go back. I hope you enjoy the journey to Venice.'

Considering what a disastrous journey he had when he finally left for Venice himself, this is unkind.

'Oh, that—' says Signor Monteverdi, reading my thoughts. 'No, it wasn't pleasant at the time. But you aren't travelling with all your worldly goods. And I—well, I was glad to get away from Mantua at any cost.'

The secretary-general's attention is distracted by a video-monitor on his desk. He shakes hands and wishes me good luck.

'Of course, Tononi was long after my time,' murmurs Monteverdi. 'Now where was he from? Brescia? Bologna? I forget.'

'Bologna,' I say.

'*Bitte?*' says the secretary-general, turning from the screen.

'Oh, nothing, nothing. Thank you very much. I'm delighted you enjoyed the concert. And for all your kindness.' Refusing to meet Monteverdi's gaze, I leave.

5.16

After a quick bite at a nearby sausage stand, I am picked up at the hotel by Maria and her husband Markus and their son Peter, who is being a bit difficult. We drive north to Klosterneuburg to collect Julia. Mrs McNicholl, happily, is out. Julia

340

emerges from the house, dressed in jeans and carrying a small hamper. I wordlessly give her her friend's fax and one of the two tickets. She opens her mouth to speak, but says nothing.

'I read it—I hope you don't mind,' I say.

'No, of course not.'

'And decided to take immediate action.'

'So I see. And, as a result, I have some explaining to do.'

'Well, better that than hesitating. It leaves at seven-thirty tomorrow morning.'

'What is this?' asks Maria, who has overheard the last few words.

When Julia tells her, she is visibly upset, but all she says is, 'This is foolish.'

Julia is silent for a while. She probably agrees with Maria and is regretting her sudden consent. Then she says: 'Maria, if it's all right with you and Markus, I'll stay over at your place tonight and get a taxi to the station early tomorrow morning. I'll have to tell my mother I'm staying with you over the next few days. But I'll give you my number in Venice—and my friend Jenny's number too—in case there's an emergency.'

'What's the use of that? How could I speak to you anyway?' Maria blurts out.

'If Michael's on an extension, he can mouth the words he hears, and I can read them off him—at least enough to get the gist of things and to respond.'

'I am glad I'm not deaf,' says Maria, by some instinct turning away so that Julia cannot read the brutal words.

At first I am too shocked to speak. Then, just as I am about to say something to Maria, I think

341

better of it. If Julia doesn't know what was said, why should I attack the remark and in effect force it upon her?

'I've brought a couple of packs of cards,' says Julia, getting into the car. 'Where are we heading?'

'How about Kritzendorf?' says Markus.

'Where?'

'Kritzendorf,' I repeat.

'Oh good!' says Julia, reaching into the basket at her feet and handing Peter a chocolate.

'Das Weinen hat geholfen,' says Peter somewhat speculatively, half to himself, as if appraising international negotiating techniques.

'What do you mean, Peter?' I ask.

'He's been very naughty,' says Maria. 'We were going to leave him at a friend's place for the day but he insisted on coming along, and cried and cried until we were exhausted and just gave in. Bad training. You don't know how exhausting children are—utterly, utterly exhausting. Anyway, when we play bridge, the dummy will have to take care of him.'

Peter, looking out of the window, has started humming.

'He's obviously learned a useful lesson,' says Markus.

'Useful for whom?' responds Maria.

It is a lovely day, though, with a restoring freshness, and our spirits soon lift.

Chestnut and lilac are everywhere, with here and there an acacia in white bloom or a linden or plane or even a willow. Julia and I hold hands. If we were alone, she would have asked me about last night, indeed she would have felt she had to, so in a way I am relieved that we have company—especially since this is not my last day with her, but the first of several.

How all fears dissolve in sunlight. The car has been parked, an ice-lolly has been bought for Peter, we have walked to the the well-trained unmeandering Danube, grass growing down to its very bank. The tablecloth is spread, and we have changed into our swimsuits, Julia into a bordello-red spare suit that Maria has brought along, I into baggy khaki exercise shorts. Cards, food, camera, paper napkins, sun-tan lotion, and a newspaper: no sign of music anywhere, no sign at all. A great white steamer hoots past. I am already in the river. A dog, not obedient to regulations, runs along the bank, barking. A sparrow fluffs itself up in a hollow of dust-fine sand. Peter, an inflated plastic band on each arm, wanders down to the pebbly edge.

'Michael, look after him, just let him wet his feet,' shouts Maria.

Peter threatens to venture out farther than is safe in this swift current, and I haul him, protesting and crying, back out.

'Crying hasn't helped this time,' I can't resist saying. He stamps his feet.

'Look. *Fukik!*' says Markus, to distract him, pointing upwards.

'*Flugzeug!*' says Peter in disgust, refusing to revert to baby-talk, though he does stop crying.

'Look at that funny bird,' says Maria. 'Funny, funny bird. Now we four are going to play bridge, and you are going to be very good and very quiet while we are speaking. Then, when we've stopped speaking, one of us will play with you until we deal again. OK? Look, a blackbird.'

'*Amsel, Drossel, Fink and Star,*' chants Peter

343

happily.

Julia looks at him, and at the blackbird, and at the Danube, and leans back on her elbows, looking irresistible and, for the moment, happy with her world.

5.17

At 7:27 the next morning, Julia rushes onto the railway platform carrying a suitcase and a small travelling bag. I wave frantically at her. At 7:30 the train departs.

Our compartment is empty except for us.

'Good morning,' I say formally.

'Good morning.'

'Do you make a habit of this?'

'I woke up late—' she says breathlessly. 'Look— we're alone. The train's covered with graffiti on the outside: it's like the New York subway, not Vienna.' Julia examines various light switches, heating knobs and speaker controls. 'It's nice inside.'

'I splurged on first-class tickets. I hope the journey's worth waiting a decade for.'

'Michael, don't be annoyed, but—'

'No.'

'Please.'

'No.'

'At least let me take care of my half. You can't afford this.'

'It's my treat, Julia,' I say. 'I'm getting a refund on my plane ticket. And besides, you've arranged for our accommodation.'

She settles herself at the window opposite me, hesitates a bit, then says: 'I had quite a disturbing dream last night. I was in the Danube, swimming, and my father was on a raft with a whole pile of old leatherbound books on it. They kept falling off and he was scrambling around desperately trying to save them. I tried to swim to him, but he kept getting further and further away. I wanted to scream for help, but couldn't. It was really horrible. I could tell it was a dream, and yet—but, well, it probably doesn't mean anything. Anyway, here we are. Let's see if it'll be a good day.' She claps her hands twice, sharply, near her left ear, then repeats this near her right.

'What on earth are you up to?'

'It's a test—a sort of hearing test. Yes, it'll be a better day than usual, I think. I was in such a hurry this morning that I forgot to do it. But of course the sound of the train might be misleading me.'

'I'm so sleepy,' I say. 'All that tension, and then a day in the sun . . .'

'I'm sure you can stretch out. Is the compartment going to be empty all the way?'

'No. Only till Villach. It's on the board just outside. Four people get on there. Full house.'

'That's still a good long time.'

'Four hours. Just before the border. How's your Italian?'

'Barely passable—and now that I can't use my ears, probably pathetic.'

'Well, mine's non-existent. What'll we do?'

'We'll do fine.' She smiles.

What could be going through her mind? Whatever she has had to endure to get to this moment, she doesn't look unhappy. She shouldn't be with me, but she is. She shouldn't be happy, but she is . . .

'I'd better look at my phrase-book,' I say. '. . . "I know a good discotheque." "Would you check the tyre pressure?" "Can I drive to the centre of town?"'

'What did you say?' says Julia.

'Can I drive to the centre of town?' How would you say that in Italian?'

'When you change the subject so suddenly, Michael, I'm completely out of my depth. Anyway, that's one sentence we won't need in Venice.'

'Just testing. Well?'

'Something something *nel centro città*. Let's talk about something serious.

'Well, what do you want to talk about?'

'Michael, what *happened*?'

'Julia, please—'

'Why?'

'I just don't want to—'

'But this is like the last time. You never talked, you never explained—'

'Oh, Julia.'

'I felt so terrible for you,' she says. 'Naturally I thought of your breakdown then. What should I have thought?'

'*This* wasn't a breakdown,' I insist.

'Can't you call a spade a spade?' cries Julia. Then, more gently, she adds, 'What is so amazing is the way you got over it. Everyone said the string quintet was truly wonderful—even my mother. If only I could have heard it.'

We do not speak for a few seconds. 'What you played saved me,' I say.

'Did it, Michael?'

'I want to thank you for *'Die Liebe'*,' I say. 'I'd never heard it before.'

346

'Nor had I. I don't even like it much, from what I can grasp of it. Quite a desperate remedy.'

'It worked.' I take her hand in mine. 'Was your mother worried when you didn't take your seat in the interval?'

'Well, it couldn't be helped. What she's really upset about is that I'm not spending these few days with her.'

'Let's draw a line under Vienna,' I say. 'A double line.'

'You talk as if it's all the city's fault,' says Julia, slipping her hand out of mine. 'As if you hated the place.'

'I don't. I—you might not believe this easily, but I love it more than I hate it. But it does things to me I can't explain.'

Over the brutal static crackle of the loudspeaker we are welcomed in German and then invited, in English, to heff a nice cherney.

Julia is unaffected by this. I think about Maria's remark.

'Julia, I've never asked you this—but is being deaf ever an advantage? I suppose you can avoid having to indulge in small talk.'

'Oh, but I can't avoid it—at least with people who don't know I'm deaf. And that's most of the world.'

'How dumb of me,' I say.

'How *what* of you?' says Julia, amused.

'How stupid of me.' She smiles. 'You know,' I continue, 'when I tuned my violin down a tone to play that Bach fugue, until I got used to reading the notes a certain way, my ears kept rebelling. I had to wear earplugs—to try to make myself deaf. But that's a pretty exceptional circumstance.'

347

'There are one or two advantages,' she says. 'In hotels I can enjoy rooms with views of the street without being worried about the noise keeping me awake. And when I'm playing I don't hear audiences coughing—or unwrapping the crinkly paper around their cough lozenges.'

'That's true.' I smile.

'No bleeps from mobile phones. No clicks from spectacles being folded after people have glanced at their programme notes. Oh yes, and I can't hear your humming any more, thank God.'

'You've convinced me,' I say, laughing.

'But I can't hear the sound of rain on a skylight either.'

If I didn't know her, I wouldn't have recognised from her voice how deeply this trivial loss seems to hurt her. She threw off the remark almost casually.

'That's sad,' I say. 'But it didn't rain on the skylight of the Brahms-Saal when we played . . . Were you disturbed by the storm a few nights ago? It kept me awake.'

'No,' says Julia, a bit regretfully. 'Actually, there is one serious advantage to being deaf as a musician, but I'll reserve that for another time.'

'Why not tell me now?' I ask. But Julia says nothing, having turned her eyes to the window.

Vineyards pass us on both sides of the train; and poppies covering a patch of wasteland flash brilliantly past. A fat man in a T-shirt walks along a forested path near the tracks. A pink hawthorn tree reminds me of London and the park.

'Are you in trouble with the others?' she asks at length.

'I don't know. Perhaps we should have agreed to stay at the Palazzo Tradonico—'

'It's better this way,' she says.

'Much . . . All I meant was, after what happened in Vienna . . . out of a sense of duty, you know . . . but I'd much rather be alone with you.'

'Will you have to do a whole lot of rehearsing?' she asks.

'No—not a whole lot. It's all old repertoire. The first performance is for some sort of birthday party given by an American woman who rents the second floor of the palazzo. Mrs Wessen. She's taken over the first floor—Piers called it a piano something—'

'Piano nobile.'

'Yes, well, she's taken it over for the do and is trying to drift-net all of Venetian society into it—Helen says they're even more fond of freebies than Londoners.'

'What is she doing? I didn't quite get that.'

'Inviting everyone who's anyone in Venice.'

'And how on earth did you all get involved?'

'Erica knows her. We're going to be performing in the *Scuola Grande di San Rocco*—but I've told you about that—and somewhere else just outside Venice as well. Erica convinced her that with a name like Maggiore, we're just the thing for a Venetian bash—and Mrs Wessen only has to pay our fee, not our fares, since we're going to be in Venice anyway. It's certainly a good thing for us too. Vienna, for all its glory, was a financial wipe-out.'

To our right is a range of low blue hills under blue skies. Slowly we advance into them, and now we are enclosed in steep green valley-banks where everything is jumbled up neatly: chalets, fields, hills, clouds, horses, cows, lilac and laburnum. It is all very Austrian, very beautiful. So this is the train

349

I am taking ten years late.

Julia nods off. I look at her for a while, happy to see her just sitting there, then get up and walk into the corridor. A cheerful American and his wife, both about sixty, are standing at a window, talking to each other. She is wearing a yellow dress and has a handbag with berries on it; he has a green bow-tie, crumpled khaki trousers, and a rich cigarry voice.

'Elizabeth, see how organised it is. Look, organised!'

'My stomach is awful,' she says.

'You're seasick?' he asks. 'Why don't you go in and rest, Elizabeth?'

She goes off; he looks around, decides I can speak English, and continues: 'Boyoboyoboy, that's beautiful—and the people live here. I love the country. To me it's . . . I can see these people . . . it's nationalism . . . if something's there they clean it up. Now New York, New Jersey, old refrigerators, old cars . . . where're the beer cans? where's the spray paint?'

'Well, there's some on the outside of this train,' I say.

He makes a gesture of tolerant dismissal. 'I had a farm,' he volunteers. 'But I sold it. I can sit on the porch with a beer in my hand and no TV and just watch the sunset, but where's the deli? where's the cigar store? That's the problem.'

'True,' I say, suddenly filled with delight for no obvious reason.

The tracks twist and list, and the train growls as it enters a tunnel.

The valley gets broader; the clouds disappear. Everything is in bloom: full-candled chestnut trees, sole poppies, unclustered, in the fields, and then whole banks of poppies, blazing red for hundreds of yards, purple lupins, white umbellifers of all kinds, and lilac in every shade from white to heavy-purple. Every so often, like some exotic conifer, a high-tension pylon appears; and tender calves, their skins fresh with the silken buff of suede, drink at the edge of a broad stream.

I go back to the compartment. Julia is awake. We do not speak much, but point out of the window from time to time at things we want to share.

'Julia, what is this great advantage to not being able to hear?' I ask after a while.

'So it's been bothering you?'

'A bit.'

'Well, you must already have some idea of it from the way I played the Trout.'

'The trouble is, I don't know what sort of thing you're thinking of.'

'Well, it's this,' says Julia. 'When I go to a concert or listen to a recording, all I can get is some general sense of what's going on. All the subtleties of other people's playing are lost on me now. So when I come to play something myself, especially something I've never heard before, I'm absolutely forced to be original . . . Not that originality by itself is enough. I'm not saying that. But at least it's somewhere to start from. With the Trout, of course, I'd heard it often enough before things went wrong—and played it. But things fade unless they're reinforced. Too many musicians, when they're asked to play something, go out and buy a CD of it, almost before they look at the score. I don't have that option. Or, rather, it isn't

351

much good to me.'

I nod. Again we are absorbed in our own thoughts, and the view outside somehow enters our absorptions. I had thought she was going to say something about suffering forcing one to understand the world. But in an odd way I'm glad she said what she did.

Klagenfurt. A large lake. Villach. But no one does in fact get on. We still have the compartment to ourselves. The border. A bloated, dissatisfied man in grey flashes a badge and bellows, 'Passaporto!' at us. I glare at him. Then I notice Julia looking at me as if she could have predicted my response. 'With pleasure, signor,' I murmur sweetly.

Chalky cliffs, high crags of rock come into view, wide screes on their lower slopes; and the milky-blue water-braids of a broad, almost dry river bed, a dusty concrete factory on its bank.

Though we are alone, we do not kiss; we are almost shy. The journey is everything it could be. The day grows warm, and I am like a torpid bee.

Soon we are in the Veneto: walls of terracotta and ochre, a red-roofed town in the shadow of a hulking mountain; elderberries along the track; gardens of irises and pink roses; the junkyards and sidings of Mestre.

As we move swiftly along the causeway across the grey-green water of the lagoon, the beautiful city draws itself into our eyes: towers, domes, façades. If a few years late, we are here at last. The two of us stand in the corridor with our luggage and look out over the water. I speak her name softly to myself, and she, somehow sensing it—or is it chance?—speaks mine.

PART SIX

6.1

Four-thirty on a weekday afternoon is no magical
time. But I stand on the steps of the station, almost
leaning against Julia, and succumb to the smell and
the sound of Venice, and the dizzying sight.

The terminal has disgorged us with hundreds of
others. It is not the high tourist season, but we are
plentiful enough, and I gape, as it is right I should,
for all of it is undisappointingly beautiful.

'So this, then, is the Grand Canal.'

'This, then, is it,' says Julia, with a small smile.

'Should we have come by sea?'

'By sea?'

'By sea at sunset?'

'No.'

'No?'

'No.'

I grow quiet. We are sitting at the front of the
vaporetto as it chugs along in its soft pragmatic
way, bumping against its landing-stages, taking on
and setting off passengers. All around is a lively,
thrumming, car-less, unhectic sound.

A breeze eases the heat of the day. A gull flies
down to the murky turquoise water, quick with
flecks of light.

Solidly, fantastically, the palaces and churches
that wall the canal pass by on either side. My eyes
take in a casino, a sign to the Ghetto, a lovely
garden with wistaria entwined over a trellis. A
small working boat, with two young men in orange
shirts, putters past the vaporetto. An elegant older
woman, with fat pearls and a brooch, gets on at Ca'

d'Oro, followed by a woman pushing a pram containing her shopping. The green scum at the edge of the water stretches up the stone steps, the striped mooring-poles.

'What would Venice do without geraniums?' says Julia, looking upwards.

I lean over and kiss her, and she kisses me back—not exactly passionately, but freely. I feel elated, and immediately begin chattering.

'Where did you stay the last time you were here?'

'Oh, in the youth hostel. I was with Maria, and we didn't have much money.

'I hope your friend's caretaker understood me. After she picked up the phone, I simply read out what you wrote. But if there's no one to meet us at the Sant'Elena stop—'

'Let's worry about that if it happens.'

'Is our luggage safe back there?' I ask. My violin case is resting under our bench, its strap entwined around my leg.

'Where can anyone run off with it?'

'Look—another gondola!' I say.

'Yes,' says Julia patiently, taking my hand. 'We've seen dozens already.'

'We must go for a ride in a gondola.'

'Michael, I can't hear myself think.'

'Well, then, you don't have to look at me,' I say, and immerse myself in the guidebook.

The stone bridge at the Rialto, the wooden bridge at the Accademia, the great grey dome of the Salute, the columns and bell-tower of San Marco, the pink-and-white confection of the Doge's palace pass over us or by us one after the other; and all so luxuriously, so predictably, so

356

languidly, so swiftly, so astonishingly that there is something about it that is disturbing, almost gluttonous. It is a relief to be in the open basin of the lagoon, unhemmed by gorgeousness.

To our right is the islanded church of San Giorgio Maggiore. I look at it in amazed recognition. 'But where is Sant'Elena?' I ask.

'Just a few more stops.'

'When I told Helen, she looked shocked, as if I was banishing myself to Clapham.'

'Exiled to Saint Helena.'

'Exactly.'

'I like Sant'Elena,' says Julia. 'I wandered over there once by mistake. It's green, and suburban, and full of families and dogs. No cars, of course— and no tourists except the cartographically challenged, like Maria and me. But it's quite close to something I want to show you.'

'What's that?'

'You'll see.'

'What is it—animal, vegetable or mineral?'

Julia takes a second to understand this, then says: 'Animal, but probably made of vegetable and mineral.'

'Well, so are we all.'

'So we are, that's true.'

'It might have been nice to stay at the palazzo, don't you think? I mean, when are we ever going to get the chance to stay in a palazzo again? If it wasn't for you, that's where I'd be: lying in a bathtub, being served champagne.'

'Prosecco, more likely.'

'Whatever you say.'

'Where is it anyway, your palazzo?' asks Julia.

'How should I know? I don't know Venice.'

357

Julia makes an impatient sound and reaches for the guidebook. 'Ah, yes, Palazzo Tradonico. It's near San Polo.'

'Whatever that is.'

'It's the biggest campo in Venice, apart from San Marco—which is the only campo that's called a piazza.'

'That's far too lucid to make any sense.'

'You're just sleepy. You've been sleepy all day.'

'You were the one who slept through the most beautiful journey in the world.'

'I took a cat-nap. For twenty minutes.'

'I don't think I'll go anywhere without you. Venice is much too confusing.'

'Oh yes you will. I'm not coming along to all your rehearsals. Here's a tip, Michael. Call one side of the Grand Canal Marco and the other side Polo. Then remember if something's on the Marco side or the Polo side, and you'll know if you have to cross the canal to get to it.'

'But why won't you come to our rehearsals? We're just having a couple—well, only three or four.'

'After Vienna, you're much better off playing without me. And without me watching.'

I shake my head.

'Do you know what that building is?' asks Julia, pointing. 'That one with the white façade—'

'I'm really not interested,' I say almost violently.

'It's Vivaldi's church,' she says.

'Oh,' I say, regretting my outburst.

'I shouldn't have mentioned Vienna,' she says. 'I'll try not to.'

'You're the one with the real problem, and I'm the one who's whingeing.'

'What happened to you was real enough,' says Julia.

'You're not unhappy I've brought you here?' I ask.

'It's good to be with you,' she says. 'And I've brought myself here.' She looks into my eyes, and I suddenly feel so joyful, I could beat drums! Ten days with her—ten days—and that too, here.

'Verdi. Wagner,' she says after a while. It has become blue and expansive all around us, and green on shore. I follow her eyes to the antagonistic busts on their pillars in the park. A tree separates them; they look out over the water.

'It's the next stop.'

We stand at the rail, looking at the grove of pine trees that fringe the waterfront, and I wonder what Sant'Elena will bring.

6.2

Signora Mariani greets us breathlessly, as if she had just spied the vaporetto and broken off in mid-sentence to run over to the metallic raft that acts as the stop. She is grey-haired and small and very friendly. She would, I think, be gossipy, if either of us were capable of gossiping with her. As we walk across the pine grove into Sant'Elena proper, she greets several curious people with bursts of explosive speech, of which I can make out no more than 'amici di Signora Fortichiari'. She nods at the greengrocer, moves me out of the path of a dog-turd, and offers, periodically and unconvincingly, to help us with our bags. She leads us up a fairly broad street to a small courtyard with wistaria

359

wrapped over its wrought-iron gate. A complicated bunch of keys is withdrawn, and we are shown how to use them at the entrance to the courtyard, at the entrance to the building, and (after a steep three-storey climb) at the entrance to the apartment.

It is a lovely, simple wooden-floored apartment with views of both the street and the courtyard where, high above a small magnolia tree, hang washing-lines laden with garments, outer and inner, of many colours—including frilly maroon underwear, belonging, to judge from the source of the line, to the neighbour diagonally across and one storey down. Julia and I look at each other in delight. Signora Mariani looks at us and laughs conspiratorially, then suddenly closes the shutters. She points out the bedroom with its clean white sheets, the telephone-and-answering-machine, the washing machine, the fire extinguisher, the vase of yellow flowers, and next to it the letter on cream notepaper from Signora Fortichiari. Then, before we know it, she is gone. Shortly afterwards the downstairs door clangs loudly and an indignant voice cries out from the stairwell.

'Stop it, Michael,' says Julia, laughing, as I draw her into the bedroom.

I nibble her ear. 'Mmm, fuzzy.'

'Don't, Michael. Let me read Jenny's note.'

'Later.'

We are lying on the bed, side by side, still almost fully clothed. Whatever she wants in the style of our lovemaking is fine by me. Today she wants me to take things slowly, not to force the pace just because it's been so long since the last time. So much has happened in between, so much unexpected strain and hope, that to have her in my

360

arms again is something I too don't want to end.

I am tempted to open the shutters, but she shakes her head when I suggest it. We make do with the light that filters in from the other rooms. I take off her blouse and press my face to her. I didn't have time to shave this morning and she complains a little.

'Your lips might be a bit gentler,' she says.

It is all a one-way conversation since she cannot read my words. She senses my intentions by touch, but can speak aloud what she feels and wants to do and have me do. She seemed shy at first, but now she is far bolder than she has ever been before—it is as if this voyage by water and this unknown room have freed her from constraint.

In the middle of it all, I have to get up to rummage around in my still unpacked bag, but even this doesn't break the flow of our excitement. She rests her head on her arm and looks at me, and when I return it is as if no doubt or thought had intervened to check our ecstasy.

Afterwards, I fetch her the note. She sits at the side of the bed; I turn on the light. She looks serious. Apparently, her friend is more or less confined to her house, since her children have measles. She doesn't want anyone to go there, but wonders if Julia can have lunch with her the day after tomorrow at the Cipriani—with me if I wish to come along. She has been assured that she herself is not infectious.

'Well, Michael, would you?' asks Julia a touch anxiously.

'No, I'd rather not,' I reply. 'And you'd rather I didn't as well.'

I'm still thinking of our lovemaking, and measles

361

is an odd intrusion.

Julia nods. 'She's a very good friend—from my schooldays. She married a Venetian about five years ago, and now she has two children, a girl and a boy.'

' "Jenny with the greasy black hair"?'

'Yes, the one who turned into a beauty.'

'I'd better not meet her then,' I say, stroking her neck with one hand and moving my fingers gently to her back. ' . . . I wonder if the others have arrived. Their flight was due to land at six. How would they get in from the airport?'

'By boat. I really hope, Michael, that you don't have any plans to meet this evening.'

'None. But I did say I'd call them. There's a rehearsal tomorrow afternoon.'

'What should we do?'

'I'm in your hands.'

'Arms.'

'To be exact. You look so gobblable.' Julia looks displeased. 'Why that grimace? What did you think I said?'

'Copulable.'

'Gobblable. With a G.'

'That's not a word.'

'It is now . . . Well, what should we do this evening?'

'We could just wander around,' says Julia. 'That's what I'd love to do. And we have so much time.'

'Not enough. Not nearly enough.'

She turns and kisses my forehead. 'You know,' she says, 'we've never danced together. Should we find a place where we can?'

'Oh, no—' I say. 'I don't know how to, you know

that. I'm completely uncoordinated when it comes to dancing. I'd feel awkward, you'd feel awkward, and it would spoil our first evening. Let's just walk around, as you suggested.'

We shower, get dressed, and wander out. The dusk is clear. From far out on the Lido opposite, a huge neon Campari sign shines out towards us. The buoys on the water light up like candles. As it gets dark we fall silent. We walk along the waterfront for a while, then wait for the next vaporetto to come and take us where it wishes.

6.3

We get off a couple of stops before San Marco, and stand for a little while before the Pietà, Vivaldi's church—or, rather, the church that stands where his church stood. On this spot my violin must often have played. Out on the black water, the façade of San Giorgio Maggiore shines out, white-lit. On this spot our quartet was conceived.

We agree to return here tomorrow, when the Pietà will, we hope, be open. Meanwhile, we stroll towards the huge square of San Marco, then through the small side-alleys. She tells me that when she was here last she never noticed that every alley has at least some light at night. It means that if there is something to say, I can always say it. But I am content to say very little.

We wander back onto the broad riva abutting the basin. Voices in a score of languages surround us or, rather, me. At night, when sight diminishes, sound should take over. But of all this—the splashing of water against stone, the tweaking of a child's balloon, wheels bumping down the steps of a bridge, the flap of a pigeon's wing, high heels against the floor of the colonnade—what does she hear? Perhaps the deep thrum of the engine of a vaporetto; perhaps not even that.

Yet here we walk, anonymous, hand in hand. That citron scent merges with the half fresh, half brackish odour of the city. I ask her if she is hungry, and she says no. How about a drink? Yes. A glass of prosecco at a bar. She is restless, and suggests a place on the Giudecca. I am happy to be led on land, and even happier to be carried by water.

The bar is brightly lit. The table next to ours is occupied by two young French businessmen with a pram containing a baby, a mobile phone, a packet of cigarettes and several magazines. An older American couple look at them curiously, then order double-decaf espressos. The grey-suited manager zips around, supervising, helping out, whipping his spectacles on and off, getting rid of a basket of breadsticks that offends him. Our prosecco comes, and we sip it and talk about nothing, about whether it is likely to rain, and what we will do if it does. My quartet and her family have never existed.

A mild-looking woman, English by her accent, seated at the table behind us, is talking to a friend: 'It's the Tradonico crowd, you know . . .' she begins and, drawn by the name, I attend. 'It's just what you'd expect of them. They—they use women for the things they can do, the clothes they can design, the jewellery they can sell, they use women as background music . . . As for the book, I'll tell you what I think: it's a newspaper article, but literature it is *not* . . . I wasn't invited, but I wouldn't have gone even if I had been . . . They throw out a peanut, and the monkeys dance . . . I *despise* them.'

Julia looks at me with curiosity, but doesn't turn around.

'It's not worth it,' I say softly, startled by these poisonous remarks. 'She's saying something about the Tradonico crowd. I suppose she means the people at the palazzo. Why have we come here of all places?'

'Maria and I came here once. I thought it very glamorous, and I just wondered if it had changed.'

We ask for the bill, and pay; or rather, she does before I can.

'You're yawning, Michael,' says Julia while we're waiting for the vaporetto.

'I must be more tired than I realised. Actually, what I am is hungry.'

The rest of the evening passes uneventfully and happily: a meal at a trattoria, a walk through small streets, a late drink at a bar. She is the woman I love, and we are in Venice, so I presume this is joy. It is. We catch a late boat back to the apartment, and fall asleep almost chastely in each other's arms.

6.4

I forgot to close the shutters last night, and the light now pours into the room. She opens her eyes, as if sensing that I am watching her, then quickly closes them again, murmuring, 'Let me sleep.'

I have not woken with her beside me for so many years. Even when we were students in Vienna, it was only on our trips to the countryside that we actually spent the whole night together.

By the time I return from the bathroom she is in a white dressing gown.

'Why do you always wear silk?'

'Silk? Do I?' she exclaims. She claps her hands twice on each side of her head.

'A good day?' I ask.

'So-so.' She smiles, then shrugs.

I explore the kitchen for breakfast food and report back that there's nothing except coffee. Should I go out and get something? Julia suggests I take my phrase-book along and point at the relevant words. I wander down to the shops and return with some bread and jam and milk. The coffee has percolated, and we sit and have some, a bit awkwardly. Sharing the morning seems more intimate, more deliciously awkward, than sharing the night.

No, it was in Banff as well that we were together, day after day for weeks on end. She told me she remembered the long cries of the trains through the distance. But what now of the calls of the horns on the lagoon?

'Cotton this morning,' says Julia as we prepare to go out.

'And even a dab of lipstick!'

'I'm on holiday.'

'Have you brought a camera?' I ask.

'Oh, we don't need photographs,' says Julia quickly. 'Anyway, Maria's taken some of the picnic . . . Shouldn't you give the others a call? You didn't last night.'

I phone the Palazzo Tradonico and get through to Piers. He tells me we're due to meet at eleven. From his tone I sense he is displeased about something, but whether it is his present

366

accommodation or my forgetting to call them yesterday or what happened at the concert or his own ambivalent memories of Alex and Venice, I cannot tell.

The three of them will naturally have been talking about me, and I wonder if they are going to present me with some sort of joint position. Julia tells me not to worry, and to be calm when I meet them next.

We walk through the greenery of our island—a traffic-less small town, smelling of cut grass—to one of the bridges that leads us to Venice proper. To our left is a backwater, almost pastoral; to our right a working canal, with shiny ventilation pipes being unloaded from a barge, and three men yelling at each other from two feet away, exchanging information rather than anger. Washing is spread across the street along which we walk, and the inevitable geraniums bloom on in their plastic pots.

We saunter along a white-gravelled walk bordered by tall lime trees with dark trunks and fresh leaves full of light. On either side of us lie unkempt gardens. At the end of the walk stands a statue—Garibaldi and a lion surrounded by pigeons, goldfish, turtles, dogs, children, babies in prams and chattering mothers: at least a hundred interdependent lives. We linger here before moving on.

'We must go via the Schiavoni,' says Julia. 'That's where the thing I wanted to show you is.'

When we get there, however, it is closed.

'But it isn't Monday,' says Julia. She bangs on the front door. There is no answer. Other tourists gather around, shrug their shoulders, confer, look at the closed door with annoyance or indifference, and turn away. Julia bangs the door once more.

'Julia, let it be.'

'No, I won't.' She looks unusually determined, even angry.

'What's so special about this place?'

'Everything. Oh, this frustrates me. No sign, no explanation, and nobody here. And I didn't even get to see my Vermeer in Vienna. Do you have any paper?'

I get a pencil and piece of paper from my violin case, and Julia scrawls something which includes the words 'telefonare' and 'pronto' on it in capitals, before thrusting it through the letter box.

'It'll be horrible if it's closed for restoration or something,' she says.

'But what have you asked them to do?'

'Phone me or face my wrath.'

'You don't have any wrath.'

'Don't I?' says Julia, half to herself.

'Even if they do phone us, I won't be able to understand them, and you won't be able to hear them.'

'We'll come to that bridge when we cross it.'

'What was that?' I say.

'I mean, we'll cross that bridge when we come to it,' says Julia, frowning at a small blue boat plying the Rio della Pietà. 'Now for your church—I mean Vivaldi's.'

6.5

But that too is closed, or effectively closed. I enter the outer door, but a huge scarlet curtain and a multi-linguistic sign bar my progress into the church proper. I can feel my Tononi moping. It is too much.

A round-faced girl sits at a counter to the right of the entrance. She is reading what, judging by the cover, looks like a horror story.

'Can't we enter?' I ask in English.

'No. Not possible.' She smiles.

'Why?'

'Closed. *Chiuso*. Many months. Except praying to God.'

'We want to pray.'

'Sunday.'

'But Sunday, we go to Torcello!'

She shrugs. 'There is a concert tonight—ticket?'

'What are they playing?' I ask.

'Playing?'

'Bach? Mozart?

'Oh!' She shows us a programme for a performance by a local ensemble. The first half is Monteverdi and Vivaldi, the second half modern music, including a piece with an English title by a contemporary Italian composer: 'Things are what they eat'. Even if I weren't with Julia, this would not be my fare.

'How much?'

'Thirty-five thousand lire,' the girl says.

'Ouch!' I ham it up, avoiding Julia's gaze. 'Too expensive. *Molto caro*,' I add, remembering a phrase.

The girl smiles.

'I am a musician,' I say, holding up my violin case. 'Violinist! Vivaldi! This is his church.' I hold up my hands in adoration. She seems amused. 'Please.'

She sets down her book, emerges from her booth, looks around to make sure no one is watching, and draws the scarlet curtain aside for a second to let us slip inside.

'There, you see,' I say to Julia. 'Charm before threats.'

'Say that again.'

'Charm before threats.'

'There was no one to charm at the Schiavoni,' she points out.

High above us on the great ceiling is a cartouche of space and light, edged with angels and musicians, at its heart a glorious effusion of pale blue, rosy ochre, and white. The Father, the Son and the dove-embodied Holy Spirit are crowning the Virgin.

As we gaze upon this in wonderment, a delirious cacophony bursts upon us from near the altar. A piano, set up on a low stage, and attached somehow to an amplifier, is being assaulted by a madman. First, an entire mountainside is blasted to bits, then a scree of demented mice roll down from the upper octaves until they are transmuted into blood-curdling bears at the bottom. Could this be 'Things are what they eat'?

Julia is perturbed too, but mainly by my perturbation.

It suddenly stops, and the pianist and sound engineer make a few adjustments before essaying once again into their rehearsal. Then there is silence again, the lid is closed—and, blessedly, the two leave as suddenly as they appeared.

'Was it really as horrible as all that?' says Julia.

'Oh, yes. Believe me. For a second I envied you.'

'Play your Tononi, then, and exorcise the church.'

'We'll be ejected. We shouldn't even be here.'

'Michael, if you don't play your violin here, you'll regret it for the rest of your life.'

'And I suppose my violin would never forgive me.'

'There you are.'

'But, Julia—'

'But, Julia, what?'

'You've got to help me then,' I say, guiding her towards the piano.

'Oh no, Michael. Oh, no. You're not going to get me to play. You know I won't.'

'You've played this before.'

From my violin case I take out the Largo of Vivaldi's first Manchester Sonata—photocopied onto a beautifully broad A3 sheet—unfold it, and place it on the piano-rack.

Julia sits down. She looks over the music for a second, swaying a little from side to side as she does so. I tune up.

'You're a bully, Michael,' says Julia very sweetly, very soberly.

I play my upbeat for answer, and she, with no further resistance, comes in at the next note.

It is rapture, and it is over soon. Nothing lovelier has ever been written for the instrument, and my violin clearly feels it has been written personally for it—for it to play here. Where else, after all, should this be performed? It was on this spot that Vivaldi tutored the young girls from the orphanage, and

371

made of them the best musicians in Europe. And since the piece was discovered in manuscript just a few years ago in the very library in Manchester from which I learned much of my musicianship, I feel it has been written for me as well.

No one interrupts us. The church is empty except for us. Only the musicians above, with their viols and trumpets and long lutes attend. 'That was perfect,' I say immediately it is over. 'Let's do it again.'

'No, Michael,' says Julia, closing the lid of the piano. 'If it was perfect—since it was perfect—it is certainly not to be done again.'

6.6

As we walk through narrow lanes and across small bridges towards the Palazzo Tradonico, I can hear a strange thumping or bouncing noise, which turns out to be the sound of footballs being kicked about by a few local kids. The palazzo is not land-locked, but its watergate opens onto a very small canal. Its main façade, grey and peeling, faces a small, irregular square, the Campiello Tradonico, which does not lie on any of the main tourist routes, and is thus an ideal refuge for a game that appears to be a sort of soccer-squash. Quite a few black-and-white footballs lie impaled on the spikes erected at the first-floor level. There they remain, deflating daily but never completely deflated, defining and adorning the palazzo like pineapples or gargoyles or other more traditional architectural excrescences.

I press the bell. A female voice says something in

372

Italian, to which I say 'Signor Holme, Quartetto Maggiore', and this results in a welcoming click. Pushing the great door open, we find ourselves in a huge, dark, empty stone hall, with a set of stairs leading up along one wall. No assisting light comes on, so we grope our way up to the first floor, where a door opens just as we get to it.

The teenage daughter of the Conte Tradonico welcomes us in, introduces herself as Teresa, and tells us that the other members of the quartet are gathered in the music room. She directs us to it, smiles, and disappears.

The gleaming, fractured ochre and black floor of the main hall runs all the way from the façade to the rear, with light pouring in from both sides. After the shabby exterior and dismal entranceway I expected nothing like this.

Each room we pass through becomes more fantastical, filled with the assorted brilliance and bric-a-brac of centuries: tapestries, gilt sofas with brocade backs, velvet chairs, doors painted with camels and leopards, a huge ornate-legged green-marble-topped table ignorant of a straight line, glass candelabra bursting into wings and flowers, clocks supported by yawning bears, a mad mélange of Chinese vases, statuettes peering and beckoning at us from every niche and paintings ranging from family portraits to small, signed pencil sketches, from milky Madonnas to a sanguinary Judith and Holofernes looking down from a wall above a dining table.

Billy appears from an inside room, and greets us warmly. 'Everything all right?'

'Yes,' I reply.

'You're sure?'

'Of course,' I say.

'We have the run of this place,' murmurs Billy.

'It's amazing!' says Julia.

'We're staying on the second floor, which is Mrs Wessen's, but it's on this floor that the concert's taking place. There's even a private garden,' he says, pointing to a little aerial bridge spanning the canal. 'It's smaller than my garden in Leytonstone, but Piers says that by Venetian standards it's a golf course.'

Julia's face lights up at the thought of escaping from all this sumptuousness into a garden. 'Let's have a quick look,' she suggests. 'Or are the others waiting for Michael? Is it all right for me to go by myself?'

'Oh,' says Billy, 'it'll only take a minute. Let's go together.'

We walk over the bridge, and are in a different, refreshingly simple world, a refuge of small-leaved trees and fragrant white flowers, ivy, oleander and cypress. A few leaves float in a shallow stone bird-bath. A bored, worn lion, forepaws resting on a shield, suns himself in front of a fountain.

There is no traffic on the small canal. It is soundless except for a little birdsong and the far bell of a church; one cannot even hear the footballs. I crush a laurel leaf, and Julia smells it from my hand.

'Well,' says Helen, who has suddenly and noiselessly appeared behind us. 'All this is very lovely, but perhaps we'd better get our rehearsal done.' She doesn't address either of us directly. As we pass over the rio, she drops a few leaves into it.

The music room contains both a piano and a harpsichord.

'You know, Julia, we should play that Vivaldi here,' I suggest. 'It makes much more sense on . . .'

'No,' says Julia quickly and sharply, looking upwards for a second. My eyes follow hers and see a huge mass of stucco putti in grey and gilt writhing down, little legs and arms and bottoms protruding off the ceiling.

'Well,' says Piers, who has been waiting for us here. 'Should we, at last, begin?' His voice is cold, and he makes no attempt to greet us.

'I'm sorry, everyone,' says Julia. 'I just came to say hello, and I'll come for the concert, but I must be off now.'

'But, Julia—' I protest.

'I've got some shopping to do,' she says. 'I've got the keys.'

'What about lunch?'

'Have it with your friends. You've been spending too little time with them. I'll wander around and see you at six at the apartment. Is six all right?'

'Well, yes, but—'

'Six, then. Goodbye.'

'We'll be done in an hour or two,' I say. 'Why not just sit in the garden and read?'

But Julia, exasperatingly, has turned away. I get up, worried that she might stumble down the lightless stairs, and get to her as she is at the door.

'Michael, go back.'

'I am going to see you downstairs.'

'Don't.'

'What on earth's the matter?'

'Nothing.'

We are now on the stairs, and it is too dark for me to speak.

'You'll find your way back?' I say anxiously, as I

375

hold the front door open.

But Julia, with a quick nod, is crossing the campiello, making no concessions to the presence or tactics of the astonished young footballers.

6.7

Billy is tinkling nervously on the piano when I return.

'Nothing the matter, I hope,' says Piers, somewhat indifferently.

'No,' I say, not delighted with his—and still less with Helen's—unwelcoming attitude to Julia.

'We haven't had time to catch up on things,' he says. 'I had a bit of a dust-up with Lothar the day after the concert. He called us up to, well, to congratulate us. The concert was, of course, a great success.'

I nod, a little warily.

'I told him that I thought he ought to have been there. He represents Julia as well as us, and he should have realised that, given the circumstances, there could have been difficulties of one kind or another.'

Piers's oddly formal speech irritates me. 'I suppose he had another engagement elsewhere,' I say.

'Yes, that's what he said.'

'Well, it's reasonable enough, Piers. He arranged everything. He even fetched us from the airport and took us for our first rehearsal. Anyway, he's based in Salzburg, isn't he? I don't see what you're driving at. I didn't know what was going to happen to me. How could he have known? He doesn't even

376

know I knew Julia before.'

'Or that you're seeing her now,' adds Helen. 'Billy, do you mind?'

Billy stops his tinkling.

'I think Lothar should have told us about Julia's problem,' says Helen. 'Don't you? It nearly resulted in disaster.'

'How can you say that?' I exclaim.

'How can you deny it?'

'Helen, think straight,' I say, very far from maintaining the calm that Julia recommended. 'That wasn't her problem, it was mine. And anyway, *I* told you about it, so what does it matter whether Lothar did or didn't?'

'It's stressed everyone out,' says Piers.

'Has this conversation been planned?' I ask.

'Of course not,' says Piers sharply. 'It's just that we're all really worried by what happened. Including Billy, who's trying not to say anything.'

'What are we rehearsing first?' I ask, looking around. 'The Mendelssohn, isn't it?'

'We've got to talk this through,' says Piers, placing his hand on my shoulder, almost as a restraint. 'If any concert required a post-mortem, it's that one.'

I remove his hand. 'There's nothing to talk through,' I say, struggling to control myself. 'Julia will not be playing with anyone ever again. All right? That part of her life is over. We won't be playing with her, so how can I get into a state about it?' I breathe deeply, then begin again. 'I am very, very sorry about what happened in Vienna. I really am. It was horrible for me, it was horrible for her, and I know it was horrible for you. I'm not making any excuses. It shouldn't have happened. I let you

377

down. But how could anything like that possibly happen again? And how can you be so unsympathetic towards her? Blame me, fine, but why her?'

There is silence for a few seconds. Neither Helen nor Piers looks convinced.

'You're right,' says Piers suddenly. 'Let's drop it.'

'Right. The Mendelssohn,' says Billy, relieved.

Helen says nothing, but nods slightly.

'The scale then?' says Piers.

We play it slowly, and gradually, almost painfully, slough off much of the acrimony that went before. I look up and see the strange tangle of babies on the ceiling again. I look down at the plain floor and re-immerse myself in the slow steps, first rising, then falling, of the scale.

'Once more,' says Billy as we get to the last note, and all of us seamlessly comply with this unprecedented request. Helen and Billy play calmly and smoothly, but Piers seems lost in a world of his own, as I remember he was when I first joined the quartet.

After the rehearsal is over, we decide we don't need another before the concert.

'Why don't we all go to San Giorgio Maggiore tomorrow?' suggests Helen, more herself again. 'We haven't done anything together this trip. We can ask someone to take a photograph of us against the columns—it would be a good publicity shot. Don't tell me you're doing something all day tomorrow, Michael.'

'I think I could make it—around lunchtime perhaps?'

'Won't the church be closed then?' says Billy.

'Well then, how about tomorrow morning?'

378

suggests Helen. 'Or even this afternoon?'

'I want to take a walk now,' I say. 'But I could meet you there at three or so.'

'Piers?' asks Helen.

'No, I'm not free.'

'You mean today?'

'Yes.'

'And tomorrow?'

'Yes,' says Piers, sounding more numb than exasperated.

'So tomorrow morning's OK then?' insists Helen.

Piers shakes his head and sighs. 'I'm busy tomorrow as well.'

'What? The whole day?' says Helen. 'What on earth are you doing? Do say you'll come, Piers. It'll be such fun. And the view from the tower's so amazing.'

'I don't want to go to that island,' says Piers, placing his violin back in its case. 'I know the view from that tower. It's etched in my head. For God's sake, Helen, don't pretend to be stupid. I won't go to that island again—not today, not tomorrow, not ever. I hate Venice. Sometimes I wish to God he'd never suggested forming the quartet at all.'

Piers walks out of the room. The three of us look at each other, stunned by his vehemence, not knowing what to say.

6.8

Julia and I are having a candlelight dinner at the apartment. She has cooked it and I have laid the table. After I tell her about Piers's outburst, I ask her why she was in such a strange mood in the palazzo. 'Was it Helen?' I ask.

'This is too much of a strain.'

'I'm so sorry.'

'I mean, it really looks beautiful, Michael, but I can't lip-read by candlelight. What was that about the moon?'

'The moon?'

'Oh, it doesn't matter. By the way, the light on the answering machine's been blinking, so we've got a message. I wonder if it's from Jenny.'

'Could be the man at the Schiavoni.'

'True.'

'In which case it'll be in Italian. How will we handle it?' I ask.

'If you listen to it after dinner and just write down what it sounds like, I'll try and make sense of it.'

I get up to turn on the light. 'There . . . but is it really very much of a strain? I mean, just being here.'

'I'm happy I'm here with you.'

'Well, but I meant, being away from—from London?'

'I miss them,' says Julia. 'But that would be true even if I'd stayed on in Vienna. But it's not just that. Today I withdrew some money with my credit card, and I thought, the records will show this took place in Venice. I'm not used to thinking in that way. It's a horrible sort of subterfuge.'

She is silent for a while.

'Has James ever—'

'Guessed?'

'No. Slept with anyone else?'

Julia weighs up how to—or perhaps whether

380

to—respond to this question. Does she think it crass? But I didn't want to phrase it in terms of faithfulness.

'Only once that I know of,' she says at last. 'Several years ago. And it was when we seemed to be closest. But that was different. He was travelling—and lonely—and it was just for one night. I don't believe he'd sleep with another woman now.'

'And how did you find out?'

'I didn't. He told me. I thought it odd at the time. I still do . . . But that doesn't excuse what I'm doing. It's far worse because I love you; how can I ever tell him that? The moment I think about things my head begins to spin. There's been a kind of clanging in my ears all day . . . I've just bought you a birthday present. Belated, I know.'

'Really? Let me see it.'

'You'll get it soon. I need to do something to it before I give it to you.'

I refill our wineglasses. 'It seems a bit unfair that you can change subjects abruptly and I can't,' I say.

'It's a small compensation,' says Julia. 'I used to be a mouse, as you probably remember, but you can't be a mouse if you're deaf. Now if I don't understand something, or don't want to understand something, I change the subject, and everyone else has to follow suit.'

'You were never a mouse!'

'Wasn't I? . . . You know, perhaps I should fax James from here. Jenny has a fax, and I'm meeting her for lunch tomorrow.'

'Why can't you simply tell him that you're in Venice? Especially since he could find out anyway.'

'Yes, you're right, why can't I?'

'Unless, of course, Maria has spoken to him and told him you're with her.'

'I think it was the putti on the ceiling of that room where you rehearsed that really upset me,' says Julia.

'What do you mean?'

'It's been more than a week now,' she says.

'Doesn't he have his grandmother fussing over him?' I ask.

'Yes. I'm sure he's not missing me at all. I can't bear it. My poor baby.'

I feel a sudden surge of resentment against this poor baby. How can I ever compete with him? How could I even think of drawing them apart?

6.9

After dinner we go out for a coffee, but only to the local square, treed with ginkgo, loquat and lime; then back home under the wistaria, careful not to bang the front door.

She holds me through the night, and from time to time says my name. She has taught me the alphabet of touch, so that in the darkness she can read from my fingers a word or two of love, enough to laugh at my mis-spellings. I find it difficult to sleep, being held. Finally, we settle into a position where her head rests on my shoulder and arm, and I sleep well.

In the morning I lazily watch her make up, my chin resting on my hand. She looks so beautiful—even more lovely here, in the light of this city by day. She asks me, a little annoyed, if I have nothing better to do. Why don't I read up on Venice? Why don't I study the 'Art of Fugue', which I've brought with me? Why don't I shave? Why don't I do anything other than watch her at her toilette. She doesn't watch me shaving, and she can't understand my fascination.

But how can I not be fascinated? We make love so easily, here at the end of Venice. We walk hand in hand: here, there, and everywhere. We are a couple: the English couple, friends of Signora Fortichiari. There is no history for me in all of Venice, except that of a promise. For her there is the memory of a visit without me, but Sant'Elena, being unfraught, unweighted, almost unvisited, has escaped even that.

The message on the answerphone was indeed from the *Scuola di San Giorgio degli Schiavoni*. The caretaker had fallen ill, and had not been able to arrange a substitute at short notice, which is why we could not get in; but someone has now been found, and the building will be open again from about half past nine.

We walk over to the Scuola. It is not crowded. Julia tells me the name of the artist whose work she has brought me to see: Carpaccio. My eyes get used to the dimness, and as they do, my mouth opens in astonishment. The paintings against the dark woodwork of the wall are the most striking I have ever seen. We stand together at the first one: a repellent dragon, attacked by St George, squirms balefully, the point of the spear breaking through its mouth and skull. A plantless wasteland of decay stretches all around. It is filled with loathsome objects—snakes, toads, lizards, heads, limbs, bones, skulls, cadavers. The foreshortened torso of a man, who looks a bit like the curly-headed St George himself might have looked had he been a victim of

383

the dragon, stares out of the picture, one arm and one leg consumed. A maiden, half eaten from below, contrives somehow to continue to look virtuous. Everything is pallid and grotesque; yet far behind this withered tree and this fatal desert is a zone of serene beauty: a scene of ships and water, tall trees, opulent buildings.

We move from scene to scene along the wall, not speaking, one painting away from each other. I trail behind with the guidebook. The tamed, shrunken dragon awaits the final stroke of its victor's sword; pagan monarchs are spectacularly converted, while a small red parrot looks out of the painting with a cynical, speculative gaze as he nibbles the leaf of a small plant; a child is exorcised of a bizarre basilisk; across the altar on the other wall, the mild Saint Jerome travels about with his still milder lion, sending timorous monks fleeing like cloned bats across the canvas; the little red parrot appears again as Saint Jerome piously dies; and then, most wondrous of all, the news of his death appears to Saint Augustine in his rich, calm study, lined with books, adorned with open music, where he sits alone with his gorgeous, impeccable, polite, adoring, curly-haired white dog, than which there is nothing more perfect or more necessary in this room, or in Venice, or the world.

A little scroll near him, no more remarkable than the open music books, states that Vittore Carpaccio made him. But is it possible? Did he who made the dragon make thee? The pen is poised in your master's hand, the light of prescient knowledge is on his face, and long late shadows jag the whole plain floor, empty except for you, O glorious mutt. How moist your nose is, how shiny

384

and attentive your eye. The painting is unimaginable without you. Christ could disappear from his niche and not be missed.

A sudden small horde of very young French schoolboys in yellow caps are discussing the paintings under the supervision of a Socratic teacher. They sit on the benches, they look around, they crowd around particular scenes. *'Chrétien . . . une bête féroce . . . jeune fille . . .'* In my mind's ear I hear a chant: *'Fou.' 'Non, soûl.' 'Non, fou.' 'Non, soûl.'* I grow agitated, then calm. We stand to the right, unobstructive. Julia is holding my hand. One little boy, in answer to a question, shyly says: *'Le chien sait.'* And he is right, the dog does know, though he is not knowing like the red parrot, whose motives I doubt. He is calm in his knowledge. He has faith in the way things are, and dignity, and devotion.

When we go upstairs, we are alone. I kiss her. She kisses me with tenderness and abandon. There is a bench by the window. A pigeon coos, the breeze ruffles the red curtain, and from across the canal comes the sound of work: they are exposing the brick of a plastered wall. We—I, rather—would be able to hear anyone on the stairs. We kiss for a long time. I sit on the bench, she sits astride me, I move my hands over her, and under her dress.

I whisper into her ear what I'd like to do, knowing she can't hear.

'Oh God—' she says. 'Let's stop at once! Let's stop!'

I can hear someone on the stairs. We spring apart, and involve ourselves in the guidebook and the panels on the ceiling, where various holy figures are going about their holy tasks.

An old man comes stiffly and slowly up the stairs, surveys us coldly, then walks downstairs again without saying a word. Even though he could not know what we've been doing, it is enough to chasten us.

Downstairs, we take a final look at the paintings. The pews are now full, with at least a hundred schoolboys chattering uncontrollably away.

We enter a side room, a sort of sacristy containing chalices, vestments, three Madonna-and-childs, and a closed circuit television in blue-and-white—which is focused on the empty bench upstairs where we were seated a minute ago.

'Let's get out of here,' says Julia, her face filled with horror, her cheeks red with shame. The old man is nowhere to be seen.

We leave quickly, walk across the bridge, and are deep in a warren of alleys before she speaks: 'It's horrible, horrible—'

'Now, Julia—'

'It's so tawdry—'

'Look, it's just one old man doing his job.'

'I'm sick of all this—' She begins to weep.

'Julia, please, please don't cry.'

'Oh, Michael—'

I hold her to me: she doesn't, as I feared she might, resist.

'Why did you leave me?—this can't go on—I hate it—and now the Cipriani—James stayed there once—' I make out incoherent words, and I speak words incoherent to her, but mostly just wait for her sobs to diminish.

We walk to the riva.

'How do I look?' she says, before getting onto the launch that will take her to the hotel.

386

'Awful.'

'I thought so.'

'You don't. You look as lovely as ever,' I say, tucking a stray hair behind her ear. 'I'll be standing here at three-thirty, waiting for you. Don't be so sad. We're both tense, that's all.'

But this is a pathetic understatement. I know it is more. Something has come undone. The little brown boat chugs off across the basin. A huge white ship moves into view. Clear blue sky, busy blue lagoon: to take my mind off what has happened, I attempt to paint the scene into my memory, taking in each element like some latter-day Canaletto: cruise-ship, car ferry, water-taxi, police launch, gondola, a couple of vaporetti, a small flat boat like a barge. But it is no use; these thoughts will not be warded off. I try to imagine myself without her. I turn away, and move onto the piazza, then the thin, twisting streets.

I stand on a little bridge over a side-canal, and view a landing-stage, its blue poles tipped with gold. Here is the watergate to the opera house: on it lie scraps of twisted metal, a wooden pallet, charred doors, a rusted bird. On the black walls graffiti proclaims: 'Ti amo. Patrizia'. This is the phoenix which burned down once before and this time has not risen. Surely what was lost so stupidly, so swiftly and in so short a time can be retrieved, redone, brought to life once more.

6.10

I see a small blue porcelain frog, and buy it for her. At half past three we meet where we parted. Julia seems calmer. We go to the island of Murano, where we have a disgusting apricot ice-cream and visit a shop full of nightmarish glassware. She tells me that measles is called *morbillo*: a pleasing fact. I suggest that she buy an Invicta backpack for Luke. Then, out of the blue, she tells me that her friend has said that I can stay on in the apartment even after she herself has left—which she is going to do on Tuesday.

'Tuesday?' I say, the blood leaving my face. 'Why so soon?'

Nothing I say can dissuade her. And now she says she cannot come for this evening's concert either. Why not? I ask. Is it the palazzo itself ? the putty putti? my colleagues in the quartet? She shakes her head—it is difficult to get an answer. She needs to send a fax, and will do so on the way back home. She will go to bed early.

Cruelly, I tell her about the sounds of Venice, and now her face goes white, though she says nothing. I describe them lovingly. How can she leave me on Tuesday? How? How? Will it be only four full days we spend together here? And today is the second of these.

During the concert my hands move competently over the fingerboard. Haydn and Mendelssohn are duly conjured up. The performance is applauded; as an encore we play a movement from the Verdi quartet, earlier requested by Mrs Wessen. Il Conte Tradonico and his Contessa act as co-hosts, exquisite in their attentions to everyone, strangers and acquaintances alike; their charm is serene, professional. A bitter brother of the count, a sculptor, wanders about morosely among the guests. I want to speak to him, but suddenly cease

388

to want to. I cannot connect the gossip in the Giudecca bar with anything I see here, or reconcile anything with anything.

The fifteen-year-old Teresa smiles at us, especially at her favourite, Billy. It is drizzling, so no one ventures across the little bridge into the garden. Prosecco and canapés are ingested in the room with the suspended grey-and-gold babies; a successful hubbub is generated. Mrs Wessen is loud in her effusions. It is a relief to know no one, to belong to no skein of society. I do not talk much with my fellows in the Maggiore beyond fixing rehearsal times for the other two Venetian concerts. I leave for Sant'Elena.

I have drunk too much prosecco; no doubt she will smell it on my skin. On the way to the vaporetto I stop by a bar to sober up, and drink a little more—strong grappa this time. I grow fraternal, voluble outside the language. I find that it is past midnight.

At night the vaporetti creep up on you on the black waters; you must not miss them.

No light slits out from behind the shutters. I can make noise in the apartment, but not light, for she is asleep, and her dreams could stall. I strip and lie down by her side. As the night progresses, for all the fractures of the day, we edge absently into each other's arms. Or so I assume, for that is how we awake.

6.11

The alarm goes off. It seems I have hardly slept. I look at the luminous digits of the clock, which say

389

05:00. She, of course, is still asleep. But if she set the alarm for such a mad hour, she must want to be woken. I wake her gently, kissing her eyelids. She complains a little. I tickle her feet lightly.

'Let me sleep,' she says.

I turn on the light. She opens her eyes.

'Do you know what the time is?' I ask.

'No—oh, I'm so sleepy.'

'Why did you set the alarm for five?'

'Oh, yes'—she yawns—'I didn't want us to miss the dawn.'

'The dawn?' I say stupidly. 'I think I have a hangover.'

'Put on some warm clothes, Michael.'

'Why?'

'Vaporetto to San Marco, by land to the Fondamente Nuove, and the six o'clock boat to Torcello.'

'Oh no.'

'Oh yes.'

'The six o'clock boat?'

'Six o'clock.'

'Coffee first then. I'll put it on. I won't be able to move without coffee.'

'We might miss the dawn.'

'What time is dawn?'

'I'm not sure.'

'Well, let's weigh a sure thing against a doubtful one, and have a cup of coffee.' But she looks so disappointed that I quickly capitulate.

There's a rustling in the pines. The sky is heavy, touched here and there with gold. The birds are making an absolute racket at the landing stage. It creaks and rocks as we gaze out towards the Lido. There is the sound of something approaching; a

390

boat, almost empty, for it is Sunday morning, and barely 5:30.

Golden lights shine across the wide lagoon; the noise of the engine rises and falls in pitch. We are soon at San Marco.

'And now?' I ask.

'Now we cross the piazza, and savour its emptiness.'

'Cross piazza. Savour emptiness. Got it.'

There is no one in the piazza except a multitude of pigeons and a man with a broom. I savour it as best I can.

A grey cat joins the pigeons; it makes no attempt at assault, and they show no sign of alarm.

'What is this lemony perfume you keep using? It's amazing.'

'It's not lemony, Michael,' says Julia irritably. 'It's floral. And it's not a proper perfume. It's just an eau de toilette.'

'Sorry, sorry, sorry. Anyway, it is gorgeous. Almost as gorgeous as you.'

'Oh, do shut up, Michael, or I'll start calling you gorgeous.'

'Before the pigeons, you mean? Well, aren't I?'

'Yes. If you like.'

'What you really mean is, be quiet.'

'Yes.'

'But I can hum?'

'Yes.

A Japanese couple, who must be as mad as we are, are out strolling. They emerge from the colonnade, and the woman persuades the sweeper to let her pose for a photograph with his broom. He hands it over. She is photographed clutching the broom with a backdrop of San Marco and a

391

foreground of pigeons.

'Where's the dawn?' I ask. The sky is becoming light.

'It's these clouds. I don't think we'll see it,' says Julia sadly.

I am still groggy. We meander on, ending up once or twice in alleys that drop off into canals. A baker's boy emerges from somewhere with a tray, a man wheels out a newspaper stand, pigeons land with a flap of wings on a huge open square. A bronze horseman surveys us from his sleepless height. We arrive at the Fondamente Nuove just in time to see our boat pulling away.

'Too late,' I say. 'And now?'

'Now we savour the sky,' suggests Julia.

'Right.'

We walk along to a bridge, and stand on it, looking northwards to the island made memorable to us by its apricot ice-cream. Our boat is moving away in its direction.

'If you hadn't been so slow . . .' begins Julia.

'If you hadn't taken so many wrong turnings . . .' I point out.

'You were supposed to be the map-reader.'

'And you were the one who claimed to know the route from experience.'

'Well, you must admit it's beautiful.'

I admit it. The sky has opened up with a burst of pale gold over the cemetery island and a clear pink flush over Murano. But the next boat is in more than an hour. It is too cold to stand here on the bridge, and too desolate to sit at the Torcello stop, so we sit at a contiguous one, where there are at least some comings and goings. The gangplanks squeal as a boat comes in. A priest in a brown habit gets off and a few blue-shirted navvies get on. The shop opposite opens, and we get some more coffee. We then go next door to a bar that has just opened, and I drink a defiant grappa.

Julia keeps her comments to herself. Two minutes before the next boat is due to leave, I order another grappa.

'Hair of the dog,' I say.

'Don't be annoying,' she says.

'Let me savour it. I've been doing a lot of savouring lately.'

'Michael, I'll leave without you.'

'Remember the train? The plane? You did catch them, didn't you, but only just.'

She glares at me, grabs the grappa off the counter, gulps it down herself, and drags me across to the boat.

6.12

Log-bundles mark the lanes in the lagoon like bunches of asparagus. Cypresses haunt the island of the dead, well-populated with the illustrious like the great graveyard of Vienna. Static foam flecks the grey water. I look back at the green-black fringe of Venice. Too soon, too soon: it is Sunday already.

A lighthouse tower, tall and white, is mollified by a frieze of the Pietà. We pass under broken factory windows, then out again into the low lagoon, almost featureless.

The airport is on my left. How small that plane is; and there she will be in two days, much smaller in the air; and there her lips, her eyes, her arms, her legs, her breasts, her soul, her shoulders, her hair, her toes, her voice, all swiftly moving away; and in the hold the blue porcelain frog which I have yet to give her.

Is the tide low? Gulls sit on the exposed mudflats of the malarial lagoon, staked with tilting towers. Look: there is a human being doing something strenuous with a pole and a white something on the mudflat to the left. What is he doing with so much effort? Need we care? Now we hoot and chug in a passage between islands. Now we are there.

All the others have got off at Mazzorbo. So what are we two doing at eight in the morning on Torcello? On two red benches sit two grey cats, tiger-striped.

The canal we walk along is dishwater grey. There is a cool breeze. Sweet birds sing, cocks crow distantly, an engine putters. We walk along the herringbone brick. Weeeee-weeeee-weeeee-weeeee-weeeee-chuk-chuk-chuk-chuk. Nothing can she hear. But she can see vines and figs, poppies, dark roses to the front of an inn; she can see a dog barking, its tail stiff, its eyes furious. Plump, well-fed three-legged dog, why do you need to growl? You sniff, you pee, you run alongside us, you bound clumsily up the Devil's Bridge. Let us through, let us admire these trees with their silver-white leaves, this early emptiness. Do not distress yourself; we will not breach the peace. Chuk-chuk-chuk. Weeeeee.

Peace in little Santa Fosca. She kneels in silence, I sit in a hail of sound. A short fat priest in black mops his brow under a white rim of hair. An old assistant wearily holds out an orange bag. The

394

week's takings pour into the bag from the boxes, one by one. Money, money, luscious lire: coins showering in, and the distinct sound of notes mixed in with them, the closing of the boxes, the shuffling and shambling; and through all this the birdsong, so distinct, and the distant engine rumbling softly through the open door.

The priest coughs, kneels before Mammon in the aisle, his back to Christ. It is a wooden collection box on a stand. Restless, I rise; to the left of the altar, Mary, twelve-star-crowned with miniature electric bulbs, holds her infant in her arms. He is a good child, he does not smirk as some do, who know they are the light of the world. To the right, a man kneels before a trusted and benevolent God; his hammer and the other tools of his work laid down, his chin alone visible as he tilts his head upwards and raises his obscuring arms in prayer.

She lights two candles, and looks at me. I hesitate for a second, then light one as well.

We walk outside, into the sunlight, and after a while into the cathedral.

6.13

In God's great barn the souls are weighed. In the fiend's lap sits the false Christ, pert and mild. Great beams thrust off the wall and strut the roof. The queen of grace, dressed all in blue, holds up her wise-faced child.

The day of doom is swathed with gold. The wild beasts hear the last trump sound and spew forth those on whom they gorged. The dead wind off their sheets. The calm damned, stoked in red flames, show no pain. In zones of black, worms pierce their eye-holed skulls.

The saved stand and praise God. This is their fate through time.

Once more she kneels. The bells toll. The priest and his small flock, no more than ten in this vast hall, take up a chant. Cease your plaint, round priest, do not sing high and low: it is out of tune and time, it is harsh to my ears.

I am bored, jarred. I make as if to go. She will not have it. I sit out the hour-long Mass, but am not here.

The bread and wine are blessed. Not sure at first, she goes to take the host. And then, praise be to God, there is no more to do but go.

But now I look and see the trance that is on her. Oh, to be moved like this, to be so struck, to feel there is this aim, this clear good at the end. I too knelt down, but not to This or That. I was not pierced as she was to the bone. What shall I say to her or she to me when we have left this place?

6.14

We emerge into throngs: cold drinks, lace tablecloths, knick-knacks; Murano glass. The desert has in an hour become a marketplace. I buy some postcards. Dad and Auntie Joan like receiving separate postcards from foreign parts. With a twinge of guilt I realise I didn't send them anything from Vienna.

We escape into the back-marshes with their brackish channels and salty air. A cuckoo sings down a third, again and again. It must have drizzled while the priest droned on; the fields are moist. Wild oats and barley grow along the path and, where it falls off into the lemon-green swamp, plastic bottles, petrol cans and broken shells of styrofoam shore themselves up in banks of debris.

For five minutes or more she does not speak.

From my satchel I take out the porcelain frog and give it to her. Its blue is the lapis of the Madonna's mosaic robe.

'This is lovely.'

'Isn't it?'

'Thank you for being so patient in the church.'

'Not at all,' I say a bit sheepishly. 'And where's my present?'

'I left it at home—I mean, at the apartment. It's ready now. I worked on it last night. Anyway, if you tried to unwrap it here, it would get drizzled on.'

'Why are you leaving Venice so soon?'

'I have to. Don't make it so hard. Please don't keep asking me why.'

'I've got to spend at least an hour practising tomorrow. And then there's a rehearsal. The time's going too fast.'

'If only there were two of me,' she says.

'Are you going back to London or Vienna?'

'London.'

'And all this will be over?'

'Michael, I'm happy here with you. You're happy here with me. Isn't that true? It's a miracle we're here at all. Isn't that enough?'

I am silent for a while and concentrate on that. Yes, it is true, but no, it is not enough.

6.15

We are sitting in the garden of the Palazzo Tradonico on a stone bench near the fountain. It is late Monday morning. The sun is bright. We are shaded by a tree, nameless to me, with glossy leaves and small, intensely fragrant white flowers. A book rests on my lap. The maker's card has fallen out of it. I pick it up: name, telephone number, the numerical address in the sestiere of San Marco, the name of the street: Calle della Mandola.

'What does 'Mandola' mean?' I ask, looking at the card.

'Mandolins,' she says. 'Or is it almonds? No, mandolins.'

'Oh, really?'

'Oh, really?' she says with a smile. 'Is that all you can say?'

'I can't say anything,' I say. 'I really can't. No one has ever given me anything so beautiful. Not even you.'

It is a handmade book from a small bindery we passed by on our first day here. Like an old music copy-book, it is broader than it is high. Its cover is a light marbled grey, its contents more than a hundred pages of heavy paper. Each page has eight blank five-line staves. On the first few pages, in her hand, and with a dark brown ink, so different from her usual blue, she has copied out from my score the first eighty or so bars—in fact, the whole of the first fugue—of the 'Art of Fugue'.

Not one note has been crossed or whited out, so far as I can tell. It must have cost her hours, to take such pains with rare clefs, yet the pages look fluid, unlaboured.

On the spine, embossed in small dull silver unserifed capitals are the words: *Das Grosse Notenbuch des Michael Holme*.

On the first page she has written: 'Dear Michael, Thank you for persuading me to come here, and for these days. Love, Julia.'

I rest my head on her shoulder. She runs her hand over my forehead and through my hair. 'You should go in. It's almost eleven.'

'Will you play it for me? We still have a few minutes before the rehearsal.'

'No. How can I?'

'I remember you playing a little of it in Vienna, years ago.'

'That was for myself. You crept up on me!' she says.

'Well?'

'I can't read these clefs fluently enough, Michael. You haven't brought your score with you, have you? It's got a piano transcription.'

'No. It's at the apartment. If I had known . . .'

'Well, there's my excuse.'

'Maybe some of it's still in your fingers?'

She sighs, and acquiesces.

We cross the bridge and go to the music room. I place my gift on the piano and stand by to turn the pages. She sits down, plays the bass line for a couple of bars, then picks at the soprano and the inner parts. She closes her eyes, and lets her hands and her inner ear remember. From time to time her fingers stop; she opens her eyes, registers a little more, and continues. What she plays is heavenly: an interrupted heaven. Finally, about halfway through, she holds up her hands and says: 'It's there somewhere, but where?'

'You're doing really well.'

'Oh no, oh no; and I know it.'

'I don't.'

'I played through this fugue that night after I heard you play it at the Wigmore Hall. I should remember it better.'

'Well, then, in London?'

She hesitates. Does that word define her unsettled, too-settled life? She softly says, 'I don't know, Michael.'

'Perhaps?'

'Well, perhaps.'

'Make that a promise, Julia. The second half of my present.'

'I can't promise. It's such a different . . . situation. I don't even know if I'll want to play this there.'

'You've taken five days away from me, Julia. Can't you give me this?'

'All right,' she says at last. 'But this isn't something I would ever play for anyone but you.'

6.16

She takes my book off the piano and goes back to the garden.

After a few minutes Helen, Piers and Billy enter, and we tune up. We are rehearsing for tomorrow's concert at the *Scuola Grande di San Rocco*. Julia's plane leaves at 6:30 in the evening; I will not even be able to see her off at the airport.

One of the pieces we are playing is the Brahms C minor that we performed a few months ago. I play it better than before because I can hardly bring myself to care. It does not knot me up with frustration as it used to. Anyway, most of myself is in the garden across the small rio. If the others sense my absence, they do not say so.

We take a break much earlier than expected. I wander into the garden. Julia must have gone inside. The book lies on the bench beneath the tree. Her bag is on the ground nearby.

I notice a sheet of paper sticking out from between the pages, and open it. It is a fax addressed to her husband in that easy, slanting hand. It is a private communication, but my shameless eyes, greedy for anything I can learn about her, compel me on.

Dearest Jimbo,

I miss you terribly—both of you. I am longing to see you again. Jenny sends her best wishes. She's house-bound for much of the day, so we haven't spent as much time together as we'd have liked to. It's tough on her; I think I mentioned her kids have measles. And though she has help, they don't want to let her out of their sight. According to her, they normally spend their time fighting—fraternally but quite fiercely. But now they're too listless and spotted to do even that. Incidentally, they are not at the infectious stage, so my two Hansen men are quite safe. I will not, like Mutti's poodles and pekes, have to be kept in quarantine.

I have been having a most wonderful time in Venice. I am so very glad I came. Vienna was becoming too stressful, and if I had gone with Maria to Kärnten, with her husband and their little son, I'd only have made myself miserable.

I needed this break. I feel so refreshed. I walk miles every day. But I miss you both and can't bear the thought of being away from you for another week, which is why I'm returning early. The other day Jenny and I had lunch at the Cipriani, and I thought of you, staying there without me and thinking of me. Tell Luke that if he forgives me for going away for so long, he will get two surprises, one small and one big, from Venice, together with a present from his Oma. A huge hug to my little Benetton bear. Not that, with his grandmother fussing over him and spoiling him rotten, he will even remember me when I return.

I'll be back tomorrow (Tuesday) on the Alitalia flight arriving at Heathrow at 7:25 in the evening. I'll look out for you, but please, darling, don't bother to come to the airport if you have work or something else on. I know I haven't given you much warning. I'll get a taxi. I don't have too much luggage.

I love you so much and think of you all the time. I hope you haven't been overworking. It is so hard not to be able to phone you. One of my worst fears is that I will lose the sound of your voice.

Lots of love,
Julia

I break off a bunch of those white, fragrant flowers. I feel ill. I feel like a thief who has entered a house to find in it goods stolen from his own.

The worn, bored lion leaning on his shield yawns as if to say: 'Well, what's the big deal? What did you expect?'

A black carp nudges an orange one aside, and continues to circle goallessly round the fountain.

I cross the bridge. From somewhere inside I hear Teresa's cheerful, rapid Italian, followed by Julia's voice, more hesitant. I can make out the words 'Wessen', 'Billy', 'Londra'. I feel sick at heart.

We continue with our rehearsal. Everything goes as it should. Our performance tomorrow should be one of our standard successes.

6.17

'What is the matter with you?' she says. She has turned on the bedside lamp and is looking at me, shocked and frightened.

I have bitten her gently before, on the side of her neck, on her shoulders, on her arms, light nips that, I hardly know how, bring out the maddening scent of her body—perhaps this is Virginie's strange behavioural bequest to me—but tonight in the bitterness of my passion I don't know what happened. I hardly felt it was love I was making to her—I was not in my mind.

'You're mad,' she says. 'Look at these marks.'

'Poor Jimbo: I wonder what he'll make of them when he meets you at Heathrow. Do you think he'll bring the Benetton bear along, or will it be past his bedtime?'

My tongue is as brutal as my teeth. She stares at me and cries out—a horrible sound of rage and hurt and disbelief and violation—then covers her face with her hands and her hair. I try to touch her. She slaps my hand away.

She begins to cry almost with fury. I try to put

403

my arms around her, but she shakes them off. I try to say something, but she cannot see my words.

Abruptly she turns off the light, and lies in the dark, unspeaking. I try to take her hand; she pushes it off. I kiss her cheek, the edge of her lips. I lick away her tears. Slowly she grows still. Again I take her hand, to spell out a word of apology. Two letters into the five she understands and withdraws her hand once more. What can excuse my gouging words?

Strangely, she falls asleep soon, and I am left wakeful, bitter with her and the world she is so enmeshed in, and with shame and regret at what I have done.

Her sleeping arms are around me when I wake, but I do not feel that I am forgiven. The bruises remain on her shoulder. They will turn yellow and stand out for days. How can they be talked away?

6.18

A walk at the end of the world, the earthquake plate, alone; the mudflats of subsidence and flood, and the hermitage of the one who found the true cross. Then in the city on the day of the earthquake was born the weak priest whose writings were dispersed, coming through hands and hands to the library of the curved wall. There they lay till ecstasy rose unheard to the crowning angels and the dove. If we were dolphins, what would we play? If we had four hands would Bach's mind have further branched? Let our thumbs be opposable at the opposite edge. Let our teeth be pulled, let us have baleen like whales, that our plankton love might grow, that we might ungnashing plash and play.

Grief and rue, grief and rue, break the erring heart in two. They cry out the flight, there she must be in 6D, viewless and hurtling on the winds. Will she land, has she landed, can she land, and have all papers stamped or surveyed? Is she of this centimetrage, and are these her birthmarks? Are her eyes gold, her hair blue? She has marbled the apartment in grey. She has written *die Liebe* into my notebook. Campari calls from the Lido, and I sing of trout at the sight. From above light darkens upon red pillars, the colour of algae, and music floats on the unsanded shelves and shoals.

Signora Mariani may make what she will of the sheets. The county Tradonico may tend his loquat groves and use a scarecrow against an avalanche. Let the smoky Käll sustain himself on Mars, and Yuko lay rue on Beethoven's grave. Let the lord of the manor of Rochdale clap his coffin into a canoe and disport himself on the waters. Let Zsa-Zsa sleep on a pillow of haddock in Maria's cello case. Let Mrs Wessen live to see her thousandth moon. Let Ysobel unknit her forehead. Let not poor Virginie weep. Let all and no things come to pass, for how will I pass these days?

An egg may not be unboiled nor trust resealed. We play here in the dark boding school where the cross tilts grossly forward, yet the people applaud. We play there in a villa in solid Italy, its rose sun-hot, its iris dying in a walled field a sixth part of Venice. Two great white dogs are there, like polar bears at sport. Cherries are ripe, and I wander within the grove, kissing them and biting them off the trees.

I have exhausted my means. I have seen a dog on

a boat, which was Carpaccio's dog incarnate. I saw it, it was small and white and faithful, and alert to the goings-on about it. It noted the worth of the woman's pearls, it weighed the grief of the Invicta'd teenager. In sluggish dyslexia under the bridges wove the S, whereon the dull barge sat, the lively dog a jewel on its prow. Its forepaws were so still. My hand was halted then, or was it later? Each beast is sad thereafter, yet how few are penitent.

See how the lightning flashes and it storms across the black lagoon to the white-lit church, its two-faced front major and minor both. There is the font in which our common caul was dipped and named, though we have bowed and fled. Piers, Helen, Billy, Alex, Michael, Jane, John, Cedric, Peregrine, Anne, Bud, Tod, Chad, James, Sergei, Yuko, Wolf, Rebecca, Pierre: what catalogues of ships and seed will fill this regiment, this firm, this sausage-skin? These isles are unserene and full of noise. A rack is winched behind that pink-white wall. A cruise-ship bellows and a sparrow screams. Green lapwater, a child's balloon, bronze bells. She reads these on my lips: her own grow pale.

PART SEVEN

7.1

'Welcome back to London, welcome, welcome, welcome. I hear it was an *enormous* success,' says Erica. 'Congratulations, congratulations, well done! Lothar was *raving* about it.'

'Lothar wasn't there,' I reply, moving the receiver a bit farther away from my ear.

'I know,' says Erica, slightly chastened. 'He was in Strasbourg—sorry, Salzburg—silly me!'

'Lunch at the Sugar Club, Erica?'

'No, no, no, just a slip. I hope Piers didn't mind. He sometimes gets his knickers in a twist about things like that. He thinks someone should be there, twisting arms, chatting up the press and the powers that be. But it was well reviewed, so he must be happy. I wish I had been there to hold all your little hands, especially during that interval, but there it is, there it is. Next time!'

'Who told you about that?'

'About what?'

'The interval.'

'No one, no one, I just picked it up from here and there. Little bird, grapevine . . . terribly dramatic, I must say. Sometimes it makes for fantastic playing, all that adrenalin floating around—flowing, I mean.'

'How far has it gone?'

'Not far. Actually, in confidence, it was Lothar, and he was told by the management of the *Musikverein*. They felt they needed to tell him; and Lothar himself is the soul of discretion—which, of course, got him into trouble with Piers. Actually, *entre nous*, I'm getting rather tired of Piers—and I hear he's getting tired of me. Is that so?' Erica suddenly sounds very alert.

'What do you mean?' I ask.

'Well, your Julia, you know. To tell or not to tell. Lothar didn't, or couldn't, and Piers felt it was a breach of faith. Poor girl's deaf as a post, surely we're entitled to know, that sort of thing. You know how Piers is. Do you think he's trying to get rid of me?'

'No, I don't think so, Erica. You're a wonderful manager. What gave you that idea?'

'Agent. Just agent. Nothing more fancy. Well, it's a number of things. The "Art of Fugue", most recently. Oh, well, I'm just sounding everyone out,' says Erica artlessly—or is it artfully? 'Piers is not a happy bunny. He never has been, has he? Though I hear he was rather naughty in Vienna after hours. And have you been good?'

'What do you mean by good?'

'Well, you define it first, you evasive boy, and then answer the question.'

'No, you define it . . . By the way, Julia is not deaf as a post.'

'No, no, of course not, of course not, but it would make for such wonderful promotion. Lothar shouldn't try to keep it quiet. What lies behind that sad smile? She plays like an angel, but can't hear a note . . . With the right build-up you could fill the Albert Hall.'

'For heaven's sake, Erica! What is this—Barnum and Bailey?'

But Erica's thoughts have run ahead. 'That's the hardest thing about you lot: how do you promote a quartet? Who is a quartet? What is its real personality? Four faceless faces. Now, if I could split up your personalities, like the Spice Girls, there could be fantastic crossover possibilities . . .'

'Really, Erica!'

'Oh, Michael, don't be so prim. I'm just thinking of ways of bringing home a bit more bacon—so to speak! Ysobel, you know, is terribly clever in that respect. But she's so fastidious musically that she manages to get away with it. Well, I must rush.'

'Afternoon nap to sleep it off?'

'Hah! And what are you doing?'

'Practising the viola. Getting my fingers used to it again after so long. It's just that one crosses over a lot more. And of course there's the vibrato—'

'Oh, you clever thing . . . so I hope to see you soon . . . be good . . . and fight my corner for me if Piers says nasty things . . . best love . . . ba-yee!' says Erica, and puts down the phone quickly.

7.2

I relive our last day in Venice, Julia's and mine.

I have a rehearsal, she a flight to catch. We are at bay, yet fear to confront each other. We are sinking into an earlier darkness, only worse. She is packing, avoiding my eyes.

What I did was unforgivable—but nor am I in a forgiving mood. The night before she gave me the book, we had made love, more at her desire even than mine. Yet, just a few hours later, such a letter to this other man: yes, yes, her husband, yes.

'How could you read that letter? How could you bring in Luke? I thought we operated at a different level.'

Why this? Am I a fork-lift?

'I don't hate him. I don't hate you. I'm sorry for what I did.'

She looks at me as if she doesn't believe me. 'I'll have to hide out somewhere and keep lying to James. I'll have to tell him I'm visiting someone or doing something. I don't understand you any more—if I ever did. What do your apologies mean? I won't even be able to see Luke.'

'I don't understand you either—if I ever did. Why are you playing with me? Why did you ask me to your house to meet your husband? I'm still baffled. Why did you come here with me if everything between us was a sham?'

The post-mortem merges with an earlier one. Were there three corners to that crisis then? Was it not just teacher and student in a war of wills? But have we not worn this cloth bare? Depression made me brutal. I felt cut off, even from her. My link with Carl too began almost like love. 'I can't take on anyone at this point,' is what she tells me I then said—but could I have said that and nothing more? Did I feel lessened by this younger woman, just a shade scornful of my ignorance? 'I thought we operated at a different level.' I never had what she took—takes—for granted.

And now she tells me what she has not read: 'Your letters were in Vienna, in a trunk. I found them last week. It was quite a shock. I'd asked my father not to send them on. I didn't know he'd stored them—anyway, they must have got there with his other papers. I found them with old dolls and other stuff my mother hadn't sorted or thrown out. I didn't read them—how could I have done? It wasn't just that you yourself were there. I feared

412

the memories that they might dredge up, ten-year-old thoughts only half true to us.'

'Was that why you decided to come to Venice with me?'

'I don't know—so much was going on—yes, probably—partly.'

'So you *did* read them.'

'No, I didn't—I began reading one. I opened it at random. I couldn't go on. *Don't.*'

But there is no one else in this apartment where we have been happy. She lets my hands rest for a few seconds on her shoulders. My palms rest on them, my fingers do not move along the marks. She read it, then, my raw remorse and sorrow. That would not have aged.

'Michael, don't write to me,' she says.

'Will you call me—or fax me—or drop by?'

'I don't know. Maybe. Yes, in time. Now let me be.' But in this I hear her father's voice: a small lie, the easier to detach herself.

She goes out to send a fax. In an hour she returns. I carry her bags to the stop. She tells me to go back. I refuse. We stand there unspeaking until the boat comes to take her to the Lido, from where she will go straight to the airport. She steps quickly onto the boat. No kiss, not even to avoid a scene.

I go to my rehearsal. I live on in the apartment in Sant'Elena. I read and walk and do the usual things. Is this what happens when your life is not in your own hands?

Yes, I have got to where I am from somewhere else. But I too am subject to higher powers—to music, to my fellows, to the life of someone who is better off without me. Even for music, can I serve her now? Sometimes my fingers move across her

413

book as if they held an unknown form of braille. Here too in London it's a talisman that calms me in these weeks I wait for her.

7.3

From her book with its grey marbled cover, laid open on the music-stand in my cell, I play the first contrapunctus, but this time with a viola. It is written out, as it happens, in the alto clef, so it is easy to read.

We have realised that we are going to need not two but three violas for our work on the 'Art of Fugue': Helen's regular instrument; the special large viola, strung low; and one for me to play where my part falls below the compass of the violin. For this I can't simply borrow Helen's regular viola, since I will also need to practise at home.

I have borrowed the viola I am playing from a dealer. It is an odd pleasure to be playing the larger instrument again after so many years. I had forgotten—not forgotten exactly, but got unused to—how much more one needs to stretch.

We are beginning—with something of a shock— to come to terms with the complexity of our project. What exactly is to be included in our recording? In what order are the various fugues and canons to be played? Where only three of us are playing, should Piers or I play the highest voice? Exactly which fugues require Helen to tune low or me to exchange my violin for a viola? What is the best pace for these pieces, to none of which Bach has assigned a tempo?

We have decided to leave all this, in the first

instance, to Billy. He is to be our researcher, ponderer, and director. If he tells us to play something funereally, we will play it funereally; if headlong, headlong. After we have tried it his way we can approve or adjust or overturn. It may be that only someone with the instincts of a composer could guide us through these musical thickets. Piers knows and accepts this. I did not realise he had been voicing his doubts about the 'Art of Fugue' to Erica yet again.

In remarkably short order—and I suspect he began working on this during our stay in Venice— Billy has produced a document of a dozen pages or so in which he has addressed most of our potential questions: exclusions, ordering, tempi, substitutions, retunings, personnel, variant readings. He talks about Bach's manuscript, the engraved edition of 1751 published a year after Bach's death, the doubtful question of whether the chorale dictated by him when he was blind and dying was intended to form part of the work, the placement of the great incomplete 'three subject' fugue which if completed would almost certainly have included as its fourth subject the main theme of the work, the researches into Bach's intended order both from general principles and from the examination of erased page numbers in the extant copies of the first printed edition, and even a few arcane questions of numerology involving the letters in Bach's name.

He has also, sweet Billy, got his computer programme to generate parts for Piers, Helen and myself in the clefs most convenient for the instruments we will be playing. This must have taken ages to key in.

We do not often practise anything without having read it through together first, and all we have ever played together so far is the first contrapunctus. But in this work, especially for Helen and (to a lesser extent) for me, there will need to be a great deal of preparation if we are to play fluently. So after I have played the first piece from Julia's book and have turned its blank pages one by one, projecting onto them the water and sky and stones of Venice, I revert to Billy's computer-generated parts.

These I scan for hours in preparation for our first rehearsal, thinking of them and playing from them till my mind and fingers stretch to conform to what sounds before my eyes and in my ears.

7.4

Write to me some word of love and comfort. Or leave a message on my answering machine. Or turn up at my door, or in my small blue screen. I wrote to you; I know the fax went through.

It is June: squirrels eat the unripe figs on the wall, dried chestnut flowers are swept to the gravel verge.

I have not heard from you. You have not replied to my unbidden fax. Are you not in town? Have you gone somewhere with your husband and his mother and your child? With his little grey blazer and little green cap, are his days no longer numbered and lettered and noted?

Where did you hide for a week till the marks were gone? Back to Vienna, to your mother's house?—you had some days to spare from those

416

you took from me. I don't forgive myself. That is not all that I have done to you.

The public squares grow garish with laburnum, and near the sunken garden the mushroom-topped may is thick-flowered with pink. The small grey monsters march in a crocodile.

White may is what I love, and lilac lilac; yet modish colours will displace them quite. I walk here and there, and you play Bach for me. Is love so light in the scale? But I see plinths and pillars and pediments from the heights of buses. It is a film over my vision: this is what the great stonemason, with his four volumes, has done to London town. Slow are such actions, but once set are set.

Cats too I see, in vision and from sight. One night, late, I saw a woman as I walked. She was on the riva by the Arsenale, and eleven cats followed her as she called and fed them. She, old woman, threw them scraps from a bag, and they mewed from gratitude and want. They were lean and full of sharpness of spirit and sore with mange, not like the well-loved Zsa-Zsa, so ill now in the north.

You said that I should wait for you to call. How many minutes are required of me who have touched you after years? Look gently on me with those blue-grey eyes. Yes, you may smile, you may well smile and laugh. Be reasonable!

Then to my mind comes the courtyard of washing and wistaria that we looked down at, from the room where we made love those days of the week and that Sunday.

I put my hand on my shoulder where your head rested. Then I say your name once, twice, a third time, a fourth. Some nights I sleep like that, remembering you; some nights I only sleep as dawn comes on.

7.5

But now I am here at her door. Luke is at school, the mother's help attacks subjunctives at the French Institute, and James flicks his abacus in Canary Wharf. How will she hear the bell? There must be some mechanism, for she is at the door. I read her face. Is she happy then to see me? Yes and no. But there is no surprise. She looks so tired; her face is drawn. Is it sleep she lacks more, or peace? She steps back, and I enter.

'You don't mind?' I ask.

'I need some time on my own.'

'Is there anyone at home?'

'No. Would I speak like this if there were?'

'Will you forgive me, Julia? I didn't mean to say what I said or do what I did—'

'Yes,' she says, too quickly.

'I don't know what got into me—'

'I've said yes. Don't go on.'

'I won't ask you why you didn't come to see me. But couldn't you have written?'

'After what happened, why should I deceive you as well?'

I say nothing, then: 'Will you show me your music room today?'

She looks at me with a sort of exhaustion. She could not have expected this question, but acts as if nothing would surprise her any more. She nods, but it is an unspoken concession—as if to give me a free choice of my final meal.

We go up the stairs. The whole of the first floor is a single room. In the middle, by an unused fireplace, stands a black Steinway. At a bay window a desk looks out over the garden of the crescent. On the desk my blue porcelain frog squats on a pile of notepaper, facing a half-finished letter. I avert my eyes.

'Working hard?' I say when we have turned to face each other.

'Yes. Vienna decided things for me.'

'So you'll play alone from now on?'

'Yes.'

'Can't you have a cochlear implant or something?' I blurt out.

'What are you talking about? You don't know the first thing about this,' she says, her anger rising. Did I think once there was no wrath in her?

Somewhere in the house a phone rings four times, then stops.

I notice the Goldberg Variations lying open on the piano. 'Well, since everything I say sounds stupid, why don't you play something?'

She sits down immediately without either protest or active acquiescence, and without bothering to open the volume plays the 25th variation: but as if I were not there. I stand, eyes closed. After she has finished, she gets up and closes the lid. I look down.

'I've been playing the first piece of the "Art of Fugue",' I say.

'Would you look up? Thank you. Yes?'

'I've been playing the first piece of the "Art of Fugue". With a viola. From your manuscript.'

She looks abstracted, distracted. The words have led her into a maze of thought.

'Will you copy the next fugue into my book?' I ask. I hardly want this, but I feel that I can keep her talking only through a series of questions and requests.

'I've been working too hard,' she says. I can make nothing of her answer.

'Chopin? Schumann?' I say, thinking of her Wigmore Hall concert.

'And other things.' She does not wish to enter on it. She looks restless. Her eyes go to the table where the blue frog rests.

'I can't sleep without you,' I say.

'Don't say that. Everyone gets to sleep eventually.'

'What should I say then?' I ask, stung. 'How's your gardening? How's your tinnitus? How's James? How's Buzby? How's Luke? In fact, how is Luke?'

'I suppose he's growing daily in academic, artistic, musical, social, spiritual, physical and moral stature,' says Julia dreamily.

I begin to laugh. 'Is he now? That's quite a lot of growth for a small boy.'

'I'm quoting from his school brochure.'

I kiss the side of her neck, where no trace remains of any mark.

'No—no—let me go. Don't be crazy. I don't want all this.'

I release her and go to the window. A blackbird is pecking at something under a rain-drenched rhododendron bush. Perhaps she feels that she has been too harsh. She comes up to me and lays her hand very lightly on my shoulder.

'Can't we just be friends?'

So here they are, at last, these words.

420

'No!' I say, not turning around. Let her read my shrug.

'Michael, think a little of me.' So, finally, I am permitted my name.

We walk downstairs. She doesn't suggest a coffee.

'I'd better go,' I say.

'Yes. I didn't want you to come, but here you are,' she says, looking miserably into my eyes. 'If I didn't love you, things would be quite a bit simpler.'

So will she visit me? May I come here again? Whatever her answer, I won't be at rest. Is it not love that knows how to make smooth things rough and rough things smooth?

She takes my hand, but not in enforced ceremony. The door opens, closes. I look down from the top step. Water, full fathom five, flows down Elgin Crescent, down Ladbroke Grove, through the Serpentine to the Thames, and double-deckered red vaporetti sputter like Mississippi steamboats down its length. A small white dog sits on the sneezing prow. Go, then, with the breathing tide, and do not make a scene, and learn wisdom of the little dog, who visits from elsewhere, and who knows that what is, is, and, O harder knowledge, that what is not is not.

7.6

We are at Helen's for our rehearsal.

'I'm going on a diet,' says Billy. 'I've been told I'm overweight.'

'No!' says Helen. 'How slanderous.'

'The doctor,' explains Billy, 'says I'm grossly

421

overweight, grossly, and my blood pressure is dangerously high, and if I love Lydia and Jango I'd better start slimming, so that's what I'm going to have to do. I don't have a choice. Last week I went to the gym three times, and I feel I've lost a couple of pounds already.'

Helen starts to smile.

'It's too horrible,' says Billy. 'He said "grossly" . . . He didn't even try to be tactful . . . Have all of you looked at my notes?'

'They're terrific,' I say. Billy bucks up. Helen and Piers nod their approval. So here we are together. I too have my family now.

'It must have taken you weeks to key all our parts in,' I say.

'Oh no,' says Billy. 'I just scanned it in from a score—just scanned it in, cleaned it up, adjusted the odd clef, and printed it out. It's amazing what you can do these days.' His eyes light up with the possibilities. 'My programme now has a playback setting for piano called espressivo—a few controlled irregularities, and you can hardly tell it's a computer that's playing, not a human being. Soon they'll perfect it, and you won't be able to tell. Performers will be redundant for all practical purposes . . .'

'I suppose composers won't,' snaps Piers.

'Oh, yes,' says Billy in joyful contemplation of his own obsolescence. 'Take fugues, for instance—you can already do all sorts of things with computers. Say you want to repeat a fugal subject at the twelfth, augmented, inverted, and with a delay of a bar and a half—touch a few keys and it's done.'

'But where's the imagination in all this? Where's the music?' I ask.

'Oh,' says Billy, 'that's not a problem. Just generate lots of combinations, vet them for harmonic compatibility, and test them out on humans for beauty. I'm sure, in twenty years, computers will out-perform us in blind tastings. Maybe we'll even have a formula for beauty, you know, based upon testing various parameters. It won't be perfect, of course, just more perfect than most of us.'

'Disgusting,' says Helen. 'Chilling. A sort of chess.'

Billy looks hurt. 'A sort of *holier* chess.'

'Well,' says Piers. 'Back to the imperfect present. This is all fascinating, Billy, but would you mind kicking off?'

Billy nods. 'I thought we might start with something that doesn't require Michael to play the viola,' he says. 'This isn't a vote of no confidence, of course . . .'

I look at him carefully.

'No, really,' says Billy. 'Really. It's just to keep things simple, you know, as simple as possible. And for a start it's probably better if Helen doesn't attempt to play with that larger viola tuned down.'

Helen nods her head slightly.

'Well,' says Billy, 'that narrows it down to contrapunctus five or nine. Does anyone have any preference?'

'You're the boss,' says Piers.

'Oh, OK,' says Billy. 'Number five. Pizzicato throughout.'

'What?' say the three of us almost in unison.

Billy is well-pleased with the effect. 'Well, what have you got to lose?' he asks. 'It'll only take three minutes or so. Right, Michael, begin,' he says, a trifle dictatorially. 'Here's the tempo.'

'Billy, you're nuts,' I say.

'We haven't even played the scale yet,' Helen points out.

'I forgot about the scale,' says Billy. 'Let's play it then. The D minor scale—pizzicato.'

'No!' says Piers, goaded into action by this sacrilege. 'We can't play the scale pizzicato. It would make a travesty of it. We'll play it arco first, and then you can do what you like with us.'

So we bow the scale first, and then Billy makes us pluck it, which is bizarre, and we follow this up with contrapunctus five. Though we don't get any true sense of the length of the sustained notes, and though the plucked violins sound pathetic compared to the cello, the counterpoint emerges with etched clarity. In addition, it's something of an exercise in intonation. We never did this when we practised the first contrapunctus for the encore. Perhaps we should have.

Billy takes us quite gradually through our paces. For the next pass we play it through with the kind of vibrato we normally use. The third and all subsequent passes are almost without vibrato: the style in which Billy intends that we should record or perform the work. It is slow going, but revealing. In an hour or so we move to the other piece that lies in our compass, and come to terms with it in much the same way.

Then, at a stroke, the quartet is transfigured—its sound, its texture, its appearance. We move directly to a piece where both Helen and I have to use deeper, larger instruments. We look and we feel oddly out of proportion: with ourselves and with the others. I play the viola I have borrowed, she what could perhaps be called a tenor viola. It makes an amazing sound, lazy and growly and very rich and weird, and suddenly all four of us are laughing with delight—yes, delight, for the world outside has thinned out of existence—even as we continue to play.

7.7

We move from piece to piece, in an order that Billy has thought through. Our session was planned to last from two till six o'clock, but we decide to continue it after dinner. Helen and Billy cook the pasta and sauce, while Piers and I attend to the wine, the salad and the table. Billy phones Lydia to say he'll be late and Piers makes a phone call too.

This impromptu dinner at Helen's is the first time for months that all four of us are—as we so often used to be—together for a meal; and it is odd that it should happen in London, rather than on the road. In neither Vienna nor Venice did we eat together. Those few days with Julia could not be spared or shared. And when she left I continued my solitariness.

Billy resists a second helping. The fact that we have several hours of playing ahead of us doesn't matter. It is still so exciting that we are playing the 'Art of Fugue', and for a recording at that, and such a relief that Helen's instrument, so improbably strung, is all that we could have wished it to be, that there is an atmosphere of celebration more than work.

'Rebecca's baby's going to be called Hope,' says Helen.

'So it's going to be a girl?' asks Piers.

'No, they're not sure. They didn't want to find out. But they're going to call it Hope anyway.'

'Stupid father, stupid name,' says Piers. 'I'm not going to the christening. Stuart's the most boring man I know.'

'You can't hurt Rebecca,' says Helen. 'Besides, he's not boring.'

'He is boring. He's a sort of microwave of boredom. You're bored to a crisp in thirty seconds. No, to a sog,' says Piers, grinding great quantities of pepper onto his pasta.

'What does he do?' asks Billy.

'Something electronic,' says Piers. 'And he talks about it all the time in a dreadful nasal voice, even when no one in the room has any idea what he's talking about. He comes from Leeds.'

'Liverpool,' says Helen.

'Well, somewhere forgettable,' says Piers.

There was a time when I would have risen to such taunts, but that was years ago.

'They've come out with a special shampoo for redheads,' says Helen.

'Good,' says Piers with patently feigned interest. 'Very good. Tell us more.'

'Do you think we should aim to perform the "Art of Fugue" on stage sometime?' asks Billy.

'Oh, Billy, give us a break,' says Piers.

'Why?' I ask. 'Let's discuss it. It's better than discussing Rebeccas and Stuarts whom neither Billy nor I know.'

'You don't know how lucky you are,' says Piers.

'Rebecca has been our friend since she was a baby,' says Helen. 'And she was Piers's first girlfriend.'

'She was *not*,' says Piers. 'Anyway, I have nothing against Rebecca.'

'Yes, I think we should perform it,' I say. 'After all, our encore went down well.'

'But can we hold an audience for that long?' asks Billy. 'The whole piece is in the same key—or at least each fugue begins and ends in it.'

'That's true for the Goldberg too,' says Helen. 'Well, it's the same tonic anyway. And pianists fill halls with that.'

'But it's also the sameness of the "Art of Fugue" that bothers me,' says Billy. 'I mean, in terms of texture—for a performance piece. On the other hand it does build up. Perhaps we could play half of it . . .'

'Why didn't you write about all this in your brief, Billy?' I ask.

'Oh, I don't know, I thought my notes were too long anyway.'

'They weren't,' says Helen.

Billy hesitates for a second, then continues. 'Personally—and this has nothing to do with Ysobel or Stratus or our quartet as such—I feel that strings are ideal for bringing fugues out, ideal. They sustain notes better than the harpsichord or piano. They express individual lines better. And unlike, say, wind instruments, they let you double-stop—as Piers and I had to at the end of the first piece today, when four parts became six. Besides, Mozart and Beethoven agree with me.'

'Oh, they do, do they?' asks Piers. 'When did you last use the celestial link-up?'

'I didn't need to. It's a well-known fact that Mozart arranged Bach fugues for string quartet, and Beethoven arranged a Handel one.'

427

We look astonished.

'It's a well-known fact, is it?' asks Piers threateningly.

'Well, perhaps not in some quarters,' says Billy with a satisfied smile.

'If it's true . . .' begins Helen, 'if it's really true, couldn't we perhaps play the first half of the "Art of Fugue", and then—after the interval—these Mozart and Beethoven arrangements? That would be a great programme, and it would give the audience a bit of variety.'

'Yes,' groans Piers, 'why don't we build our whole life around fugal programmes?'

'Fugues are so empowering for the middle voices,' continues Helen, a bit smugly.

'Empowering. Empowering,' says Piers. 'Who's been talking to you about empowerment? No, don't tell me. I smell sandals.'

'Oh, Billy,' says Helen suddenly, 'I've got the ideal dessert for you. It'll take me thirty seconds precisely.'

She jumps up, goes to the freezer, then to the microwave, puts it on for about ten seconds, and emerges with five yellow cherries on a plate, which she places in front of Billy.

'What are these?' he asks.

'Yellow cherries. No calories to speak of.'

'But what have you done to them?'

'Eat them quick, then ask. Quick.'

Billy puts one gingerly into his mouth, then rolls his eyes back in ecstasy. He eats another, and another, till they are all gone.

'They're a miracle,' he says. 'It's like molten cherries outside, and crunchy sorbet inside. Marry me, Helen.'

'You're already married.'

'So I am. How did you do it?'

'Bought them, washed them, froze them, microwaved them. That's it.

'You're a genius.'

'I call them cerise microsorbet. I'm thinking of starting my own school.'

'That would be great,' I say. 'A string quartet cooking school. Helen could be the director, Piers and I the students, and Billy the guinea-pig. Erica would have no problem with a brand image then.'

'Why does Erica need to brand us?' asks Piers.

'Oh, she just thinks that we need something to make us better known to the musical public. String quartets are hard to promote.'

'That's Erica all over,' says Piers. 'I've been wondering about her. I think we should consider getting another agent.'

Billy, Helen and I, in different ways, demur.

'I wasn't happy about this trip,' says Piers. 'We barely broke even financially, and—well, there were other things as well.' Piers avoids looking at me. 'Now we've got the clarinet quintet coming up with Cosmo. We've played with him before, so we know he's OK, but if we hadn't, how would we know? How can we trust our agent if she doesn't inform us fully?'

'Erica didn't know about Julia,' I say. 'Be fair, Piers. Lothar knew, but decided he couldn't tell. If you're thinking of getting rid of anyone, it should be him. Except that you won't, because he's the best agent in Austria.'

'I'll have some more cherries,' says Billy quickly.

Helen prepares some more of her creation, and each of us gets a helping this time. She pours out some grappa she bought in Venice, and good fellowship is restored.

The second half of the rehearsal begins. But now I cannot forget the world outside, and from time to time I am attacked by small panics lasting a few seconds each, when my hand but not my mind is on the notes before my eyes, and I sense the grey bathroom near the Brahms-Saal closing in on me.

7.8

I get back home late at night and check my messages.

'Michael, this is James; James Hansen. I need to speak to you. Please call me on my *office* number,' begins the message. There is a brief pause and a rustle of paper. He gives me his number, and adds, rather brusquely: 'I'd appreciate it if you'd call me as soon as possible.'

There is another message after this, but I can't take it in, and have to rewind the tape to get it. Something about an overdue score from a library. I close and extend my left hand, which is bothering me a bit—the rehearsal was long, and I'm not yet used to playing the viola again.

Why is it he and not Julia who has called? Why does he want me to call him at his office? What has Julia said to him?

My thoughts are interrupted by the phone. Who could it be at this hour? It must be eleven o'clock.

'Hello—Michael?' says my father's voice.

'Dad? What's the matter? Is everything all right?'

'She's dead—Zsa-Zsa's dead. This afternoon. I

430

called but I kept getting your machine.' My father's voice is querulous, tearful.

'I'm so sorry, Dad.'

'I don't know what to do.'

'Did you have to have her put down?'

'No—she just lay down under the table like she usually does after lunch, and an hour or two later we found her there.'

'Oh Dad. I'm so sorry. She was a wonderful cat.'

'She could have died in my lap.' I can hear my father's voice breaking. 'I remember the day when your Mum named her.'

'How is Auntie Joan?'

'She's upset,' he says, trying to pull himself together.

Poor Zsa-Zsa. Poor old faithful, aggressive, salmon-filching, territorial, canny cat. But she had a long life and an eventful one.

'Dad, I'll come and visit you next week. Or at the latest the week after.'

'Do come, Michael, please.'

'Dad, I'm sorry I haven't visited . . . Where do you plan to bury her?'

'Now it's funny you should ask,' says my father, cheering up. 'We were just talking about it. Joan thinks we should cremate her, but I think we should bury her in the garden.'

'Not near the gnome, I hope.'

'Not near the gnome?'

'No,' I say firmly.

'But that's in the Boyds' garden anyway,' he says.

'I know, but it's two feet away from ours, and half facing it.'

'Where do you suggest, then?' he asks.

'In a flower-bed.'

'All right, I'll think about it,' says my father. 'Thank you for calling, Michael. I was very upset, and if you hadn't called I was thinking of calling you even though it's late.'

'But I didn't,' I begin to say, then stop. 'That's all right, Dad. Bye, then, Dad, goodnight.'

'Goodnight, Michael,' says my father, and hangs up.

I am tired: mind, hand and heart. I drift off, thinking: what does her husband want to speak about?

My dreams, though, are of Zsa-Zsa. At one point I say to her—her head is resting on my arm—look, I know this is a dream, Zsa-Zsa, and you are dead, but I'd like to continue it with your permission; and somehow I manage to do so.

7.9

I dial James Hansen's office number quickly; but before anyone lifts the receiver I hang up. After a few minutes I dial again. His secretary puts me through to him.

'Thank you for getting back so soon, Michael,' he says. 'It's Julia's birthday in less than a week, as you perhaps know, and I'm throwing a party for her—and I wondered, since you are such good friends, whether you might be able to come . . . Hello, Michael, are you there?'

'Yes. Yes, thank you, James, I'd love to come.'

'Well, then, Wednesday, seven o'clock or so. But it's to be a surprise, so I'd be grateful if you didn't mention it to anyone.'

'Where will it be?'

'At home. A neighbour in the crescent is keeping the caterers and the food and drink in readiness, so I hope Julia won't cotton on to what I'm doing. I'm trying to keep numbers down to about a dozen, because, well, she can't concentrate in crowds—so I haven't asked your colleagues in the quartet.'

'No, I—I see why, I mean, that's a good idea.'

'I hope the weather's better than today.'

'Yes.'

'Well, I'm really delighted you can come. See you in a few days. It was good to meet you the last time.'

'Yes, well, thank you. My—my very best to Julia.'

'Well, that'll have to wait, wouldn't you say?'

'Oh, yes, naturally. But how did you manage to get my number?'

'The way anyone would. The phone book.'

'But of course.'

I put down the phone, dazed with relief. Yes, I will go—yes, I tell myself, I *will* have to go, for anything else would be inexplicable. What will she say when she sees me? What will I get her as a gift? Has she told James about the blue frog that he must often see? She couldn't have. I would have sensed it, surely.

7.10

Wednesday comes. I have put down my gift, shrouded in paper, on the table near the door. I am shaking hands.

But today he is not so delighted, not so cordial at all. He is polite, no more. He does not scowl, but is cold. The weather is marvellous and the guests spill

433

out into the garden. Dark venous roses bloom. Waiters top the drained flutes, and Julia, who has not dressed for the occasion, is looking lovely.

What is the explanation for his manner? Is it something at the office? Is it a tiff ? If it was anything else, something pointed at me, could he not have phoned and told me that the whole thing had been called off? Am I not, for him, at the periphery of things?

Julia laughs, talks, then sees me—and looks distressed. Luke comes over to me and we talk for a while. What did the monster eat after he had all his teeth taken out? The dentist. Buzby bounds about and Luke runs after him. I stand aside and watch.

After a while, Julia comes up to me and says, without even a greeting, 'Michael, I don't know why James invited you—but I think he knows about us, somehow, I'm not quite sure how. These last couple of days he hasn't been himself.'

His eyes are on us from a distance.

'I'm certain he didn't know last week,' I say. 'Are you sure?'

She nods.

'Has he said anything?' I ask.

'No—nothing directly.'

'Not such a happy birthday after all.'

'No.'

'I'm going to Rochdale in a few days. Come with me. You used to say you'd go there with me—that you wanted to see where I was born and brought up.'

'I can't, now or ever.'

'Oh, Julia, it's not good, is it, what's happening?'

'I don't know what's going to happen . . . I'd

434

better talk to the other guests now.'

'I've left my present on the table.'

'Thank you.' She cannot meet my eyes. What will she say when she discovers it is a bonsai, twelve years old, that needs to be watered once every two days? If she does not tend it, it will certainly die.

I wait till she finally looks up, and say: 'I'm going to make some excuse and go. But please come and see me. Please.'

Even as the words leave my mouth, I think: what am I, a lapdog?

'Yes, yes, I will—just leave me alone, Michael.'

'All right,' I say. 'I'll go up and beard James.'

'No. Don't,' she pleads. 'Just mingle and avoid him. I don't know how he knows. Perhaps I spoke in my sleep—perhaps Sonia said something—or Jenny—oh, how grim all this is.'

'Julia, we're both transparent people.'

'Are we?'

'I love you. Is that transparent enough? He can't lip-read, can he?'

'I must go,' she says. 'But please don't leave immediately. It'll look odd. Goodbye, then, Michael.'

She leaves me. After a few minutes of tippling and nibbling with people I'll never know, I take my leave of Luke and, on the way out, of James.

'Have you said goodbye to Julia?' he asks. 'You must say goodbye to Julia.'

'I told her I'd be going early, so she knows I'll be slipping off.'

'What a pity. Something come up?'

'Yes, some work.'

'What are you working on?' he asks. Is he toying with me?

'The "Art of Fugue". We have a big rehearsal tomorrow, and I'm woefully unprepared.'

'Julia's fond of that—as you probably know,' says James. 'Plays bits of it sometimes. Quite subtle music, isn't it?'

'Subtle?'

'Oh, there's so much more going on than one senses at first. Of course, I'm not a musician; I don't know if I'm using the right word . . . but then, Julia tells me she's pretty glad on the whole that I'm not a musician. Kind of paradoxical. If I had been, I would have been able to make music with her. On the other hand, when she lost her hearing, perhaps I wouldn't have encouraged her to continue. Of course, it's a hypothetical question, but it's a relief for me to discuss it with someone who's in the know.'

'Yes. I'm so sorry, James. I must be off. Thank you. I've enjoyed the party.'

He eyes me evenly and reaches out his hand. I shake it, and go.

7.11

I have come, as promised, to Rochdale again. My father has aged since the Christmas holidays.

We are sitting in Owd Betts at two in the afternoon, and his tears fall onto his stratified sole. It is cloudy outside. There is a pearly light in the lower half of the sky, and a dull gleam on the reservoir.

'It's only a cat, Stanley,' says Auntie Joan. 'It's not Ada.'

This distracts my father enough to make him

glare.

'Give over, Stanley, you've seen enough turkeys die in your time.'

'Auntie Joan,' I protest.

'It's good for him,' says Auntie Joan unfeelingly. 'He's been like this for days. Doesn't say a word. It's unhealthy. And it's boring for me. Your coming has done him good, dear.'

'I hope so. Dad, why don't you get a kitten? I'll get one for you.'

'Don't suggest it,' says Auntie Joan firmly. 'If I die first, what'll become of it? And if he dies first, I don't want to have to deal with it.'

I am silent in the face of her brutal logic. It strikes me that one of her most admirable skills is taking charge at a scene of death and bustling everyone about till they face things. This could be because her husband was an undertaker in Balderstone.

'And what's the matter with you?' continues Auntie Joan. 'Has she left you?'

I put down my Guinness. 'Who?' I ask.

'Whoever she is. You get these hangdog looks all of a sudden.'

'Auntie Joan, what exactly happened to that couple who went to Scunthorpe?'

'Well, he got a divorce and married her, of course. But the poor wife never got the full insurance on the shop. The lorry-driver's insurance company paid out a bit and then refused to pay any more.'

My father has started humming one of Gracie Fields's more risque songs. One stratum of his stratified sole has disappeared.

'There wasn't any embalming in those days,' says

437

Auntie Joan for no obvious reason. 'They gave him a tumbler of whisky when he went to the house, that's how they greeted him, and he just went ahead and dressed the corpse. No embalming. They kept it at the house and then buried it.'

Dad's ginger and lemon pudding arrives in a lake of custard, to his evident delight. The ghost of Zsa-Zsa no longer hangs over the meal. Auntie Joan reverts to her more customary mixture of gossip and reverie, and stops bullying us.

'Don't forget, Stanley,' she says, turning suddenly to my father who has meanwhile perked up, 'life's worth complaining about.'

I like it here, even if I nearly banged my head against the low beams when we entered. Owd Betts is for me a sign of friendly hope, though it stands so exposed on the moors, at the crest of the road. When we were at school, a friend and I did a sponsored walk from Blackpool to Rochdale. We were bussed out and dumped on the seafront, and told to find our way home on foot. Lashed by rain, blistered, exhausted and starving, we finally passed Owd Betts and felt for the first time that the end was in sight. I remember the shock in Mum's eyes when I got home. I slept for three days.

I think back on those times, so far removed from these, when my heart neither knew of nor yearned for love. What would I have thought if an outsider had intruded on my parents' marriage? James has been deft; he did not mention Luke.

'I'm going to walk back,' I say.

'Whatever for, Michael?' asks my father.

'I want to walk off my Guinness.'

'Who'll drive us back?' demands Auntie Joan.

'You will, of course,' I say with a smile. 'You

438

drove us here.'

'But it's miles. It'll take you hours.'

'Just a few miles. I'll be home by evening. I've been in London too long. I need it.'

'Well,' says Auntie Joan, 'don't blame me if you fall down a mineshaft.'

I pay, see them into the car, and watch it weave a little uncertainly down the road. Auntie Joan may have arthritis but she is as reluctant to share the steering wheel as the stove.

Beyond Owd Betts there is a roadblock for some reason, with police in lime-green jackets busying themselves turning cars back towards Rochdale. A man in a little one-horse sulky is protesting, but to no effect. There must be an accident further down. I leave the road and walk up into the hills.

7.12

From high up here the sign of Owd Betts, the inn itself, the road with its buttercups and thistles and weathered, blackened gritstone wall, the reservoir, the lime-green jackets distance themselves, and all there is is grass and wind.

The sound of cars disappears, but I hear the hooves of the horse through the violent sough of the wind. It is drizzling a little, so I may not be in luck, but there to the west I see a small cut of blue.

The air is fresh and sharp and the ground is a subtle chart of tussocks and black earth: hundreds of different grasses, some tipped with feathery brush, some with minute white four-pointed stars; low bilberry bushes with their berries still green— all rippling with or resisting the flapping and rushing of the wind.

I crouch in a hollow; the wind slackens; I lie in it, damp though it is, and the wind dies, and the horizon dies, and there is nothing but silence and sky.

From somewhere a cow lows; and then through it comes a wheedle-wheedle sound, a whistle of joy and energy that becomes a frenzied untrammelled song that rises higher and higher as the lark itself spirals unseen into the low grey sky.

Perhaps I will see it when it plummets. No, I would have to stand or scan; and I am happier to lay my arm across my eyes—or view the sky through my fingers.

Now two, now three, and now, though the sky is scarcely brighter, legions of larks rise up from the damp earth in careless counterpoint, each retaining its self even as it merges with its fellows.

But why can the lark not be itself alone, uninvested, uncompared even by those who love it most?

Type of the wise who soar, but never roam;
True to the kindred points of Heaven and Home!

O stodgy git.

Like a high-born maiden
In a palace tower,
Soothing her love-laden
Soul in secret hour
With music sweet as love which overflows her bower.

O gushy twit.

He rises and begins to round,
He drops the silver chain of sound
Of many links without a break
In chirrup, whistle, slur and shake . . .

Ah, now that, now that is it.

7.13

I have driven Mrs Formby up to Blackstone Edge and beyond, where the road cuts into the blackened rock. The stone walls end, the moors continue unmarked, the pylons march far into Yorkshire.

We talk about the music the quartet is preparing. When I tell her of the planned recording, her face lights up.

She asks me what has brought me to Rochdale this time. I mention my father and aunt and Zsa-Zsa. Besides, I say, I don't need a reason to come home. She seems unhappy and uncomfortable, and my own heart sinks.

'Michael, the violin, I'm afraid it's no good. Blood is thicker than water, and . . .'

I nod.

'In fact my blood is a bit too thick. Hypertension. Though why, I don't see. I'm a calm enough person.'

'I do hope you're all right.'

'Yes, I'm fine, I might live to be a hundred. Well, as I was saying, Michael, I'm not very fond of my nephew, but there it is.'

'I was afraid of this.'

'But you came to see me nevertheless.'

'Well, of course. And besides—'

'Yes?'

'You asked my father for my number some months ago, so I imagined you had something to say to me.'

She is silent for a while, then says, 'I didn't have the heart to call you. Well, what are you going to do for a violin?'

'I haven't thought it through yet.' I am silent for a while. 'When do you want it back?'

She looks puzzled, almost as if she hasn't understood the question.

'Mrs Formby, you must know that I have it here,' I say desperately. 'I always bring it with me when I come to Rochdale. It's yours, it always has been. But I wonder if I could keep it for just a few more months. Till we've completed our recording. I wonder if you could grant me that period of grace.'

'Oh, but the trust isn't set up yet. It'll be a few months in any case.'

'Thank you.'

'No, Michael, no—don't thank me. This must be hard.'

I nod. 'Well, 'tis better to have loved and lost, though, isn't it, Mrs Formby, than never to have loved at all?'

What am I saying? Why is she smiling?

'How are you rehearsing the "Art of Fugue"?' she asks.

I tell her about how Billy is structuring things, about Helen's deep viola, about my own viola-playing, about Piers's doubts, about Ysobel Shingle and Erica. She is rapt.

'How low do you have to go?' she asks.

'Usually F, but sometimes—for two or three

442

pieces—E or D.'

'Didn't you tell me that you tuned the lowest string of our violin down to F at the Wigmore Hall recital, and that you were able to play it instinctively with that tuning?'

'Yes.'

'Why don't you do the same now?'

I look at her. Indeed. Why don't I? I have, in fact, thought about it before, but never very seriously. It does have its advantages, though: apart from the three pieces where I go so low that I would be compelled to use a viola, I can stay with the violin throughout. The texture of our quartet would be more consistent on the whole. On the other hand, it would be a bit odd to play with a variant tuning more often than with the standard one—especially as it could unsettle the violin for other rehearsals and concerts.

But now what matters most is that I get to play my fiddle, however it is tuned, as much as I can contrive to in our last months together.

'Mrs Formby, I think that's a really good idea.'

'I'm so sorry about all this, Michael. I don't want you to think I haven't thought about you.'

'No, no, Mrs Formby. Don't say that.'

I tell her about my walk yesterday, and the larks. Behind her thick spectacles her eyes grow wider, and she smiles.

'He rises and begins to round,' she prompts.

'He drops the silver chain of sound,' I continue, and we recite it in alternate lines, unerringly.

'Till lost on his aerial wings,' she says at last, and sighs.

I am silent, and after a while, almost inaudibly, she herself murmurs the final line.

443

7.14

What are my assets then, my means? My bow is my own, my furniture, my books, £4,000 in savings, and what I own of my mortgaged flat. No car alas, nor patron either.

On my return to London I talk to Piers, who is himself looking for an instrument. He says nothing, then simply: 'My dear Michael.'

He tells me of a fund—I have heard of it before—that makes small loans at low interest rates to musicians seeking to buy instruments. But by themselves these loans are not enough.

Might my bank help? If I could pay for it, perhaps I can keep my violin after all. Piers doesn't know. His didn't.

Over these two years he has been to all the dealers in London but has found nothing he can afford that he likes enough. Now he has taken to attending violin auctions in the hope of a fortunate encounter. I should do the same, he says; we can examine instruments together, and play them, and bid for what we like and can afford. Am I interested? But it can break your heart, he warns; so far he has liked three fiddles, and been outbid for each.

Or perhaps I can get an instrument made for me by Sanderson along the measurements of my violin. *The* violin; *the* violin. Practise that.

Time is not with me. Unlike Piers, I am not upgrading what I already have. I will be left with nothing in my hands by the end of this year.

444

7.15

I do go to my bank. I make my case. I am asked for documents and proofs. I return in two days.

I meet a cheerful young man from whose vocabulary the first person singular has been expunged. He shakes my untrembling hand. Do sit down. Please. We do not believe in desks. Coffee? Yes, and sugar, please, for all three Fates lie in this grateful cup: vegetable bean, animal milk, mineral spoon. I read my grounds and the iris flecks of his friendly, pitiless eye. From him I learn that the bank has considered my problem. The bank recognises my fidelity. The bank appreciates the fact that I have never been overdrawn. The bank values me as a customer. The bank will not help me.

Why? Why? Is it not a tool of my trade? Do you not find my word or credit good?

Mr Morton—I think that's his name—explains that my income is low. My income is uncertain. I have no institutional affiliations. I am not even a permanent member of the Camerata Anglica. I am an extra, to be called upon as and when required. My mortgage payments are too high. The bank believes that the combination of my existing mortgage payments and the estimated payments on a loan for a fairly expensive instrument would leave me with very little to live on. The bank, in fact, is thinking chiefly of my interests.

But surely my interest lies in repaying any loan you make me.

Will anyone stand surety for you if you fall behind in your payments? Well, Mr Holme, we are sorry, but our guidelines . . .

So is that it, then? Will I lose the touch of it, the

sound of it, the sight of it? I really can't bear the thought of that, Mr Morton. I have had it for as long as I can remember.

Norton.

I'm so sorry. I'm so sorry. The forms have crushed themselves within my hands.

Now please remain calm, Mr Holme; let's have a look at your assets. Perhaps you would consider selling your flat? The bank is, well, associated with a residential sales company. The bank would be delighted to help.

I need a window. Where?

The bank should warn you, however, that your equity is not substantial, that the property market is volatile, and that there are, as we are sure you are aware, certain costs and commissions involved.

Is that what I must do then? What solution else? Is it the fault of the computer? Or is it Head Office? Why must there be no window in a manager's office? Is it a guideline? Why must this thing of wood undo me?

He will clone me a clone from woods both hard and soft; he will varnish it with resins from the argosies of Venice: sandarac, dammar, mastic, colophony. He will string it with the guts of beasts. Three hundred years of sweat and tears will rain acid into it, a year for every day, three hundred years of music will sing through its serpentine mouths, it will be mine again; the unique will be replicated.

Or I can go to the rooms with Piers, and stretch my hand forth with its urgent digits—I want that— or that—or that.

But it is my Tononi that I want, which is too dear. Sell, beg and borrow as I may I cannot stretch so far.

7.16

My dear Michael,
   I said I would visit you but I can't. I can't take the strain of it any more. I can hardly play the piano these days. It seems as if my heart stops when I play.
   Things are pressing down on me. Please don't reply to this or see me or ask me to explain. I won't say I will always love you. It will sound too false. It's not false at all—but what good will it do you or me to know it or say it?
   I feel as if I am a prisoner in my mind and in this room. You have seen it now, so you can imagine me at my desk or at the piano. I wanted you to see it but now you are too much here, as everywhere else in my life. I have to learn peace again, for my own sake—and for Luke, and for James, who looks lost and tired. I have become restless with you, and uncertain, and afraid, and guilty, and unsustainably, stupidly full of joy and pain—none of which is anyone's fault but my own. Don't ask me why or how, because I don't know myself. I know that I cannot cope with seeing you or knowing that it is possible to see you.
   I, of all people, who have a Before and an After, should have known that you can't relive your life. I should never have come backstage that night. Please forgive me and, if you are as little capable of forgetting me as I am of forgetting you, at least think of me less often

with each day and each year.

Love—yes, you know what I feel. I may as well set it down again—

Julia

7.17

This is not true. But I saw the letter come through the slot. I saw her slanting hand and tore it open.

The lift. No. Stop it, recall him, undeliver this. Unpost, unwrite, unthink it.

Julia, rethink this for pity's sake, and for God's, in whom you trust. I will be deaf to it, I will ignore it. How about that? I will not re-read it, as I am re-reading it now. I will put on some Schubert. The Trout Quintet, blithe and lithe, the little fishes conjured from no vasty deep. This you played, and this, and this. It makes me gag. I hurriedly shave. My heart's blood stubbles my chin, but look, it is smooth again, and clean, and whole. None of this need be or have been.

I will journey on a double-decker bus to find you where I once saw you in the choked road. The summer leaves obscure the Serpentine. Only through knowledge do I divine the water beyond, as I trust in your kindness. Will you let my plant live, that was entrusted to your care? Of it you have not said a single word.

The Angel of Selfridges is not in the giving vein. Is it that we have offended?

Maculate with the black dregs of chewing gum, how grubby is the pavement all around. This is not the place.

448

Your address is known to me, so now in the bright day I am at your door.

7.18

Julia stands before me, her son at her side. I hear the qualities in her voice. For the words I care nothing.

Luke addresses me and I smile, unhearing, uncomprehending. 'But shouldn't you be at school?' I ask.

'It's the holidays.'

'I'm going to borrow your mother for a little while, Luke. We have some music to discuss. Is your Nanny in? Good. I promise to bring her back.'

'Can't I come too?' he pleads.

I shake my head. 'No, Luke, it's boring. It's worse than scales. But very important.'

'I could play with Buzby.'

'Darling, it's not a good idea,' she says. 'It slipped my mind that I had to go out. I'll be back soon. Oh, Michael, I forgot. I've still got your record.'

'I can always take it later.'

'No, now would be best, I think,' she says lightly. A quick smile at Luke. She is back in half a minute, with the LP of Beethoven's string quintet in its white inner sleeve.

'Julia, keep it.' No, this intensity will not do.

'No, Michael, I won't,' she says. She thrusts it into my hands.

Luke looks alarmed. 'How soon is soon?' he asks.

'Just an hour, darling,' says Julia.

We are walking up a hill and down a hill and into a park in which peacocks preen and cry. Her face says, I will indulge him for one hour and no more, and make things clear. There will be no interminable codas. In the Japanese garden we sit where others sit, on a gentle slope near the waterfall.

'Say something, Julia.'

She shakes her head.

'Say something. Anything. How could you do this?'

'How could *you* do this?'

'I had to see you. You can't mean it.'

Again she shakes her head.

'Have you been able to practise?' I ask.

'Michael, I don't want to see you again.'

'How is the tinnitus?'

'Didn't you hear what I said?'

'Didn't you hear what *I* said? How is the tinnitus? How is it? Are you hearing better or worse? Will you play with me again? There's a problem with the Tononi, Julia—I need to think things through.'

'Michael, I can't, because of a series of your problems, be forced to play with people.'

'With *people*?'

'With anyone. I am not, I am not ever, I am never going to play with anyone again.'

'What does he mean to you? Does he mean what I mean?'

'Michael, stop this.'

'What's happening to us?'

'Us? Us? What us?'

'Julia.'

I close my eyes. I bow my head. The cataract

450

sounds in my ears. 'I'm not taking you away from anyone,' I say at last. 'I'd be content just to—'

'We're going to Boston for a month,' she says.

I stroke the grass with my palm. 'How do you know he knows?'

'He's injured. I can see it, and I can't bear it. In the worst days, when I could hardly recognise myself in the mirror, I saw in his eyes that I was myself. He helped me through. I can read him, Michael.'

'How did he find out?'

'Michael, can't you understand—all this is beside the point. Perhaps no one else said anything. People who have lived together for years can sense such things. Perhaps he just heard the falsity in my voice.'

'Can *you* hear that in *his*?'

'Michael!'

'You'll cope without me, Julia. I won't without you.'

'Michael, don't make things more difficult.'

'Have you ever danced with him?'

'Danced? What sort of question is that? Did you say danced?'

'Do you love him?'

'Yes. Yes. Yes. Of course I do.'

'But you married him—' I stop.

'On the rebound?'

'I wasn't going to say that.'

'You were. Or words to that effect. It's only partly true. I liked him from the start. He isn't volatile—like me. He isn't moody—like me. He doesn't ask questions that come out of nowhere. He comforted me. He made me happy. He kept me sane. He gave me courage.'

451

'And I can't? I didn't?'

'I love him now. I can't live without him. What's the point of explaining these things? Or Luke. How could I have been so stupid—worse than stupid, so selfish, so self-indulgent, so reckless? I can't cope, you know, Michael. I seem to, but I don't. He can't even hear the sound of his parents talking to each other at night, when the lights are off. All children hear that. I hate my deafness. If I were blind I would have coped better. If it weren't for music I'd be a mess.'

I can't follow this, I can't unravel this. It goes too far back into the separate hinterlands of our lives.

'You're an only child. So am I—that's part of it,' she says, her voice quieter once more.

'Part of—do you mean part of the problem?'

'I want to have another child. Luke needs someone to share me with, or he'll grow up to be as selfish as I am.'

'Why not apply this kind of logic to James? Why doesn't he need someone to share you with?'

She doesn't bother to respond to this. 'I must get back,' she says.

'So we're not to see each other again?'

'No.'

'You'll pray for me, of course—as you did on Torcello.'

'Yes. Yes.' She's crying now, but she still has to look at my face for my words.

'An odd God to make you deaf.'

'What a cheap and easy thing to say.'

'Possibly. But it's not so easy to rebut it.'

'And cruel.'

'What do you think you're being? You think I'm like some—some porcelain frog that you can pick

452

up and smash down when you lose interest in it or decide it's inconvenient? How could you tell me all that in a letter, Julia? Couldn't you at least have—'

'OFF the grass. OFF the grass, please. OFF the grass.' A stern dumpling of a policewoman is doing her prohibitory rounds. The quiet couples scatter. We stand up.

'But why?' I ask the woman, dazed. 'Why?'

'There's a sign there. OFF the grass, please.'

Beyond the grass are smooth stones, the zen margin of the pond. I will touch you. Guide me.

'And the stones?' I ask.

'The STONES?' The policewoman turns to stare.

'There's no sign regarding the stones, is there?'

'Michael,' says Julia, her hand on my arm. 'Don't argue with her. Please. Let's go.'

'Thanks, Julia. I'm living my own life now.'

'I'm TELLING you, OFF the stones.'

'If there's no law, what does it matter what you say? What would you do if I did step on the stones?'

'I'd . . . I'd . . . I'd PROCESS you,' the woman says, pointing her finger at me.

Off she goes, disappearing along the path. We brush ourselves off, and stand facing each other for a minute. I will not kiss her. It is peace I need. I will go down to the water's edge and touch the smooth round stones.

Julia is holding the record out to me once more. This is the music that we both once loved. This is what I lost, then found.

I look at it, and at her, and fling the wretched taunting thing into the pond.

It sinks. I do not turn to see her expression. I

453

leave her there and walk away.

7.19

The streets are full of noise. I sit in my nest above the world. The wind flaps against the panes, but apart from that there is nothing.

My eye falls on her book, her paper-knife. No, let them be, why rail against these things?

There are no messages on my phone. I turn off the answering machine. From time to time it rings. I do not answer it. Whoever it is tires of waiting.

I sit and let the sky darken.

The sky is grey, the room is not yet cold. Let me sit in silence. Let my head drop on my chest. Let me, abjuring hope, find peace.

7.20

The phone rings madly, maddeningly. I let it ring. It continues ringing, twenty, twenty-five rings, each drilling into the pulp of my brain. Finally I pick it up.

'Yes? Hello.'

A woman's voice: 'Is that the London Bait Company?'

'What?'

'I said, is that the London Bait Company? Why don't you answer the phone?' It is the braying, hateful voice of the deep South.

'Do you mean 'bait' as in catching fish?'

'Yes. Of course.'

'Yes, this is the London Bait Company. What

were you looking for?' My voice must sound quite wild.

'Trout pellets.'

'Trout pellets? I wouldn't recommend them.'

'Why ever not?'

'It's better to tickle trout.'

'I didn't exactly ask for your advice . . .'

'I'm new at the job. What particular trout pellets would you like?'

'What on earth do you mean?'

'We have small, medium and large; coffee, chocolate and liquorice flavoured; ribbed, textured, extra-strength—'

'Look here, this is the London Bait Company, isn't it?'

'Well, no, as it happens it isn't, but from the number of calls I receive it might as well be.'

'How dare you speak to me in this manner? This is sheer harassment.'

'May I remind you, madam, that it was you who called me. I have a good mind to dial 1471, get your number, and play *'Die Forelle'* to you every midnight.'

'This is absolutely intolerable. I shall report you to your manager—to the police.'

'You can do whatever you fucking well like, madam. Just stop ringing this number. I have had a hard day, one which I wouldn't wish even on you. The love of my life has left me and the police have threatened to arrest me, so your menaces hold no terrors. And I wouldn't recommend trout pellets because the latest research shows, madam, that 99.93% of those who used trout pellets in 1880 have subsequently died.'

There is a gasp at the other end of the line, and

it goes dead.

I turn off the ringer and sit still, hour following hour, listening to nothing, waiting for nothing.

PART EIGHT

8.1

Only my daily rigours keep me clear. We meet, the four voices, and enter a braid. So I play, and I am praised by my fellows, and I bow, I bow, for only sorrow moves me cleanly through these lines. My violin senses where I am veering, and keeps me to the path that is direct and spare. How few months we have together.

Sun-up, sun-down. I practise duly what I must. We perform, and the mad fan reappears to taunt us with adoration. Will nothing be done about him? What hath closed Helen's eye? In the green room we are quizzed and questioned. I am out of all this.

My violin, I am sad like you, and yet I thank the moon for these few months of grace. Your strings are true. How will the chartered surveyor smile on you? He will have you appraised and divided, back and belly, between his daughters. Your golden grain will milk him his balances. How thick, how sour must blood be, that it can corrode all propinquity?

I must use the dumb-blind alphabet at night. My one hand will speak to its partner and know what it is doing. Sensile, sensate, sensory, sensible, sensitive. I retain two others unsaid: sensuous, sensual. Two escape me still—sensive, sensal—for I am uncertain as to their meaning; that then is nine. As for sensational, it is a doubtful case, and I would leave one finger uncorresponded. She can play on two manuals as I can not, but what will stir her stereocilia in their ruined bath? Moon-rise, moon-set. In Boston too the weeks pass at this pulse.

Need I list the vegetation that the Gulf Stream gifts the squares of London? Shall I blotch the invariant calendar with dyes and juices? The golden husks of lime-keys were gathered in piles along the kerb. The acres near the Round Pond grew dust-white with flower-of-grass. All this, it seems, happened from new moon to new moon. But then the rain was a patter, almost a crackle, in the sycamore behind me. And now it is more a sort of steam, mixed with the pollen of lime blossom, rising from the grass and resting below the lowest boughs.

8.2

Hawthorn is green in berry, and pyracantha ripe. My feet have lost their hold, my hands scrabble for purchase. The days swelter and they make Carnival in the streets. I said I could not sleep without you, yet I do. Is it not to be wondered at?

We are at Denton's auction house now, and I am here to see Piers bid, for I cannot yet take what I must soon take, a step such as this towards infidelity. Piers is indifferent towards his violin. But now he has seen and held and heard one that he loves, has borrowed it from Denton's and played it with us for a couple of days. It is a burnished red with black crackling. Sadly—or, rather, happily for Piers's hopes, because this reduces only its monetary worth—its scroll is not by the original maker. It has a grand, unplaintive tone, slightly too penumbra'd with richness and resonance for me, but Piers loves it with the passion of sudden and, yes, attainable love. With all his savings and borrowings he can just about reach the estimated price. The auctioneer's 15% will stretch him on the rack, but he knows that this is what he must have. He will spend years paying it off.

It is marked in the auctioneer's catalogue as a P. J. Rogeri. Henry Cheetham, the green-suede-jacketed, urbane, avuncular head of the musical instruments department at Denton's, has collared Piers. Indignant snorts, anxious consultations of his watch and managerial glances around a room adorned with fiddles mark his monologue, so confident, so confiding.

'Oh, yes, the dealers say we auctioneers are in it for the quick buck, but I don't see any dealers starving in attics, do you? At least in our case everything's transparent. The price is the highest bid at an open auction—plus our, well, pretty modest commission when you come to think of it. Well, all right, we collect from buyer and seller, but, you know, overheads and so on. And we certainly don't get into the sorts of shenanigans that *they* do. Dealers! Compared to them we're bloody saints! . . . Well, good luck, Piers, old chap, I do hope you're not outbid. Too bad about the last time. I've a feeling, though, that you were being preserved for this one. Just look at that purfling— that grain—that glow! What tone. What timbre. What, er, what a *terrific* old fiddle this is. You were *made* for each other. Ah, two-forty. I'd better go down. You've registered, haven't you? Good . . . good . . . very good indeed! Piers is a pro!' he adds confidentially to me. 'He'll teach you the ropes. Or should I say strings? Ha ha ha!' And, well-pleased with this last, he walks magisterially out of his office, leaving Piers sick with anxiety.

'I bet Henry's telling everyone it's *made* for

461

them. I bet he is.'

'I suppose that's part of his job.'

'Whose *fucking* side are you on, Michael?' says Piers with miserable viciousness.

'Hey, come on now,' I say, placing my arm on his shoulder.

'It's twenty minutes till the auction begins. How am I going to get through it?' he demands. 'I can't concentrate on the newspaper, I don't want to make small talk, and I don't dare to have a drink.'

'How about doing nothing?' I suggest.

'Nothing?' says Piers, staring at me.

'Yes,' I say. 'Let's go downstairs, sit down, and do nothing at all.'

8.3

At 3 p.m—the auctioneer ascends his podium in the great room downstairs. He passes his right hand through his greying blond hair, taps the microphone placed at the front of the lectern, nods at a couple of faces in the audience. A young man in a green apron—he looks like a butcher's boy, I think with a start—stands in front of the podium. He holds up the objects announced and sold: at first, a few books relating to the art of string playing; then bows: silver-mounted, gold-mounted, bone-mounted. The butcher's boy holds them from the frog and the tip, rather gingerly. The auctioneer's eyes are languid and alert, his voice coaxingly brisk. His suit is dark grey and double-breasted. His gaze moves swiftly from the floor where we sit to the bank of telephones to our left.

The price of a bow rises swiftly from a starting

price of £1,500, less than half its lower estimated value in the catalogue.

'Two thousand two hundred here now . . . yes, against you, in front of me . . . two thousand four hundred . . .' A young woman on one of the telephones nods. 'Two thousand six hundred . . . yes. No? No? Two thousand six hundred once; twice,'—he taps the hammer lightly on the lectern—'sold for two thousand six hundred pounds to . . . ?'

'Buyer number two hundred and eleven, sir,' says the woman on the phone.

'Number two hundred and eleven,' repeats the auctioneer. He pauses for a sip of water.

'Do you really want to sit through all this?' I ask Piers.

'Yes.'

'But you said it would be two hours before the Rogeri comes under the hammer. Isn't all this just a sort of preamble?'

'I want to wait. You can suit yourself.'

He bids for nothing else. He wants nothing else. He torments himself. But he follows the prices, and points out to me that things are going, on the whole, for less than their lower estimates. It bodes well for him; don't I agree? I nod. I've never been to one of these things before. I am hardly capable of holding his hand through this auction, so jittery am I myself.

The secret, says Piers, is to calculate the total cost including commission and tax at each level of bidding, decide the most you are willing to pay, and stick to it, no matter how hectic the bidding or how tempting the prize. With a pencil he circles the figure he will refuse to go beyond, and underlines it

463

for good measure.

He points out the dealers at the front. Despite the chasm between them and the auctioneers, they are quite happy to procure what they desire in enemy territory. An hour into the auction, a brittle middle-aged woman, heavily lipsticked and mascara'd and with a laugh like a slash enters, preening and basking. She represents one of the wealthier dealers. A bearded, humbler fellow responds to her witticisms with a stifled giggle. She bids for a few items with a nod of her head, picks up her seven shopping bags after half an hour and hangs visibly about the corridor for a bit before leaving.

Who are these others around us? I recognise a woman who is an amateur violinist and part of the management of the Wigmore Hall. I see Henry Cheetham sitting discreetly to one side. I recognise a couple of faces from orchestra or session work. But London is a musical universe, and who the others are I do not know.

The auction has moved from cellos to violas to violins.

'Ladies and gentlemen,' the auctioneer is saying, 'do call out if you have the slightest doubt that I've noticed you. Fingers are sometimes difficult to see, especially behind a catalogue, and it's very awkward having to reopen a bid once I've closed it. Well, I shall take that bid at nineteen thousand pounds with apologies to the gentleman here in front . . .'

Piers is looking ill. He is taking slow breaths to calm himself. One violin, estimated in the same range as the one he wants, goes for just over its lower estimate, and his shoulders relax. The auction, so slow before, is careering along at a mad pace. Before he expects it—for in his nervousness he has stopped following the order in the catalogue—the Rogeri is on the block.

In his hands it was as if it belonged to him. But now it is the aproned lad who holds it up before us.

Its red-brown grain flares out through its ground of gold. It is not ashamed of its 'later Italian scroll' nor does it deign to care whose chattel it is to be. Messrs Denton and Denton will sell it to whoever's need is greatest, whoever's purse is deepest, whoever will most recklessly mortgage his future, whoever is of its desirers the most pound-puissant.

Piers bids nothing till they have expended themselves competing on the phone and on the floor. Its estimate is £35,000 to £50,000, because of that blessed unoriginal scroll. But they are already at £28,000, the price at which the other one was sold.

There is a pause, and at last he raises his paddle. The auctioneer looks relieved.

'Thirty thousand from a new bidder. I have thirty thousand here in the middle. Any advance on thirty thousand pounds?' Someone behind us raises a hand, for the auctioneer's eyes move to the back of the room. 'Thirty-two thousand. I have thirty-two thousand.' His eyes focus on Piers, who nods slightly. 'Thirty-four, I have thirty-four thousand.' His eyes zigzag back and forth between the only two bidders remaining. 'Thirty-six . . . thirty-eight . . . forty.'

I read the signs of Piers's confusion in his hands clutching the catalogue, in his breathing, so deliberately slow. 'It's against you, sir,' the auctioneer is saying, pointing, ballpen in hand, to

465

where he is sitting. 'Forty thousand against you; do you wish to bid?' It is all Piers can do not to turn around to face his unseen rival, who is so precipitately gobbling away huge chunks of his savings and earnings with each bid. He nods, slightly, calmly.

'Forty-two thousand,' says the auctioneer. 'Forty-four. Forty-six. Forty-eight.'

The bidding pauses as the auctioneer looks at Piers and waits for his bid. Finally, Piers nods.

'Fifty thousand,' says the auctioneer imperturbably. 'Fifty-two. Fifty-four. Fifty-six. Fifty-eight.'

'Piers!' I whisper, shocked. He has gone ten thousand pounds beyond the figure he circled.

'Do I have an advance on fifty-eight? At the back?' The auctioneer waits. There is a deep silence in the room. By now it is clear that these are two musicians, not dealers, bidding against each other, for they have far exceeded what is rational for resale. This piece of maple and spruce before them is not something that will pass into their hands and out again.

A mobile phone bleeps stridently; bleeps; bleeps; bleeps. Heads turn towards the source of the sound. Piers's paddle falls to the floor. The startled boy in the apron twirls the violin around, then back again. The auctioneer frowns. The bleeping stops as suddenly as it began.

'I imagine that has been detonated here by Christie's,' he says, to perfunctory laughter. 'Well, after that little intermezzo, perhaps we should continue. Fifty-eight. I have fifty-eight. Do I have sixty at the back? I do? Sixty. Sixty-two?' He looks at Piers, whose shoulders have slumped.

466

'Don't go on, Piers,' I whisper. 'Something else will come along at the next auction.'

But Piers looks up at what the butcher's boy is holding, and nods once more.

'Sixty-two. I have sixty-two. Sixty-four? Sixty-four. Sixty-six?'

Piers nods, white-faced.

'Sixty-six. Do I have sixty-eight at the back? Sixty-eight.'

'Shit,' whispers Piers to himself. The woman in front of him half turns around.

'Don't do it, Piers,' I say. He glares at me.

'I'm sorry, sir, was that a bid? Do I have seventy?'

'Yes,' says Piers aloud for the first time, in a calm, anguished voice. Is he giving himself away? If so, good. Let the other bastard have it, Piers. Don't ruin yourself.

'Seventy. Seventy-two at the back? Yes, seventy-two. Seventy-four?'

I say nothing. I have undermined him enough. Piers is silent. The auctioneer's acute eye is on him, appraising his struggle. He does not rush him. His ballpen is poised in his hand. Finally, Piers nods once again.

'Seventy-four. Seventy-six? I have seventy-six. Sir?'

'No! No!' I whisper to Piers.

And at last Piers shakes his head, defeated.

'Seventy-six. Any other bidders? Seventy-six once, seventy-six twice, sold at seventy-six thousand pounds to buyer number . . . one hundred and eleven.'

The gavel descends. A hubbub breaks out in the room. The next violin is displayed.

Piers is sighing a long, half-sobbing sigh. In his eyes are tears of frustration and despair.

'Lot number one-seven-one. A very fine and rare Venetian violin by Anselmo Bellosio . . .'

8.4

'That concludes the sale for today.'

Ten minutes have passed since the Rogeri was sold. Piers is still sitting as others get up all around him.

We too get up at last. A young woman standing near the door is being congratulated. She, however, looks shattered. This must be the unseen bidder at the back. She looks at Piers and opens her mouth as if to say something in consolation, then thinks better of it.

Piers stops and says, 'Forgive me for bidding so long. I wanted it so much. Forgive me.' Before she can respond or he break down, he walks into the corridor.

'Dear chap,' says Henry Cheetham, waving as he advances towards us. 'Dear chap. What can I say? There it is. She felt it was made for her. There you have it: everything in the doldrums, and then suddenly—frenzy! Quite electric.' He takes out a maroon pocket-handkerchief to dab at something invisible on his chin. 'If it's any consolation,' he adds, 'I'm sure she would have gone much higher. Well, it's a rum world. But nil desperandum and all that . . . see you, I hope, at the next . . . er . . . ah, hello, Simon. Excuse me.'

Suddenly I see Mrs Formby's nephew putting my violin under the auctioneer's hammer, and I feel a

468

visceral urge to smash his smug face to pulp. My heart is racing, my fists clenched against someone I hardly know.

Piers puts his hand to his forehead. 'Let's get out of here.'

'I've got to pee. I'll be back in a minute.'

As I make my way through the dispersing crowd, the girl from the Wigmore Hall whom I had noticed in the crowd greets me.

'Hello, Michael.'

'Hello, Lucy.'

'Exciting, wasn't it?'

I nod, but say nothing.

'Sorry about Piers.'

'Yes,' I say. 'Were you also bidding for something?'

She nods. 'Nothing in quite the same range, though.'

'And did you get it?'

'No. Not my day either.'

'Bad luck. I'm sorry, I must rush off to the loo. Oh, by the way, Lucy, I wonder if you could do something for me. When the tickets for Julia Hansen's concert go on sale, would you keep one aside for me? I know that these things sometimes disappear quite fast.'

'I'd be happy to.'

'You won't forget?'

'No. I'll make a note of it. You played with her in Vienna, didn't you?'

'Yes. Yes. Thanks a lot, Lucy. See you.'

'You don't know, do you, that she's changed her programme?'

'Has she? Good. Schubert replacing Schumann, no doubt.'

469

'No. She's playing Bach.'

'Bach?'

'Yes.'

'Bach? You're sure?' I stare at her.

'Of course I'm sure. She faxed us about a week ago from the States. I can tell you that Bill wasn't delighted. If you've agreed to play Schumann and Chopin, you shouldn't suddenly spring Bach on us. But, well, she explained the reasons: the range of octaves is smaller, more within her . . . you *do* know, don't you?'

I hesitate, uncertain for a second what her question means, then nod. She looks relieved.

'I shouldn't be saying all this,' she continues. 'I just assumed you knew about her, well, difficulty, since you've played with her. But it's to be kept firmly under our hats. Her agent insists that we can't say anything. But can I ask you something in confidence? There was no problem with her playing in Vienna, was there, Michael?'

'No. None.'

'Odd piece to choose, though, for our concert, I thought—the "Art of Fugue".'

'No—no—not the "Art of Fugue"! It couldn't be that. Surely not?'

'Well, one certainly doesn't hear it too often,' she says. 'I looked in the clash diary. Doesn't seem as if it's being played anywhere in London that month. In fact, I can't remember the last time I heard it played live on the piano. But one can never be too sure. One doesn't hear a double-bass concerto for a year, and then suddenly, presto: three double-bass concertos by three different musicians in a week. What's the matter with you, Michael? Are you all right? You look as if you've

470

seen a ghost.'

'I'm fine,' I say. 'Just fine.'

I get to the toilet. I enter a stall, sit down, and stare at the door, my heart thumping sickly, erratically in my chest.

8.5

At home I try to practise this but cannot. My hands will not deal with it. The finger pads refuse to touch the strings. I force them to, and hear the sound before I bring my bow to bear. But now my ears repel it. This goes beyond sense. I, who have loved the 'Art of Fugue', can play no part of it even to myself. I'll practise scales and wait for this to pass.

Yet in rehearsal with the others tonight the fit still grips my hands. We play the scale but even here the notes I play are foreign to myself. Can they not hear this? Then Billy tells us which fugue we're to play.

I try to tune the string down. After a minute the others look at me, bemused. It seems too low for F now, now too high.

'Ready?'

'Yes.'

Now Billy nods. Mine is the third entry of the four.

'What are you playing at, Michael?' This from Piers.

No, no, I am playing at nothing, I am playing nothing, this something has me right along the nerve. I cannot breathe, and all along my arms I feel the fine hairs rise.

471

'For heaven's sake, what's the matter?' says Helen.

For everything has stopped. Why have I not come in? I thought that I was playing but am not.

'Michael,' says Piers, 'get a grip on yourself.'

But I have lost the link from eye to hand. A simple trick, and within my powers on Monday. It is the hammers, not the bow, that sound the strings. I see the very room where as we play she plays. But no, she sleeps in Boston, well espoused.

'Here, let's try it again,' says Billy.

I make a sound, but such a sound as stops the others dead, mid-note. These bones, so many, in these much-trained hands have lost clean action, and this mind is smudged.

'God damn it, Michael,' says Piers, 'this isn't going to be another Vienna, I hope.'

'Should we try the first fugue first?' asks Billy. 'Just to break ourselves in again. After all, we know that one perfectly.'

'No, not that fugue,' I say. 'I'm sorry, I . . . I'll be fine in a day or two.'

It was that fugue that coiled all this around me. It led her to me, and that night, she played it. It is the unpaid remnant of the gift she promised me and then defaulted on.

'Well, what should we do?' says Billy. 'Should we rehearse something else? But I don't know if we've got the music. And there's so much work to be done on this . . . Erica says the producer and maybe even the sound engineer want to set up a meeting with us soon. Time's short. Perhaps we should just barrel ahead.'

'I don't know if I'm up to it today,' I say. 'I seem to be having a bit of bother with this piece.'

'I wouldn't call this just a bit of bother,' says Piers. 'If you're going to make a habit of this, it's going to be impossible for everyone.'

'What do you mean?' I ask.

'I think you should consider all this seriously. We've contracted to record the "Art of Fugue". The Maggiore is not going to put on a slipshod performance.'

'Shut up, Piers,' says Helen, flushed with anger. 'Don't make silly threats. Do you think Billy—or I—or Michael—would allow anything sloppy to go out under our name? We'll meet here the day after tomorrow at three—agreed? Get some sleep, Michael—you look burned out. I'll phone you later. You must let us help you if there's anything we can do.'

I loosen the bow. I place the violin away. I leave quickly. I do not look at any of them. As for myself, I need to slump, to sleep. I must restore these arcs into a vault. Under the clustered cherubs gilt and grey, I too must dream of some perfected heaven.

8.6

A message from Helen on the phone. I don't answer it. A card from Virginie, travelling with friends. A letter from Carl Käll. I leave it sealed. Why should I come to terms with the whole world?

It is a brutal place. A swan was killed last night on the Round Pond. Its throat was cut. Yet surely a gondola is as beautiful as a grand piano, a peacock's legs as ugly as a swan's. Its pimpled carcass lies preserved in ice.

Why must she spin me down into this place? I

should consider all this seriously. These are my options: yes, and no. If I could play this thing, would I not stay? For its own sake, if not for all of us? But I can't play two bars and not seize up.

I will apply my balms: a walk in the park, but not by the Orangery; the chess puzzle, covering with my hand the screed on bridge; the sage Wodehouse, not the unsettled Donne; the blackbird on my street, neither lark nor nightingale. How late must he be musicking this year?

I wake up to the sound of the first contrapunctus: louder and louder she thumps it out, for she cannot hear it. She has made me redundant, she has downsized me. The small grey suits are back, so she is back. Day by day, in every way—academic, artistic, musical, social, spiritual, physical, moral—the children of Pembridge School get better and better.

More news. They are tearing music out of the lives of poorer children. Now children, say your L M N. Literate, Musicate, Numerate. Now once again, all together: Illiterate, Immusicate, Innumerate. These sainted powers will starve you of music as surely as the damned. Leave music to those who can afford indulgences. In twenty years no butcher's son will be a violinist, no, nor daughter neither.

I cannot play it, for all this two days' grace—nor would I play the serpent or the shawm if you gave me two months or twenty years. What has possessed me lies outside my hold. It is a piping Pembridge child that says: so did you know my mother before I was born? Was there such a time— before I was born? Tears fill his eyes that such a thing should be.

What is the difference between my life and my love? One gets me low, the other lets me go. O Luke, O Luke, rack me no riddles more. Why were you not my son?

8.7

Winters will pass, and lips remain unkissed, and heart unsoothed, and hands and ears unlinked. No mystery must remain. I rip Carl's envelope open with my fingers. What is this?

Yes, this is just by way of follow-up. He got my letter, which he considered kind and untrue; indeed, its loud tact made it less than kind. He knows perfectly well what I felt towards him. Senility, he would point out, does not invariably accompany decrepitude. He will not repeat regrets, but simply say that he has decided at last that the quartet is in fact my true home. He exhorts me to remain where I am. Perhaps his contribution to musical posterity will be a bloodline of second violinists. I will no doubt have heard that Wolf Spitzer is now a member of the Traun Quartet. Nothing of his own health or plans or deeds. No request for a response. End of letter.

Strange missile, coming at a time like this when no one could have known, not I, not they, that anything would be amiss among us. He has decided; that is just as well. For Wolf I must be and am glad, but in myself I burn that this man still should claim the right to bless or blast what I may do or not.

Late at night, thirst wakes me, and then I cannot

sleep. By my bed lies the book inscribed and scored by her. With water on my fingers I move along my part. Page after page I hear my smudging notes. The staff dissolves, the heads and stalks blur into mire, the water in my glass grows turbid brown. The wetness seeps into the neighbouring voices, onto the pages not yet traced and bleared. As if in worn-down braille my fingers touch my name, that once you wrote; and look, I cannot read it any more.

8.8

When I tell them, Helen speaks first.

'Michael, take a week off and return—you can't mean you want to leave us. What about our solidarity of the middle? We can't do without you. I can't, I know. What will we do about Bristol next week? About everything that's been booked. It would make me sick to play with someone else.'

'I didn't mean what I said, damn it,' says Piers. 'You're crazy, Michael, to think I meant it. All I meant was we couldn't make a bad CD. Are you threatening to take off just because of something I said? Helen's been giving me hell even before you burst this bombshell. OK, you've lost it for a while, but it'll come back to you. You're obviously going through some sort of crisis. You're not the only one among us who has caused a problem. It's happened before. We worked it out. We'll work it out again. We're not that fragile.'

But there's no point; the braid has been untwined. I've thought it through and through. Think of Stratus, I tell them, think of Ysobel. How often do these chances come? A second violin, well, you found one once.

Billy is sad. He doesn't say too much. He sees more clearly than the other two that it's no use, that things are too far gone. 'Last in, first out,' he says. 'We'll miss you, Michael.'

They will all miss me, none can wish me luck. Why would they when I'm doing this to us? Round and round we talk, but nothing moves.

I am no use, dead-fingered, to you now. I can't even survive an interval. Play on without me, as for a minute you played in the hall where she will play. It is an aimed shaft, it has hit home. No, not even that; all this is collateral to her aims. But she must salvage, must she not, her life?

Tell them I'm ill; give Erica my love. What's lapsed has lapsed. It's fugue I suffer from. Even this fiddle that I play must go. By night, by day, I am half flesh, half wood.

8.9

No, says Erica, how can she represent me now? There are no mwah-mwahs for me: she speaks most sternly. A foolish thing, irreparable harm, career. They will find someone else, they'll have to, you've made them; but how about you? I'm fond of you, Michael. How can you let this happen to yourself?

Now Helen calls again, refusing tears. What will my work be? Will I make ends meet? Where is my anchor? Why not stop this now? But I've been through these reasonings myself. It's true, I didn't share your meals in Venice, but as we strayed we saw Augustine's dog.

It was once a cat, you know, she says sadly.

A dog.

A cat, though, once.

I saw a dog. She saw a dog. It was a dog. I even saw it on a barge one day in tender replica, alert.

A cat, originally, in his sketch. In the BM, I think.

No, that's not true. I will stop up my ears. Dear Helen, tell me that it is not so.

Why not face facts? Why argue *this* right now?

8.10

The violin on the pillow next to mine, I sleep and wake and sleep again. Outside in the untravelled trees the migrant birds rest. In whose hands will it sing? How can I play without it? How with it? I tune it well, and it sounds well again. I cannot support it, or claim it, or bear it.

Blizzard confetti slew about me: fax paper, tufts of a white dog's fur, snow on a carpark, the ivories she plays. If each voice in her hands were a city, which would have which part? She is going deaf and it is I who cannot play the things she does. What suasion will you use on one who lacks a will? 'This isn't something I would ever play for anyone but you.'

Besides, it is not merely in my mind. This thing I hold is coming half apart. This is no mere tinnitus in my head. It hums, it keens, it has the buzzing bane. The swollen belly chafes the fingerboard. Sanderson will see it, he will see to it, he will judge its ills, he will press it, prod it, patch it into good humour. It has cause to keen, these are our last few months. But why this sudden mutiny at this time?

8.11

Mrs Formby died yesterday.

Auntie Joan phones to tell me. Apparently, she had a stroke a fortnight ago, which impaired her speech. Yesterday morning she had a second stroke, and died as she was being taken back to hospital.

I am glad she was not bedridden for months or years and was clear in mind and speech till almost the end. As with my mother, her end was swift.

I wish I had known she was so ill. Auntie Joan and my father themselves didn't know about the first stroke. I would have gone up to see her one last time, and have played a little for her. For her the Tononi would have sung anywhere—house, hospital or Blackstone Edge.

Her Tononi. I grieve for it, and for myself. It won't be months now but weeks before it is reclaimed from me.

I will not go to her funeral—a cremation, says Auntie Joan. Mrs Formby hated funerals—was impatient with the well-wishers who came to her husband's, and never went to those of her friends. The chartered surveyor will be there, a cat from Cheshire, dreaming of cream. His wife will be muted, looking to her husband for guidance. Their three yowling daughters will postpone their scratching and sulking till the drive back home.

Into his hands I will deliver my beloved fiddle.

I loved Mrs Formby. She woke me to the joy of music. In her passing I am to taste its sorrow.

8.12

'Please be more mechanical,' begs the conductor, for we are recording a Mozart piano sonata fluffed up by some creative sicko into a concerto minus the piano. This is called Be Your Own Maestro. Young pianists with ambition will play their sonata to the accompaniment of an orchestra. Mozart leaves something to be desired: the sicko has added new tunes to him, and the triangle goes tink tink tink. The Camerata Anglica is playing, and most of the players are gagging. But this is meat and mortgage to me now: up my bow goes, and down, in perfect rhythm and intonation.

I thought that I might buy a violin once. Now when the mail drops through my door I think: no Rochdale postmark, please. One day's grace more.

I see white hairs. Those that I see I pluck. I get the usual headaches. Now I think: cat or dog? cat or dog?

How fares the Maggiore minus me? How have they patched things up? Helen still calls me sometimes, but to ask how I am coping, not to draw me back.

In the British Museum Print Room the daylight pours through the roof. Carpaccio's box is brought. His sketch is clear.

Augustine has no beard; the music's blank.

And it's a cat that holds the floor. No, not even a cat, not even that but some sly stoat or weasel on a leash!

Why? Why? Why? Why? I have taken much, but this touches more than me. The poor dog will weep that there was a time before he was born. Stoat!

Stoat! Stoat!

Stoat, do I wrong you? Are you an ermine, winter-white? You have no tail-tip, but this is a sketch: the astrolabe's an O, the music blank. Pure, chaste and noble in the winter months, you spoil in summer and revert to stoat.

Where was that dog that solaced me conceived? Must he grow rank, lanky and feline-clawed? Upstairs we kissed, not knowing we were viewed.

Zsa-Zsa, you have died. Old widow Formby has died. Does Carl too speak like the light of a dwarf from beyond the grave? Outside the Print Room is a map of Venice. Of this and other matters I must inform her. She would want to know. On Oxford Street our gondolas passed by. She raised her veil, and swiftly she was gone.

Last night her hands moved in among the keys. What was she playing that appeased my dream? Bach, to be sure; but I had not heard it before. How many chambers does one's heart require to play such music? Was it something he wrote in the years immediately following his death?

8.13

Strange to be a man and never grow big with child. To feel a part of you opening, and a part of you leaving, and howling as if it were not a part of you. Then it puts on a green cap and a grey suit and has friends. All these are waiting on the Pembridge steps for pieces of themselves to emerge, and to all of them this once happened.

It is the time for conkers and their hedgehog casings. Plane leaves, lime leaves twirl and whirl.

What does young Luke of Boston think of conkers? What does his Oma from Klosterneuburg, the 26th district of Vienna under the Reich, think of conkers? She stands beneath the bloodbeech, muttering. Chestnut and poplar line the Danube there.

Oh, it is 3:45. They emerge and are precisely kissed, but where is Luke? That is her car, parked there. She comes out and rushes up the steps. Luke is there, and she. Their faces speak their happiness.

She is on the pavement near the car. She does not see me and she cannot hear me. This must be reconfigured. Verdi cannot read Wagner's lips, nor the lion the griffin's.

I am in eyeshot now. She starts. How blue are her attentive, panicked eyes.

'Michael.'

'Hi, Julia. You know, that Carpaccio dog—'

'What?'

'You know, in Venice, at the Schiavoni—'

'In Venice, where?'

'In the Schiavoni—'

'Get into the car, Luke.'

'But Mom—it's Michael. I want to—'

'Get into the car at once.'

'Oh OK, OK, don't get mad.'

'What's all this about? Why are you bothering us?'

'But all I wanted to say—'

'Yes?'

'That dog was originally a cat. Or a stoat. Or ermine. It wasn't a dog at all. I saw the drawing, the drawing he made himself.'

'Michael, what exactly have you come to say?'

I need to say so much that I say nothing. Maggiore, Formby, Tononi, Augustine . . . names in a phone book, how can they break her heart?

'Well, what? Don't just stand there.'

'I—'

'Michael, this is hopeless.'

'I thought you said you'd always love me.'

'I didn't think it would come to this.'

'Julia—'

'Don't. Luke can see you. Stay where you are.'

'I had a letter from Carl Käll.'

'Michael, I'm sorry, I can't stop to talk.'

'The bonsai—'

'Yes,' she says bitterly. 'Yes. It's well. It's very, very well. A brilliant present. I suppose I should thank you.'

'Why are you playing the "Art of Fugue"? What are you trying to do?'

'The "Art of Fugue"? Why? Why not, for heaven's sake. I love it too. Now I've really got to go, believe me. And, Michael, you are bothering me. Do you understand that? You are bothering me. Don't, please don't stand in wait for me again. I don't want to see you. I don't. I really don't. I'll break down if I do . . . If you love me that's not what you'd want. And if you don't love me, just go and get on with your life.'

She covers her eyes. 'And no, for God's sake don't tell me which is true.'

8.14

Three weeks have passed since I met her. I am removing items one by one from the addresses in my mind.

No, I have no use for this vision, I can dispense with this fact: rooms, books, meetings, the flecks in her irises, the scent of her skin: let them be hauled away on weekday mornings, let them float off in helium balloons.

I too believe, at last, that I can build on nothing, that there is nothing to build on. It has taken time, for hope has well-cased germs. As for myself, I think: if I left this darkness and this blankness, it would not make the universe sneeze. I would be free of dreams and thoughts and Be Your Own Maestro. My father, though, would grieve. Auntie Joan would grieve. As autumn deepens, rings form round my eyes.

What can't be disposed of must be placed in deeper storage. I will hire a warehouse in the suburbs and in it lay all undesired entities: scent, sound, sight, inclination.

It is Saturday morning, but I don't swim. From the bridge I watch the light play on the water, on the wake of the Water Serpents beyond the Lido. I read the helpful warning on the bridge: 'Danger. Shallow Water. Do Not Jump from Bridge.' No, no, I am a swimmer, I will live to be arthritic.

This is my best-loved tree, the plane—all knots and knobbles and peeling bark. But why look here? In all my years on the moors I never found a lark's nest. Here too I hear not hooves but yapping. It is a quartet of dogs—a small white dog, a vast brown one, the limper of the Devil's Bridge, a fox-like interloper. They bark, they sing, they sniff. She flings her slipper into their number and with musical cries they rip it into shreds. They have no sense of who met whom, of what lies above our world or in our hearts. They are full of charm; in their eyes is love and ice.

There are a hundred kinds of deafness. The

484

more tense I am, the less well I hear. So it makes sense to put one's acts in order.

Concentrate on these few things: the bread, the papers, the milk, some vegetables, some food to microwave, the book you will read tonight. Read words again: you have no quartet to play, no music to look over. Defer till its own time the work you do.

Tune the strings, though. Play scales. More than father, mother, friend or lover, it has companioned you. The residue now rests in weeks, in days. Play scales on it, things that may bring you calm. Remove the chin-rest, feel its wood again.

Balance your books. Ride buses. Walk. You are in the lonely majority. Which of these sitting around you belong to your unselect fraternity? The chatterer, the smiler, the silent one who looks ashamed in a crowd?

That conductor—that schoolgirl whispering, *'Fou!'*—that man selling outdated diaries from a stall—that salesgirl with dark hair like Virginie's?

8.15

'Just flying off the tables they are, the T-shirts. Can't get enough of them.' She smiles at me.

'Do you have any large ones in that dark reddish colour there?'

'The russet? Just what's on the table, I'm afraid. We emptied the stockroom this morning.'

'Ah . . .' There is even something in her face which keeps me here.

'Too few of the large,' she says. 'It's not the right mix. We've complained to Head Office.'

'Ah, yes, Head Office. That and the computer.'

'May as well blame someone!' she says, laughing.

'Sorry, it's not my fault, the computer's down.'

'Sorry, I'm taking my lunch break. It's Head Office.'

'Well, if there's no russet, I'll have a black. Sorry, this five-pound note is forged. It's the computer.'

'You'd be surprised!' she says, looking at it intently. 'There're a lot of them going around.'

I suspect the shiny penny she returns me.

'Better bite into it,' she suggests, giggling. 'It may be chocolate.'

'Sorry, we don't serve chocolate pennies on Saturday.'

'It's Head Office,' both of us say, laughing.

'When does Head Office let you off this evening?'

'I have a boyfriend,' she says.

'Oh—' I say. 'Oh.' All laughter has left my voice.

'Look here,' she says, coolly, 'I think you'd better go.'

Not fear of me, but a different fear, of the fragility of trust. She will not fraternise with customers for a while.

'I'm sorry,' I say. 'I'm sorry. You're so nice. I just thought—'

'Please go. *Please.*'

She does not look around for a supervisor, but at the table with the T-shirts, russet, black and grey.

8.16

At 1:30 at night, restless, I walk to the rank of phone-booths by the recycling bins. Even at this hour there are a few people wandering here and there on the streets. I press the numbers.

'Hello?' A soft, sweet voice, a slight Irish accent.

'Hello, I wonder if I could speak to Tricia.'

'This is Tricia's number. Can I help you?'

'I, well, I saw—I just saw your card in a phone-booth, I mean her card, and I wondered if she might be free soon—well, in the next half hour or so . . .'

'Yes, my darling, she would be. Where are you now, sweetheart?'

'In Bayswater.'

'Oh, that's very close. Let me tell you about Tricia. She's an English girl, long blonde hair, blue eyes, very nice legs, clean shaven, 36-24-36.'

'How old is she?'

'She's . . . twenty-six.'

'And how much, I mean . . .'

'From forty to seventy pounds, my darling.'

'Oh. And that would include . . .'

'Massage to start with, and then oral, and intercourse,' she says sweetly.

I am silent, then say: 'Should I take your address?'

'Yes, my darling, it's twenty-two Carmarthen Terrace, flat three. Just press the buzzer below.'

'I'm sorry, I'm—I don't know how it works. Do I pay you before?'

'Whatever you like, love,' she says with a smile in her voice. 'The only thing I do insist on is that we use protection.'

'Are you Tricia?'

'Yes, I am. I look forward to seeing you soon, sweetheart. Thank you for calling.'

8.17

What she does not feel, she feigns. She is about 35, attractive, practised, sweet. All that I have withheld for months forces itself through me. Afterwards I begin to weep. She does not shoo me out but offers me a cup of tea.

'It's someone you care about, darling, isn't it?'

'I don't know.'

'You don't have to say anything.'

I don't. She doesn't. We sip our tea calmly enough together. The phone rings, and she says to me, 'Would you like to take a shower and get dressed, darling?'

'Yes. Yes. I need a shower.'

The pink of the bathroom, my face in the mirror, the small ragged Winnie-the-Pooh on the sill, the cloying smell. I feel a frightful nausea wrench my guts. I get to the toilet bowl and retch. Nothing comes up. In the shower I boil the skin off myself, steam all this away.

I am dressed. I mutter my thanks and am about to leave.

'You haven't paid yet, sweetheart.'

I pay what she asks, and say goodbye. I am sick at heart, sick to the heart. Has this been me this hour? 'Don't lose my number, sweetheart. Do come again,' she says, and lights the stairs.

8.18

My diary service fills my days with dates: jingles for ad companies, background music for movies. I sit around in a recording studio in Wembley, working out a chess puzzle, reading the newspapers. People have heard the news about the Maggiore, but they leave me alone. I overhear someone mention Julia Hansen once, but the rest is absorbed in a general tuning-up.

Lucy from the Wigmore Hall phones to say she has kept aside a ticket for Julia's recital on 30 December. Or was it two tickets I wanted? I thank her, but tell her I will be out of town. Let someone else have them.

'Oh, where will you be going?'

'I don't know—Rochdale, I suppose, for Christmas.'

'I'm sorry you're no longer with the Maggiore.'

'Well, that's the way things go. Fresh woods and pastures new.'

'I hope I haven't disturbed you, Michael.'

'No. No. Not at all. Not at all.'

She rings off and I take stock of things. The stockroom was emptied this morning, yet there are all sorts of things in it already gathering dust: a porcelain frog, a stuffed stoat. I find myself on the Number 7 bus.

Behind the British Museum is a small photographic department. I get two prints made of the drawing, one to be sent to me, one to her. I will examine the stoat at my leisure. Let her share my delectation and my musings.

A kind woman in the Print Room gets out an old article containing the two pieces of music, one sacred, the other secular, standing open at St Augustine's feet. I gaze at them till I can hear them in the silent room. I orchestrate them at whim: strings, woodwinds, voices, lyres.

These days I leave half my letters unopened. I

avoid Holland Park, whose stones one may not touch. Mnozil's has new management, and I myself am purged, expurgated. All things must pass, all flesh is grass.

I dream of Carl. He is listening to me play a dog-food jingle. He leans his head back in ecstasy. 'Sustain,' he says. 'Always sustain. Your playing, which never displeased me much, now brings tears to my eyes. But do you know, I prefer Bach.'

'That's a subjective judgment,' I say. 'But, if you like, here is some for you.'

He grows infuriated. 'That is not Bach, that is a Bachlein,' he thunders. 'Give me Johann Sebastian.'

'I cannot get him under my fingers, Herr Professor. Julia McNicholl has taken him from me.'

He grows apoplectic. 'I will not have this. I will not have this. I will throw you out of my class. You have reacted badly to my letter. That was wrong, very wrong. You will leave Vienna at once—by the town sewer.'

'I will never leave Vienna again—'

'Very well, then,' he says sadly. 'Very well then, indulge the whim of a dying man. Play the dog-food aria again. And with less feeling. We must learn to respect the composer's intentions.'

'As you say, Herr Professor,' I reply. 'But why bother to predecease me?'

8.19

The doorbell rings. It is the registered letter from Rochdale.

I sign for it. I leave it unopened on the counter

in the kitchen. Those tangerines are mouldy. I must clean out that bowl.

Is this what it is like? You stand there in the dock, and while the judge intones something, you notice that the dark, almost purple lipstick of the woman in the second row is smudged.

They have come for custody. Please let us be for a day. I do not contest anything. The child is asleep. He will wake of his own accord in his own time.

Shall I play you and then give you up? Shall I give you up unplayed, so that the memory of our parting is not marred with sounds, so that Bach is not joined by other losses: Mozart, Schubert, all that gives me life.

What would I play if not that, where would I play if not here? 'Tea for Two' chez Tricia? The dog-food aria for my old, tired teacher? The untrembling scale with my estranged friends? 'The Lark Ascending' in honour of a dispersed spirit?

I take it out, I tune it up, I close the door of my cell. In the darkness I play it, and I do not know what it is I am playing. It is a medley of something, it is an improvisation such as I have never played before, it comes more from its own heart than from mine. It is a lament, but I sense with a feeling of having been abandoned already, that it is not for me.

But now it has swerved into the Vivaldi Largo that I played on that miraculous day, there in his church. I play it, it plays me, and in the darkness of my cell I know that I will not hear the repeat, that it is time to cease, to beg the guardian gods of the woods from which it sprang that in its future life— and may it live another two hundred and seventy years—or more, or more—it will be treasured by its owners and fare well.

Farewell, then, my violin, my friend. I have loved you more than I can say. We are one being, but we now must part and never hear our common speech again. Do not forget my fingers or our voice. I will not hear you, but remember you.

8.20

Dear Mr Holme,

You will doubtless be aware of the recent death of Mrs John Formby (Cecilia Formby). I understand you were a close friend of the deceased, and I would like on behalf of my firm to offer you our sincere condolences.

Varms & Lunn have acted as Mrs Formby's solicitors for many years, and she named my partner William Sterling and myself as her executors.

Mrs Formby's will was lodged together with the relevant documents at the District Probate Registry ten days ago. Probate has now been granted.

In a codicil to her will drafted by this firm under her instructions and signed a week before her death, Mrs Formby left an old Italian violin (Carlo Tononi, circa 1727) to you, free of tax.

I understand that the violin is presently in your possession. You may continue to look after it for the executors until the administration of the estate has reached the point where its ownership can be transferred to you.

It has been some weeks since Mrs Formby's

492

death, and there has been some delay in informing you of the terms of her will. Part of the difficulty arose from the fact that in her codicil Mrs Formby gave an address for you that no longer exists.

Mrs Formby also left a note for you, which I enclose. She was incapacitated physically in the days immediately preceding her death, though her mind was entirely sound and her intentions clear. She dictated this note to me in hospital. Since her speech was somewhat slurred, I read it back to her to ensure that there were no errors in my transcript. I then had it typed out, and she signed it.

If you have any questions about the bequest or any other associated matter, either immediately or for any reason whatever in the future, I hope you will have no hesitation in getting in touch with us.

Yours sincerely,
Keith Varms

enc: letter to Michael Holme Esq from Mrs John Formby

8.21

My dear Michael,

I fear I've caused you a great deal of anxiety in the last year owing to my uncertainty about my violin, and I'm sorry. I sensed your distress when we spoke of this matter earlier this year, and it was honourable of you not to attempt to influence my previous decision, and to accept it without questioning.

You have been a true friend of mine since you were six or seven years old, and we have seen each other pass through both good times and bad. I want to help you increase the good times, and this is the best way that I can think of to ensure this. Besides, I can't bear to imagine my violin passing by sale into the hands of a stranger when it's been played by you for so many years.

I hope you'll forgive my signature. I am afraid I'd no longer be any good at Vaughan Williams's high trills.

I send you my love, though by the time you receive this, the ashes of that 'I' will be scattered—quite contentedly, believe me— around Blackstone Edge.

Goodbye, my dear Michael, and God bless you.

Yours,\
[illegible]

8.22

Not me, but you, Mrs Formby, if he exists. I can't sleep tonight for restlessness. I am filled not with relief but disbelief. I don't even take my violin out again. This can't be true, yet is. It was lost to me, that now is found.

Your words have given me life and taken sleep away. The park gates open at first light. Slate-grey and coral, dawn is reflected in the pool. The flowers have been turfed under in the sunken garden. The chack of a squirrel, the splash of a small duck, a blackbird hopping about beneath the thinned-out linden hedge: this is all. I am alone with this troubled joy.

Let me report to you from my world. The views have widened as the world's grown bare. Someone has sprinkled orange lentils on the ground beneath the sycamore. The corporate pigeons waddle and strut among them. Cold fat black crows stand still, uncawing, watchful.

As for music, the grey geese cry above the Round Pond. They fly low, then rush feet first to settle on the water. The swans sleep safely on, their heads tucked into their feathers.

What possessed you to repossess me of it, you who were close to death and lacked clear speech? Is it the violin alone you want to give me, or must I learn some lesson from the world?

8.23

The voice on the telephone is taut with repressed fury.

'Michael Holme?'

'Yes.'

'This is Cedric Glover. We met briefly at my aunt's place last Christmas—Mrs Formby. I am her nephew.'

'Yes. I remember. Mr Glover, I am very sorry about your aunt's death . . .'

'Are you now? I'm rather surprised, considering how well you have done out of it.'

'But—'

'My aunt was an old lady, and not in full possession of her faculties. It was easy enough to prey on her.'

'But I didn't even know she was ill—I never visited her—to my great regret.'

'Well, someone did. My wife was there almost the whole time—taking care of her, as only family can—so I do not see how she managed to contact her solicitor and make this ungrateful codicil. But she could be quite guileful.'

'I had nothing to do with this. How—how did you get my number?'

'Do you really mean to dispossess my daughters of their education? Do you really believe my aunt meant to do that?'

'No, I—'

'The decent thing to do would be to return the violin to the family without making a legal issue of it, which I can assure you I am quite prepared to do.'

'Please, Mr Glover, I loved your aunt. I don't want to cause bitterness—'

'I would strongly advise you then not to cynically and selfishly hold on to what does not belong to you, either in ethics or in law. It is clear that she was disturbed in her mind in her last days, and suggestible in the extreme.'

'Mr Glover, I suggested nothing. I didn't even know how ill she was. She wrote me a kind and lucid letter. I want to believe the words she wrote.'

'Yes, I have no doubt you do. Did she sign it?'

'Yes.'

'Well, if the signature on the codicil is anything to go by, you will understand on how weak a footing you stand. It was the scrawl of a feeble-minded child. Why, her mind was so far gone that she gave a carpark as your address. A carpark!'

496

'Please, Mr Glover, don't say these things. She was my friend. How can I give up what she has given me?'

'Given? Given? I am afraid that you are labouring under a misapprehension. While her mind was sound she did not intend to give you anything. She intended to put the proceeds from the sale of the violin into a trust for me and my daughters, and I know that she told you of this. I am a reasonable man, Mr Holme. I disapprove of what my aunt has done, considering all we did for her, but I forgive her because she did not know what she was doing at the time. However, I may as well tell you that if we cannot come to some sort of compromise on this matter, you will lose both the violin and a large sum of money in legal fees besides.'

His words are more than bluster, and I am filled with terror. And then there are his wretched, wretched daughters: can I really rob them of what is theirs by right and live in peace? What will I feel each time I raise my bow?

'What do you suggest then, Mr Glover?' I say quietly. 'What can I do?'

'I have drawn up a deed of gift for a half-share in the violin . . . It requires your signature. It can then be sold and the proceeds justly and equally divided.'

'But I can't do that—I can't sell my violin.'

'Your violin. I see it has not taken you so very long to assume possession.'

'The violin. Her violin. Whatever you like. I love it. Can't you understand that? It would kill me to give it up for money.'

He is silent for a few seconds, then says, with

cold exasperation: 'I have one final offer, Mr Holme, and this really is my final offer. You must at the very least return to my family the forty per cent of the violin's value that you have taken from the rest of the estate.'

'Mr Glover—I have taken nothing—'

'You have indeed taken something, and a great deal at that. Are you aware of what the words "free of tax" mean? They mean that while most of the estate—whose value is deemed to include that of the violin—is charged inheritance tax at forty per cent you are to be charged no tax at all. No tax at all, none, none! We, in other words, are paying your tax for you. You have a legal and moral duty to return that tax. Can you in your right mind believe—and do you expect any court to believe— that my aunt intended that we should support you?'

'I don't know—I don't know what to believe. I don't know about these things.'

'Well, I suggest you think about it, but not for long. I am speaking from my late aunt's house. You have her telephone number. If I do not hear from you within twenty-four hours, I will put the matter in the hands of my solicitors. Goodbye, Mr Holme.'

I rest my forehead on my hands. I do not go to the soundproof room where the violin lies. After a while I go to the bedroom and stare at the ceiling. The light plays on the wall; a helicopter clatters past. I am tired now beyond the point of sleep. One way or another I am to lose it after all. Mrs Formby, as you love me, tell me what to do.

8.24

I phone Varms and Lunn and speak to Mr Varms, who is more nasal than I expected from the writer of the letter. I thank him, and I tell him how amazed I was to receive his letter.

'Mrs Formby rather thought you might be,' he says.

'You visited her in hospital. Was she in much pain—or difficulty?'

'Some difficulty. Not much pain. She insisted on going home as soon as possible after her first stroke. She was at home when she died—or possibly in the ambulance that was sent to her house to fetch her. As such things go, she went quickly.'

'I'm glad.'

'But not, if you take my point, too quickly. She had time to take stock of things and do something about them.'

'Yes. I see . . . Mr Varms, I don't know how to say this. I have just had a phone-call . . .'

'Yes?' Mr Varms's nasal voice becomes almost oboe-like with alertness.

'From her nephew, a Mr . . .'

'Glover. Yes. I've met the gentleman.'

'In which he told me I had no right to the instrument. He said a number of things . . .'

'Mr Holme, I was a little concerned that he might be tempted to do something of the sort, which is why I phrased my letter to you as I did. Let me assure you—er, reassure you that there is no substance whatever to his threats and claims, which he made at some length before me, and which I dissuaded him with difficulty from presenting to

499

the Court. He wanted to contest the codicil, which had, in the usual way, been witnessed by two independent witnesses, one of whom was Mrs Formby's doctor. I explained to Mr Glover how expensive the exercise would be for him, how likely it was to bring other parts of his late aunt's will into question and thus delay probate on the whole, how vigorously the witnesses and I would confute his contentions, and how little chance he had of succeeding in his object. I took the liberty of, er, apprising him that Mrs Formby's intentions were restated in no ambiguous terms in her note to you, though I assure you I did not let him read that note, whose contents I was privy to only because she could not write it herself.'

'Mr Varms, I had no idea of all this. You have been very kind . . .'

'Not kind at all, I assure you. Just carrying out my duty as Mrs Formby's executor—and as the recipient of her instructions in drafting her will. Did he have anything else to say?'

'He said I should at least return the tax he's paid. He said I had a legal and moral duty . . .'

'Mr Holme, no legal duty exists. I cannot advise you on the moral issue, if you can call it that, but I can inform you that the estate was not a small one. Mr Glover, as residuary beneficiary, will receive a good deal of money, tax or no tax; and I understand from his rather, er, self-confident conversation that he is no pauper anyway.'

I begin to laugh, and Mr Varms joins in.

'So you didn't take to Mr Glover,' I say.

'Well, he spoke rather slightingly of his benefactress, hardly an endearing thing to do.'

'I hope he wasn't rude to you.'

'He was more than polite after our first meeting. Ingratiating, in fact, as I have often found to be the case with threatening people whose threats don't work. Oh, there is one more thing I should tell you. It was not Mrs Formby's intention to give you fifty per cent or sixty per cent or some other proportion of the violin. She was, if I may say so, quite an astute lady, and recognised that any loan you might have to take out would run counter to her purpose, which was, if you will forgive my speaking in these terms, to give you happiness, not anxiety. Well, I was rather expecting your call, Mr Holme, though I hope you can see why I couldn't warn you of his. If he pursues his stated intention, I could not of course advise you myself in a legal capacity, but I would be happy to put you in touch with another firm of solicitors. However, I do not think that will be necessary. I suspect that a firm answer will put an end to these vexatious claims. Mrs Formby was determined to add that codicil, and she understood every word of it. I hope you enjoy the violin.'

'Thank you, Mr Varms. I don't know what to say. Thank you very much.'

'Not in the least.'

'Are you fond of music, Mr Varms?' I ask, I don't know why.

'Oh yes, I am rather fond of music.' Mr Varms suddenly sounds flustered and eager to close the conversation. 'Er, is there anything else? Please do get in touch if there is.'

'There's nothing else. Once again, thank you.'

'Goodbye, Mr Holme.'

8.25

Mrs Formby:

I know you are dead and cannot read this. I wish I had known of your stroke.

My life had shelved towards desolation. Thank you for not forgetting me and for assuming, though I did not visit, that I had not forgotten you.

I will drive to Blackstone Edge at the right time each year. I will take your violin with me whenever I come up north.

I never asked you where or from whom you bought it. That history has ended with you.

What little I ever did for you is over, but what you have done for me will last till I too go.

May something of your memory advise me, when I come to die, into whose hands I should deliver it.

Both your friend and your fiddle thank you— from soul and soundpost respectively.

8.26

One night I wake up in a cold sweat, with the pulse of my heart in my ears.

I had a dream. I was in an underground station, Holborn, I think. I was standing at the bottom of an escalator, busking with my Tononi. On the descending staircase were clumps of strangers, interspersed with people I recognised, who travelled down two by two. Billy's son Jango passed by hand in hand with Mrs Formby. She dropped a coin into my cap, and continued to talk to him. I knew in advance that Carl would be there, and he was, with his protégée, Virginie. He nodded at me and said something through bluish lips. She looked happy, and passed by unspeaking.

I was playing long slow chords on the open strings. When I tired of one fifth I moved to another. Julia's mother, wearing a tiara and holding Carpaccio's little dog under her left arm, descended, handcuffed to the Holland Park policewoman. Had she breached some quarantine regulation? I knew that all this was a passing show, that I could turn it off at any moment. I was in, not of, the dream.

But as the couples passed, sometimes with many strangers in between, I grew more anxious. I was racked between hope and dread, because I thought I might see Julia herself, and I did not know who would be standing with her. Yet among the many tedious people from my past who floated down, cousins and maths teachers and orchestral colleagues, she did not appear, and my heart sank.

I got onto the ascending escalator to find her. At the top it halted, then turned back downwards. But as I descended, the escalator shaft grew narrower and darker and I was alone. Everyone else had disappeared and except for my violin, which I had been ceaselessly playing, there was silence. Deeper into the earth the escalator descended, far past where it had previously stopped; and I could do nothing to stop it. I was no longer playing the three calm open chords, but a line of compelling, terrifying music that I only gradually recognised as my single, unsupported line of the 'Art of Fugue'.

I half choked, half cried aloud. But I could not escape from its grip or my descent. The violin, like

503

some bewitched broom, played on and on, obsessed, and if it had not been for a car alarm, far below on the real street, chipping through the casing of my dream, I would have descended forever into endless night.

8.27

Do not dramatise this. It's just love, it's not a limb. How far does this indulgence, this sensitisation extend? It will not stop you from making a living. Is all this worthy of your violin? As for those lost to you, consider where their happiness lies. 'For God's sake, Michael, haven't you hurt her enough?'

Let your body stir, if your mind is still becalmed. Swim. No, now, like her, I can't cope with a crowd. But you do, don't you, when you play as an extra fiddle in an orchestra? How about walking? Walk to what you can walk to. Walk around if you have nowhere to go. It is five in the morning, but this is wintry London, there is no Venetian dawn. The drifters out of the night pass those who are drifting into the day. There are footsteps behind me, but I do not turn my head, and they dissolve.

Consider your students again. But I do. I spend hours mulling before and during and after their lessons: Elizabeth's wrist action, Jamie's arpeggios, Clive's sight-reading skills. I have no will to be impatient.

'Why don't I see that pretty lady, Michael?' snickers the brat, who has grown fond of the violin, who knows why. 'Jessica, yeah, see, I remember her name.'

'She doesn't come here every day, you know,

Jamie.'

'*Must* I prepare this by the next lesson?'

'Yes,' I say, thinking of Carl. 'You *must.*'

I smile at him, and he, surprised, smiles back.

On those evenings that I am not working, I read, since I have nothing to prepare with my fellows, or for them. This is another life, one with north-facing windows. The light is blank and does not burn.

I come across these lines I half-recall from my schooldays, it must be twenty years ago:

But never either found another
To free the hollow heart from paining—
They stood aloof, the scars remaining,
Like cliffs which had been rent asunder;
A dreary sea now flows between;—
But neither heat, nor frost, nor thunder,
Shall wholly do away, I ween,
The marks of that which once hath been.

I do not visit Tricia again. A sexless calm: to this favour have I come.

8.28

Near the Greek church the trees are evergreen. 'Persistent' is what Virginie used to call them.

The children of Archangel Court press all the buttons in the lift. Giggling, they wait for a reproof from me, and scowl now that it's clear I'm in no hurry.

The girl at Etienne, gathering her courage, asks me why I always buy seven, then tells me I should never freeze croissants.

Rob won ten pounds in Wednesday's lottery draw, and spent his winnings on lottery tickets.

Mrs Goetz tells me I should accompany her to a homeless shelter one Saturday night when I'm not working.

Dave the Water Serpent bumps into me on Queensway. 'Hey, Mike, where've you vanished?'

But I have not. I am here, and I observe the world and its doings. One morning the phone rings.

'Michael Holme?'

'Speaking.'

'Fisher. Justin Fisher.'

The name—the voice—it is the sticky fan! 'It was very disturbing yesterday,' he plunges in. 'Quite hopeless! But what's the point of telling them? Such a hash of the Boccherini. But they said they hadn't thrown you out. It was a young woman—not a patch, I'm afraid, not a patch on you: like suet after souffle. No, no, no, it won't do. Think what you owe Art. And they say you're spending much of your time with the Camerata Anglica. Really now—even the name, half Italian, half Latin!'

'Mr Fisher—'

'In the Emperor Quartet last night they kept tuning and retuning, and it quite broke my mood. Of course, they're unsettled. How can you play with a sore thumb or a sore heart? I spoke to a violin-maker the other day, and he says he's met you. Let him be, he said: quartets last longer than fiddlers, and fiddles last longest of all. Such cynicism. But that's the way of the world nowadays. I kept thinking: is he serious on the surface and mad underneath? Or vice versa? Anyway, I couldn't get much sense out of him. So I thought I'd try the

506

telephone directory. Stop me if I'm holding forth too long. Are you *yawning*?'

'Not at all. I've just been—'

'Well, that's all I have to say,' he cuts me off petulantly. 'I'm not going to take up any more of your valuable time. But if I don't see you there instead of that suet, you can be sure I won't be laying any more burnt offerings on the altar of the Maggiore. Return, and forthwith. Goodbye.'

8.29

Am I so islanded then? Time has passed: seconds, hours, months. The day I set my eyes on her last year has gone. It is December now. I walk, but note the leafless season less. In the lobby of Archangel Court Mrs Goetz decorates the Christmas tree. Who ties the baubles to the Hansen fir? She? Or she and he? Or both of them and Luke?

Invited to Nicholas Spare's party, to my own surprise I accept. I can leave without disruption. None of the others will be there. Piers will surely not be invited. Mince-pies and tuneless carols are right for me, and the company of people I do not much know, before my journey north. At least this much is true: where once I scourged myself, I see no point.

It is not as cold as it should be. I play scales on my violin for an hour or two or more. It makes me concentrate, it gives me comfort, it relieves me of thought. Sometimes faces come to me: among them my mother's, and my first violin teacher other than Mrs Formby, a young man very keen on scales himself.

I meet my neighbours in the lobby, and I think: What misery lies behind that smiling face? What happiness behind that mournful one? Why should the first be likelier than the second? Will compelled laughter toughen the heart to rubber?

8.30

Nicholas Spare has forgiven Piers for last year's delinquency, for why else would he be here at his annual bash? And Piers has presumably forgiven Nicholas his violent anti-Troutism.

We have white wine instead of red fruit-punch this year. Piers looks sloshed already. Before I can think of anything to say, he has crossed the room and almost pinned me to the wall.

'Michael!'

'Dear boy!' I mutter in embarrassed mimicry.

'Now, now, no making fun of our host. He's feeling depressed this year, not aggressive.'

'Oh, why?'

'He can't find love, not even on Hampstead Heath.'

'Ah, that's serious,' I say. 'And how have you been? How have all of you been?'

'Michael, come back.'

I sigh, and gulp my wine.

'Well, all right, all right,' continues Piers. 'I won't say anything for the moment. But how have you been? No one has seen you for ages. No one knows if you're alive or dead. Why are you hiding away? Can't you at least meet us? Helen's depressed. She misses you. We all do. She gave up calling after you stopped replying to the messages she left. Well, what is your news?'

'The good news? or the bad?'

'The good. Save the bad for the next time we meet.'

'I've got a violin.'

'Oh, wonderful. What is it?'

'It's a Tononi.'

'Carlo?'

'Yes.

'But that's the same as your last one.'

'That's because it is the last one.'

'You mean you bought it? How could you afford to?'

'Piers, it was given to me.'

'Given? How? By the old biddy up in Yorkshire?'

'Don't call her that.'

'Sorry. Sorry.' Piers holds up both hands, splashing a bit of wine onto the front of his shirt.

'She died. She left it to me.'

'Oh shit!' says Piers. 'Everyone inherits things except me. Oh, I don't mean that. I'm really happy for you. Really. To old biddies. May they all die quickly and leave all their money to starving fiddlers.' He raises his glass.

I laugh and rather treacherously raise mine.

'Actually, I shouldn't complain,' says Piers. 'I've got a violin too. Or at least I think I do.'

'What is it?'

'An Eberle. An exceptionally fine one.'

I smile. 'Well, Piers, congratulations. I felt really bad that day at Denton's. Eberle's Neapolitan, isn't it? Or is it Czech? Wasn't there a Czech Eberle too?'

'I've no idea. This one's from Naples.'

'Oh, by the way, Mrs Formby lives—lived—in Lancashire, not Yorkshire.'

'Just to put the record straight?'

'Exactly.'

Piers laughs. 'You see? We can talk. You've got to hear it, Michael. It's got a lovely tone—balanced on all strings, warm but clear. It sounds amazing in E major, if you can believe that. In a funny way, it's the opposite of the Rogeri. Perhaps that would have been too resonant for me. Especially for the Bach recording.'

'Did you get it from a dealer or at an auction?'

'Neither.' says Piers. 'It's an odd story. Actually, I feel a bit of a profiteer in a friend's misfortune. Luis. You know Luis, don't you?'

'No'.

'Oh?' says Piers, looking surprised. 'Well, anyway, he was forced to sell it, and offered it to me, since he knew there'd be no dealer's commission that way. He'd taken out a big loan to pay for it, and for all sorts of reasons couldn't keep up with the payments. The final blow for him was when the LSO screwed him over.'

'How was that?' I ask, deeply grateful to be talking about the London Symphony Orchestra and an unknown Luis rather than the Bach recording.

'Well,' says Piers, 'old Luis went for an audition, played well and was offered a trial as number four in the Firsts. His first real chance to play with them was going to be a tour in Japan and a few connected concerts in London the week before. He got out of a whole lot of pretty lucrative work in order to do it: poor benighted dago, he's always been in love with the LSO. Then, less than twenty-four hours before they were due to begin playing, someone from the board phoned him up to say that they had filled the position the previous week, but Luis could tag along if he wished. No regrets, no apologies—nothing.'

'What reason did they give?' I ask, interested despite myself.

'Apparently, two other violinists had been on trial for that position for a while, and the board was "under pressure" to decide quickly between those two without considering Luis.' Piers tries to indicate the quotation marks with his fingers—a hazardous procedure.

'But why offer him a trial in that case?' I ask. 'Or book him on the tour?'

'Search me. Search them. Their board is run by the likes of you and me, just ordinary oppressed musicians who think the world gives them a raw deal.'

'Why didn't he just hold his nose and go along if the money was so important to him?'

'That's exactly what I asked him. I suppose I would have. After all, every world has its sleaze, and a lot worse goes on than that. But he said he had his honour, and he didn't want to start hating the orchestra whose sound he'd loved ever since he took up his little quarter-sized fiddle. Perhaps he's right. Perhaps if all of us had a bit more pride, they wouldn't treat us that way . . . Oh, God knows. I suppose it's no fun being crapped on, even by your favourite elephant. But this wasn't the only pressure, just the last straw. Anyway, I told Luis that I loved the Eberle, and that I'd buy it from him like a shot, but that if he wanted to buy it back within six months, I'd let him. He protested nobly and started blubbering, but I told him to shut up—

511

I'd feel like a heel if I didn't give him the option. But, well, I also had to tell the poor bugger that after six months, I'd have bonded with it too deeply to give it up. Bonded! I'm beginning to talk like Helen.'

'You, Piers, take some getting to know.'

'That's a nice remark from someone who's been married to me for six years.'

'Well, divorced now.'

'Yes.'

The respite is over. There is no getting around it.

'Well, how have my other spouses bonded with their new second fiddle?' I ask as casually as I can. It doesn't come out casual, though, but almost coldly offhand; and unjust. For them the trauma of divorce leads straight on to the traumas of wooing and engagement and shotgun marriage.

Piers takes a deep breath. 'We've tried out a number of people; more women than men, as it happens. I thought Helen wouldn't want to disturb the balance, but she's been quite keen to. She doesn't want another man to replace you. She's taken to yelling at me. She's even broken up with Hugo; well, thank heavens for that. She's really upset still . . . Of course, because of the recording, we can only try out people who play the viola as well.'

'And Stratus?' I ask, side-stepping what I can't engage with.

'Well, they've very decently agreed to keep the contract warm,' says Piers. 'But I associate you with the "Art of Fugue", Michael. So do we all. It's not just that you're a fantastic player, it's that you're part of us. God knows how we'll manage to get the

512

feel of it without you. Everyone else is on probation. They're all sort of OK, more than OK, but we couldn't play the scale with any of them.'

I feel the pricking of tears behind my eyes.

Another expansive gesture, more spillage of wine. 'Hey, Michael, steady on, I don't want to upset you twice in one evening.'

I look away for a moment.

'You're a selfish bastard,' says Piers suddenly.

I say nothing. How I have let them down. If the 'Art of Fugue' falls through, will Helen ever forgive me?

'It's still open. It's still open,' he says. 'Just about. But we can't play with a temporary second much longer. And we can't keep everyone hanging either. It's not fair on them.'

'No.'

'We'll have to decide by the end of January.'

'Yes. Well—'

'Michael, tell me one thing: is it just the "Art of Fugue"? I mean, it's not as if you can't play at all, is it?'

'I don't know. I really don't know what it is. I wish I knew. I've had six years with all of you that I wouldn't exchange for anything. When I saw you here this evening I wanted to leave. I knew I couldn't avoid the subject, but we've been through it now. So please, Piers, let's change it.'

He looks at me coolly. 'All right, then. Billy's son got meningitis a few weeks ago.'

'What? Jango? Meningitis?'

Piers nods.

'Oh no. I can't believe it. Is he—is he all right?'

'Well, you've been out of touch with the world so long, how would you know what to believe or not?

But yes, he's all right. One day he was fine, the next on the verge of death. Billy and Lydia were totally freaked out. They've still not recovered. But the little bugger's in perfect health again—as if it had never happened.'

'Piers, I'm getting out of here. I need to take a walk and get some fresh air. I don't think I can face the carols.'

'Who can!'

'I'm a selfish self-centred bastard.'

'Selfish? Why selfish?' Piers looks innocently surprised. But didn't he call me that himself a minute ago?

'I don't know,' I say. 'Anyway, I don't think I want to hear any more tragic stories. But how is Billy generally? I mean, apart from that.'

'"Apart from that, Mrs Lincoln, how did you enjoy the play?"'

'Oh, come on, Piers.'

'Well, he's inflicted his piece on us.'

'Oh. And?'

'Well, you won't know what it's like, will you, until you rejoin us. Or should I say 'unless'?' Piers is eyeing me cynically. 'On second thoughts, perhaps that's a disincentive.'

I laugh. 'I—well, I miss all of you. I even miss our sticky fan. When's your next concert? No, not your next one—I'm going to be in Rochdale till the thirtieth—I mean the next concert after that.'

'The second of January—the Purcell Room. But isn't the thirtieth when—'

'Yes.'

'So you're not going to hear her?'

'No.'

'What's happening in Rochdale on the thirtieth?'

514

'Nothing.'

'No, perhaps six years is not enough time to understand someone,' says Piers, looking at me with troubled concern.

8.31

Susurrus, sussurus, the wind in the poplars, electric-pitched. The swans hiss at me. They swim between the ice-floes on the Round Pond, and the sky is as blue as in summer.

Panes of ice, frosted and clear: the wind pushes them onto the southern shore. They slide upon each other, give gently and break clean. Seven layers thick, half-beached, they lie as clear as glass and creak and shift as the water moves with the wind.

No, not like an un-oiled door; more like a tired boat. But no, it's not that, it isn't quite that. If I were not reading these surfaces, could I interpret their noises? Creaking, rippling, shifting, easing, crackling, sighing: this is not something I have heard before. It is a soft sound, easy, intimate.

This is the spot where I learned she could not hear. I break a sliver off; it melts in my palm. I met her in winter, and lost her before winter came.

No, on that day, I will not be here, within the reach of sound.

The ice shifts like a skin upon the ripples of the pond, and the swans move lightly on the winter water.

8.32

Once more I am going north from Euston.

For much of the journey I sleep. My destination is where the train, in the announcer's locution, terminates.

It is a cold morning, three days before Christmas. I am giving myself a day in Manchester to visit my haunts, and will drive to Rochdale tonight.

I return the music to the library. I close my eyes while a blind man taps his cane along, tracing the curve of the wall.

At the cathedral I touch the beasts carved on the misericords, the unicorns and dragons.

Near the Bridgewater Hall I stand by the huge rounded touchstone and look at the basin formed by the canal below.

What keeps me in London? Why not come back home?

Nothing essential to my heart keeps me in London now. All those who love me have died or are very old. Dad and Auntie Joan are in Rochdale. Before my college years I came to Manchester. Even if my speech throws up only the odd Lancastrian trace, once here my ears relax into the lilt; they are at home with Bacup and Todmorden and all the names that aliens distort.

If I lived in Manchester, say, or Leeds or even Sheffield, I could visit them and spend more time with them—a weekend a month, even more perhaps, not three or four uncertain times a year. I could sell my flat and buy something cheaper here. But then, why not live in Rochdale itself, with its moors all around, and no Park Polizei to say: do

516

not trespass, do not sing, do not shout for joy or grief, do not touch the stones, do not feed the larks Christmas pudding?

No, not Rochdale, with its meccano guild, drystone walling, badminton, German shorthair pointer club. Not Rochdale with the heart torn out of it, the claustrophobic market, the murdered streets of my childhood, gutted into vertical slums. Not Rochdale to commute from to the city where I work.

What work though? The Hallé perhaps, who filled the elephant ring with magic sound? A bit of teaching, something linked to my own old college? Some work with an itinerant trio I could form? I formed one once, I could do so again. Who would the pianist and the cellist be? There'd only be one work I'd never play.

London is a violin jungle. In its heartache, in its busyness lie its varied pickings. But I have ceased to swim in the Serpentine and have grown scant of breath. It is no longer, if it ever was, my home.

I embrace the touchstone. I press my forehead and my face against it. It surrenders no swift answer. It is very smooth, very cold, and in its heart very old. The snow falls all around me and swirls above the basin of the canal.

8.33

It's a quiet Christmas. Snow falls intermittently. Zsa-Zsa lies under the garden she once roamed. My father has formless anxieties, then is cheerful. I do the shopping in my white rental car and get an un-Christian parking ticket. Auntie Joan creates

517

her usual vast repast. We talk of this and that. I do not say I'm thinking of a move.

Afterwards, I drive around in the falling snow.

The cemetery is covered in white: the graves, the tops of gravestones, the flowers placed there a few hours ago. I lose my bearings: have they moved a hedge or is it just the snow that's muddling me? But here it is: a grey headstone engraved by Auntie Joan's husband's friend, a monumental mason: 'Treasured memories of Ada Holme who fell asleep' on such and such a date, with space for a name or two below.

On my mother's grave I place a white rose.

Snow has closed some of the roads, but not the road to Blackstone Edge. I drive past Mrs Formby's: a notice tells me it's for sale.

On Blackstone Edge I crumble some Christmas pudding, warm in its foil, onto the snow. The moist black crumbs will melt through to the black earth of the moor. But of course the larks left months ago. The snow has stopped falling, and the view is far and clear. Yet I cannot see even a raven or a carrion crow.

I get the violin from the car. I play a little from 'The Lark Ascending'. And then I tune down the lowest string to F.

My hands are not cold, nor my mind agitated. I am in no dark tunnel but the open moor. I play for her the great unfinished fugue from the 'Art of Fugue'. No doubt it makes no sense by itself, but she can fill in the parts that I can hear. I play it till my part runs out; and listen till Helen too has ceased to play.

8.34

On the 30th I take a train down to London. It is a clear day with the odd cloud. By the time we get to Euston it is dark. I have no luggage, not even my violin.

I go directly to the Wigmore Hall. The evening's concert is sold out.

The young man at the box office says he was surprised, given the nature of the work. He thinks there may be another factor. ' "The concert by the deaf pianist", you know, that sort of thing. A bit off-putting, I think, that some of them don't even know her name. But there it is. It's been sold out for weeks. I'm very sorry.'

'If there are any returns . . .'

'We usually do have a few, but it all depends on the concert. I really can't guarantee anything. The queue's just along here.'

'Haven't you kept any tickets aside for—you know, the odd patron or benefactor or whatever?'

'Well, not officially, no, we don't officially do that kind of thing.'

'I've played here before. I'm—I'm with the Maggiore Quartet.'

'I'll do my best,' he says, and shrugs.

There is an hour to go before the concert. I am sixth in the queue. But fifteen minutes before the concert only one ticket has been returned. The lobby has filled up with people hailing each other, chatting and laughing, buying programmes, collecting their pre-paid tickets. Again and again I hear her name, and the word 'deaf', 'deaf', again and again.

I start to panic. I leave the queue and stand

outside. The night is windy and cold. I ask everyone who comes in, passes by, programme in hand, or even goes down by the outside staircase to the restaurant below whether they have any tickets to spare.

Two minutes before the concert I am beside myself. Two warning bells have rung—and now the third.

'Oh, hello, Michael, so you've come after all. Piers said . . .'

'Oh, Billy, Billy—I've been standing here—I—oh, Billy—I was so shocked to hear about Jango.'

'Yes, he gave us quite a scare. Lydia wanted to come to the concert, but decided to stay with him. She's the one who's been hit hardest by this. We'd better go in.'

'Her ticket. Do you have a spare ticket? Billy?'

'No. I returned hers a couple of days ago . . . You mean you don't have a ticket?'

'No.'

'Take this.'

'But Billy—'

'Take it. Don't argue, Michael, or neither of us will get in. They'll close the doors in half a minute. The lobby's almost empty. Don't argue, Michael. Take it and go. Go.'

8.35

I am in the front row of the balcony. A murmur fills the hall. I look down on the heads of the crowd below. In the fifth row I see a small boy, I would think the only one here, and next to him his father.

She enters, looks at them and smiles. For a

moment, for more than just a moment, she casts her eyes around, troubled, searching, then sits down at the piano.

She plays without the music, her eyes sometimes on her hands, sometimes closed. What she hears, what she imagines I do not know.

There is no forced gravitas in her playing. It is a beauty beyond imagining—clear, lovely, inexorable, phrase across phrase, phrase echoing phrase, the incomplete, the unending 'Art of Fugue'. It is an equal music.

Rain begins to fall. It strikes the skylight with a faint patter.

After the eleventh contrapunctus is the interval.

Now will come the chaos: the uncertain ordering of the pieces when I return—and here, in the foyer, the chatter of gossip and praise. I cannot hear any more.

I push through the crowded lobby into the rain. I walk a long while, through the streets, the darkness of the park. Once more I stand by the Serpentine. The rain has washed my earlier tears away.

Music, such music, is a sufficient gift. Why ask for happiness; why hope not to grieve? It is enough, it is to be blessed enough, to live from day to day and to hear such music—not too much, or the soul could not sustain it—from time to time.

AUTHOR'S NOTE

Music to me is dearer even than speech. When I realised that I would be writing about it I was gripped with anxiety. Only slowly did I reconcile myself to the thought of it.

Friends and strangers have helped me in this work: string players, often those in quartets themselves or who, because of their involvement with early music, have had to deal with the problems of variant tuning; pianists; other musicians, both players and composers; makers, repairers and sellers of instruments; those who aid or attempt to aid the creation or dissemination of music—teachers, critics, musicians' agents and managers, executives of record companies, managers of halls and festivals; those who know the places I have written about better than myself—Londoners, Rochdalians, Venetians and Viennese; those who understand the world of the deaf—medically, like the many doctors who have advised me, or educationally, in particular my lip-reading teacher and her class, or from personal experience of deafness.

Many people talked to me about the world of these characters; a few about the characters themselves. A number of friends generously agreed to read the first draft of the manuscript—a task I can hardly bear to do, even for my own work. Others forgave me for disappearing in script, voice and person from their lives.

At the cost of redundancy I would like most particularly to thank three musicians—a pianist, a percussionist and a string player—who helped me, in quite different ways, to go where imagination alone could not have taken me: to get some sense of what it might be like to live, to have lived, and to expect to continue to live in the zones that lie at the intersection of the world of soundlessness with those of heard, of misheard, of half-heard and of imagined sound.